GRAY DAVIS

For testimonials from law enforcement,
visit Carolyn Arnold's website.

CAROLYN ARNOLD

ELEVEN

HIBBERT&STILES
PUBLISHING INC.

2019 Revised Edition

Hibbert & Stiles Publishing Inc.
hspubinc.com

Names: Arnold, Carolyn, 1976
Title: Eleven / Carolyn Arnold.
Description: 2019 Hibbert & Stiles Publishing Inc. edition. | Series: Brandon Fisher FBI series ; book 1

Identifiers: ISBN (e-book): 978-0-9878400-6-6 | ISBN (4.25 x 7 paperback): 978-1-988353-71-5 | ISBN (5 x 8 paperback): 978-1-988064-06-2 | ISBN (6.14 x 9.21 hardcover): 978-1-988353-16-6

ELEVEN

Dedicated to George Arnold,
my husband, best friend, and greatest supporter.

One

Nothing in the twenty weeks at Quantico had prepared me for this.

A crime scene investigator, who had identified himself as Earl Royster when we'd first arrived, addressed my boss, FBI Supervisory Special Agent Jack Harper, "All of the victims were buried—" He held up a finger, his eyes squeezed shut, and he sneezed. "Sorry 'bout that. My allergies don't like it down here. They were all buried the same way."

This was my first case with the FBI Behavioral Analysis Unit, and it had brought me and the three other members of my team to Salt Lick, Kentucky. The discovery was made this morning, and we were briefed and flown in from Quantico to the Louisville field office where we picked up a couple of SUVs. We drove from there and arrived in Salt Lick at about four in the afternoon.

We were in an underground bunker illuminated by portable lights brought in by the local investigative team. The space was eleven feet beneath the cellar of a house that was the size of a mobile trailer. We stood in a central hub from which four tunnels spread out like a root system. The space was fifteen feet by seven and a half feet and six and a half feet tall.

The walls were packed dirt, and an electrical cord ran along the ceiling and down the tunnels with pigtail light fixtures dangling every few feet. The bulbs cut into the height of the tunnels by eight inches.

I pulled on my shirt collar wishing for a smaller frame than my six foot two inches. As it was, the three of us could have reached out and touched each other if we were so inclined. The tunnels were even narrower at three feet wide.

"It's believed each victim had the same cuts inflicted," Royster began, "although most of the remains are skeletal, so it's not as easy to know for sure, but based on burial method alone, this guy obviously adhered to some sort of ritual. The most recent victim is only a few years old and was preserved by the soil. The oldest remains are estimated to date back twenty-five to thirty years. Bingham moved in twenty-six years ago."

Lance Bingham was the property owner, age sixty-two, and was currently serving three to five years in a correctional facility for killing two cows and assaulting a neighbor. If he had moved in twenty-six years ago, that would put Bingham at thirty-six years old at the time. The statistical age for a serial killer to start out is early to mid-thirties.

The CSI continued to relay more information about how the tunnels branched out in various directions, likely extending beneath a neighboring cornfield, and the ends came to bulbous tips, like subterranean cul-de-sacs.

"There are eleven rooms and only ten bodies," Jack summarized with impatience and pulled a cigarette out of a shirt pocket. He didn't light up, but his mouth was clamped down on it as if it were a lifeline.

Royster's gaze went from the cigarette to Jack's eyes. "Yes. There's one tunnel that leads to a dead end, and there's one empty grave."

Jack turned to me. "What do you make of it?" he asked, the cigarette bobbing on his lips as he spoke.

Everyone looked at me expectantly. "Of the empty grave?" I squeaked out.

Jack squinted and removed the cigarette from his mouth. "That and the latest victim."

"Well…" My collar felt tighter, and I cleared my throat, then continued. "Bingham had been in prison for the last three years. The elaborate tunnel system he had going would have taken years to plan and dig, and it would have taken a lot of strength. My guess would be that Bingham wasn't working alone. He had help and, after he went to prison, someone followed in his footsteps."

Jack perched the unlit smoke back between his lips. "Hmm."

I wasn't sure how to read *Hmm*, but the way his gaze scrutinized me, I was thinking he wasn't necessarily impressed.

"Anyway, you'll want to see it for yourself." Royster gestured down one of the tunnels and took a step toward it. "I know I haven't seen anything like—" Royster didn't catch his sneeze in time, and snot sprayed through the air.

Ick. I stepped back.

More sniffles. "Again, sorry 'bout that. Anyway, this way."

Jack motioned for me to follow behind Royster, ahead of him.

I took a deep breath, anticipating the tight quarters of the tunnel.

Sweat dripped down my back, and I pulled on my collar again.

"Go ahead, Kid," Jack directed.

He'd adopted the pet name for me from the moment we'd met, and I wished he'd just call me by my name.

Both Jack and the CSI were watching me.

The CSI said, "We'll look at the most recent victim first. Now, as you know, the victims alternated male and female. The tenth victim was female so we believe the next is going to be—"

"Let me guess, male," Jack interrupted him.

"Yeah." Royster took off down the third tunnel that fed off from the bottom right of the hub.

I followed behind him, tracing the walls with my hands.

My heart palpitated. I ducked to miss the bulbs just as I knew I'd have to and worked at focusing on the positive. Above ground, the humidity sucked air from the lungs; in the tunnels, the air was cool but still suffocating.

I counted my paces—five, six. The further we went, the heavier my chest became, making the next breath less taken for granted.

Despite my extreme discomfort, this was my first case, and I had to be strong. The rumor was you either survived Jack and the two years of probationary service and became a certified special agent or your next job would be security detail at a mall.

Five more paces and we entered an offshoot from the main tunnel. According to Royster, three burial chambers were in this tunnel. He described these as branches on a tree. Each branch came off the main trunk for the length of about ten feet and ended in a circular space of about eleven feet in diameter. The idea of more space seemed welcoming until we reached it.

A circular grave took up most of the space and was a couple of feet deep. Chicken wire rimmed the grave to help it retain its shape. With her wrists and ankles tied to metal stakes, her arms and legs formed the human equivalent of a star. As her body had dried from decomposition, the constraints had kept her positioned in the manner the killer had intended.

"And what made them dig?" Jack asked the CSI.

Jack was searching for specifics. We knew Bingham had entrusted his financials to his sister, but when she passed away a year ago, the back taxes had built up, and the county had come to reclaim the property.

Royster answered, "X marked the spot." Neither Jack nor I displayed any amusement. The CSI continued. "He etched into the dirt, probably with a stick."

"Why assume a stick?" Jack asked the question, and it resulted in an awkward silence.

My eyes settled on the body of the female who was estimated to be in her early twenties. It's not that I had an aversion to a dead body, but looking at her made my stomach toss. She still had flesh on her bones. As the CSI had said, *Preserved by the soil.*

Her torso had eleven incisions. They were marked in the linear way to keep count. Two sets of four vertical cuts with one diagonal slash through each of them. The eleventh cut was the largest and was above the belly button.

"You realize the number eleven is believed to be a sign of purity?" Zach's voice seemed to strike me from thin air, and my chest compressed further, knowing another person was going to share the limited space.

Zachery Miles was a member of our team, but unlike Jack's reputation, Zach's hadn't preceded him. Any information I had, I'd gathered from his file that showed a flawless service record and the IQ of a genius. It also disclosed that he was thirty-seven, eight years older than I was.

Jack stuck the cigarette he had been sucking on back into his shirt pocket. "Purity, huh?"

I looked down at the body of the woman in the shallow grave beside me. Nothing seemed too pure about any of this.

"I'm going to go," Royster excused himself.

"That's if you really dig into the numerology and spiritualistic meaning of the number," Zachery said, disregarding the CSI entirely.

Jack stretched his neck side to side and looked at me. "I hate it when he gets into that shit." He pointed a bony index finger at me. "Don't let me catch you talking about it either."

I just nodded. I felt I had just been admonished as if I were his child—not that he needed to zero in on me like that. Sure, I believed in the existence of God and angels, despite the evil in the world, but I didn't have any avid interest in the unseen.

Zachery continued, "The primary understanding is the number one is that of new beginnings and purity. This is emphasized with the existence of two ones."

My eyes scanned Zachery's face. While his intelligence scoring revealed a genius, physically, he was of average looks. If anything, he was slightly taller than Jack and I, probably coming in at about six foot four. His hair was dark and trimmed short. He had a high brow line and brown eyes.

"Zachery here reads something once—" Jack tapped his head "—it's there."

JACK AND I SPENT THE next few hours making our way to every room where Jack insisted on standing beside all the bodies. He studied each of them carefully, even if only part of their remains had been uncovered. I'd pass him glances, but he seemed oblivious to my presence. We ended up back beside the most recent victim where we stayed for twenty minutes, not moving, not talking, just standing.

I understood what he saw. There was a different feel to this room, nothing quantifiable, but it was discernible. The killer had a lot to say. He was organized and immaculate. He was precise and disciplined. He acted with a purpose, and, like most killers, he had a message to relay. We were looking for a controlled, highly intelligent unsub.

The intestines had been removed from nine of the victims, but Harold Jones, the coroner—who also came backed with a doctorate unlike most of his profession—wouldn't conclude it as the cause of death before conducting more tests. The last victim's intestines were intact, and, even though the cause of death needed confirmation, the talk that permeated the corridors of the bunker was that the men who did this were scary sons of bitches.

Zachery entered the room. "I find it fascinating he would bury his victims in circular graves."

Fascinating?

I looked up at Jack, and he flicked his lighter.

He held out his hands as if to say he wouldn't light up inside the burial chamber. His craving was getting desperate, though, which meant he'd be getting cranky. He said, "Continue, Zachery, by all means. The kid wants to hear."

"By combining both the number eleven and the circle, it makes me think of the coinherence symbol. Even the way the victims are laid out."

"Elaborate," Jack directed.

"It's a circle which combines a total of eleven inner points to complete it. As eleven means purity, so the coinherence symbol is related to religious traditions—at minimum thirteen, but some people can discern more, and each symbol is understood in different ways. The circle itself stands for completion and can symbolize eternity."

I cocked my head to the side. Zachery noticed.

"We have a skeptic here, Jack."

Jack faced me and spoke with the unlit cigarette having resumed its perch between his lips. "What do you make of it?"

Is this a trap? "You want to know what I think?"

"By all means, Slingshot."

There it was, the other dreaded nickname, no doubt his way of reminding me that I didn't score perfectly on handguns at the academy. "Makes me think of the medical symbol. Maybe our guy has a background in medicine. It could explain the incisions being deep enough to inflict pain but not deep enough to cause them to bleed out. It would explain how he managed to take out their intestines."

Was this what I signed up for?

"Hmm," Jack mumbled. Zachery remained silent. Seconds later, Jack said, "You're assuming they didn't bleed out. Continue."

"The murders happened over a period of time. This one—" I gestured to the woman, and for a moment, realized how this job transformed the life of a person into an object "— she's recent. Bingham's been in prison for about three years now."

Jack flicked the lighter again. "So you're saying he had an

apprentice?"

Zachery's lips lifted upward, and his eyes read, *Like* Star Wars.

I got it. I was the youngest on the team, twenty-nine this August, next month, and I was the new guy, but I didn't make it through four years of university studying mechanics and endure twenty weeks of the academy, coming out at the top of the class, to be treated like a child. "Not like an apprentice."

"Like what then—"

"Jack, the sheriff wants to speak with you." Paige Dawson, another member of our team, came into the burial chamber. She had come to Quantico from the New York field office claiming she wanted out of the big city. I met her when she was an instructor at the FBI Academy.

I pulled on my collar. Four of us were in here now. Dust caused me to cough and warranted a judgmental glare from Jack.

"How did you make out with the guy who discovered everything?"

"He's clean. I mean we had his background already, and he lives up to it. I really don't think he's involved at all."

Jack nodded and left the room.

I turned to Zachery. "I think he hates me."

"If he hated you, you'd know it." Zachery followed behind Jack.

Two

S alt Lick, Kentucky was right in the middle of nowhere and had a population shy of three hundred and fifty. Just as the town's name implied, underground mineral deposits were the craving of livestock, and due to this, it had originally attracted farmers to the area. I was surprised the village was large enough to boast a Journey's End Lodge and a Frosty Freeze.

I stepped into the main hub to see Jack in a heated conversation with Sheriff Harris. From an earlier meeting with him, I knew he covered all of Bath County which included three municipalities and a combined population of about twelve thousand.

"Ah, I'm doing the best I can, Agent, but, um, we've never seen the likes of this before." A born and raised Kentucky man, the sheriff was in his mid-fifties, had a bald head and carried about an extra sixty pounds that came to rest on his front. Both of his hands were braced on his hips, a stance of confidence, but the flicking up and down of his right index finger gave his insecurities away.

"It has nothing to do with what you've seen before, Sheriff. What matters is catching the unsub."

"Well, the property owner is in p-pri-prison," the Kentucky accent broke through.

"The bodies date back two to three decades with the newest one being within the last few years."

Harris's face brightened a reddish hue as he took a deep

breath and exhaled loud enough to be heard.

Jack had the ability to make a lot of people nervous. His dark hair, which was dusted with silver at the sideburns, gave him a look of distinction, but deeply-etched creases in his face exposed his trying past.

Harris shook his head. "So much violence, and it's tourist season 'round here." Harris paused. His eyes said, *You city folks wouldn't understand.* "Cave Run Lake is manmade but set in the middle of nature. People love coming here to get away. Word gets out about this, there go the tourists."

"Ten people have been murdered, and you're worried about tourists?"

"Course not, but—"

"It sounds like you were."

"Then you misunderstood, Agent. Besides, the counties around here are peaceful, law-abidin' citizens."

"Churchgoers?" Zachery came up from a tunnel.

"Well, ah, I wouldn't necessarily say that. There are probably about thirty churches or so throughout the county, and right here in Salt Lick there are three."

"That's quite a few considering the population here."

"S'pose so."

"Sheriff." A deputy came up to the group of them and pulled up his pants.

"Yes, White."

The deputy's face was the shade of his name. "The in-investigators found somethin' you should see." He passed glances among all of us.

Jack held out a hand as if to say, *By all means.*

We followed the deputy up the ramp that led to the cellar. With each step taking me closer to the surface, my chest allowed for more satisfying breaths. Jack glanced over at me. I guessed he was wondering if I was going to make it.

"This way, sir."

The deputy spoke from the front of the line, as he kept moving. His boots hit the wooden stairs that joined the cellar to the first floor.

I inhaled deeply as I came through the opening into the confined space Bingham had at one time called home. Sunlight made its way through tattered sheets that served as curtains, even though the time of day was now seven, and the sun would be sinking in the sky.

The deputy led us to Bingham's bedroom where there were two CSIs. I heard footsteps behind me: Paige. She smiled at me, but it quickly faded.

"They found it in the closet," the deputy said, pointing our focus in its direction.

The investigators moved aside, exposing an empty space. A shelf that ran the width of the closet sat perched at a forty-five-degree angle. The inside had been painted white at one time but now resembled an antiqued paint pattern the modern age went for. It was what I saw when my eyes followed the walls to the floor that held more interest.

Jack stepped in front of me; Zachery came up behind him and gave me a look that said, *Pull up the rear, Pending.* Pending being the nickname Zach had saddled me with to remind me of my twenty-four-month probationary period—as if I'd forget.

"We found it when we noticed the loose floorboard," one of the CSIs said. He held a clipboard wedged between an arm and his chest. The other hand held a pen which he clicked repeatedly. Jack looked at it, and the man stopped. The CSI went on. "Really, it's what's inside that's, well, what nightmares are made of."

I didn't know the man. In fact, I had never seen him before, but the reflection in his eyes told me he had witnessed something that even paled the gruesome find in the bunkers.

"You first, Kid." Jack stepped back.

Floorboards were hinged back and exposed a hole about two and a half feet square. My stomach tossed thinking of the CSI's words, *what nightmares are made of.*

"Come on, Brandon. I'll follow behind you." Paige's soft

voice of encouragement was accompanied by a strategically placed hand on my right shoulder.

I glanced at her. I could do this. *God, I hated small spaces.* But I had wanted to be an FBI special agent and, well, that wish had been granted. Maybe the saying, *Be careful what you wish for, it might come true,* held merit.

I hunched over and looked into the hole. A wooden ladder went down at least twenty feet. The space below was lit.

Maybe if I just took it one step at a time.

"What are you waiting for, Pending?" Zachery taunted me. I didn't look at him but picked up on the amusement in his voice.

I took a deep breath and lowered myself down.

Jack never said a word, but I could feel his energy. He didn't think I was ready for this, but I would prove him wrong—somehow. The claustrophobia I had experienced in the underground passageways was nothing compared to the anxiety squeezing my chest now. At least the tunnels were the width of three feet. Here, four sides of packed earth hugged me, as if a substantial inhale would expand me to the confines of the space.

"I'm coming." Again, Paige's soft voice had a way of soothing me despite the tight quarters threatening to take my last breath and smother me alive.

I looked up. Paige's face filled the opening, and her red wavy hair framed her face. The vision was replaced by the bottom of her shoes.

I continued my descent, one rung at a time, slowly, methodically. I tried to place myself somewhere else, but no images came despite my best efforts to conjure them—and what did I have waiting for me at the bottom? *What nightmares are made of.*

Minutes passed before my shoes reached the soil. I took a deep breath when I realized the height down here was about seven feet and looked around. The room was about five by five, and there was a doorway at the backside.

One pigtail fixture with a light bulb dangled from an electrical wire. It must have fed to the same circuit as the underground passageways and been connected to the power generator as it cast dim light, creating darkened shadows in the corners.

I looked up the ladder. Paige was about halfway down. There was movement behind her, and it was likely Jack and Zachery following behind her.

"You're almost there," I coached them.

By the time the rest of the team made it to the bottom, along with the deputy and a CSI, I had my breathing and my nerves under control.

Paige was the first to head around the bend in the wall.

"The sheriff is going to stay up there an' take care of things." The deputy pointed in the direction Paige went. "What they found is in here."

Jack and Zachery had already headed around the bend. I followed.

Inside the room, Paige raised her hand to cover her mouth. It dropped when she noticed us.

A stainless steel table measuring ten feet by three feet was placed against the back wall. A commercial meat grinder sat on the table. Everything was pristine, and light from a bulb reflected off the surfaces.

To the left of the table was a chest freezer, plain white, one owned by the average consumer. I had one similar, but it was the smaller version because it was only Deb and me.

My stomach tossed thinking about the contents of this one. Paige's feet were planted to where she had first entered the room. Zachery's eyes fixed on Jack, who moved toward the freezer and, with a gloved hand, opened the lid.

Paige gasped, and Jack turned to face her. Disappointment was manifested in the way his eyes narrowed. "It's empty." Jack patted his shirt pocket again.

"If you're thinking we found people's remains in there, we haven't," the CSI said, "but tests have shown positive for human blood."

"So he chopped up his victim's intestines? Put them in the freezer? But where are they?" Paige wrapped her arms around her torso and bent over to look into the opening of the grinder.

"There are many cultures, the Korowai tribe of Papua New Guinea, for example, who have been reported to practice cannibalism even in this modern day," Zachery said. "It can also be involved in religious rituals."

Maybe my eyes should have been fixed on the freezer, on the horror that transpired underground in Salt Lick of Bath County, Kentucky. Instead, I found my training allowing me to focus, analyze, and be objective. In order to benefit the investigation, it would demand these three things, and I wouldn't disappoint. My attention was on the size of the table, the size of the meat grinder, and the size of the freezer. "Anyone think to ask how this all got down here in the first place?"

All five of them faced me.

"The opening down here is only, what, two feet square at the most? Now maybe the meat grinder would fit down, hoisted on a rope, but the table and the freezer? No way."

"What are you saying, Slingshot?"

My eyes darted to Jack's. "I'm saying there has to be another way in." I addressed the CSI, "Did you look for any other hidden passageways? I mean the guy obviously had a thing for them."

"We didn't find anything."

"Well, that doesn't make sense. Where are the burial sites in relation to here?"

"It would be that way." Zachery pointed at the freezer.

We connected eyes, and both of us moved toward it. It slid easily. As we shoved it to the side, it revealed an opening behind it. I looked down into it. Another light bulb spawned eerie shadows. I rose to full height. This find should at least garner some praise from Jack Harper.

"Nothing like Hogan's Alley is it, Kid?"

Three

Hogan's Alley, originally named after a comic strip from the late 1800s, is a mock town used by the FBI in Quantico, Virginia as a training ground for future special agents. Placed on ten plus acres, the government built it with the aid of Hollywood set designers. The fact that Jack mentioned it by comparison silenced me.

I locked eyes with him before studying the size of the hole. It was just large enough for the freezer to fit through if turned.

"This guy did a lot of planning," Paige said. She moved closer to the tunnel entrance. "He definitely didn't want to get caught and probably never thought he would. That could be the elevated thinking of a narcissist."

Jack watched her speak, and something about the way his eyes fell, tracking to her lips, made me wonder about the nature of their relationship.

"Well, I'd definitely peg him as a psychotic, too. Narcissists usually only kill if it's the result of a personal affront, but this man gutted his victims and ground their intestines. Who knows if he ate them!" A visible shiver ran through Paige, and for some reason gauging her reaction intensified the severity of the situation.

Up until now, the training had taken over. I had cataloged the victims as fictional, not once living and breathing individuals. With the snap back to reality, I became aware of the presence of death and the way it hung in the air like a suffocating blanket. My stomach tightened, and I felt sick.

"Question is," Zachery began, "did these people threaten him in some way? Were they random, or were these planned kills? The patience he seemed to execute with the cutting and burial indicates he was very organized. I'd almost lean to believe that they were planned, not random."

"It could be that they reminded him of one person who wronged him. That's not uncommon," Paige offered.

I was frozen in place, unable to move and incapable of thinking clearly.

The CSI hunched over and shone a flashlight into the opening. "It spreads out after a few feet. It almost looks as high as it does in here."

"I want to know what happened to the intestines," Jack stated matter-of-factly. "Slingshot, any ideas?"

"The guy knew he was going to prison and had them cleaned up?"

"But why?"

I wanted to say, *What do you mean, why?* I thought the answer was obvious, the question rhetorical, but I focused on Jack's two words. There was little risk that this room would be discovered even if the bodies were, and if the bodies were, what was a little ground-up human intestine? Another toss of my stomach brought bile into the back of my throat. "I'm not sure."

An ominous silence enveloped the room as if we were all absorbed in contemplating our mortality. The human reaction to death and uncertainty, of wanting to know but not wanting the answers, of sympathy for those lost yet relief that it wasn't us.

The CSI made his way through the opening. His flashlight cast more light in the dimly lit space. I followed and heard the rest of the team shuffle in behind me.

After a few feet, I could stand to full height.

The CSI looked up at the lit bulb. "The guy thought of everything."

The electricity that had been run down here was basic and minimal. A band of wire ran from the *meat room* to here, but it wasn't so much the wiring that garnered my attention.

To the side of the room, there was a stretcher with metal straps and stirrups. Beside it was a stainless steel tray with a single knife lying on it. Just as with the table and meat grinder, light reflected off it. A roll of plastic sheeting stood vertically beside the bed.

"This just keeps getting creepier." Paige took up position beside me.

"Say that again," Deputy White said. "'Scuse me." His face paled and he slapped a hand over his mouth.

Jack was the last to come through the tunnel. Even he paused when his eyes settled on the items in the room. "What do you make of it, Kid?"

Why am I the only one who needs to provide answers?

"He killed them here." I pointed back to where we came from. "Ground up their intestines in there." I felt sick.

"Whoa, nicely put, Pending," Zachery said.

"And how did he get them down here?"

"Well, there's got to be another way in. The freezer alone discloses that, and I mean obviously, he wouldn't be able to make the victims go down the ladder, past the meat grinder." I took a deep breath, hoping this was the worst case I'd ever have to deal with. "There has to be another way in here, a passageway that connects to the burial sites."

Paige said, "Bingham—"

"You assume," Jack corrected her. "Maybe he worked with someone from the start. They picked the victims and brought them here."

She disregarded him. "Bingham brought them down through the passageway that comes off the cellar. Maybe he drugged them or held them at gunpoint—"

"Or knife point."

Paige rolled her eyes.

I looked forward to the day I could express myself in that

manner to the supervisory special agent.

"Whatever. The point is he had a system worked out. Bring them down, bring them in here, cut them, kill them, gut them—"

"You're assuming he didn't gut them while alive."

The deputy tightened the placement of his hand over his mouth and swiveled his hips to the right.

"You said kill them, and then gut them?" Jack asked.

"Either way." A large exhale moved her hair briefly upward. "Gut them to kill them. There, you happy? He's one sick son of a bitch either way."

"And he just went away on a fluke charge, killing cows and assaulting a neighbor." I knew once the words came out I should have thought them through. Deputy White looked capable of hauling me to the field and flogging me.

"Cattle are a v-very important investment 'round here. Farmin' is what we people do. It's to be respected an' so is the livestock."

The hint of a smirk dusted Jack's lips. My discomfort brought him happiness. I felt my earlobes heat with anger.

"I didn't mean it like that."

"Then what did you mean?" Both the Kentucky-bred deputy and the local CSI kept their eyes on me.

"He has ten bodies buried underneath his property. Ten *human* bodies. There's a freezer which seems to have been used to hold the unspeakable." My arms pointed in both directions. "Numerous passageways, all the secrecy. Who was this guy really? And don't say a killer because I think he was more than that."

"What are you saying, Slingshot?"

"He didn't kill them like this for no reason." I gestured toward Zachery. "Maybe it's something to do with that coinherence symbol of his, or maybe it has something to do with the health profession, but whatever it is, it was for a reason. This guy had something to say."

Zachery stepped toward me. I moved back. He said, "The

killers always have something to say."

"Well, I believe this one has more to say than most." All of them watched me as if I were about to shed light on the case. I wish I were.

Four

They say when you've seen as much as Jack nothing surprises you anymore. The cruelty and evil of the world hold no impact, but, even if it was just a flicker in his eyes, this case affected the man.

The rumor was Jack came to the FBI as a former sergeant major of the 7th Special Forces Group. In the 1980s, he had played a critical advisory role in the training of the Salvadoran military to deal with counter-insurgency. His last deployment had been Operation Just Cause, also known as the Invasion of Panama in eighty-nine. When he retired from the military the following year and came to the FBI, he was given a pass straight to supervisory special agent.

"So the guy gets his victims down here, but how? I mean there has to be a connection between this room and the burial sites," the CSI said.

Jack fished out a cigarette. "That's an obvious observation."

The CSI held up a hand, pointed at the cigarette. "Not down here please."

Jack's eyes narrowed, and he placed it unlit in his lips. "Well, I suggest you and your CSI buddies get on finding the connection between the rooms. It's got to be a large enough opening that the freezer could fit through it—"

"Could it be this easy?" I left the group, following the wiring on the ceiling and rounded a bend to the left.

"Slingshot, don't go wandering off—" Jack came up behind me, his words dying on his tongue as he looked on what I had found.

Smoothed concrete filled a space in the wall the size of a doorway.

"This location would line up with the tunnel that seemed to lead nowhere," Zachery said.

Do I sense excitement in his voice? My chest tightened, and my next breath stalled. I needed out of this place. I needed to go above ground.

"This would make sense," the CSI said. "In the tunnel that's a dead end, the wire disappears up into the dirt."

"Hmm." Jack glared at the investigator. "The killer knew we'd catch on to what he had going. If the last murder was done after Bingham was in prison, his apprentice—" Jack glanced at me, and Zachery smirked "—came back to clean up the mess. He knew that Bingham's sister died and the property would be reclaimed."

"But why not close off access to everything?" I asked the question. "Why not cover over the empty grave? Why not block off the entrance from the cellar?"

Jack's lips curled upward. "You have to ask that?"

"He had a message to send," Paige said, stepping forward. "This isn't over yet. The unsub plans to kill at least one more, and they want us to know it."

"But why wouldn't they just keep up the payments. He had something going here," I countered.

"It was time to move on. Maybe the apprentice isn't from this area but traveled here. With Bingham in prison, they could have started to kill in their hometown."

"So this other killer has money for travel," Zachery observed. "It fits the profile for a serial killer—mobile."

"And by all appearances the unsub plans to kill again if he hasn't already. They saw merit in what Bingham had done and respected him. Someone like that would want to let Bingham know. They'd likely be in contact. We'll need to get a copy of Bingham's visitor log at the prison." Jack passed a glance to the CSI and flicked his lighter.

"Please, don't—"

Jack put the lighter back in his pocket but continued to let the cigarette bob on his lips as he spoke. "We'll get a media blackout in place and call it a night. We don't need details of the find getting out. It would cause panic, and worse case, scare off the unsub. He'll lay low, and we'll never find him. In the morning, the kid and I will go to the prison. I want you two," he addressed Paige and Zach, "to talk to the man Bingham assaulted."

Five

The Eastern Kentucky Correctional Complex is a medium-security prison and thirty-one miles from Salt Lick. Some prisons in Kentucky house death row, a punishment still enforced in the state. I had no doubt that once all was proven, Lance Bingham would have his suite upgraded, a last meal granted, and a lethal injection shot straight through his veins.

A guard at the front gate let us pass with a flash of Jack's creds, and after we relinquished our guns, we were on our way to meet with a monster. I had studied a lot of serial killers, their methods, their means, their trophies, and their messages. I had spent hours studying their faces and peering into their lifeless eyes void of compassion, but that had been through the pages of literature or through video. I wondered how much different it would be in person.

We were led into a meeting room used by lawyers to confer with their clients. Jack offered me the chair, and he paced behind me. The door opened, and two security guards entered, securing the prisoner by a grip on both of his arms. His hands were bound together in cuffs at the front. I wondered if the security here was always this intense, or if they were putting on a show for the FBI.

Lance Bingham had round-framed glasses that covered from his brows to his cheekbones. The silver hair on his head and face resembled steel wool, wiry and unkempt. His physique was trim and muscular.

His eyes met mine, and the corners of them creased as he smiled at me. His eyes, unlike the photos of killers I had studied, possessed awareness. His gaze reached inside my head and gripped onto my innate fears.

"Sit," one of the security guards barked, shoving Bingham into the chair across from me.

Bingham leaned his torso as far over the table as he could before sitting down. His breath swept across my face. "You're a little young'un, ain't ya?"

In the few seconds it took the guard to secure his cuffs to the restraint on the table, I looked back at Jack who bobbed his head to direct my focus forward. I knew this. My training and exercises in interrogation had prepared me for this. In fact, I had excelled in this part of the course.

"We're good here," I said, releasing the two security guards. I noticed the glance they passed to Jack as if looking to him for reassurance of my directive. He must have backed me up as they left the room.

Bingham smiled. "I killed two cows." A Kentucky accent inflected his speech, even though we knew he was born in Sarasota, Florida—coincidentally, my hometown.

"We're not here about the cows."

"Then what possibly could you all be here for?" His index finger tapped the table.

It was uncanny to hear a friendly phrase native to Kentucky, such as "you all" coming from this man's lips, a man who had tortured, murdered, and disemboweled at least nine people.

"We found the burial sites."

Bingham sat back. The smile remained tattooed on his lips like the permanent grin painted on the face of a clown.

"You know what I'm talking about."

"You'll have to clarify that, officer." He continued tapping the table with his finger.

"FBI Special Agent Brandon Fisher," I corrected him.

"Well, how-howdy Special Agent Fisher."

My earlobes heated with anger. He kept mind-piercing eye contact. I wanted him to avert his eyes, even blink for an extended period to create a barrier between his mind and my thoughts.

Empathize and establish a groundwork. Build on their ego.

"Your basement bunker. Genius really."

"Can't say I know what you're talking about." More finger tapping.

My eyes wanted to sag, to shut, to close, but I fought the urge. "Ten bodies were found buried on your property." I fanned out the crime scene photos on the table. My stomach flopped knowing I was sitting this close to the man responsible.

His eyes were unwavering. "Beneath my property you say?"

"You tortured them." I pointed out the incision marks on the most recent victim. "You killed them. You tore out their intestines. We found your meat grinder and the freezer."

"But you never found anything to prove I did it, I assume."

"It's your property, your responsibility."

Bingham laughed. "You can't prove nothin'."

Although the training prepared me to handle real life situations, it was quite another to be staring into the eyes of a sadistic killer as opposed to those of a colleague.

"Do you recognize her?" I put a fingertip on the photo of the most recent victim. Her face had been brushed of dirt, swept as if she were an object and not once a living human being.

"Can't say that I do." A smile lingered.

"That's enough!" Jack roared from behind me and came over to Bingham. He held him by the scruff of the neck. Eye contact with Bingham was broken as his face contorted, and he fought for oxygen.

"You killed those people. You won't even have a fucking chance to rot in this hellhole. I'll make sure they inject you, and we'll be in the front row watching you take your last breath. Tell us the fucking truth and maybe that won't happen."

Bingham's arms pulled back, his constraints allowing him little advantage in the struggle with a free man. A guard peeked through the window in the door but stepped back when I brushed him away with the wave of a hand.

Bingham's face flushed from a pale pink to a bright red.

"Who is she?" Jack held his face inches from Bingham's.

Bingham gasped for breath and Jack eventually let go. He stepped back.

"I might recognize her." The southern accent was gone.

Jack went back for his throat.

"Go ahead. What have I got to lose?" Bingham laughed, and his eyes returned to mine. They latched on as a life-sucking vine does to the brick of a house, destroying the mortar, crumbling it to a fine powder. "I killed cows. I assaulted my neighbor."

"You must think we're idiots." Jack looked at me. "He thinks we're idiots."

"I'll talk to the young'un, not you." Another series of finger tapping began.

"We're not negotiating with a murderer."

"You haven't proven that I am."

"It will only take a brief amount of time, and I assure you that your ass with be in that execution chair." Jack gestured between us and repeated his earlier words, "The two of us in the front row."

"You're extremely aggressive, Special Agent." Bingham spoke to Jack yet his eyes were on me. The smile had disappeared from his lips, but the wildfire in his eyes sparked with amusement. "You leave. I'll talk to him."

My heartrate sped up. The government believed in me, and the least I could do was muster enough confidence.

Jack straightened up. "You have two minutes. After that I'll be coming right back in that damned door, you understand?" He passed me a glance, one I was certain not to miss. His eyes said, *Are you ready for this, Kid?* before he left the room.

"He doesn't have faith in you."

"This isn't about me."

"But yes, it is, Special Agent Brandon Fisher. It most certainly is about you." The smile spread across Bingham's lips again.

"You said you recognized her."

"I could have been mistaken." He cocked his head, pointed to my wedding band. "You married, Special Agent?"

If he were trying to manipulate me or divert my course, he wouldn't meet with success. "These people were found under your property. Forensics will tie you to the murders, the torture."

"Does your wife know about her?"

My thinking process faltered at his question for a second. "You said you recognized her."

"I said I could have been mistaken." He maintained steadfast eye contact. "My guess is she doesn't know."

"The most recent victim was murdered while you were in prison. This one." I glanced at the photograph on the table.

"Certainly you can't pin that one on me."

"Who do you have working for you?"

A proud grin ate his mouth.

"You had a partner who killed with you."

"Will your wife divorce you when she finds out about the other woman?" Bingham clasped his hands.

"Mr. Bingham, your life is on the line—"

"As is your marriage. Confess, come clean of your sin and be forgiven."

How did this man know about the affair—or he was messing with me, taking a gamble on the statistics of the failed marriage arrangement of the twenty-first century?

"You tell me to confess? You don't even know me. Follow your own advice; cleanse your soul. You murdered ten people—"

"You just said nine."

I stared blankly at him.

"You said someone else killed another while I was in prison."

"You tortured them, you killed them and tore out their intestines, maybe ate them." My words paused as Bingham sat back; the intensity in his eyes was stronger than before.

"Who said I did that after they were dead?"

"You're confessing to the murders?"

"No, I never said that, but why assume their intestines were removed after death? How can one know true punishment for sin when dead?"

I quoted the only scripture I knew, "The wages of sin is death."

His crooked smile enlarged. "You know your Bible, yet you preach and do not apply—one of the greatest sins." Bingham leaned across the table, and for some reason I found myself moving toward him. "Set things right before you meet with punishment."

Something in his eyes and his body language made me uncomfortable. "Are you threatening me?"

"The Lord works in mysterious ways."

The door opened and Jack walked through. "Time's up."

"THAT SON OF A BITCH threatened me."

Jack laughed.

"You think that's funny?"

"I find it amusing how worked up you're getting." Jack's walking pace for a man almost twice my age proved a challenge to keep up with. "He definitely has obsessive compulsive tendencies."

Jack's comment came at me from an unexpected direction. He didn't look over at me when he spoke but kept his eyes straight ahead. We walked through a seemingly unending series of corridors in the prison.

"Can you tell me why I said that?"

"What, the OCD thing?"

"Yeah."

My mind was fixated on Bingham's threat housed in a few words, *Set things right before you meet with punishment.*

"Did you learn anything in there?" Jack stopped walking and faced me.

With the absence of our tapping shoes hitting the concrete floor, the prison was silent. "I learned a lot."

"You don't have to whisper, Slingshot."

I let out a deep breath.

"Hmm." Jack tapped his pocket. He craved another cigarette. I wondered how he had lived as long as he had without developing lung cancer or emphysema. "I'm waiting."

"He didn't deny the murders. In fact, he toyed with the idea. He wasn't disgusted by human remains or repulsed by the mention of removing intestines. He seemed intrigued by it." I thought back to his words, to his permanent smile, and then how it had expanded. "He experienced pride when I mentioned a tenth body and asked who helped him out." I took a deep breath and continued. "He didn't like it when I said the intestines were removed after death."

"Sounds like a confession to me."

"But not the way he continued to play it. I know he did it, you know he did it, but until we can prove that, there's nothing we can do to him."

"Well, then I guess it's best that we get on proving it. We know he's not going anywhere. What else did you get out of him?"

"He's religious. He told me to—" I stopped there. Jack didn't know about my extramarital affair, and I didn't think it would please him to know it had been with Paige.

Jack just watched me, his eyes saying, *Continue.*

"He believes in confessing sin to be forgiven. He said that if the intestines were removed after death, then the sinners would have been taught nothing."

"So he believes he's doing the Lord's work. Zach could be on to something with the religious connotation. Did he confirm the identity of the female vic?" Jack paused a few seconds. "You didn't push him."

"I tried to get it out of him but ran out of time. You came in."

Jack's face tightened, and he massaged his left temple. "Hmm."

"We'll find out another way."

"We'll find out another way?" Jack mocked my words. He pointed back down the hallway. "You had the opportunity to find out in there. You don't let opportunities go. It may be the last one you get."

I took another deep breath. The threat issued by Bingham had receded to the background. My foremost concern now was keeping my job. "He's religious. Based on his talk about sin, confessions, and forgiveness, I would say he's Catholic."

Jack didn't say anything but kept eye contact.

"He talked about people being sinners and needing to be punished. Maybe these people were from his church? He knew their secrets and made them pay for them?" I paused for a few seconds. "And why did you say OCD?"

"He tapped his index finger on the table eleven times. Two groups of five and one single."

"Just like the cuts on the victims. Two groups of five, one final—" My words faded, and my stomach tossed as Bingham's threat returned to the foreground.

Six

The prison warden could have been a basketball player; his height of about seven feet dwarfed both Jack and me. Maybe adding to the perception was that he was string-bean thin. He wore a salmon dress shirt, which complemented his dark skin, with a navy tie to match his pants. His suit jacket hung over the back of the chair. He carried his authority confidently as if he were molded for his position. His name was Clarence Moore.

"Sit, please." Moore gestured toward two chairs opposite his desk. "I've pulled the records you requested." He extended a folder labeled Lance Bingham to Jack, who passed it to me.

I opened it, and the first sheet inside was the visitor's log. "He only had one visitor?"

"That's right. Seems he ain't that popular."

"Lori Carter, that's Bingham's sister, right?"

"Yes, sir. She only came once jus' after Bingham was sentenced."

Lori had been married to Travis Carter up until he went missing in eighty-six. She never remarried.

I looked at Jack. "She probably came to sort out his affairs. She was paying for the property up until she died last year." I directed the next comment to the warden. "Was their interaction recorded?"

"Unfortunately not. It would violate his privacy rights."

It seemed unfair a man of Bingham's history would be worthy of any privacy. Of course, at the time of his conviction no one had known about the bodies under his property. I flipped through the few sheets in the folder.

Moore continued. "Unless it's a lawyer or law enforcement, there's always a guard in the room—ya know jus' to keep an eye on things. He might have heard somethin', but he's retired now."

"We'll need his name." Jack crossed his legs.

"Of course." Moore pulled a business card from the holder on the desk and scribbled a name on the back of it. "I wouldn't normally give you his home number—"

"Violation of privacy," Jack said.

"Exactly, but, given the circumstances…" A hand gestured forward, and his eyes added, *Because the FBI is interested, I'll make an exception.*

"Does Bingham attend any of the religious services you offer here?"

"That should be in the file."

I continued reading through it. When Bingham had been booked three years ago, he came in with a watch, a pocketknife, identification, and numerous wallet-sized photos. "The file mentions photos. What were they of?"

Moore leaned forward. "We don't catalog in that detail, but I can have it released to you with a warrant. Why are you guys interested in Bingham, anyhow?"

Jack uncrossed his legs. "Let's just say it involves more than dead cows."

Moore sat back. "He killed someone?"

"We're not at liberty to say."

Moore studied Jack's eyes. Seconds later, he picked up the water bottle on his desk and drained half of it. He roughly swallowed the last mouthful. "I'll get you a copy of the photos."

Jack continued. "What about access to the internet? Most prisons allow their inmates computer time."

"Yes, and we do. As you'll notice in the file there, Bingham took advantage of this."

I traced a finger along the printout as I recited, "Every day about ten in the morning, and in increments of thirty minutes each of those days."

"That's right."

"And I assume no recorded history due to Bingham's privacy rights."

A smile spread on Moore's lips. "That we are allowed to do. When inmates sign up for computer time, they have to sign a waiver. Included with this is authorization for us to monitor, track, and record their browsing history."

"We'll need a list of that," Jack said.

"Of course."

"What about Twitter, Facebook, and other social networking sites?" I asked.

"He did have a regular habit of logging onto Twitter."

"Do you know what his logon information was?"

Moore's face contorted. "I thought it was in the file there. Uh, if I remember right, he used the name, 'The Redeemer.'"

WE WERE IN WITH WARDEN Moore for about thirty minutes, but of everything that was said, the last two words he spoke stuck, *The Redeemer*. "This guy took it upon himself to exact vengeance and hold sinners accountable for their actions. Maybe he was a former priest."

The SUV's lights flashed as Jack pressed the key fob to unlock it. "What have we got in the file?"

I looked over at Jack from the passenger seat. "It tells us where Bingham was born, also when he moved to Salt Lick."

"Things we knew already." I shook my head. "I find it strange there aren't more addresses on file. Don't most serial killers move around a lot?"

"Just because more places aren't mentioned in a file doesn't mean Bingham was stationary."

"Guess that's true, but those tunnels wouldn't have made themselves, and even though we know he had help, I think it's safe to say he was in Salt Lick as long as the record says."

"Hmm."

"Both parents were dead by the time he was twenty. His sister Lori would have been sixteen, four years between them." I read more from the file, still deriving facts we already knew. "Bingham worked as a farmhand. He was strong, used to manual labor." I paused and connected eyes with Jack. "It explains how he'd have the strength for all that digging and how he could have overpowered his victims."

"I don't think he needed physical strength when it came to them."

"You're thinking he drugged them."

"Possibly, but I also believe the guy is a master manipulator. Once we know more about the victims, we'll have a better idea."

I flipped a page in the report. "Bingham works out in the prison gym every day. It would explain why he's in good shape."

"We also know the guy is an obsessive compulsive, and he likes things a certain way. What does the file say about Bingham attending religious services?"

I shuffled through the sheets. "Every Sunday."

"So he is religious. He also has narcissistic qualities. He convinced himself he was in control of our meeting by requesting that I leave."

"I witnessed pride when I brought up the other killer. He loved the thought of controlling someone else."

"But there's still a lot more to fill in. We need to know what he's twitted—"

"You mean tweeted." My statement earned a glare.

"Find out who he's in contact with."

"Who follows him," I corrected Jack. For some reason, those three words brought back Bingham's threat. Jack must have sensed it.

"He's behind bars, Slingshot."

I tried to let Jack's words comfort me, but it wasn't much Bingham that I worried about as I did the killer who roamed free.

Seven

J ack and I were making our way back to Salt Lick. He had his window cracked, but it did little to ease the secondhand smoke billowing from his mouth. By the end of the probationary period, I'd probably have lung cancer. Life could be unfair like that. While Jack would live to see a hundred, I'd be dead by thirty.

"How are you coming with the twit thing?"

"Twitter," I corrected him again. The generational gap drew a distinct line between those from the dark ages and those who were hitched to technology. "We know he goes by The Redeemer, but, just for the heck of it, I searched for users with the handle Redeemer in it. Most of them are churches. There's also a newspaper."

"Maybe Bingham belonged to one of those churches." Jack directed the hands-free system to dial Nadia Webber.

Nadia worked out of our home office in Quantico as a technical analyst.

She answered on the second ring.

"I need you to get together a list of the churches in the area around Salt Lick, take in all of Bath County. I believe there should be a list of about thirty, according to the good sheriff anyhow. I also want to know if any are of Catholic denomination or go under the name of Redeemer."

"Of course."

"Give that information to Zachery." Jack hung up and turned to me.

"I can see his history." I had clicked the link to his profile on Twitter. "There's not much here. His last tweet—"

"I like twit better."

I'm sure you do…

"Was two weeks ago," I paused for a second. "The file says he's on Twitter every morning, but I guess he doesn't have a lot to say—or maybe he sends personal messages and deletes them afterward."

"What was his last tweet?"

"He quoted a scripture."

Jack rolled his eyes.

"You don't believe in God?"

He sucked in on his cigarette and crushed the glowing butt in the SUV's ashtray. He didn't say anything.

I studied Jack's profile for a second. "Bingham's last tweet said, 'Let the words of my mouth and the meditation of my heart be acceptable in thy sight, O Lord, my strength and my redeemer.'"

"I hate it when cases cross over like this." Jack rolled up his window, but I kept mine lowered. "Now we're not just dealing with a psychopath and narcissist, we're likely dealing with a religious fanatic. They're the worst kind." He looked over at me. "Welcome to the FBI."

I METHODICALLY WORKED THROUGH THE list of Bingham's two hundred followers, curious what they were tweeting and where their interests lay.

"How do you know so much about this Twitter anyway?"

I glanced at Jack, not sure whether to explain.

"You have an account." He pulled around a slow-moving tractor and headed down the side road back to the house from hell.

"I used to."

"You still do."

I turned to face out the window and watched the cows in the field. A few of them were lying down. Rain was coming.

"Kid?"

"I don't use it much."

"Hmm."

"I started it as an experiment."

"Uh-huh."

"You don't believe me? That's all right. I just thought I'd see how many I could get to follow me."

"How many?"

I looked down at Bingham's following.

"Not as much as the psycho killer, I take it. Maybe you need to spout scripture."

This man made me pull on every portion of self-control I possessed. He could never know why I had started on Twitter or the people with whom I connected online.

"You're part of a knitting club. Not many sign up with Tweeter?"

"Twitter," I corrected him again, "is the site where when you share a brief message, it's called a tweet. What's so hard—"

Jack's lips curled upward.

"You're testing my limits."

"Not hard to get there either, is it?" Jack's face turned serious as he parked the SUV and took his keys from the ignition. "If you're not secure with who you are, this job will eat you alive."

"It's—" My words stopped there. My eyes were on the screen. "Jack."

"Yes." He stuck his head into the vehicle through the opened door.

"He just twitted, I mean tweeted."

"So much for just ten in the morning." Jack tapped the clock on the dash. Two in the afternoon.

I read off what Bingham had shared.

"What the hell is 'Confess, repent, respect the authorities, and vengeance is mine' supposed to mean?"

"I believe they're a bunch of scriptural verses melded

together. He's ordered a hit on me."

"You're overreacting."

"He told me that I would need to confess my sins to be forgiven. He went further to say that if I didn't, I would be punished. He's identifying me with his—" I paused, trying to think of another word, but couldn't conjure one. "His apprentice, whatever you want to call it. I don't think he expected them to carry on his work or even to get a partner along the way for that matter, but I definitely believe he knows who it is."

Jack activated the hands-free and connected with Nadia again. "Work your way through Bingham's followers, get together a list of names, IP addresses, and track these people down to their hometowns."

"I'm working on it, sir."

"And also track down the family of Travis Carter, Bingham's sister's in-laws."

"Of course."

"One more thing. Check the system again. See if you can find any more addresses associated with Lance Bingham. For some reason, I believe there should be more than two."

"I'll get this information to you as soon as I can."

"Make it even faster than that." Jack disconnected the call.

"So you know what IP addresses are but don't know what Twitter is?"

Jack passed me a glance before he got out of the SUV.

Eight

We reentered the house in which the unspeakable murders had taken place. Chills ran through me as I realized the man responsible no doubt fantasized about my life ending in the same manner.

Jack led the way down the stairs to the cellar, and I wasn't sure if I had the fortitude to go underground again. Despite being chilled from fear, sweat dripped down my back.

We stopped in the cellar to speak with Royster, the CSI with the allergies. He possessed a dislike for Jack as evidenced by the scowl that formed when he saw him.

"You guys find where the concrete door lined up for certain?" Jack asked.

"Of course." The CSI turned to me and said, "From the burial side, it was covered with packed dirt. Once it was removed, it revealed cinder blocks that were stacked to create the barrier."

"Made it simple. Then all he had to do was smear cement on the other side," I said.

"Excuse me, gentlemen." The chief coroner, Harold Jones, came up from the passageway. He and his assistant were carrying out the remains of a victim.

"How many more to go?"

Jones stopped near Jack, still holding onto the stretcher with the body. "Quite a few. The remains are aged and require a delicate touch—and there's been a lot of trace evidence to collect and catalog for the investigators. It all takes time."

"What do we know for sure?"

Jones nodded to his assistant, and they set the body down.

"He tortured them over a period of time," Jones said, his face paling. "He took time with them. The wounds were inflicted at different stages. There's only a slight variation, and someone with less experience may not have even noticed. Open it up, Jacob." His assistant opened the bag and Jones pointed at the incisions. This body was older and had decomposed significantly, but there was some skin left on the torso. "This victim is male, estimated remains are six years old, but like the most recent vic, his rate of decomposition was slowed by being buried and protected from the elements. Anyway, see here how the abrasion is less evident than this one, and so on."

I didn't see it but took his assessment. "Over how long of a period do you think he tortured them?"

Jones looked at me. "Over a period of at least ten to twelve days."

"Eleven days."

"Yes." Jones gave me a look that said, *That would be the number between ten and twelve.*

Jack patted his shirt pocket and pulled out his cigarette pack. The CSI watched his every movement and seemed ready to stop him should he actually light up. Jack stuck an unlit one in his mouth and turned to me. "Like I said, OCD." The butt bobbed as he spoke.

"So what's this guy's fascination with the number eleven?" I asked. "We figure that out, and we'll be on our way."

"I told you. It's the coinherence symbol." Zachery came up from the passageway with Paige behind him.

"We still don't have anything to prove that—"

I was interrupted by the ring of Jack's cell phone.

He answered and backed away a few steps. "And when can we expect the photos...Okay." He hung up and all our eyes were on him. "That was Moore," he looked at me. "The warrant came through already, and they're working on scanning the wallet photos. They'll be forwarded to us shortly."

"There's also something else you might be interested in knowing, Agent." The coroner's sharp eyes focused on Jack. "Upon closer examination, the victims were still alive when their intestines were removed."

I choked on my saliva and coughed to clear it.

"And not that I'd have to tell you, but based on the killer's pattern, the next victim would be male."

Zachery's focus was on me. "Something wrong there, Pending?"

"He believes Bingham threatened his life." Jack smiled in the smug way only he could achieve.

"I fail to see how that's funny."

"It's not funny per se, but it's entertaining. What would make him want to kill you?" Zachery slipped a hand into a pocket.

I passed a glance to Paige, but she was looking at the body.

"He wants Slingshot here to confess his sins."

Paige's eyes shot to mine and pain surged through them. It was the same look she had given me when I had told her it was a mistake, that I was a married man, and that I loved my wife. What were the chances that I'd be assigned to her team? I had hoped to never see her again.

"Sins? Do you have any, Pending?"

"Well, if that is all, I'll be getting back to work, Special Agent Harper." The coroner, not amused by the banter, bent to lift the stretcher. "Jacob." His assistant lifted the other end.

The coroner and his assistant left the cellar, heading for above ground while the CSI disappeared down the ramp.

Jack pulled out his lighter, flicked it, and put it back in his pocket. "How did you guys make out with the neighbor?"

"He's still bitter. Says that Bingham is one crazy son of a bitch." Paige put a hand on her hip above her holster.

Jack's lips gripped on the cigarette as if he were taking a drag on a lit cigarette. "It seems Bingham likes to go by the name of the Redeemer."

"That makes sense now. Nadia called with a list of churches, said that you told her to call, and she specifically mentioned there weren't any named Redeemer in the area," Zachery said.

"It's his Twitter name, but there's a reason he picked it."

"Maybe he considers himself a savior of sorts?" Paige offered. When we looked at her, she shrugged.

"With Bingham being on Twitter, there's a good chance the unsub already knows about the find and us." I relayed Bingham's last tweet and the mention of secular authorities.

"He tipped the guy off," Zachery said.

"But he might not know all the details, and he doesn't know that we know about Twitter or even him necessarily—" Jack's ringing cell interrupted. He answered. "Okay... How are you making out with everything else?... As fast as you can." He hung up and looked at Zachery and Paige. "So what all did Nadia tell you about the churches?"

"Like the sheriff said earlier, there are quite a few in the county. We have the names and locations now. Paige and I can go check them out, see if Bingham was a registered member with one of them."

"Visit the priests, elders, or whatever they call them. Start here in Salt Lick first, work your way out. Also speak to more of the neighbors, find out what they have to say about Bingham." Jack held up his phone and addressed me, "And you and I, well, we've got the address for Travis Carter's mother, and she lives right here in Salt Lick."

Nine

Travis Carter's mother, Ellie, had survived her husband of eighteen years. At the current age of sixty-five, she had never remarried but shared an address with a man by the name of Stewart Carlson.

They offered us a glass of iced tea which we appreciatively received as the humidity had increased with the promise of incoming rain. We sat at their dining room table with Jack and I facing each other, and the couple positioned at each end of the table.

"We understand your son was married to Lori Bingham," Jack said, using Lori's maiden name.

"That's, uh, right. What about her?" Ellie fidgeted with the glass of iced tea, spinning it around in her hand.

"How long were they married?"

"Too long." Ellie paused and took a swig of her drink. "She told lies about him."

"What sort of lies, Mrs. Carter?" I asked.

"Oh, please don't call me that. It's still Carter, but 'Miss' will do just fine." She spun her glass again. "She was a good girl at first. The perfect find for my Travis, but as time went on, she claimed he beat her. My boy wouldn't lay a hand on anyone, let alone a woman."

"How was his childhood growing up?" Jack asked.

Ellie's eyes snapped to him. She stopped spinning the glass. "If you're implying that I was abused, Travis witnessed it, and carried on the family tradition, you're sadly mistaken."

"If you know my Ellie, she wouldn't put up with that type o' shit," Stewart backed up his woman.

"How was Travis's relationship with Lori's brother, Lance Bingham?"

"Now that man, he sends shivers through me," Ellie said.

I straightened in my chair. "Why is that?"

"You ever meet the man?" I'm sure my eyes communicated the answer. "I guess you have. Anyway, I think he's the one who put Lori up to rattin' on Travis."

"Your son went missing back in eighty-six," I said.

"Yes. February eleventh of that year."

"The file reads the twelfth." Another instance of the number eleven made a bead of sweat form on my brow, or it could have just been the stale air in the farmhouse.

"Well, that's the day we reported him missing. We gave him a day to see if he'd come back."

"We?"

"Lori said he went off to work like any other day, only they never saw him at work. She spewed nonsense about my son having run off with a girlfriend." She solidified eye contact with me. "My Travis would never have done that, either. They wouldn't pronounce him until ninety-three. They said seven years had to pass first, not that you ever get closure without being able to..." Her words stalled as if she couldn't bring herself to say *body* in reference to her son. Her eyes smeared with suspicion. "Why are you around here asking questions about my boy anyway?" Her eyes lit. "Did you find him?" She looked toward a framed photograph on a sideboard.

"Is that your son?"

"Yes. He was handsome, wasn't he?"

I saw a man in his mid-twenties, a smile forced for the camera. Nothing about him stood out to me except for the glint in his eyes. Something lurking there made me question his character. I simply nodded in response to Ellie.

Jack's cell phone chimed, notifying him of a text message.

He pushed some keys and scrolled down the screen with a fingertip. He looked at me. "It's time we let these two get on with their day."

"Oh, please, you never answered what made you come by." Ellie extended her arm and rested a hand on Jack's forearm.

"We're investigating his disappearance." Jack rose to his feet, and she pulled her arm back.

"We'll let you know if we find anything," I added. Jack corrected me with a look that said, *We don't promise anything.*

When we got into the SUV, I did up the seat belt and looked over at Jack. "What was the text message?"

"The photos from the prison came in, and Travis Carter was one of them."

AFTER A FEW HOURS, Paige and Zachery had visited neighbors in a five-mile radius from Bingham's property. Most of them only knew Bingham from occasional run-ins at local stores but nothing much beyond that. They described him as keeping to himself and pretty much a loner. One older lady had commented, *Why move to a small town if you don't want connections with your neighbors?*

"Why do we get stuck doing all this?" Zachery drove while Paige sat in the passenger seat.

"We're the lucky ones."

"Huh, I don't see it that way."

Paige didn't really care what she did as long as she kept busy and intrigued—and, to her, finding out more about Lance Bingham proved intriguing. Bingham wasn't everything that occupied her focus. She missed Brandon and what they used to have. Even though it was brief and forbidden, his passion for life was contagious. Somehow, with him, despite all the negative and evil in the world, she felt some hope.

A few raindrops hit the windshield.

Zachery looked over at her. "You're awfully quiet."

"I'm just thinking."

He put his attention back on the road, and she was thankful

he didn't push her to speak her thoughts. She recalled how Brandon had looked at her when he and Jack had returned from visiting Bingham—how he mentioned confessing sin and stared at her. He regretted everything while she just wanted to resume things. She had also noticed something else. There was definite fear in Brandon's eyes.

JACK PULLED INTO THE PARKING lot of Betty's Place, which announced itself as a variety store and a restaurant. He activated the hands-free and asked for Doctor Jones.

"Special Agent Harper, I will call you once I have more news."

"The first victim you placed time of death at around three decades ago."

"Yes, as we've discussed."

Jack passed me a glance. The timeline aligned with when Travis Carter went missing. "And this victim was male, correct?"

"Yes." Impatience dripped from every word out of the coroner's lips. "Age approximately mid-twenties."

"I'm forwarding you some pictures. Please let me know if any of these match the victims. I'll mark the photo I'm especially curious about."

"You do realize that it will take more than a photo. I cannot confirm anything without tying DNA to the remains, dental records, health records, or other means of comparison."

"Start with facial structure similarities. Just do your best, doc." Jack disconnected the call, pulled out his cell, and tossed it to me. I caught it by reflex. "You hungry?"

It was hard to believe one could find their hunger when facing a case like this, but when asked the direct question, my stomach growled. "I could eat."

"Good. You forward those pictures to Jones—" he pointed to the cell in my hands "—and I'll get us something." Jack got out of the SUV.

I found it strange that Jack left me his cell phone when he

could ask the store clerk if she recognized any of the people in the photos.

I pulled the keys from the ignition and went into the store. There was one other car in the parking lot when we pulled in, and I assumed it must have belonged to a person who worked here. So much for their tourist season.

A bell chimed over the front door when I walked in. The store housed a small restaurant. A few tables were at the back of the store along with a chalkboard noting their daily specials. Today's special was hot dogs with fries and a side of coleslaw.

"Can I help you?" a voice called out from behind the checkout counter. I couldn't see her but knew by the fragile fluctuation to her tone that she was older. I noticed the top of Jack's head and maneuvered around a display at the end of an aisle.

"Oh, there are two of ya." The woman was barely five feet tall. Her eyes were friendly, but the look on her face indicated she wasn't impressed by feds being in her store.

I moved beside Jack and noticed he held another cell phone. His eyes went from it to me and then to the older lady. He pointed to a couple of subs stacked with meat and wrapped in cellophane that he had on the counter. "Hope that will be fine."

It seemed like a simple statement, but his head was slightly cocked to the right and his eyes sparked with reprimand.

"I just thought you might need your cell," I said, starting to explain why I had left the car.

He took the cell from me and stuffed it into a pocket. "I was just telling Mrs. Miller here about our investigation and asking her if she recognized any of these photos."

The older woman smiled at me awkwardly. "I only recognize the one."

"This one." Jack held up the phone, displaying the photo under discussion. I expected to see Travis Carter, but it wasn't him. "Mrs. Miller said his name is Kurt McCartney."

"He lived in Salt Lick back around ninety-three," Mrs. Miller began. "I only remember because it was the year Ellie Carter's son, Travis, was pronounced dead. How sad for a mother never to have closure. I just assumed that man—" she gestured to the phone "—had moved on. Not everyone can handle living in a small town. He wasn't here too long."

Personally, I'd go crazy living in a small town where everyone knew my business and where I had to drive miles to reach my destination every time I got in the car.

"You mentioned that you remember McCartney because of Travis Carter's death announcement. How are the two connected?" Jack asked.

I glanced at Jack. *Impressive.*

Mrs. Miller glanced between us. Her eyes said, *You're investigating more than missing persons.* I thought she was about to call us out, but instead she said, "I had just found out the news, and Kurt came in the store. He was an outsider at the time, really, but when he asked what was wrong, I told him." She offered a sincere smile. "I also remember the last name because of the famous McCartney. Kurt's first name was harder coming to me. He just wasn't that open, but he seemed like a nice man."

"So you didn't know of anyone who would have had an issue with him?"

She shook her head. "No, not at all. I knew he was married but never met her. Kind of strange for 'round here." Her brow creased, and her eyes narrowed. "Is it really missin' persons you're investigatin'?"

Jack dropped a ten-dollar bill on the counter and grabbed the subs. "Oh no, that's the god-darn truth."

A gasp escaped Miller's mouth, and a hand went to cover it. It slowly dropped. "Why, I never!" She shot me a look as if I should apologize for Jack's language.

"Thank you for your help, Mrs. Miller."

It was raining when we got outside, and the air was thick with humidity. Jack cranked the AC in the SUV. It blew out warm air for about sixty seconds. "You didn't trust me, Kid?"

Another car pulled into the lot. I watched as they parked beside us.

"I've been around a lot longer than you." He put the SUV into gear.

"I know—"

"I was serving in the military when you were in diapers."

"I know you could pretty much be my grand—" I left it there when Jack's head snapped to face me.

"Don't push it."

I smiled and killed it with a bite of my sub. Maybe if I had my mouth full of food, I wouldn't say anything to get into more trouble. I sneaked in a sideways glance and caught a hint of a smile on Jack's lips. Maybe I had actually impressed him back there—just maybe.

Ten

Rain hit the windshield as if a heavenly dam had released and combined with the grit from the road it smeared it with a chalky coating. Night had finally set in and had blanketed the county in blackness. No street lights or illumination from buildings compensated for the moon that lay buried in the sky behind a duvet of clouds.

After we had grabbed something to eat, I forwarded the pics to Jones, tagging the one of Kurt McCartney. He had texted a reply, *It won't be today.*

We followed up with Nadia to see how she was making out with tracking down the Twitter followers and gave her a new task of pulling the background on Kurt McCartney.

Jack and I found Jason Michaels, the retired prison security guard and paid him a visit. He didn't remember the interaction between Bingham and his sister, but oddly recalled Lori Carter fidgeting a lot, and he said that she wouldn't look him in the eye.

Jack and I met Paige and Zachery at Done Right BBQ, a restaurant that came highly recommended by the sheriff. When we got there, it wasn't any surprise where the man may have gained part of his paunch. Ribs and huge pieces of meat slathered with barbecue sauce cooked to perfection and served with a side of fries were the main feature of the menu. I didn't think I was hungry until we pulled up to the place. Mouthwatering aromas saturated the air outside the restaurant.

We all ordered and updated each other on our findings from the day.

"There're still a lot of people to visit, but we don't seem to be getting anywhere." Zachery stuck a french fry in his mouth. "Seems to me you guys were to come back and help us out with that." He looked at me, and then to Jack. "Ah, you were trying to be nice, you don't do door-to-door. I should know that." He smiled.

Jack tapped his shirt pocket.

I pointed to a sign on the far wall. "No smoking."

"Don't you seem to know everything? Surprised you haven't solved this thing yet," Jack said with a crooked grin.

I chose to ignore the mockery. "If Travis Carter can be confirmed as the first victim, we have a direct connection to Bingham." I took a sip of water. The steak was delicious but a larger portion than I was used to, and it was sitting heavy on my stomach. Jack had ordered a plate of wings and had me wishing I had.

"And if Bingham knew about the abuse against his sister, which we assume he did, based on what Ellie Carter told you," Paige started. "Maybe he played the role of Redeemer, but instead of forgiving sins he extracted punishment for them."

That mouthful of water went down hard. Paige looked at me as if she knew I was thinking of Bingham's words, *Confess your sin and repent or be punished.*

Her eyes remained fixed on mine. I took another swig of water and signaled the waitress for a refill.

"Take it easy, Slingshot." Jack tore off a piece of meat.

You'd think I was drinking booze...

"I'm just surprised you're able to put down your smokes long enough to eat." The words, intended to come out in a joking nature, came out more sarcastic. Everyone went quiet until Jack laughed.

"The kid thinks he's a comedian."

"Hey, I thought it was pretty funny." Paige smiled.

"Well, you would." Jack put another wing to his mouth.

The laughter died. More wasn't being said. Did everyone know about our past affair?

"So the Redeemer threatened you," Zachery said. "Quite the excitement for your first day in the field."

More glances were shared between Paige and me. It didn't escape Zachery who was about to say something when the waitress came to the table and topped up my water.

"Besides water, what do you suggest?" Jack wiped his fingers on a bunched-up napkin.

"Around here we like Ale-8-One," the waitress said. "Or just Ale-8 as we call them."

"And that is?" Jack asked.

"A soft drink."

"Sure, I'll take one of those," Jack said.

The waitress smiled and nodded, looked around the table. "Anyone else?

I shook my head. *No thanks to the sugar and caffeine.*

"I'll just take more water," Zachery said.

She topped up his glass and turned to Paige.

"Okay, I'll try it," she said.

With the waitress gone, it left us to face the reality of our day. I never had the illusion the world was a brilliant place free of evil, but being confronted with it to this degree made me appreciate what I did have—a happy marriage and a peaceful home life.

Jack's cell rang. He checked the caller ID. "And here he said he wouldn't have an answer for us today." He answered, and less than a minute later hung up. "That was Jones."

I leaned forward and turned to face Jack who was on my right. "Cause of death?"

"He'll start autopsies tomorrow and take a look for facial structure similarities to the pictures of the two men we've identified from Bingham's photos—Carter and McCartney—but he does have something for us—"

"Kind of crazy that someone would put themselves in the

place of God to decide guilt or innocence," Paige interrupted Jack.

"It wouldn't be the first in mankind's history," Zachery said.

"I know that." Her brows furrowed, and she pointed her fork at him as if threatening to stab him with it.

He held up both hands in surrender, and the waitress came back with the Ale-8-Ones. She stood there waiting for them to try the drink she'd suggested.

"Here goes," Paige said and held her bottled soda to Jack's.

They both took sips and Paige lowered hers first, licking her lips. Jack pressed his lips together and nodded.

"What does it taste like?" I asked.

"Like…citrus…and ginger?" Paige seemed unsure and looked at Jack, then the waitress.

"I'd agree." He took another swig. "It's good."

The waitress smiled and left. With her gone, Zachery picked up the conversation where we'd left off. "It's referred to as the God complex. They believe they can accomplish more than is humanly possible, and that they're above everyone else. In fact, it's not uncommon for serial killers to have an elevated opinion of self that motivates them to exact punishment, payment, or retribution for acts committed either directly against them or society in general."

Paige looked at me, and it felt like she read my mind. I had enough of trying to justify multiple murders for one day. I drained my water, wishing we could just get out of there.

"So do you guys want to know the reason Jones called?" Jack cupped his hand around his soda bottle and sat back. "Or we can continue to jabber all night." A subtle hint of a smile. "Remember the knife on the table in the—"

"Kill room," I interjected. He glared at me for the interruption.

"It wasn't a match to the wounds on the last victim."

Paige straightened and leaned in toward the table. "The unsub we're looking for didn't kill with that knife?"

"Doesn't look that way."

"Then they still have it with them. It's intended for use on the eleventh victim," she mumbled. The implication in her eyes said I could be the next victim. I swallowed decisively.

"We know that the unsub has intentions to kill again if they haven't already." Jack passed Paige and me a glance. "We have to stop them—"

"First we have to find them." The obvious slipped from my lips.

Jack gave me a look I had a hard time interpreting. I summoned the waitress to get the bill, hoping to dismiss any awkwardness. Jack lifted his bottle in a cheer gesture and drained it. As his arm came down, he was looking at me. "Alarm goes off at five, so you better be bright-eyed and bushy-tailed."

THE CAVE RUN LAKE LODGE where we were staying was a fifteen-minute drive from the restaurant. It was a two-story building with sixteen rooms. Sheriff Harris had gotten us in and called it a blessed miracle as most accommodations were already booked up with tourists. He also commented that the only saving grace was that most visitors preferred to stay in one of the numerous cabin resorts in the county.

My room was number eleven, and after today, I felt more than a twinge of superstition as I turned the key in the lock. I dropped my luggage bag on the bed, and it didn't make an impression. The bed was hard, but I was so tired I doubted it would matter.

When I had left home yesterday afternoon, I had told Deb I wasn't sure when I'd return. She wished me luck, but I sensed insincerity in her tone of voice and body language. She had braced herself against the doorframe as she normally would to wave goodbye, but as I had pulled out of the driveway, she never did.

I fished my personal cell from a pocket in the bag and saw four missed calls and two messages. One was from my friend

Randy whom I hung out with back in Florida. Hearing him made me homesick for my younger days. Debbie had called three times and had only left one message consisting of two words: *Call me.*

I looked at the time on the alarm clock. *9:30 PM.*

I dropped onto the bed and dialed home.

Eleven

L oud banging on the door startled me from sleep straight into a seated position. The clock read five fifteen.

What the hell happened to the alarm? Shit!

I opened the door to Jack, who was dressed in black slacks with a silver shirt. He looked down, and I realized I was just in boxer shorts. "Rise and shine, Kid."

"Just give me five minutes."

"Hmm."

I closed the door on him and hurried around the room to see if I could beat some sort of record for getting dressed. I went into the washroom and wiped a fingertip across my teeth. I needed to brush them, but I didn't have time. I hoped I had gum.

Five minutes later, I opened the door to see the rest of the team assembled in the parking lot. They all had coffee cups in their hands. The sun hadn't risen yet, and the lights mounted on the hotel cast the only illumination.

"Decided to return, after all, Pending?"

I stuck a piece of gum in my mouth, realizing that the moment I drank coffee the refreshing effect would be compromised. *Oh well.*

"Sleeping Beauty must have slept good, boss."

"There was a problem with my alarm." I wanted to add a bit of flair to the statement, possibly add knucklehead, but I resisted the urge.

"Next time make sure there isn't." Jack headed to the driver's seat. "I want us all back at the crime scene. I want us to study it, breathe it, and analyze it. Until some other people wake up, there's not much else we can do."

"Course, boss." Zachery and Paige got into the other SUV and drove out before Jack even had the keys in the ignition of ours.

The day was going to be a scorcher, and the rain from the night before only seemed to intensify the humidity. All I wanted was the vehicle's AC on.

Jack did up his seat belt and faced me. "There are a few things that bother me. One of them is tardiness."

"My alarm—"

"I don't want excuses."

I buried my sour facial expression into the lip of the coffee cup and took a sip.

As we pulled into Bingham's driveway, any hunger that had my stomach growling ceased. Instead, my insides churned at the thought of what lay beneath the ground—the tunnels, the burial chambers, the victims who had been tortured and murdered—all of it had etched permanent residence into my memory.

Two deputies were in charge to watch the place. They waved us past while they stayed in their cruiser, likely comfortable in the car's air conditioning.

We let ourselves in and headed to the cellar. My chest tightened, thinking about going further down, but we stalled there to talk. I took a deep breath.

Jack had an unlit cigarette dangling in his mouth, even though he had smoked one on the way over. "Now, I thought it would be best to immerse ourselves in Bingham's and our unsub's state of mind. What do we know about Bingham, The Redeemer, as he terms himself?" He turned to me.

The coffee hadn't infused me with sufficient caffeine yet.

"Time to wipe the sleep out of the eyes, Pending."

I disregarded Zachery and answered Jack. "We know that Bingham and his sister lost their father when he was twenty. The mother had died years before that." Everyone watched me. "We know that he came to Salt Lick from Sarasota, Florida where he was born and grew up."

"His family life seemed normal, straightforward—at least what can be discerned from a file," Paige said. "Unusual for a psychopath."

"What makes you conclude psychopath?" Jack turned to her.

"You're kidding, right?"

Jack's sour expression disclosed he was serious. I remembered Jack had referred to Bingham as a psychopath yesterday. He must have wanted Paige to justify her conclusion.

"Besides the violent nature of the murders and his disconnect from society? Brandon, you said that he seemed proud someone was killing for him since he's been in prison. He feels nothing for his victims."

"Psychopaths are normally of above-average intelligence. The construction of the underground passageways, the fact they didn't collapse or meet up, tells us Bingham is intelligent. The unsub likely is, too," Zachery said.

"He also exhibits psychopathic behavior, including the art of manipulation," Jack added.

I looked at Jack. "He did make you leave the room. It could also explain how he was able to get his victims to come with him and go down the passageway. He lured them with false charm perhaps?"

Jack cast me a sideways glance and said, "He saw you as someone he could manipulate. You're younger than me, obviously, a new *special* agent." Jack mocked my words from yesterday when I had corrected Bingham. "He saw your pride yet tried to demean you."

"I didn't let him."

"Psychopath," Paige said with a smile, trying to ease the

tension between Jack and me.

It seemed to have worked as Jack continued. "He wants to have control over everyone he comes across. He's obsessive compulsive as evidenced by his fascination with the number eleven. OCD is a narcissistic trait, but he definitely exhibits characteristics of a psychopath. I got an e-mail from Nadia last night that had more background info on Bingham. His mother was Robin Bingham and she married Lance's father in forty-nine, a month after Lance was born. Now Bingham's file doesn't show any criminal activity prior to more recent events."

"He likely just wasn't caught before now."

Jack nodded in agreement to Paige and opened the discussion to the rest of us. "What about other narcissistic characteristics he displays?"

"Bingham worked as a laborer for local farmers, helping out where he could. That aspect doesn't sound like a narcissist," I said.

Paige latched eyes with me. Her next words contradicted my sentiment. "Mr. Thompson, a neighbor who Bingham did work for, commented yesterday that Lance would talk about a day when he'd have his own farm. His words were: 'Then I won't have to report to the likes of you.'" Paige's eyes showed an apology.

"What about Twitter? He seeks contact, not necessarily a connection, with the outside world, but he doesn't do so in order to learn what's going on. He joins a social network where people can follow him, feed his ego, and make him feel important. That is a typical narcissist."

Zachery's eyes glazed over. "I know what he is. It makes perfect sense."

"By all means, share it with us." Jack pulled the cigarette from his mouth.

"He's a malignant narcissist. They can demonstrate psychotic behavior and a schizoid personality, so Bingham's really a concoction. His follower, the unsub, is likely submissive, easily manipulated. They likely idolize Bingham."

"I've heard of malignant narcissism, but isn't it pretty hard to discern from regular narcissism?" Paige tested Zachery's assessment.

"Yes, in fact, while you'll find narcissistic personality disorder defined in *The Diagnostic and Statistical Manual of Mental Disorders*, you will not find malignant narcissism. These people are simply diagnosed as having a narcissistic personality disorder, but with the other factors we've discussed, it seems like a plausible fit for Bingham. A schizoid person usually prefers to isolate themselves. It doesn't seem like Bingham had any close friends, and he wasn't involved with anyone. Many schizoids prefer to masturbate over dealing with the complications and social aspects of finding a partner."

Paige's face crunched up. "Prefer not to think about that part."

Zachery shrugged a shoulder.

"Hmm." Jack connected eyes with me before he turned and walked down the passageway. Zachery followed after him.

I wasn't sure how to read his eyes. Was he disappointed in my contribution about Twitter and connections? Should I have said more? Maybe I would have if given the time.

Paige put a hand on my shoulder but shrunk back after making contact. "He was impressed by what you had to say."

"He didn't sound it."

"If you're looking for praise, and a 'Well done,' you'll never hear it."

"I thought whenever he said, 'Hmm,' it was a bad thing."

She smiled. "It can be, but you will get to recognize the difference."

"If you say so." I took a deep breath and headed underground. Melding with the suffocating effect of confined spaces were the flash nightmares of Bingham's sick perma-smile.

In the main hub, Jack flicked his lighter and put it back in his pocket, more or less for something to do with his hands, I assumed. "Now the thing that's been bothering me is why take out their intestines. They are enormous, and it would be messy."

"The large intestine alone is about five feet long. That's not even mentioning the small intestine that is the length of twenty feet or more depending on the person. The basic math is roughly ten times longer than a person's height."

All of us looked at Zachery.

"The large intestine contains a type of bacteria that can break down molecules the human body can't break down itself."

Paige's face scrunched up. "I could have handled not hearing all of this."

"Oh, that's just the beginning—"

"End of it, if I have any say," Paige rushed out. "Disgusting. Do you really think Bingham and his follower ate the intestines? Why not the heart, brain, or other organs? Why where the shit passes through?"

The coffee rose into the back of my throat. I swallowed quickly.

"Maybe he didn't eat the intestines," Zachery said, "but then why remove them, why the grinder, and why the freezer?"

None of us said anything. I focused on trying to breathe as my heart kept tapping as if preparing for a major heart palpitation. Paige crossed her arms, her eyes looking down a tunnel. Jack pulled out his lighter and flicked it again.

"And here's another question," Zachery continued, "where are they now?"

WE SPENT THE NEXT HOUR and a half working the crime scene. Zachery was fascinated by the pristine state of the area given the bloodshed that would have transpired here. I kept trying to put that aspect out of my mind.

We went down the fourth tunnel, and through the uncovered doorway that led to the *kill room* under Bingham's bedroom.

Being enclosed in this type of a prison ignited my compassion for the victims. The coroner had confirmed that they were disemboweled while alive. Again, the threat Bingham had extended on my life gave the scene personal impact.

Bingham never expressed any remorse, but, in contrast, joked about the fact that the intestines were removed. An innocent person, a normal person, when confronted with a find like that under their home would be disgusted and scared. They'd realize that it would likely only be a matter of time before they made it to death row, but Bingham had been calm, even proud of being accused. How his smile had grown at the mention of someone following in his steps. He thought of himself as untouchable.

Jack had sent an e-mail to Nadia to research any unsolved cases that were similar to what we found here. He believed that Bingham had killed before Salt Lick, Kentucky.

"What would motivate him to kill these people?" I asked the question we were all contemplating.

We were all standing in the "kill room" beside where the stretcher had been. It had been removed as evidence.

"Sometimes we never get the why, Kid."

"Hope I'm not in-interrupting anything." The accent pure Kentucky. Deputy White entered the room. "You feds git an early start to the day, don't ya?"

None of us said anything.

"Anyway, the sheriff's upstairs, and there's fresh coffee. We came by earlier, saw your fancy SUVs out front. Harris thought it'd be nice if we got y'all a coffee and came back."

"Thank you," Paige said, offering a sincere smile.

She looked like she'd had a rough night's sleep. Her eyeliner was applied a bit thicker, her lids painted heavier.

"How's things goin' anyhow?"

"We think we have an ID on the first vic. Jones still has to confirm," Jack offered the information.

White's feet twisted in the dirt as he glanced back down the tunnel from which he had entered. He aligned his eyes with Jack's. "And who's that?"

"Travis Carter, Bingham's brother-in-law." Jack watched the man's reaction closely.

White's mouth formed an *O*.

"You knew him, I take it."

"I believe most of us deputies did," he continued, realizing all of our eyes were on him. "He beat up on Lori. Now she never filed any charges, but it was d-def-definitely Travis that did the damage to her."

Jack turned to me. "I guess Ellie's precious son would after all."

I took a deep breath. I had likely met the family of a victim. My eyes welded to where the stretcher had been, where the victims had been constrained and forced to stay for a period of days while Bingham mutilated and eventually disemboweled them.

The deputy twisted his feet again, jacked a thumb over his shoulder. "Well, that coffee ain't gettin' any fresher."

SHERIFF HARRIS STOOD IN WHAT had served as Bingham's living room, decorated with only a rust-colored floral sofa, an old tube television, and a fold-up TV tray.

"Good mornin', y'all. Fresh coffee." Harris held onto a coffee cup and lifted a finger to point toward the counter in Bingham's kitchen. "At least it was twenty minutes ago."

"They think they know who the first victim was." Deputy White took a draw on his coffee. It was quiet enough in the room to hear his thick mustache hairs scrape the plastic lid. He pulled back from the cup slowly. "Travis Carter."

"Travis?" Sheriff Harris's legs gave way slightly. His height dropped a few inches as his knees buckled.

Paige stepped toward him. "Sheriff?"

He held up a hand to her. "I knew the boy since he was knee high to a grasshopper. It was terrible what he did to his lady, but he was a misled young man." Harris turned to me. "He only knew what he was taught."

"His father abused his mother?"

Harris nodded. "All the time, and Ellie was a good lady, still is."

Jack fished a cigarette out of the package, lit up, and looked at me. "Ellie lied to us."

Deputy White's eyes flashed with disdain, snapping to the amber butt.

Harris spoke up, "Well if she did, it was for a damn good reason."

"You consider any reason good enough to justify lying to a federal agent?" Jack exhaled a puff of white away from the group of us.

"I'm not saying that. All I was sayin' is she'd have a good reason."

"To protect her involvement?"

I noticed Paige's and Zachery's heads turn. Even they seemed surprised by Jack's lack of candor. It made me think of what he told me: *Sometimes you have to play dirty to get the answers you need. We're not special agents to make friends, we're not here to bring healing to the world, we're here to bring the guilty to justice and make them accountable.* Dramatically, he had taken a drag on his cigarette after the speech.

"That's insanity. Why would she kill her own son?"

"It doesn't mean she took part, maybe she knows something she's not telling us."

"Why am I feeling attacked?"

"Why should you feel that way, Sheriff?"

The sheriff took a draw on his coffee, swirled it around his mouth before swallowing it. "Ellie and I, well, we were a couple. Now that's a while back now, before her dead husband. Can't believe she picked him over me. Anyway, I jus' know her is all."

"Hmm."

There it was again. I thought back to how he responded that way to me. Maybe there was a difference to the inflection. This time Jack's fix on the man cemented the fact he held suspicions of something. "Hmm" meant he wasn't buying it.

"Anyway, the county would like to treat you to breakfast if you're interested, your whole team." He swept a hand out to encompass all of us.

"We don't have time."

"You don't have time to eat? Wow, you city folk really don't take time for nothin', do ya?" He laid a splayed hand over his round stomach. "How's a man, or woman—" he smiled at Paige "—s'posed to survive without fuel in his system?"

Jack looked at all of us and after thirty seconds nodded his approval for breakfast. I found myself thankful as all the talk of food had made my hunger return.

"We have to make it quick."

"But of course." It was Sheriff Harris's turn to add a sardonic nature to his statement.

Twelve

Deputy White had a way of pulling food off the fork with his teeth, not his lips; every mouthful was accompanied by a small scraping sound. For the first five forkfuls or so, I watched, wondering if he'd take the hint as to how annoying the habit was. He didn't seem to notice.

"They've got the best flapjacks here." The sheriff cut off a triangle-shaped wedge, stuffed it into his mouth.

We were at Betty's Place. She was moving around like a woman half her age, splitting her time between the kitchen and checking on her customers.

There were eight tables and the six of us took up two of them pushed together. The other six tables were full, save one where the couple was standing to leave. No one was waiting to fill it. Either tourist season was not as busy as Harris had led us to believe or we were here too early.

"So you had a relationship with Ellie Carter—" Jack brought an abrupt ending to his sentence as he lifted a coffee mug to his lips.

"Well, she wasn't Carter back then, Eldridge." Harris's eyes went back to his plate as he took another stab at his flapjack, which must have been his fifth one.

I had finished my breakfast some time ago. Food was simply something my body required. I didn't find enjoyment in having a long, drawn-out meal. That was one area where Deb and I differed, and where I made the sacrifice every anniversary, birthday, and Valentine's Day. She liked passing time at fancy restaurants.

Deputy White elaborated for the sheriff. "She hurt him real bad—"

"Wayne, that's none of your business."

Jack's phone chirped with notification of a text message. He lifted it out of its holder, read it, and then looked at us. "Nadia's finished running the photos through missing persons. The only one it recognized was Travis Carter. The record also confirmed what Ellie told us. He was reported as missing in eighty-six, pronounced in ninety-three."

"I told you, she's not a liar, Agent."

Jack didn't look at the sheriff but continued speaking to us. "We could be looking at victims who didn't have family or connections. Otherwise, they all would have been reported."

I thought of Kurt McCartney, a married man. I hesitated to correct him but wondered if this was another test. "I don't agree." The words came out bluntly. Everyone's eyes went to me. Even the sheriff, who had a forkful, paused it en route to his mouth. "Kurt McCartney was a married man, so why wasn't he reported missing?" As I continued talking, some more things became evident. "We don't even know for certain that the people from the pictures were all victims of the Redeemer. We're assuming that. Maybe some are intended targets?"

"Hmm."

I glanced at Jack, not knowing how to interpret that one.

"The Redeemer?" Harris rested the full fork on the edge of his plate, took a napkin, and wiped his hands.

"That's what he calls himself on Twitter."

"Twitter?" Deputy White leaned forward, waved a hand. "I know what it is, but who has time for such foolishness?"

Jack passed me a look.

I responded to White, "It's popular and honestly doesn't take a lot of time—"

"Well, that's what we call a load of shit ready to spread

on a field, Agent. It's time away from family. That's most important."

"It takes seconds to post something that's on your mind, share a link. There's a great part of the population that are online with it. I hardly think it's harmful, or wasteful to spend time social networking."

"What do you have to social network for?" White asked the question, and everyone faced me.

My eyes met with Paige's. "That's his personal life. Let's focus on the case."

"Sounds like it could be interesting, Slingshot."

"Come on, Pending, don't hold out on us."

I looked around the table, appealed to the sheriff to bail me out of this one. He sat back waiting for an answer. I guessed I didn't help him when it came to Jack's grilling him about Ellie. "I'd prefer not to answer."

"He dresses up My Little Ponies and puts them up for sale." Zachery laughed.

"He what?" The deputy chuckled.

"Oh, some people pimp them all out, put jewels on them, paint them, you name it. People sell them, people collect them." Zachery turned to me. I glared in return.

"It's not that."

Paige said, "What does it matter? We've got ten murders to solve, likely one to prevent. Maybe Brandon's right, the photos weren't of victims only, but also of intended targets."

Zachery let out a rush of air as if disappointed his fun had ended.

"Very valid point and one I had considered myself. First, I wanted to make sure they weren't in missing persons," Jack said. "I e-mailed Nadia to look into that last night."

Paige pushed her plates out from her, leaned forward, and crossed her arms on the table. "Makes complete sense, but now that we know they're not in the database, we need to find out who they all are."

"If they're not all victims, it really shows how arrogant

Bingham is. He thinks he's untouchable," I said.

Deputy White's eyes rolled back. "The man's in prison."

"He believes he'll get out. He still feels he's above the system."

"Based on what?"

"Attitude. Projection." I paused, certain the deputy would add something, but he didn't. "I know it hasn't been confirmed that Travis Carter or Kurt McCartney were among the bodies found, but it makes me wonder if his targets are out there walking around. If we find the people in the pictures, we might prevent another murder."

Paige nodded. Zachery's expression was hard to read. Jack stared into his coffee.

"Really, where is McCartney's wife in all of this? She didn't report him and she's not among the photos."

Betty Miller came over to the table. "I hope all was good here." She smiled sincerely, sharing it with all of us at the table.

"Delicious as usual, Betty." The sheriff patted his stomach.

The woman stood at the edge of the table. An awkward silence filled the space.

"Is there something you want to say?" The sheriff put a hand on her shoulder.

Betty Miller looked from him to Jack. "I know it ain't polite manners to eavesdrop, and I didn't mean to." She bunched up the front of the apron she wore around her waist, twisting it in her hands.

"It's okay," Paige assured her.

Betty stopped twisting the fabric and wiped her hands on the apron. When she removed them, the apron was still starch white. She looked to Jack. "You said missing persons, and I know that's what you and him—" she nodded toward me "—were in here asking about yesterday. Those photos you—"

The front door chimed, and she lifted on her toes to see who it was. She smiled as she waved the person over.

Rounding the aisle was a woman with delicate facial features, her nose slightly upturned. It seemed like her pace stalled when she noticed the rest of us. Her eyes went to the floor.

Betty wrapped an arm around the woman and squeezed her. "Everyone, this is Nancy Windermere. She's a friend of mine."

A hand went up and waved timidly, followed by a weak, thickly accented, "Hi."

"I did some jaw-flappin'," Betty said, holding less shame in that than overhearing a conversation. "I told her about the special FBI agents up here in Salt Lick, what y'all are doin'." Betty squeezed the woman tight before releasing her. "It's all right, Nancy, go ahead."

Nancy slipped a hand into the oversized purse she carried. It was knitted out of variegated wool of bright pinks, greens, and yellows. She pulled out a five-by-seven photo and extended it to me.

The photo was of a woman in her early twenties, maybe as young as twenty. She had long, platinum blonde hair, which she wore with the sides pulled back. She was smiling large enough to disclose two deep-set dimples.

"That's Sally," Nancy said, her voice barely loud enough to hear.

"This is your daughter?" I asked.

Nancy nodded. "I was hoping that you could help me find her."

The sheriff chose now to stand. The deputy followed behind him. I sensed this was an arranged meeting. He might not have known when we'd show up, but Harris was aware that Nancy Windermere wanted to talk to us.

Harris put on a hat and tipped it to us. "We've got work to do out there, and it's gonna be another scorcher. Good day, y'all."

With them gone, Betty slipped into one chair and Nancy the other.

"Did you file a missing persons report, Mrs. Windermere?"

I asked.

"You can just call me Nancy, please. Nothin' so formal." Her eyes looked around the restaurant. "But, no, I didn't." The photo of Sally had made its way around the table, and Paige extended it back to Nancy. "No, no, please keep it. That is a copy for you."

Instead of pushing the issue about why she hadn't filed a report, I thought I'd go about it from another angle. It seemed the team left the talking to me. "When was the last time you saw your daughter?"

"Three years ago." Nancy clasped her hands over the purse she had placed on her lap. "February eleventh."

Different year of course, but February the eleventh was the same date that Travis Carter had last been seen. "Did she have any new friends?"

Nancy's lashes soaked with tears. "I know you found something at the Bingham property. People talk. We might talk slower, but we ain't stupid." She put a hand over her nose and mouth, wiped downward. "What did that man do to my baby?"

I looked at Jack, who nodded for me to continue. "We haven't been able to identify who was found as of yet."

Betty leaned forward. "But you did find more than one, didn't you? All those pictures you showed me. Are they victims?"

"We're not confirming anything at this point."

"Which is governmental talk for puttin' a lid on it." Betty huffed, crossed her arms, and turned to Nancy.

"I just want to know what happened to her. I know that she wouldn't have run away. I know that will be your next question. She was engaged to be married."

"We're going to need his name."

"Course." Nancy went into her bag and pulled out a piece of notepad paper. She handed it to me. "I wrote up everything. His name was Colt Smith. His family grew up 'round here. Doc Jones helped birth him."

How ironic that the man who was now undertaking dead bodies had at least once played a role in bringing life into the world.

"And he and his family are still around in the area?"

"Yes, course. They live on Caney Avenue. Colt does, too. He married another woman a year ago, though. He's a young man, needed to get on with his life." Her eyes went vacant. "I wish I could. Please find out what happened to my little girl."

"I assure you, we will do the best we can."

Nancy placed a hand on my forearm and squeezed. "God bless you."

I smiled at her, but there was at least one more question that needed to be asked. "Mrs. Windermere—" Her eyes chastised me to be less formal. "Nancy," I corrected, "I realize it might be hard on you, but what specific memories do you have of that day?"

"Do you have children, Agent? You look young enough to still be considered one, not much older than my Sally."

I shook my head, conscious of Jack's eyes on me. Mark one off for the old man. I was young, was that a crime?

"She went out of town to the next county over, shopping for decorations. She called from the store and sounded so happy." Nancy's eyes welled with tears again. "That was the last I heard from her."

"What about that morning when she left? How did she seem to you?"

"Jus' like normal, I s'pose."

"She wasn't anxious, upset? She didn't complain about anyone watching or following her?"

Nancy went quiet. "Did Lance kill my baby girl?" Tears fell down her cheeks. She pulled her hand back.

"We're still investigating who, and what exactly happened."

"As Betty asked, is there more than one?"

I did my best to redirect. "What about Lance Bingham? Did your daughter know him?"

"Course. We all attended the same church."

"Which church?"

"Lakeview Community."

"Is it Catholic?"

"No, but it's Christian." Arms crossed.

"We will look into this for you, Nancy."

She blinked hard and rose along with Betty.

"Breakfast is on the county. Sheriff Harris settled up already," Betty said.

The two women walked away, leaving three pairs of eyes watching me. Zachery shook his head, Paige looked at me with some sort of empathy, and Jack's jaw sat askew.

"You two checked with the churches here, I thought."

"We did, even Lakeview, but Bingham wasn't a member," Paige said.

"And no one knew him?"

"They heard of him but didn't know him."

Jack fished out a cigarette. "It's time to go."

Thirteen

Y ou can't promise anyone anything, first rule," Jack said with a lit cigarette pressed between his lips.

The four of us were standing near the SUVs in the parking lot.

"All I said is we would look into her missing daughter."

"What you, in effect, promised is something that might not even factor in to this case." He took a solid drag from the cigarette, letting the ash build up on the end.

"But she very well might."

"You a gambler, Kid? Because that's what you just did."

"Her daughter knew Bingham, went to the same church—"

"But three years ago, Bingham was in prison. If, and I'm using that generously, if the girl is the last victim, it wasn't Bingham who killed her." He dropped the burning cigarette to the dirt and extinguished it with a twist of his shoe. "Their prior relationship might not mean anything. We don't give people false hope." Jack turned to get in the SUV.

"And what's wrong with false hope? Isn't hope of any kind better than none?"

Jack stopped moving and didn't say a word. Zachery watched me with large eyes, and Paige's movements froze with the SUV door open and her hand on the handle. Seconds passed.

"Seriously." I knew the single word came out as a desperate appeal.

Jack got into the SUV and slammed the door.

"Shit!" I stomped a foot into the dirt of the parking lot and found myself turning to Zachery for reassurance. He shook his head and got into the other SUV.

IT HAD ALREADY BEEN DECIDED before I got a lesson on what to say and what not to, in which direction we would be heading. Jack and I would be seeing Colt Smith, Sally's fiancé, and Paige and Zachery would be paying the guy's parents a visit. I found it interesting how something *that might not even have to do with the case*, as Jack put it, had us literally spinning wheels on the gravel to investigate it. Of course, I kept that part to myself.

We now knew the name of the church that Bingham had attended, the Lakeview Community Church, a non-Catholic denomination. We may have wrongly assumed he had an affiliation with Catholicism, but then maybe we just had to look further into his past. It was also entirely possible we were off base altogether. That's the thing with assembling a profile: it was a work in progress.

We had forwarded the photograph of Sally to Jones for comparison to the most recent victim. Jack activated the hands-free and called Jones to see how he was making out. Jack had to leave a message, and that didn't improve his mood any.

We pulled up to the address indicated for Colt Smith and were about to get out of the SUV when the phone rang. Caller identity read Nadia Webber. Jack answered by saying, "You got the Twit thing figured out?" He looked over at me. He had intentionally referred to Twitter incorrectly.

"I have something better than that. You also asked me to dig into any open cases that show similar MOs to this case. I found one in Sarasota, Florida, sir."

"What are we looking at?"

"Eleven bodies."

"Ah, shit."

"The murders date back to seventy-one."

"Bingham would have been twenty-two at the time," I said.

"Tell them to forward all the information they have on the case."

"Have already." She paused only a few seconds. "I also have accessed Lori Carter's medical records. She was admitted to the hospital eight times. She had stitches to her cheek once. The last time her nose was broken."

"Is there a record of any charges against her husband?"

"No, nothing."

Jack disconnected the call and leaned back into his seat.

The curtain in the front window of the house pulled back, and a woman looked out. Jack either didn't notice or didn't care. He carried on as if we were parked in an abandoned lot.

"Bingham has no next of kin, and no children on record." Jack ground a palm into the steering wheel. "With the empty grave and the similar murders now in Florida..." His words trailed off, and he picked up seconds later. "The unsub would have admired Bingham, possibly hung around him."

"No one's mentioned anyone like that."

Jack fished out a cigarette and lit up. He put the window down and blew the smoke out the window. "Well, Kid, we're gonna have to find them."

"What if the unsub was connected to Bingham originally through his sister, Lori Carter. We could find out if she was a member of Lakeview Community Church, find out who her close friends were. It could be a place to start."

"Hmm."

Was he giving consideration to what I had said?

"We need to know who the other people in those pictures are," Jack said.

"Yeah, great idea, but how do you intend to find out? We already know they're not in the missing persons database."

Jack put the SUV into reverse. Dust from the graveled driveway kicked up into the air.

"Aren't we going to talk to Colt Smith?"

Jack drove with his eyes straight ahead, determination lighting a fire in them.

AN HOUR LATER, we sat in the visitor's room at Eastern Kentucky Correctional Complex. Jack told me he would be taking the lead on this. The door opened, and the same guards from yesterday led Lance Bingham in.

His eyes instantly latched to mine. As they secured him to the table, across from Jack, he looked at me. A smile spread across his mouth. "Confess your sins yet?"

Jack slammed the flat of a hand against the table. Bingham never flinched. His eyes stayed fixed on mine.

Jack spread copies of the photos on the table. "These were on you when you were booked. Who are they?"

"If you confess your sins, you will be forgiven." He directed the comment to me.

"He was twenty-three when he went missing." Jack pressed an index finger to Travis Carter's photo. "He was your brother-in-law."

Bingham adjusted his focus to Jack. "He wasn't worthy of her."

"Is that why you killed him?"

"Who says I did?"

"We know he beat your sister, got her admitted to the hospital. You think of yourself as the Redeemer. Were you your sister's savior?"

Bingham's eyes lit and narrowed as a lizard's. "You've been doing your homework."

"We know you love Twitter—"

Bingham laughed. "So impressive you found out about Twitter seeing as I sign away my human rights to log onto the internet."

"It allows you to feel powerful, needed, and influential," Jack said, dragging out the last word, "and you especially like feeling that way."

"You think you know someone." A sardonic smile sat on his lips.

"What about him?" Jack pointed to the photo of Kurt McCartney. There was no reaction on Bingham's face. "You know all of these people—"

"Says who?"

"You carried them on your person. They were your trophies."

The statement warranted another laugh. "Maybe I'm lonely. Carrying pictures of strangers makes me feel a connection to others."

"We know about the other murders."

"You said there were ten bodies under my house. I have no idea how they got there." He scanned the table for a few seconds, two of them were spent on Sally Windermere.

We took the photo given to us by Sally's mother and printed it in wallet-size to place among the ones taken from him at the time of booking.

"You knew Travis Carter. Why carry the picture of a man who beat your sister?"

Bingham shrugged. "He was family."

"But you also knew her, didn't you?" Jack put a finger on the picture of Sally. "And before you lie to us, we know you did."

Bingham opened his hands, palms up on the table. "I didn't have that picture. Where did you get it?"

"She is dead." Jack stretched the truth.

Bingham looked at me, a sick smile on his face. "You haven't answered me. Have you confessed your sins?"

I moved forward three steps. This man wasn't going to hold power over me, despite the evil in his heart, the intent in his eyes, and his outreach to the world. "Have you?"

Bingham's face cracked into a wider smile before transforming into laughter.

OUT IN THE HALL, Jack patted his pocket but didn't pull out

the cigarette pack. "He said he didn't have the picture of Sally. We know he didn't at the time of booking because we slipped it in there, but he recognized her. He also made it sound as if it were in the past tense. His words were, 'I didn't have that picture.' Maybe he didn't at the time of booking, but the unsub sent it to him since he's been in here?"

I paced, my skin jumping from nerves. I had stood my ground with a serial killer. "He mentioned connection when it comes to the pictures. Those people mean something to him. I believe the fact he came back with 'You think you know someone' was his way of confirming he likes to be influential, just as you accused him of. I believe both connecting and influence mean the same thing to this guy. He's not capable of a relationship unless he's able to manipulate it."

"He's not remorseful even for Sally, and we know that he knew her. In fact, he's void of emotion except for pride which surfaces when discussing the victims."

"And yesterday, when the truth came out that one of the murders happened while he was in here, he was proud—and did you see his face when you called him the Redeemer?" When I stopped talking, silence ate the space between us before I spoke again. "Okay, let's assume Bingham has a photo of Sally. We know he didn't have it at the time of booking, so how did he get it?"

Jack addressed the guard. "We need to speak with the warden again."

"Course." The guard's voice was deeper than one would expect given his smaller stature. He took us through the labyrinth of corridors with which we were unfortunately becoming familiar.

Clarence Moore looked up from his monitor to us in the doorway. "They asked to see you," the guard said, slinking back into the hallway.

Moore stood. "Agents? I thought I had provided everything you asked for."

"We need to see Bingham's cell."

Moore tossed a pen he held in his hand to the desk. "I'm not sure what y'all think it's going to tell ya, but I can take ya there."

Moore still didn't know the details of our investigation, and it was better that way. The fewer people who knew, the less possibility there was of it leaking to the media and, in turn, reaching the unsub.

Minutes later, we were stepping into the Redeemer's cell. As Moore informed us, he shared the space with an inmate by the name of Tim Johnson. Johnson had been put away for armed B&E that had him holding a gun on the homeowner.

Bingham hadn't returned from his trip down the hall, but his cellmate was sitting on the mattress picking at his fingernails. He didn't move when our shadows broke his light.

"Johnson, out!" The guard bellowed. Johnson kept picking at his nails. "Don't make me come in there an' drag yo' ass out!"

Johnson stopped moving, and with his eyes on us, rose to his feet. He turned around and held his hands behind his back.

The guard made it to Johnson in a few long strides and cuffed his hands. "You think yo' so fuckin' smart."

"Ass-ault." Johnson laughed as if he was drunk.

The guard pulled on him and took him to the hall.

"Did you see that? Ass-ault." Johnson only stopped cackling long enough to repeat himself.

A look passed between the guard and Johnson. This time Johnson shut up.

Jack went into the cell first. Johnson was on the bottom bunk which meant Bingham would have crashed on the upper one.

Beside Johnson's mattress, there was a crayon drawing of a girl in a triangle dress with a stick-figure dog beside her. Green strokes made for grass under their feet, and the words, *I love you, Daddy*, were scribbled on it.

I turned to face Johnson who was looking down the hallway as if scheming a run for freedom. If he had a child, why would he risk everything to wind up here?

Jack looked at the ceiling of the cell, hunched, and looked behind the urinal and under the sink. He snapped on a pair of latex gloves and pulled out Johnson's mattress. He looked behind it, underneath it, around it. In this medium security prison, the mattresses came free of the metal frame. He lifted up a paperback novel. The cover showed a hand holding a gun. I shook my head. That was what had landed him here in the first place. Jack put it back in place, the mattress on top of it.

I put gloves on and went to slide a hand under the edge of the top mattress. Jack pulled my arm back. "Don't ever go in blind."

His sour expression and the warning in his words halted my movements.

"You lift that end. I'll lift the other."

I followed Jack's directions, and the mattress was on the floor seconds later.

I stepped up on the railing of the bottom bunk to get a good view. What I saw made my pulse speed up. "There's a lot up here."

Jack hoisted up on the frame of the bottom bunk. "Good thing I stopped you, Kid." He held up a small razor.

"Where would he have—"

Jack angled it. "It's from shaving."

"They let them have razors?"

"Medium security. Just like they're allowed playtime in the yard, on the internet, and in the library." Jack took a dig at the justice system, the same one he stood to defend. "He broke the blade from the holder. He probably has a system worked out. Usually inmates are allowed to purchase razors but have to return the dull ones to get new ones."

"That's reassuring." I rubbed my stomach, thinking back to the victims and how they suffered. "Arm a serial killer with his ideal weapon."

It went silent between us for a few seconds as we looked over the rest of what lay exposed on the metal slab. There was a King James version of the Bible along with a book on the history and meaning of the coinherence symbol. All I could think is how Zachery would never let us hear the end of it once he knew his theory had complete merit, possibly even factoring into the killings, but even though the two books were dog-eared and had worn edges, what had our attention was the spread of photographs.

"Where would he have gotten all of these?" I asked.

"His apprentice." A smile cracked Jack's lips, and with the expression came the realization he only seemed amused when it was at my expense.

"Thought we were going with follower now."

"It's all right, Kid. Don't get all excited."

There were easily twelve photos on the metal surface. They were of a mix of men and women, just the way he preferred to kill, in alternating sexes. Most of them were unfamiliar faces.

"The Sarasota murders?"

Jack held one up of a young woman.

"Sally Windermere."

Jack let out a rush of air. "You might be able to make good on your promise yet."

In a way, I didn't want to be right in this instance. I hoped that Sally had fallen in love with someone new and had taken off, even though logic dictated the odds of that were minimal. Coinciding with logic was the reality that Sally Windermere may have been victim number ten, the result of Bingham's follower, the one free to kill again.

"We'll need to find out where he got these photos. Someone from the outside world brought them to him."

Jack stepped off the bedrail and moved to the guard who held onto Tim Johnson. "Take him somewhere else for a bit."

"Where—"

"Don't care, really, but we'll be taking all this shit with us."

The guard let out a sigh and pushed Johnson down the corridor ahead of him.

With them gone, Jack was silent. His eyes were taking in the space, and he was analyzing everything.

"These pictures are probably of his other victims, the murders from Sarasota," I repeated my earlier statement.

"Bet you they are."

WE FOUND CLARENCE MOORE BEHIND his desk. His hand moved a pen rapidly across a page. A flick of a wrist, a few loops of ink, and the sheet was turned over and placed on top of a pile to his right. He looked up at us when we entered his office.

He gestured for us to sit across from him. "I heard you found items of interest."

Jack nodded. "We'll be taking all of it with us."

Moore clasped his hands and leaned across his desk. "What do ya want with a man like Bingham anyhow?"

We had never given Moore the truth of the investigation. All he knew was the FBI had their attention on Lance Bingham, and it involved more than the murder of cattle.

Jack glanced at me as if to say, *Pay attention*. "The details of our investigation are of the utmost sensitivity. There is a media ban in place, and should you leak any of the information we give you, you will be punishable by the law. Do you understand that?"

A slow nod was Moore's reply.

"Lance Bingham is a serial killer."

It had Moore reaching for his water bottle. He took a swig and wiped his mouth with the back of his hands. His eyes peered straight ahead. "What is he doing here then? We're only a me-medium security prison. We ain't equipped to deal with—"

"We still have to prove it."

"You still have to prove it?"

"Ten bodies were found under his property."

"No way. Lance isn't that smart."

"People are not who they project, especially serial killers."

With the term serial killer being used again, Moore's eyes moistened not from fear but I suspected from intrigue.

"We'll be taking what we found in his cell," Jack repeated his earlier statement. "We also need to be informed when he gets mail and what he's received. Is this something that you can handle?"

"Course. All prisoner mail is opened, and the contents checked."

"We'd like to be the ones to give final approval on whether it gets delivered to him."

"I'll see what I can do."

"We need you to figure it out." Jack kept eye contact with Moore.

Moore picked up the pen and scribbled something in a notepad. His handwriting angled to the left and was tightly compressed letters. I looked at the writing on the form he had been working on when we had interrupted him. There it was larger with more swirls. This change showed that Moore had closed emotionally from what we told him.

"When was the last time he received mail?"

"If you'd excuse me for a moment." Moore picked up the telephone receiver and hit a few buttons. He spoke into the receiver, "Anita, I need to know the last time an inmate received mail." Moore rattled off a prisoner number. "That's right, Lance Bingham." Moore cupped the receiver and said to us, "It should only take her a few sec—" He spoke back into the receiver, "Today...okay, and it hasn't been distributed yet?" Moore shot a glance at Jack.

"Have her bring today's mail to us."

"I need you to bring it to my office...Yes...I know it's not the norm...Thank you." Moore hung up. "That was the mailroom supervisor, and she'll be here in a few minutes with it. She had said the last package before today was March 2008."

Sally Windermere went missing February 11, 2008. Bingham was booked in January of that same year.

"She'll need to know the details of your investigation as well."

"Not going to happen—and you're not going to tell her either. The fewer people who know, the better."

"But if we have him in prison, what is the big deal? What is the leak y'all are worried about?"

Jack relayed the fact we suspected the use of Twitter to communicate with another killer.

"We'll remove his right to access the internet."

"You'll leave everything the way it is. If you take the privilege away, it will only tip off the unsub and make them run. Did she say what type of package came in today?"

"Just an envelope that would fit a greeting card. We open all the mail, and when deemed safe, it's approved and forwarded to the inmate."

"Wonder if it's a photo." Jack turned to me, and I knew what he was thinking. The mail from 2008 wasn't a coincidence. The unsub had sent the photo of Sally Windermere to let Bingham know that the job was done. Did that mean all the people in those pictures were dead, or were some intended targets?

"Did she say where the package came from?" I asked.

"Every piece of mail has to pass certain requirements such as having a postmark and a full return address. We'll see when she gets here."

Jack addressed me, "We know not all those pics were mailed, so how did Bingham end up with more photos?"

"His sister visited not long after he was booked," I said, glancing to Moore, then back at Jack. "She could have brought them when they met." Back to Moore, "Is that possible?"

Two raised palms in the air. "It's possible. Like I said, it's confidential what happens in there."

"So people could bring in whatever they want to?

Weapons? Drugs?" Jack asked.

"All our visitors are checked, but photos wouldn't get our attention."

"You said that conversations aren't recorded, correct?" I said.

"Correct, and we don't videotape them either. The only person who could say would be the security guard and that's if he stayed in the room. It's that name I gave you before."

"We saw him, and he didn't remember any of their conversation."

"Well, then I'm sorry, but y'all are out of luck."

A rap on the doorframe caused us to look up. A woman stood there. Her dark hair was drawn back into a neat ponytail that reached her shoulders, and bangs framed her face. Her figure was trim and her clothing fit snugly, hugging her curves. "I have what y'all are looking for."

My stomach turned, fearing it contained another photo. Had we delayed too long? Was another life lost?

"Gentlemen, this is Anita Abrams."

She stepped into the office and extended a hand, first to Jack and then to me. She smiled.

"These men are Special Agents of the FBI."

Anita withdrew her hand from mine but held eye contact.

"I'm Special Agent Brandon Fisher, and this is Supervisory Special Agent in Charge Jack Harper."

Jack reached for the envelope and ripped the edge where the prison employees had resealed it with their tape.

"You can't do that—" Anita's words stopped there.

Jack pulled out the contents. It was a photograph.

Anita looked from it to me. "I thought you looked familiar."

Fourteen

I lunged for the photo. "What the hell—"

Jack asked Anita, "Does the mail department wear gloves?"

"Yes, of course."

Jack addressed Moore, "Do you have a plastic bag?"

The warden shook his head and lifted his shoulders. "Anita?"

"I can get you something."

"How the hell did he get my picture, Jack?" I bumped his shoulder. "Let me see it."

Jack's eyes were saying, *Keep it cool.* He held it out so I could look at it.

Strength left my legs, and I felt the color drain from my face. "That's my Twitter account pic."

"Why would Bingham be getting a picture of you?" Anita's soft voice didn't serve to calm me but had the opposite effect.

Our heads turned to face her. Jack stood. "We're going to have to ask you to keep all of this confidential."

"Sure."

"And we need you to leave now." He moved forward until she backed up into the hallway, and then he closed the warden's office door.

"Where did it come from? Why me?" The Redeemer's words kept replaying in my mind as a never-ending audio reel. *Confess, repent, and be forgiven. Don't confess and be punished for your sins.*

Jack dropped back into his chair. "There's no return address on the envelope but based on the date of the postmark it was mailed Monday, the same day as the find. How is it even possible that it made here that quickly?"

"He could have dropped it in a local delivery mailbox," Moore said. "It's a different box at the post office that allows for faster mail delivery."

"It's someone local!"

I was trained to remain calm under pressure but confronted with an issue like this it was too much. I knew I raised my voice. I knew it displeased Jack as evidenced by the sour expression on his face. His lips contorted almost as if he were biting the inside of the bottom one, his jaw tight, his eyes fixed and pointed.

Jack looked at the envelope. "It's postmarked with zip 40360."

"That's Owingsville, not too far from here," Moore said.

"Why was this piece of mail approved?" I asked the question of Moore.

"Maybe they assumed that it was a photograph of a family member."

"Is the mailroom in a habit of assuming? And no return address? Shouldn't that alone be enough to reject the mail?"

"I'm not sure what to say. Human error?"

"If anyone was aware of Bingham's file, they'd know he doesn't have any living relatives. The single photograph would have been deemed more suspicious, possibly even considered a threat of physical harm toward the person in the photo."

"Our mailroom personnel can't remember the background of every inmate. Again, I'm not—"

"Not sure what to say," Jack intercepted and rose to his feet.

My attention stayed on the photograph. As we had discussed before, the pictures were not necessarily of his victims, but possible future targets. I swallowed hard.

Jack headed for the door and addressed Moore. "You let us know if he gets anything else. We'll want to look at it first. Make sure he still has Internet use rights."

"Course."

"And we're taking this with us." Jack placed the photo back inside the envelope.

Minutes later we were in the SUV, and I turned to Jack. "The pics are not all trophies."

He slipped a cigarette from the pack and lit up.

I glared at him, but he didn't seem to notice as he inhaled deeply and exhaled, filling the car with white, polluted smoke. I reached over, turned the key in the ignition and put my window down. "Why do you have to smoke all the time?" I asked, agitated.

He tapped the ash in the tray and took another inhale.

I let out a deep breath. "He's going to have me killed."

Still no reaction from Jack, just a slow and steady hand up, cigarette sucked on, exhale of white smoke, ashes tapped off in the tray.

"The killer was in Salt Lick," I said. "They know about the discovery."

"He was at some point. We figured that."

"I don't understand why you're not taking this seriously."

He stopped moving, his arm paused midway to his mouth. "I take this very seriously."

"You sure aren't giving me that impression."

"Listen, Kid, getting yourself all worked up doesn't accomplish a thing."

"I'm the target of a psychopath."

"That hasn't been proven yet." Another draw on the cigarette.

My hands balled into fists on my lap. Jack noticed. His eyes dived there before returning to look over the parking lot.

"We need to find this person," I ground out.

"And we will."

"I guess. Why should you be worried? It's not your picture."

Jack laughed so hard it forced a deep cough from his lungs.

"What's so funny?"

"You're not so good under pressure, Kid. You'll have to work on that."

"Why are we just sitting here?"

"You wanted to talk."

"Ah." I groaned. "Our best lead to this killer is that piece of mail." My mind went to the photograph, to the envelope, the defilement of evidence. It hadn't even occurred to me at that moment because when I noticed the picture all common sense left me. "You tampered with the evidence. There could have been prints."

"I sit here listening to you sulk, whine, and panic, but I draw the line when you insult my skills. I've been an agent almost as long as you've been alive." He snuffed out the cigarette, pushing it down hard enough to crumble the entire remains to ash.

"Then you should have known better."

"May I remind you that you report to me."

"You do every opportunity you get." The words slipped out, and I wished instantly that I could retract them. I glanced out the window, then back to Jack. "Maybe I'm just being a little—"

"Paranoid?" Jack paused. "Are you going to be able to keep a cool head for this case and pull yourself together?"

Seconds passed. I answered, "My life was threatened."

"Hmm."

"No, hear me out. It's not like that happens every day." Jack's eyes met mine. "I'm fine now." He studied my expression and had me questioning my resolve.

WE LEFT THE PRISON AND touched base with Paige and Zachery. They had ended up visiting both Sally Windermere's former fiancé and his parents due to our last-minute detour but didn't come out any further ahead. No one seemed to know much about other people in Sally's life. Everyone described her as a good girl who would never run off and hurt people like this. They didn't know of any enemies or people that held anything against her. We filled them in on everything that happened at the prison and arranged to meet them back at Betty's Place in about an hour.

I held the laptop and powered it up. My mind was on my Twitter account and on Bingham's followers. I wanted to know if he had said anything else. The mail intended for Bingham lay on the back seat sealed in an evidence bag. "What about your prints?"

Jack had lit another cigarette the minute we stepped up into the SUV. It was almost gone now and it was only five minutes later. "What about 'em?"

"They've littered the evidence."

A smile lifted Jack's mouth. "We're back to that? You worry too much, Kid. With technology these days it's not going to be an issue."

"They can lift prints even if they're layered?"

"Yep."

"Huh."

"See I've been an agent longer than—"

"I know, 'Almost as long as I've been alive.'" I parroted.

The onboard phone rang. Jack answered, "Speak to me."

"Special Agent Jack Harper?"

"This is. You're also on speaker with Special Agent Brandon Fisher."

"Doctor Jones here."

I straightened out, paused my efforts to log online.

"The oldest vic could be the man whose picture you forwarded me. Facial structure matches that of Travis Carter."

Jack pulled onto Highway 460, merged with the traffic.

"We'll need DNA from his mother for cross comparison."

"DNA on a skeleton?" I whispered the words, but the

doctor heard.

"It's called mitochondrial DNA. It's passed on from our mothers. It is taken from dead cellular debris such as bone and hair. Now, this victim's x-rays also show a broken tibia and carpal bone. Both sustained years prior to death."

"His shin and wrist bones," Jack clarified. "So if we can verify that Travis Carter had these injuries—"

"That's correct. Along with a DNA comparison, we'll have our certainty. I've already ordered his medical history and should have it soon."

"Keep us updated."

Jones disconnected the call.

I logged onto my Twitter account. No new followers and no new mentions, which meant no one was addressing me. I searched the Redeemer to see if there were any new posts, and there weren't since yesterday. Jack glanced at the screen, back to the road.

"Nothing new there—" My eyes were on the messages tab along the top. "I think I know how he identified me to his follower." I dialed Nadia on the onboard system. Three rings later, she answered. "I need you to hack the Redeemer's Twitter account and look at his private messages."

"Sure. Is there something specific I should be looking for?"

"You'll know it when you see it."

"Okay."

"How are the rest of the background searches going for the followers?" Jack asked her.

"I've waded through the first hundred. Still working on it. This isn't TV where they solve a murder in an hour." The tapping of keyboard keys came over the hands-free.

"Don't have to tell me that." Jack's voice held a smirk.

"If you were here I'd slap you for that." Her fingers paused a moment but started up again.

Jack laughed, but it stalled when I looked at him. Apparently, I wasn't supposed to know he was capable of laughter. My focus went back to my profile page. Bingham's follower knew who I was.

"Oh, here we go, I'm in."

"Nad—"

"He's got a few." She rhymed off snippets of messages. "'Happy to have such a righteous person to follow, thank you for being a role model.'" She'd read the last one slowly. "Do you think—"

"What's the background on that one?" I asked.

"Devin Mercy."

"Interesting last name," Jack said.

More keys were tapped on the keyboard. "Five backgrounds come up with that name."

"Narrow it down to anyone in the Salt Lick area. Try Owingsville, postal 40360."

"Zero."

"What about Sarasota?"

"Ah, zero."

"Shit. Are there any links to pictures or names mentioned in any of these messages?"

"Not that I see. Is something wrong?"

Jack told Nadia about my picture being mailed to Bingham.

"Oh my God, Brandon. Jack, what—"

"We've got it under control."

Glad you *do.*

Maybe it was because he wasn't completely attached to the newest member of his team.

"We've got the photo and its envelope on the way for the LPOU." LPOU stood for the Latent Print Operations Unit. "Stay on top of them for the results." Jack hung up and glanced over at the screen with my profile. "Sixty followers? You twit regularly?"

"Are we back to that? I *tweet*, sometimes, not often."

"About what?" He looked at the screen. "Your logon name is WordAddict. Are you a writer or something?" Jack laughed.

It was time for a subject switch. "Why are you set against having and providing hope?" I referred to this morning when Jack gave me a hard time over a promise to find Sally Windermere.

"So you're a writer." Jack pulled out another cigarette and lit up.

I took a deep breath and tried to conjure self-control.

Fifteen

Paige and Zachery were in the corner table of Betty's Place waiting for us. It was the best we could do for a conference room around here. Two plates on the table were empty, with the exception of leftover coleslaw in small ramekins and four red plastic toothpicks.

"Hope you don't mind, we went ahead and ordered something." Zachery drew back on a can of pop.

"Looks like you ordered and ate." Jack pulled out a chair from the table, letting it scrape across the floor. He dropped onto it.

"Triple deckers," I said.

"Two layers of turkey, bacon, and cheese wedged between three slices of whole wheat. You should try one, Pending."

"I'm not that hungry—"

"He feels his life was threatened," Jack interrupted.

"Come on, why would someone throw away their life killing you?"

I studied Paige's eyes. They communicated vulnerability and empathy. Her hair framed her face with loose curls. I remembered putting my hands in that hair, sweeping it back from her face, taking her lips, kissing her neck. Her eyelids fell slowly as if she were thinking the same thing.

She ended the eye contact. "There's no need to be like that, Zach."

"Why are you sticking up for him?"

"I take it seriously. Brandon is a Special Agent just like the rest of us—"

"Pending."

Undeterred, Paige continued. "We're family. We look out for each other. What if it was your picture?"

The smile faded from Zachery's face.

"Yeah, not so funny now."

Jack leaned back into his chair. "This is normally when I'd say we don't have time to eat, but seeing as this is our only meeting place—"

My phone rang, and the tone told me it was my personal cell and that it was Deb.

"Are you going to get that?" Jack asked.

I pulled out the phone and clicked ignore.

"Not important, Kid?"

My eyes were on Paige. Hers went to the table.

The ringing started up again.

"Sounds like you better get that."

I walked away from the table and answered. "I told you I'm in the middle of a case—"

"Are you going to be home tonight?"

"We talked about this."

"Brandon, I didn't realize you'd be away for days at a time."

"We talked about the possibility."

Silence.

"I've got to go."

"Brandon?"

"Yeah."

"I love you."

To hear her voice change from confrontation to this tugged at my heart. My life was threatened. Who knew what tomorrow would bring? "I love you, too. I'll be home as soon as I can." I hung up the phone and headed back to the table.

"That wasn't personal was it, Kid? We're on a case."

"It won't happen again."

"Hope it doesn't."

I was learning something else about supervisory special

agent Jack Harper. He ran his team like a dictatorship.

JACK AND I BOTH ENDED up eating a triple decker sandwich, following in the shadows of our colleagues. All I could think about was my photograph having been sent to Bingham. I swallowed in large bites and washed them down with chugs of water. I never took a lot of time to eat, but this was a record.

"If we could even connect victimology we'd have a better chance of catching the unsub," Paige said. "All we know right now is the first victim was likely Bingham's brother-in-law, and the most recent seems to be Sally Windermere."

Zachery gestured toward the Bible and reference book on the coinherence symbol we took from Bingham's cell. They sat on the table in plastic bags. "I think this is more about divinity. Bingham views his killing as a higher calling. It's given away by his handle, the Redeemer. He's taking it upon himself to save people from their sins."

"Let's talk about Sally Windermere then," Jack challenged. "Why a young girl who wasn't even married? What sin could she possibly have committed?"

Paige put a hand through her hair and tucked a strand behind an ear. "We're pretty confident Bingham killed his brother-in-law. We know the man had beaten his sister, but we also know that the last kill at the burial site didn't have their intestines removed—different killer, possibly a different motive?"

Zachery shook his head. "I'm not buying that part."

"And why's that?" Paige rested her chin in a cupped hand, her elbow braced on the table.

"The unsub is a follower. He respects and follows Bingham's lead. I believe they kill for the same purpose."

"Okay, I agree with the part that the unsub follows Bingham's lead—"

"Bingham controls everything."

"Stop agreeing there." Paige sat back. "If he did, the last vic would have been gutted. She wasn't."

"The other markings on the body are the same, the burial is the same. What we need to know is why she was targeted, and we'll have a better chance of finding our unsub. We need to think exactly like Bingham to draw the unsub in."

Paige let out a rush of air.

"You don't agree?"

"No, I do. Maybe that's the problem." A smirk creased the edges of her mouth. "I hate it when you have a point."

"It happens too often?" Zachery's smile grew and faded just as quickly. His eyes glazed over and he looked at me. "He told you to confess your sins and be forgiven."

"Yes."

"Evidence seems to lean toward him killing for a sense of righteousness. Think of the seven deadly sins in the Bible."

Jack tapped his shirt pocket and looked around the place.

"It's been a long time since Sunday school." I said.

"Don't get smart, Pending. The seven deadly sins are wrath, greed, sloth, pride, lust, envy, and gluttony."

"Okay, well we don't think Travis was killed for any of those reasons." The minute the words came out, I knew I should have given it more thought. "Wrath."

"Exactly." Zachery pressed a pointed index finger onto the cover of the Bible. "And think of yourself being a young girl, shouldn't be hard to do." He smiled. I cocked my head to the side. "She's engaged to someone she loves. Where does that lead?"

"Lust," Paige answered. "She fornicated."

Zachery snapped his fingers. "Yes. Nancy Windermere said her daughter knew Bingham. Maybe he sensed it off her, or she told him."

Everyone went silent, and Jack's phone rang.

He answered, "Nadia, you're on speaker." He pushed a button and placed the cell on the table.

"Okay, you're going to love me."

"We already do," Zachery said.

"Oh, I mean even more—"

"Nadia." That was all Jack needed to say.

"I'm still working my way through all the Twitter followers, but I came across one I know you'll be interested in."

"Name?"

"One thing at a time. I logged onto his Twitter account. Now there wasn't anything that stood out to me at first, but I went to his messages again and there was a new message in there." Nadia's voice shrank. "It was about you, Brandon."

My heart palpitated. "What exactly?"

"It was from the Redeemer to a profile name of HighScore. The message was just your name without the at symbol."

"He was pointing me out."

"But there's more. I found out the guy's real name, pulled a background. He lives in Owingsville. That's in Bath County, too, only about eight miles west—"

"That's where my photo was mailed from."

She was quiet for a few seconds. "Now there's more. His real name is Earl Royster—"

"The CSI," I cut Nadia off and turned to Jack. "He led us through the tunnels, filled us in on the find. He's the one who had the allergies and kept sneezing."

Jack rose to his feet. "Let's go pick him up."

"Forwarding you all his info and address now."

Jack's cell chimed with notification of the message, and Nadia disconnected the call.

I found it hard to move. To think we had all been so close to a killer and didn't even know made me realize what some assumed about FBI Special Agents wasn't true. They weren't a type of superhero. They were just people who possessed flaws, some of which could get them killed.

"Hello."

I turned and saw Betty, but not before I heard Jack say, "Mrs. Miller, are you okay?"

"Oh, I'm fine." Her body quivered as if fighting a chill. Her hands rubbed her arms. She looked around the space which was barren except for us and an employee. "I know you're not investigatin' missin' persons. I can handle it. Was Sally one of the victims?"

Paige extended a hand to Betty's shoulder. The older woman moved out of reach. "As I said, I'm fine dear."

Paige stepped back. "Why don't you sit down?"

"You people are treatin' me like a child. I'm a grown woman. I can handle the truth."

Jack gestured to a chair that remained pulled back from the table. "What have you heard?"

She reluctantly sat down, and the rest of us joined her. "Ten people murdered. All buried beneath that man's property."

"Where did you hear that?"

"People 'round here talk even when they're not s'posed to." Her eyes flitted to each of us. "Oh God!" A flattened hand clasped over her mouth. Her head shook. She must have read our eyes. "Y'all know sometimes I wish people were wrong. Bingham killed all of them?"

"We're working on investigating who killed those people and why."

"Why? Does that matter? Just lock up the son of a gun for life."

"It doesn't necessarily work that way. In order to get answers, sometimes we need to know why."

She crossed her arms.

"You can help us, though."

"How's that?" Her eyes snapped up to meet Jack's.

"Did Kurt McCartney go to Lakeview Community Church?"

"My, that was a long time ago, but ya know? I think he did. Like I said, they weren't in town long."

Jack looked to the rest of us. "What about Earl Royster?"

The older lady thought for a while. "Yes. Why do you ask?"

"We need you to keep this quiet, Betty. Don't be telling anybody about what we've spoken about."

She nodded.

OWINGSVILLE HAD A POPULATION OF about fifteen hundred, making it larger than Salt Lick but still only large enough to make a pinprick on a map. We all piled into one SUV, leaving the other at Betty's Place, and headed to Earl Royster's house on Harrisburg Road.

Jack drove and somehow managed to only smoke one cigarette en route. I didn't look forward to peeling my clothes off tonight at the hotel as the stench of cigarette had leeched into the fabric yesterday and I expected the same would be true today.

We rode in silence, the rest of the team likely thinking about the case, analyzing all the details of what we knew so far, and speculating. All I could think about was confronting this son of a bitch. While the rest of them didn't seem to take the threat to my life seriously, I did. I was surprised by the fact they didn't view the photo or the single-worded Twitter message as threats. My concern was over my wellbeing and Debbie's. If Bingham had communicated to the other killer about me, was she safe? My personal phone rang again.

Jack turned his head to look at me in the passenger seat. "She's calling again?"

I pulled out my personal cell and chose Ignore.

"Take that as a yes." Jack's eyes were on the road now.

I looked out the window to the fields that extended to the horizon in all directions.

"She has a hard time adjusting to you being on the road?" Paige's voice sliced through the tension.

"We're not used to being apart."

The onboard system chirped, and Jack answered. It was Nadia.

"Jones contacted me with the medical records for Travis Carter. He shares the same injuries as the first victim. He said if we got a DNA sample from his mother we'd have absolute certainty."

"He told us the same." Jack ended the call.

"We'll need to notify Ellie Carter that we found her son,"
I said.

Jack turned to face me. "We will but not yet."

"She's been waiting years for closure."

"Then a few more days won't matter."

"That's your comeback to that?" I spat.

"It doesn't benefit our case to let her know yet—"

"Watch out!"

Jack swerved the SUV just before hitting the loose gravel
on the side of the road. "You're going to have to learn to
watch your mouth, Kid."

My earlobes heated as if on fire. I was tiring of being called
Kid or *Slingshot* all the time. I had gone through the training
and the education. I had been deemed worthy of being a
special agent. Why was it so hard for the man to show me
some respect?

"We're here." Jack pulled the SUV in front of a modest
bungalow with a chain link fence that surrounded the
property. There was no driveway, but the Nissan registered
to Royster sat out front.

"Doesn't look like much," Zachery stated the obvious.

"He wouldn't be able to afford much." Jack pulled the keys
from the ignition. "Zach and Paige, you watch the perimeter
in case the guy makes a run for it." He looked at me before
reaching for the door handle, his eyes going to my seat belt.
"You coming?"

As I unclipped the belt, I wondered what had made Jack
so nonchalant, uncaring, and opposed to hope. I'd find out
whether he wanted me to know or not.

"Now you let me do the talking. You're too involved," Jack
said, a hand going to his holster.

I couldn't argue. The patterns taught us Bingham had
an order of doing things, alternating male and female. The
next victim would be male. All I could think about was the
freshly dug grave that didn't have an occupant. I didn't want
to be the one pressed into it. I didn't want to become number

eleven.

Jack unlatched the gate with one hand and held his gun raised in the other. I had my hand on my holster and followed behind.

"Whatcha doing over there?" A man called out from across the street.

"FBI business. Please go inside," I said.

"Earl's police."

Jack spoke to me with his eyes on Royster's house. "You take care of it."

I hurried across the street. "We need you to go back inside your house."

"You're mighty young, ain't ya?" He moved to look past me.

I followed his gaze. Jack was just on the other side of the gate.

"What business do y'all have with Earl?" His brows sprouted silver hairs, easily the length of an inch, and they bobbed as he spoke.

"It's a private matter, but I ask that you either go back inside your house or leave—"

A gunshot pierced the air.

Glass shattered.

I pushed the man down flush with the road and huddled over him. As we lay there, I looked across the street. A bullet had fired through Earl's front window.

Everything turned to silence. We waited it out for what seemed like seconds that turned into minutes that turned into hours.

"In the house," I directed him. "Stay low."

The man nodded, willing to comply now. I walked with him, both of us hunched down as if in a room with a low ceiling. "Do you have a back door?"

"Yes."

We went through a fence gate to the back of his house. "Anyone else at home?"

"My wife."

Behind the shelter of the house, I straightened out. "Both of you go into the basement and wait for this to be over."

The man slowly resumed full height, his focus on me. His eyes were saturated with fear and uncertainty, belief and mistrust. "Are you going to kill him?"

"We will do what we need to." I spoke the words and anticipated his reaction would be completely different from what it was. I thought he'd shake his head over the loss of life, but instead he put a hand on my shoulder and thanked me for saving his life.

"You go protect us, son."

"Yes, sir."

As I hurried back, in a hunched-over posture, all I could think about was *loss of life*. My heartbeat tattooed a thumping rhythm in my ears. My vision blurred from adrenaline.

Another shot fired.

My feet froze to the ground. The bullet whizzed by me.

I was the target! Shit! Fuck!

I took a deep breath. I had to keep moving. The son of a bitch was obviously a bad aim with a firearm—maybe why his preference to the blade. I set off at a run.

"Put the gun down!" Jack's yell bellowed through the street.

Another round fired.

More glass shattered.

It halted my pace as a hiccup does a clean breath. A kickback of adrenaline was all that propelled me forward.

"Put the gun down!" Jack yelled again and hunched down beside the front stoop.

"I didn't do anything." The voice came from inside.

Jack yelled to me, "Keep alert!"

I pulled my gun from its holster, ready to fire. My training took over, willing my extremities to move while inside I feared the taking of a man's life. Even knowing this man had inadvertently threatened mine, I found it hard to contemplate ending his.

"Put the gun down. Come out with your hands in the air!"

Sobs came from inside the house.

"Come out with your arms in the air!"

"It was just…a joke." Earl's speech was fragmented by deep-throated sobs.

"Come out now!"

"No. I can't. Y'all will kill me."

"We just want to talk." There was a slight difference in Jack's tone of voice. His words spoke of reassurance, but he would pull the trigger, without hesitation, and kill this man if he had to.

"It wasn't—" More sobbing. "I didn't mean for it to come to this."

My eyes scanned the neighborhood. There were no more nosey neighbors checking out the situation. The shots fired must have been enough to turn most of them wise and retreating into their houses.

"This doesn't have to end badly." Jack moved closer to the door.

"Stop!"

Jack's hand was on the door handle. He pulled it back.

Earl had moved closer to the front door. The front window had been completely destroyed. The tempered glass had fractured into large beads, leaving only grilles and the vinyl sash.

"You don't know what it's like to be me." More sobs.

"Let's talk, Earl. You tell us." Jack's tone softened. His strategy was at work in front of me. Define a level of correlation, make the unsub comfortable enough to let his guard down.

The door handle turned. As it did, my stomach turned with it. Flashbacks invaded my thoughts: the burial site, the victims, the stretched corpses tied inside of a circular grave, the slashes in their torsos, the death slice to their gut, the man who had stood across from me in the underground bunker just two days ago sneezing from allergies.

The door's seal broke, and it opened. Earl stood there in plaid boxers. Tears had stained his cheeks and carved crooked trenches down his face. His left hand held a gun.

"Put down the gun." Jack held his at the level of Earl's forehead.

Earl's arm moved upward.

"Put it down!"

"I didn't mean to do it! I swear!"

Jack held out his other hand, flattened palm toward Earl. "We can talk, but you need to put the gun down first. This doesn't have to end badly."

"No one was supposed to get hurt." His eyes went to me. His arm continued to rise until he had the barrel of the gun pointed at his own forehead. He spoke to me, "It was supposed to be funny."

"Don't do this."

Again seconds transformed to minutes, minutes to hours, as I watched his finger on the trigger, waiting for him to pull it back. We needed to do something and stop this from happening.

"Think about your wife," I said.

Fresh tears fell. "What are you talking about?"

"Your wife. You don't want to leave her alone."

His arm faltered, the gun moving down slightly before he corrected the alignment. "I'm not m-married."

As he spoke, I caught a glimpse of moving shadows behind Earl. I tried to bury the recognition, as I knew it was Paige and Zachery. "Did you help kill those people, Earl?"

The gun shook. "No."

"Were you going to kill me?"

He made eye contact with me. "No."

"Why send the picture to Bingham?"

"I was told to." He steadied his hold on the gun.

"Do you do everything Bingham tells you to?" I knew I treaded on uneasy ground, but I needed to keep him talking, distracted from Paige and Zachery, who were moving up on him from behind.

A fire of defiance sparked in his eyes.

"You've known Bingham for a long time?"

Earl swallowed deeply, audibly.

"You don't think he killed those people?"

Earl's arm dropped, the gun no longer pointed at his head. Zachery swept in behind him, but his shoes made a noise when he reached the vinyl flooring. Earl spun and raised his gun on Zachery.

The shot fired.

Earl fell to the floor.

The entryway froze in silence as we each faced our own mortality. Another man dead, a man who hadn't needed to die.

Earl lay on the floor, blood pouring from the bullet hole at the nape of his neck—a death shot. Zachery bent forward, hands to his thighs, breathing deeply. No doubt he contemplated how he almost lost his life in the line of duty. Jack held his gun, smoke billowing from the barrel, to his side. Paige had a hand on Zachery's shoulder and looked at me.

Jack pulled out his phone. "This is FBI Supervisory Special Agent Jack Harper, send a forensic team and get the coroner." He gave them the address and hung up.

"He didn't have to die," I said.

"Us or them. I'll always pick us." Jack stepped over Earl and put his gun back in his holster.

Sixteen

Within the hour, Harrisburg Road was full of activity. Jones hunched beside Earl Royster and looked up at me. "The man didn't stand a chance." The coroner's eyes were misted over.

Truth was I didn't like dead bodies when I knew what their voices had sounded like before leaving us. I could handle seeing the ones in the grave, only imagining, not knowing what they sounded like, who they had been. As we had waited on Crime Scene and the coroner to arrive, I had spent most of the time watching Earl as if he would somehow sit up and breathe again. Somehow, his death paid for the sin of the threat against me.

"Kid." Jack gestured for me to follow him.

I maneuvered around Earl, doing my best not to contaminate the scene.

"You don't think he killed the girl, do you?" We stood in the dining room.

"No." I didn't even need to give it more thought.

"How do you explain the picture of you?"

I didn't really have an answer to that.

"He shot at you."

"But he missed."

Two crime scene investigators came over to us. One was about the same age as I was. His eyes were full of tears; though he let none of them fall. He addressed Jack. "I hear you killed Earl."

"I did." Jack didn't flourish his response by adding details, by attempts to justify his action.

The CSI held eye contact with Jack, took a deep breath, and walked away. His colleague followed.

The emotional impact left in their wake, of what wasn't being said, was more powerful than what a thousand angry words would have contained.

Jack patted his shirt pocket, and dropped his arm without taking out a cigarette. "So are you going to answer the question?"

"How can you not have any feelings? A man is dead; you shot him." I pointed toward the CSIs whose backs were to us. "Those were his friends, probably from childhood."

"We're here to do a job. Can you handle that?" Jack's eyes hardened. I tried to read them, to see if there were more layers to the man than what he projected. I was shut out.

"Yes."

"All right then. Answer the question. Explain the picture of you, and why you think Earl was innocent and not Bingham's follower in the murders."

"We discussed the traits this type of killer would possess."

"Such as?"

"He'd likely be a psychopath, unfeeling. Earl was afraid."

"Keep going."

"He didn't want to talk. A narcissist would do their best to talk and manipulate their way out of a situation. A narcissist would love themselves too much to hold a gun to their head even if trying to establish an upper hand."

"Okay, then why the picture of you sent to Bingham?"

"Just as he said, it was supposed to be funny."

"Hmm."

"Bingham is the one with control and power. He definitely fits the profile of a narcissist. He takes pride in maneuvering events to please himself. He basks in glory when people follow his lead. He only surrounds himself with those who build him up, feed his ego, and give him that power."

"Okay, so take Bingham out of the picture. What does this tell us about his apprentice?"

"He's a follower, weak."

"Now, we're getting somewhere, Kid."

"Earl could have been the apprentice." My legs felt weak.

Jack pressed his lips and nodded.

At that moment, I felt stupid and naive. I should have known better. My head turned back toward Earl's body. Now instead of looking on the man with sympathy and compassion, rage and redemption cluttered my vision, just as Jones and his assistant enclosed Earl in a black bag.

"He was going to kill me."

I turned back to Jack, who lifted a shoulder. "Guess we don't have to worry about that now."

Jones walked over to us. "I'm taking him back to the morgue. The cause of death is no mystery." He took pause, his attention going back and forth between Jack and me. "However, there will still be a full autopsy."

"I would expect no less," Jack said. He had turned over his firearm as per protocol. Any time a gun was fired, it needed to be confiscated for review to determine whether it was a *good shot,* in other words, justifiable.

"Earl was a respected member of this community, Agent. He will be missed." Jones's Adam's apple bobbed heavily. "He was born here."

Jack said nothing, and I knew there wasn't anything he could have said. An apology would have presented itself insincere at best. Jack had already said it best to the team: *Us or them. I'll always pick us.*

"I better git goin'. The bodies are piling up in my morgue." Jones walked away, limping to the right side, as he always did. Somehow it seemed more apparent today, but maybe it was sorrow adding weight to his steps.

"Boss." Zachery came into the dining room. With a gloved hand, he held up a book. "It's on the coinherence symbol."

Zachery had fallen into a subdued, quiet role since Earl

had raised the gun on him. Even his eyes were vacant of their usual jovial spark.

Paige came up to us, breathless and rushed. "We'll be sending his computer to Nadia, but there are some documents on there." Her voice lost its strength. One look at Jack and she regained it. "Pictures of the burial site, and the victims. Pictures of all of us taken at the crime scene. He had captions under all of us."

"What was mine?" I asked.

Paige avoided eye contact with me.

I came to within inches of her face. "What was it?"

"'Sinner.'" She let out a jagged breath. Her eyes lifted to match mine. "'Sinner who must be punished.'"

To again be confronted with my sin, my mistake, felt like a bruise that would never heal, a bruise repeatedly hit. I walked away.

"Brandon," Paige called out after me. I suspected Jack and Zachery were watching me.

I went into the main bedroom and found the CSI who had confronted Jack a few moments ago and pushed him against the wall.

"What the—"

I tightened my grip. "Tell us what you know!"

His face wrinkled up. "I don't know what you're talking—"

"Get your fuckin' hands off him!" The other CSI, who had been beside him in the dining room, came into the room and pulled back on my left shoulder.

Wrong move! I spun around. My fist connected with his jaw.

A hand went to cradle his face for a second before he started after me. "You little f—"

Jack came into the room, but his image was blurred by the rage pumping through my system. I turned back on the first CSI. He punched me in the gut, doubling me over. His knee met my chin. Each blow only strengthened the fight within me, infusing more adrenaline into my veins. I straightened out and went to strike him back, but I had taken a pause for too long.

He was lying on the floor, curled into a fetal position. Blood poured from his nose, and he spit blood on the carpet. The other CSI whose jaw I had hit was sitting on the edge of the bed with his hands up in surrender.

Jack's knuckles were bloodied. He yanked me out of the room, through the house, and onto the back deck. He dragged me along so quickly that I never got a flat foot planted beneath me, only moved heel, toe, heel, toe. He pushed me back from him.

His cheeks were red, his breathing deep. "You ever pull a fuckin' stunt like that again you'll be off the team. You hear me?"

"They know something!"

"Do you hear what I'm saying?" We were inches apart. Jack's voice projected loud enough to reach the end of the street.

"Royster shot a gun at me three times!"

"And he missed every time." We stood facing each other in a deadlock. "He's trained in weapons. If he wanted to kill you, you'd be dead."

"It doesn't explain the pictures on his computer, the caption, the photo he sent to Bingham in prison."

Jack faced heavenward.

"I know he said he didn't mean anything by it, but how can you not mean anything when you fire a gun?"

"You're not going to get anywhere with your hotheaded temper. Fuck your red hair! Do you think they're going to want to talk to us now? You've probably shut them up for good."

I let out a deep breath. "They'll talk to us."

Jack held up a hand to silence me. "You pull something like that again or force my involvement, you're finished. Do you hear what I'm saying?"

Shadows moved on the other side of the patio doors.

Paige and Zachery came into view. Somehow, I picked up on Paige's concern through a pane of glass.

"I said, 'Do you hear what I'm saying?'"

"Yes."

"Yes, what?"

"Yes, I hear what you're saying."

Jack slid open the door and went back into the house. Paige stepped onto the deck and closed the door behind her. Zachery followed Jack.

"Are you okay?" She extended a hand to my shoulder but pulled it back before making contact.

"Yeah, I'm fine." I couldn't look in her eyes.

"If it makes you feel better, I'm on your side."

I lost the fight and looked at her. The way the sunlight hit her face, the paleness of her skin, the soft curls that framed her face, how her lips were swollen as if she had spent hours kissing swept me back into a memory. I turned away, not able to allow myself to get sucked back in. I heard Debbie's voice, and the way she, just hours ago, had said, *I love you.*

"I can't do this." My jaw tightened. I swallowed hard.

"I know." She licked her lips and bit down on the bottom one.

"I've got to get back in." I jacked a thumb toward the house.

"Yeah." The disappointment in her voice was evident, yet I had nothing with which to melt it away.

Jack stood in the doorway to Royster's bedroom, his back to the hallway. I came up behind him. Zachery was inside the bedroom, his arms crossed. He gave me a look that condemned me to a life of pushing papers while Jack just ignored me. I wasn't sure which was worse.

The one CSI sat on the bed with a hand cradling his jaw, his gaze on me. "Just keep him away from me."

Jack's eyes flittered to me for an instant, a barely measurable amount of time. "How close were the two of you to the vic?"

"You mean the man you shot." The younger CSI, who had been flattened to the floor when I had left, was now leaning against the far wall.

Jack didn't say a thing.

"Earl and I were close."

"I asked how close."

Zachery brushed between Jack and me to leave the room. He mumbled something to Jack on the way about how he was going to look at the computer with Paige and see what else he could find.

"We go back to school years." The CSI's arms crossed.

With the motion, my mind went to the evidence collected in the case. These men were part of the forensic investigative team. If they knew of Earl's involvement or were even involved themselves, everything would be compromised. "Did you know he was working with Lance Bingham?"

All three pairs of eyes, including Jack's, shot to me. Again, the younger CSI spoke, "Hell no."

"Are you saying that to protect a memory or yourself?"

"Is this guy for real?" He shared scoffed laughter with the other CSI.

"Answer his question," Jack said, cutting their mockery short.

"Kev—" he nodded to the CSI sitting on the bed, rubbing his jaw "—Earl and I, none of us was involved in no murder."

"You didn't know that your best friend was working with a serial killer?"

Kevin made eye contact with the younger CSI. "Charlie, maybe we should say something—"

"Damn right, you should say something!" Jack took a few steps forward. The anger radiating off him now paled by comparison to the wrath he had projected when he had verbally lashed me.

Charlie pushed off the wall with his leg. "It's not like we know something. He's just been different for a while, but, I mean, that's to be expected."

"To be expected," I said, hoping he'd continue.

"Well, his younger brother went missing a while ago now."

"Do you think he suspected Bingham of something and got close to him?"

Charlie placed a hand on his hip, flexed his hand, and then tapped his fingers there. "Six years ago, Robert, that was Earl's brother, left for work but didn't return home. When police followed up, his workplace hadn't even seen him that day."

"Somewhere between home and work, he went missing," I summarized.

Charlie glared at me. "Very good." He continued. "We all did what we could for Earl, but it was hard on him. Robert was the only family Earl had left. We all have families," he gestured a hand between him and Kevin. "Kevin has a wife and kids. I have older parents I care for. Things are busy in life even here in the country." He looked at Jack and me as if ready to defend his statement. "Lance was there for him when the rest of us couldn't be. He didn't have family responsibilities."

I recalled the body Jones had shown us in the cellar. It was a male and dated back about six years. Maybe that had been Robert Royster.

"Oh, good God." Kevin's face paled. His eyes weren't focused on anything for seconds as we waited for an elaboration. "Lance told Earl that wherever Robert was, he was at peace."

There was a rap of knuckles on the doorframe. Zachery stood there. "You're going to want to come see this."

PAIGE LOOKED UP FROM BEHIND the desk in the office. "Wait until you see all this for yourselves."

Earl's office was organized. No stray paper littered the surface of the desk, filing cabinet, or bookshelf. I traced a hand over his collection of fiction and recognized some of the authors. Earl Royster had a fascination with science fiction. I noticed the void where the book on the coinherence symbol must have been.

"These were found in a folder called miscellaneous," Paige said as she moved over to make room for Jack and me behind the desk. Zachery was already there.

The images that filled the screen were familiar, but only vaguely. There was a picture of a circular grave, but it had stakes in the ground. The last one left empty didn't have them. "These were taken before a victim was placed inside?"

Paige faced me. "Yep."

We had held eye contact for a second before I turned to Jack. "He was in on this."

"Hmm."

I took it mostly based on facial expression, the downward curvature of his mouth, that my response didn't impress him.

"We need a little more than this, Pending," Zachery said. "Maybe there's another explanation. What if he thought Bingham had his brother? He snoops into the guy's house when he's helping a farmer and finds this."

"Still doesn't explain why he wouldn't report it," I said.

"Earl was a submissive person," Zachery began. "Bingham would have easily overpowered him mentally."

"So you're suggesting that he found out Bingham killed his brother and was okay with it?" Paige straightened out, crossed her arms. "I'm not buying it."

I got involved in the debate. "The guy isn't exactly an innocent. He shot at us. He risked not only my life but his neighbor's. Heck, he pulled a gun on you—" I gestured to Zachery "—or have you forgotten already?"

"Cool it. All of you. None of this is getting us anywhere," Jack reprimanded.

"No, there's more than just this. He was watching Bingham." Paige glared at Zachery and, based on the intensity, I couldn't help but think better him than me. She moved back, placed a hand on the mouse again, and clicked on another photo. "Bingham outside his house. See the fields, I recognize those."

"You recognize fields out here in the middle of nowhere?"

"Enough, you two," Jack said. "Focus on the case."

"The corner of the building matches the board exterior of Bingham's house, as well," Paige defended herself, "but there are all sorts of these pictures." She kept clicking, and images followed each other on the screen. "In all of these, Bingham didn't have any idea the photos were taken. But, this one…" she straightened up. "In this one, well it's obvious he did."

The two men were in front of Lakeview Community Church. Bingham was taller than Earl by about four inches and had his arm around Earl's shoulders. Both men were smiling.

"They look like the best of friends. How can you be friends with the man you suspect of killing your brother?" I said. "Maybe he just got too close, and Bingham started having control over him."

Zachery headed for the door. "I'll be back in just a second."

"I know that look anywhere. He believes he's on to something," Paige said.

The image remained on the screen—the smiling faces, the presence of the church. The portrayal cast a drastic contrast between life and death, good and evil.

"Okay, so I'm Earl. I found the burial sites years ago, yet I don't say anything to the sheriff. Why?" I attempted to run through the scenario aloud.

"Because he became involved." Paige's eyes lit, and she tapped her head as if to say, *Duh*.

I cocked my head to the side. "It just seems like we're making a lot of excuses for him. Bingham held power over him; Bingham made him do it even if that meant his silence. I just don't understand why he wouldn't have reported it. We're talking about his brother."

"Maybe he stayed close because he wanted to take care of Bingham in his own way," Paige offered.

"Or he knew there was something a lot larger going on."

Both of us looked at Jack who had spoken.

I picked up on his thought, "What if all his snooping brought him to that discovery? I mean, he obviously found an empty grave." I gestured to the monitor referencing the photo we had seen there. "He could have been so close with Bingham by that point, he never even realized he was being brainwashed to keep quiet."

"Brainwashed? Huh. Kid, that's the best you got?"

"You know what I mean. Bingham exerted an influence."

"Okay, how and why?"

"Narcissists only surround themselves with those who empower them and make them feel a sense of elevated importance." They both kept watching me. "Bingham benefited from the relationship. Earl allowed himself to be manipulated until he could get a handle on what he discovered."

"Before he knew it, he was Bingham's apprentice," Jack said.

"Let's just rephrase the entire thing. Bingham has named himself the Redeemer; let's officially call his *apprentice* 'the Follower.'"

"You distanced your phrase from Royster, why?"

My eyes went back to the screen. "Because I don't think he is the Follower."

"He shot at you, at all of us. Why then?"

It didn't take any time for me to calculate the answer. I was staring at it. "He knew we were going to find all this, and his life would be over anyway. It's pretty clear to conclude he knew what was going on, but was he actually involved? We'll have to prove that."

"Hmm."

Something told me Jack was impressed this time.

Zachery sprang around the doorframe holding a picture frame. "I thought I remembered seeing Royster smiling in another photograph. Paige, bring up that one of him with

Bingham again."

"It's still up."

Zachery shoved between Jack and me and held the photo out toward the screen. "Just as I thought. Compare the two pictures, focus on Royster's smile."

The framed photo was of Royster with a man who had similar features. This must have been his brother. Both men held up a bottle of Ale-8-One to the cameraman who took it at the perfect moment. Each of them had sharp eyes and bright smiles. By comparison to the one with Bingham, it was simple to see the difference.

"Royster's smile is forced in the photo with Bingham."

"So the question still is why hang around with a man you suspect of killing your brother?" Paige asked.

"Well, two reasons that I see: one, to gather enough evidence to bring him in—"

"He had that. Remember the picture of the grave," I interrupted Zachery.

"Bingham convinced him it wasn't anything or threatened him in some way. It doesn't mean he saw any victims. Maybe Bingham didn't know that Royster was onto his little operation, or possibly Royster was planning on taking revenge himself but was waiting for the perfect time."

Seventeen

Paige pushed Zachery closer to me, pretty much checking him with her shoulder.

"No reason to be so pushy."

She ignored his protest and moved the mouse on the screen. "There is another folder that I haven't been able to get into—" Her words hung out there as she found the folder, hovered the mouse over it, and then double-clicked. A window came up, requesting a password. She addressed me, "I can't break it."

"Why are you looking at him," Zachery said, sounding offended.

"You seriously have to ask? You might be a genius when it comes to what you've read in a textbook from twenty years ago, but you don't know your way around a computer."

I squeezed between the two of them. "Can I?"

Paige let go of the mouse.

I entered the source code for the folder and found the password. Seconds later, the folder was open.

"Impressive, Pending." Zachery smiled at Jack. "He knows what he's doing—sometimes. How did you know how to do that any—" Zachery's words died on his lips as the first picture filled the screen.

A young girl we all knew as Sally Windermere was tied to the stretcher in the kill room. Her eyes were blindfolded, but the shape of her jaw and the upward turn of her nose made her identity unmistakable.

"He was there," Paige said.

Zachery leaned in toward the monitor. "Forget that he was there, he was the one who killed her. Bingham was in prison."

I stepped to the side, and Paige brought up the next photo. It was a picture of the ground and the tips of two boots. It was a lower resolution when compared to the other photos. "Taken with a phone? And why a picture of his feet?"

I glanced over at Jack to get an idea where he was in all of this. He had retreated to the far corner of the room. He directed my attention back to the screen with a pointed finger. At first, I didn't know what he was trying to communicate, but as I studied the picture, it became apparent. The toe showing on the left was a right foot, the one on the right, a left.

"Bingham has two followers who kill for him." The realization caused internal panic. If Bingham wanted me dead, he still had someone else to carry out that wish.

"Someone else was definitely there with him, and he took a picture of the feet to prove it. Was Royster involved with the torture and killing, or did he just get in too deep? Maybe it was: keep Bingham's secrets or become victim number eleven," Paige offered.

"At this point, it's hard to know," Zachery said. "It is possible that Bingham had that much power and influence—and as for two followers, it wouldn't be the first time a serial killer had that much control. Look at Robin Gecht. He led three other men in the brutal murders of at least seventeen women." He glanced at Paige. "I won't go into the details of the mutilation, but they were known as the Ripper Crew or Chicago Rippers."

"I know it has to be bad when you don't go into details." Paige's eyes made the daring request for Zachery to continue.

"Not getting into it, but the thing is, when it comes to killings involving more than one accomplice, they feed off each other. What one might not do if they were alone, they're not afraid to do with an audience. Both the participant in the murder and the spectator experience power and excitement."

"I know we keep mentioning that maybe Royster kept quiet because Bingham threatened him, myself included, but if Bingham wanted to, he would have killed him," Paige said.

"Not necessarily."

"I know that serial killers normally have a certain type of person they go after, and maybe Royster didn't fit that bill. Still a narcissist isn't going to have their plans ruined or exposed by anyone. They would do anything to stop that from happening."

Jack pulled out a cigarette and perched it in his lips. "Also, at the time, Bingham's next victim was slated to be a woman. Based on this pattern, he wouldn't deviate from that."

Zachery straightened out. "Bingham demonstrates compulsive traits, such as his fascination with the number eleven. Once something is set in his mind, that is the path he follows. He's one extremely organized and controlled killer."

"We know that Bingham assaulted his neighbor, but who ratted him out for killing cows?" Jack took the cigarette out of his mouth, pointed it toward Paige and Zachery, before placing it back.

"We'll get right on that." Paige left the room with Zachery.

Jack and I worked our way through about fifty photographs. Some of them were out of focus, blurred as if taken while moving. Others were too dark to distinguish anything, but one thing was certain, there were no more of any victims. Most of them focused on Bingham or his property.

Jack stepped forward, closer to the monitor. The cigarette from at least thirty minutes ago remained pressed in his lips. I imagined the tip must have been soggy. "Stop there. Enlarge it."

It was a photo of Bingham dumping the contents of a white plastic bag into a pig's feeding trough. "That doesn't look like it came from any feed store." My stating the obvious earned me a glance from Jack and a *Hmm*. Somehow his exhalation reinforced the dark reality. "He fed the intestines of his victims to livestock."

Jack didn't say anything. His eyes were fixed on the screen.

"He'd grind them up," I said, my stomach tossing further, "and put them in the freezer until he could feed them to the animals. The freezer would keep the smell down."

Paige walked into the office, Zachery trailing behind her. She spoke, "Royster reported the dead cows. The call came in on a tip line—"

"For murdered livestock." Jack's sarcasm got a smile from Zachery.

"For crimes in the county. Anyway, the call came in as anonymous, but the operator knew Royster. The rumor got around he was the one who squealed on Bingham."

"And no doubt that got back to Bingham. It couldn't have made him too happy, but it would have reestablished control," Zachery offered.

"Reestablished control?" I asked.

Zachery gave me a look that said, *I don't have time to elaborate on everything I say.* "Yeah, his power over Royster had slipped, but this gave Bingham an opportunity to remind him of what he was capable of. A realigning if you would."

"We need to find out a connection between the victims, establish a timeline." Jack looked at Paige. "We need you to get access to the records from that crime stoppers line. Maybe dead cattle weren't the only thing Royster called in about, but before you go, take a look at this. Either of you recognize it from speaking with the neighbors?" Jack directed their attention to the monitor.

Both Paige and Zachery shook their heads.

A knock on the doorframe had us all looking up. It was the younger CSI, Charlie. His face was pale. "You guys are going to want to see this."

HE LED US DOWNSTAIRS TO the laundry room. Dirty clothes

were strewn on the floor, and clean ones overfilled a basket on the dryer. The dryer was pulled out and the CSI named Kevin, the one I had hit in the jaw, was hunched behind it.

"You told us to search the entire place. Still never expected to find something like this. I find it hard to believe that Royster was involved."

Eleven photographs were taped to the cinder blocks of the basement wall. They were laid out in order of mutilation. The first picture showed one slice in the torso, the next one to the right, two, and so on. The victim was Sally Windermere.

"How could someone be pressured into doing this?" Paige's voice was near a whisper.

Jack flicked his lighter but never lit his cigarette. Instead, he tucked the lighter back into his shirt pocket. "We're going to need to give notification to Sally's mother." He paused and glanced at me. "Since you made the promise, you can do the job."

The academy had prepared me for situations like this, but I never looked forward to putting that knowledge to use. I nodded.

"What's going on down here?" Sheriff Harris came into the room.

"Nice of you to show up," Jack said.

Deputy White had come by when Jones had been here but had left in search of coffee. He said something about not sleeping much at all after witnessing what he had yesterday.

We filled the sheriff in on what we'd learned up to this point. On our way in from Quantico, Jack had gone over how important it was to cooperate with local law enforcement but had added the stipulation, *if it would benefit the investigation.* Jack had never shared the fact we believed another unsub was roaming free.

Harris rubbed his jaw and placed his other hand on his rounded belly where he moved it in a circular motion. "I find all this hard to believe. Earl took it real hard when his brother went missin'. I just don't see him being this kind of person."

"Usually the ones we'd least expect are the really sick ones," Jack said.

Harris shrugged in response to Jack's statement. "It's just you think you know somebody. Do you think he took part out of fear for his own life?"

"Hard to say, but what might have started off as finding justice for his brother turned hellish quickly. We do believe that he suspected Bingham of killing his brother—"

"Oh, yeah, that's not a real surprise. Earl talked about Bingham all the time."

"All the time? And you only think to mention this now?"

"Honestly never thought anything of it, but yeah, we'd meet up sometimes at the Pig Sty." He must have noticed our questioning expressions. "It's a family-run restaurant with darts and pool tables. Anyway, he'd say that something wasn't right with the man, but then, after a while, he stopped saying things like that. He started praisin' the man, saying that he was a hard worker, focused. Guess you guys will be headed out now seeing as you know your unsub is dead."

"Not yet. There are still questions we need answers to. There are also numerous photos on Royster's computer. One I'd like you to see."

I wondered if Jack was going to show him the one of the two work boots, and the fact we suspected another killer. Instead, he showed him the one of the pig trough.

"That's old Gord's place. I only know 'cause of the marking on the trough."

There was painted lettering that had worn from exposure to weather, but it looked like it read, *Maggie.*

"That's the name the missus gives all their sows. Anyways, Gord lives a couple miles down the road from Bi-Bingham's property. He's the largest pig farmer in the area. He sells the meat to some big fancy food producer."

"And Bingham worked for him?" I asked.

"Yeah, at least a couple o' seasons."

Jack pulled out his cigarette and lit up.

Sheriff Harris's eyes went from the amber butt upward to meet Jack's eyes. "Guess I better git on over to Nancy's to let her know about Sally." He stopped in the doorway and turned around. "Do y'all know if one of the victims was Robert?"

PAIGE AND ZACHERY STAYED BEHIND to ensure that the evidence was collected and handled properly. With such a small community and their connections, Jack thought it best not to leave things in the hands of Royster's friends. I agreed with him. After all, we didn't know who else was in the photograph with Royster.

Jack and I loaded into the SUV and headed for old Gord's place. The man's last name was Coleman, and the farm had been in the family for generations.

I studied Jack's profile which looked much different without a cigarette dangling from his mouth. I thought about how investigations were like a poker game, deciding what to expose, what to conceal, and when to do either.

Jack must have sensed me watching him and glanced over. "I want to know why you asked Royster about his wife. You knew from the file he wasn't married."

"I thought it would distract him enough to gain control of the situation."

"Risky."

"But it worked."

"Hmm."

This time I could swear he was impressed. I wondered if I should keep a logbook. At least I'd know if I was coming out ahead or falling behind.

THE COLEMAN FARM, although two miles from Bingham's property, could probably be smelled from there if the wind were blowing just right. The summer breeze was ripe with the stench of pig manure.

I glanced in the rearview mirror at the forensic investigation van following us. We had one of the CSIs come with us to collect trace evidence from the pig trough. Jack said for speed's sake we'd have to trust one of the locals for this.

I knew Jack didn't like questions that pulled on hypotheses. He preferred calculated facts built upon evidence, but I asked the question I was thinking anyway. "Think we're going to find anything?"

"Guess we'll find out."

My question really only served as a brief filler for the awkward silence that kept resurfacing. Even though my confronting the CSIs had been addressed with a threat to my job, Jack hadn't put it behind him. "You're still mad at me."

Jack pulled into the gravel driveway designated by a red mailbox at the road that read, *Coleman Family Farm*. The farmhouse and barn were set back from the road. The fields stretched to the left and right borders of the property.

"You're not going to answer me."

He parked beside a John Deere tractor and behind a battered Ford pickup. "You've got to move forward, Kid."

"So it's behind us? I don't think it is."

"Well, then, Kid, that's your issue." Jack got out of the SUV. The door closed heavily behind him.

Stepping out in the evening air, my eyes watered at the pungent "fresh air".

The CSI got out of the van behind us, seemingly impervious to the quality of the air. He didn't even appear to take shallow breaths.

"Go in ahead of us. We'll be there soon." Jack directed the CSI toward the barn and tapped a hand on the box of the pickup.

The CSI stopped walking and held his evidence collection kit with both hands. "Shouldn't we wait until we have permission?"

I gave the CSI merit for standing up to Jack while he was

trying to appeal to his sense of right and wrong.

"You let me worry about that."

"What the heck are you people doing?" The voice came from a woman in the direction of the farmhouse, but I couldn't see her.

Jack and I moved toward the house. My personal phone rang with Debbie's tune. Jack didn't say anything but looked from it to me. There was no way for me to win in this situation. It was either enrage Jack or upset my wife, but seeing as my current company was Jack, that made the decision easy. I unclipped the cell and chose ignore.

"You have a warrant?"

As we rounded the truck, we saw her. A woman of about five foot two with a slight build stood on a mound of grass, an apron wrapped around her small waist. She watched the CSI heading toward the barn. "What are you doing back here? You people were already here—"

The CSI swung the barn door open, and it made a deep moaning sound. "What the heck." She went after him. "You better be happy Gord's gone to visit a neighbor tonight."

"Mrs. Coleman," Jack said.

"You would be right." She stopped quickly enough that I imagined one leg poised mid-stride. She turned around and came toward us.

"Lance Bingham worked for you."

"Yes. I told all this to some lady. She's with you. FBI." The three letters came out tainted with disdain. City folk, especially feds, interfered with her peaceful life.

"What did he do for you exactly?"

"Like I told her, he fed 'em, cleaned stalls, did some fixin' of things."

"Did he feed the pigs?"

"Course." Her brows pinched downward as if to say, *What are you getting at?*

"What did he feed them?"

"Oh no, I'm not sayin', but it's dang expensive stuff. To sell 'em for food, we don't have a choice. The industry has high standards, but they pay good, too."

I was going to be sick between the smell and the likely possibility people consumed pigs that had eaten human intestines.

"Did this food come in white plastic bags?"

"Course not." Her hips swayed to the right, both arms crossed over her chest. "Why are you askin'?"

"We suspect that Bingham was feeding them something else."

A raised finger came out, removed only a few inches from Jack's nose. From there it changed direction and pointed at me as she accused, "You're here to shut me down. Some big fancy wig has a baby brother or family member wantin' to get into the farmin' business."

"I assure you we're not—"

"Don't lie to me, Agent. I know your types—ruthless. You care nothing about other people's welfare." She turned toward the barn. "Git that man outta there before I call the sheriff."

"The sheriff sent us."

"Like hell he did." Mrs. Coleman stormed off toward the house, the strings from her apron gaining hang time from the gusts of air formed in her wake.

"Come on, Kid. Let's go to the barn."

"Are you sure we—"

Jack kept walking. I looked back at the house expecting the screen door to open with Mrs. Coleman coming out riding on a broomstick. She might have been a little woman, but she had a wild look in her eyes.

"No need to be afraid, Kid. I'll protect ya."

"I'm not."

"Uh-huh."

There were a couple exhalation words worse than *hmm*. Jack had just said one. With it, there was no room for misinterpretation. It conveyed disbelief and mockery wrapped up in a concise package.

We walked through the barn. The fumes were intense, but they didn't assault my sinuses the way I had expected them to. My sinuses must have been scorched and no longer a reliable sensory function, but what was worse was that the stench had converted to a tangible quality, coating my tongue. A deep exhale made me cough and the scent came up as a flavor from my lungs.

The feeding trough for the pigs was located at the back of the barn. The CSI was standing at the doorway to the pen. He turned around as we approached. "I'm not going in there."

"You are."

"You can't make me, Agent." The CSI pointed to a large sow with piglets nursing from her at the far end of the enclosed area. "That sow will kill me if I step in there. Can't you see the way she's looking at me?"

"It's all about perception. She senses fear, she'll charge you. Be dominant." Jack opened the gate. "Now, get in there."

"This ain't a dog."

"They belong to the mammal family, can't be much different."

"I'm not sure if I'm the right person for the job." The CSI stepped into the pen, and Jack latched the gate. The sow lifted her head and assessed the CSI. "See, I'm going to die."

Jack pumped a hand on the man's shoulder. "I have faith in you."

The CSI took another step toward the trough. His feet sank into the muck and made a suctioning noise as he lifted them out. "Oh, this is—" The CSI grunted.

At the end of the pen, the sow wasn't moving.

"You can do it."

I laughed unable to hold it in any longer.

"Hey, you think this is funny? Get in here with me."

"No way."

"Maybe that's not a bad idea." Jack turned to me. He

watched my expression sober. He smiled. "Don't worry, Kid, I wouldn't want the smell and mess in the SUV."

I watched as the investigator made it closer to the trough. His feet sank further into the muck with every step.

"Maybe you should have worn boots." Jack picked up a couple of thigh-highs that were in an empty stall to the right.

"Now you bring those out." The CSI teetered from side-to-side, as he pulled his feet out, careful not to lose balance. "My wife's gonna kill me."

"You're almost there, only about six more feet."

The sow let out a grunt, and the piglets shifted. The CSI froze.

"Pull back the attitude a bit. She's starting to view you as a challenge."

He never looked at Jack, but I could feel the man's energy. Jack was on his shit list. The thing was Jack wouldn't care. I actually had the feeling it fueled him.

"Okay, I'm here."

The sow had her attention on the CSI who was at her feeding trough.

"Just move nice and slow. No fast movements."

"I'm gonna die." The CSI faced heavenward and said some words that were only disclosed by his moving mouth.

"What do you expect he's gonna find anyhow?" I asked.

Jack pulled out a cigarette and lit up.

"I understand you want to find some trace of DNA, human blood, but it's been exposed to the weather for years. How do we even know it's the same trough? Maybe it looks like the older one."

"A man of little faith."

"I find it odd a non-religious person like you has said faith twice in the last few minutes."

"I'm almost done." The CSI sounded panicked. "What's it doin'?"

"You're fine, she hasn't even moved." Jack exhaled a puff of smoke. "DNA can be obtained years after the fact. A little disappointed you didn't know that."

"They don't teach us everything at the academy." I noticed he never touched on my personal observation of him.

"Your response to not knowing something is to blame the academy?"

"I'm not blaming them—"

"Sounds like that's what you just did."

"Sometimes I think we need to work on our communication skills. You don't even call me by my name. It's Brandon, by the way."

I received a blank stare in response. Seconds passed before he spoke. "We're not a couple, Kid. I'm your boss and you're part of my team."

"We still need to com-mu-ni-cate." I dragged out the word.

"Aren't we doing that right now?" Another pull on the cigarette.

"Can you guys stop talking and keep an eye on that pig?"

Jack waved a hand. "She's fine."

"Yeah 'cause she sees somethin' new on the menu."

Another grunt came from the sow. This time she moved. The piglets danced around her.

Jack calmly smoked his cigarette. "You're doing great."

The CSI stopped moving and looked at me. "Why are you doing this to me?"

The sow stirred more. The piglets squealed, creating a small ruckus.

The CSI looked over his shoulder.

I said to Jack, "Maybe we should get him out of there."

"He'll be fine." He dropped the cigarette to the barn floor and extinguished it with a twist of his shoe.

"Oh, dear God." The CSI moved quickly, swiping at the inside of the trough and put what looked like large cotton swabs into sealed cylinders.

"Make sure you get at least six. Get them from the bottom and the cracks."

The investigator never looked up, just kept moving. "If I

die, tell my wife I loved her."

"You're not going to die. You're doing great."

Maybe Jack's past had rendered him a tinge insane. There was something about his eyes and the way they glistened, that told me he enjoyed the present situation. It was a similar look to the one he had given me when he said it wasn't a big deal my photo had been sent to Bingham.

"Maybe you should get out now." If Jack mistook my logic for weakness, so be it. I didn't want to watch a man be attacked by a protective sow.

Jack faced me. "You're calling the shots now?"

"He's been in there too long as is. Look at the sow, the piglets. It won't be long until they get curious—"

"Oh, shit!" The CSI dumped his swabs into the case he carried on a strap over his torso. One of the piglets bounced around his feet, squealing as if announcing danger to the mother.

The sow let out a scream that pulled from the realms of science fiction, both high-pitched and eerie. The hairs on my arms rose.

"Okay, time to come back," Jack said.

"Oh, now's the time? I'm going to die!" The CSI waded his way back through the knee-high muck that threatened to suck him in like quicksand and hold him captive for the angry mama pig. He glanced over his shoulder. The sow moved at a good pace across the pen, the mud not having the same limiting effect on her.

"You can make it. Come on!" I stood in front of the gate, ready to unlatch it. Jack stepped to the side. He had a grin on his face.

The CSI lost the battle and fell over, elbow to muck. His arm sank in, making it hard for him to regain full height.

"Move it!"

The man's face was now sheer panic. Enlarged eyes screamed, *I'm going to die.*

The sow was closing the distance at a fast rate. The CSI

wasn't going to make it.

"You only have ten more feet." I didn't want to tell him the sow only had about that to reach him. "Come on!"

The piglets squealed as the sow charged toward the CSI.

The CSI lifted his legs high, mocking an athlete who warms up with jogging on the spot, their knees to mid-chest.

"Three more feet." My arms instinctively reached outward. The CSI made it within reach, and I pulled him to the gate. Fortunately, the piglets danced around the sow and slowed her pace. I unlatched the gate and swung it open. "Get in here."

The CSI came through so abruptly, he lost his balance and fell to the floor.

The sow reached the gate by the time I had re-latched it. Her wild eyes penetrated mine. She just might have killed him.

The CSI rose, bracing his hands on his thighs, and heaved for a solid breath. I expected him to yell at Jack, but instead he straightened out and let out a wail, "Yeah! What a rush!"

My forehead compressed, and a smile grew on my lips. Jack was laughing.

"See, I told you you could do it."

"I feel so alive! Woo." His last word was spoken at a lower volume. His euphoria was crumbling. He looked down at his clothing which was caked with mud. "My wife's gonna kill me."

"What the hell were you doing in there?" Mrs. Coleman moved through the barn toward us as if she simply hovered over the ground. A finger pointed to the pigpen. Her attention was on the CSI. "You get to that trough by bending over from the outside of the pen. You trying to die?"

"No, ma'am."

"Well, you be thankful you ain't. Maggie has attacked before." The arm and the pointed finger dropped to her side, but Mrs. Coleman wasn't finished. "And now you've gone upset my pig." She moved to the gate, snapped her fingers and pointed to the back corner. The sow obeyed.

"See, like a dog," Jack whispered to me.

I passed him a quick look, hoping that Mrs. Coleman didn't pick up on what he had said.

Two hands went to her hips. "I talked to the sheriff. He said to let you men do what needed doing." She passed a condemning assessment to the CSI's muddy clothing before settling her eyes on Jack. "Seems you already have. Now, is that all?"

"When did you last replace the trough?" Jack asked.

"Troughs last a long time. That one over there has been around at least eighteen years."

"This would be the same one that Bingham put the feed in," I said.

"Yes, that it would be."

"What happened to end Bingham's employment here?"

Her arms crossed, but she looked me in the eyes when she answered. "Lance had a temper. I mean most of the time he was fine, somewhat easy to manage. Periodically he'd git in moods."

"And that's all?"

"You mentioned plastic bags?"

Both Jack and I nodded.

"I caught him dumping from those into the troughs. You tell a soul, I'll deny it."

"Do you know what it was?"

"Nope, but I know it wasn't approved by the FDA. That's what mattered to me. Not long after that, I had a few pigs take sick, real sick. I had to have 'em put down."

"As far as you know were any of the pigs who ate what Bingham fed them sold for human consumption?" Jack asked.

My stomach tightened with nausea as it had earlier. We really had no idea what we put in our mouths these days.

"I told the sheriff I couldn't trust you. He said I could. You just want to shut us down."

I tried to calm her down. "If anyone is responsible it would be Bingham."

"But it's my farm, my reputation. Word gets out, and we're destroyed. Twenty generations of Colemans destroyed under my management."

"It doesn't have to get to that."

Mrs. Coleman had remained silent for at least thirty seconds before she spoke. "Some were set to go to slaughter the next day."

Jack bobbed his head. "We'll be leaving now."

"You're going to shut us down, aren't you? What did Bingham feed 'em? Please let me know." Mrs. Coleman trailed behind us.

Jack turned around. "Honestly, we don't have an answer for that right now."

She pointed a finger to the CSI, who was headed out of the barn to the driveway. "But that's what he was doin'? Tryin' to figure it out? Lance hasn't worked here for about six years."

"When we know something, you will."

Jack led the way, and I walked behind him. Mrs. Coleman stopped at the entrance to the barn, arms still crossed.

The CSI was loading his evidence kit into his van. He slammed the back of his van shut when we approached. He addressed Jack, "What is wrong with you, anyway?"

Jack didn't say anything.

"Did someone hurt you as child?" The CSI didn't look at Jack when he spoke. When it was apparent Jack wasn't going to participate in the conversation, he got into his van.

Jack and I loaded into the SUV. He turned the radio on at low volume and pulled out another cigarette. Those lit sticks seemed to be the only thing that held Jack together.

"Did someone hurt you?" I repeated the CSI's question and flicked the radio off.

Jack turned it back on and turned up the volume. He maneuvered the SUV around so he didn't have to back out the entire length of the driveway.

I turned the radio off again. He put his window down, blew a puff of smoke out of it, and turned the radio on, louder than the last time.

"Why do you do this every time someone has a question about you?" I raised my voice over the music and studied his profile. It revealed nothing. I turned the radio off, which got me a death glare. "Just a question. When we find out Bingham fed her pigs human intestine, are you going to tell her?" I watched Mrs. Coleman from the rearview mirror. She remained at the edge of the barn.

"She'll find out."

"But not from you?"

"We all have jobs to do. Shutting down farms isn't mine."

"You told her when we know something, she will."

"And that, Kid, is not a lie."

Eighteen

Paige knew when Jack took her to the side saying he needed to speak with her that it was going be something she might regret agreeing to. When she had first joined the academy, she knew it was going to be hard work. She'd have to prove herself as strong as a man and even more intelligent. After all, it was still a male-dominated world.

The intelligence aspect had always been relatively easy. Strength was something she continued to battle with but not so much the physical as the emotional. She tried to keep that concealed under layers of bravado.

She knew Jack saw the glimmer of vulnerability in her, but he respected her enough to ignore it, and to her, it wasn't as if she were fragile. She was human. She had compassion despite years on this job. In a way, maybe that was more a strength than a weakness anyhow. It allowed her to keep perspective.

Being a woman brought with it a preconceived notion that dated back before women's liberation, that they were gullible and fickle creatures ruled by emotion. Even a modern man who considered himself untouchable by a woman could easily be swayed by sweet words, tight clothes, and slit eyelids. Of course, the easiest flirtation that would never grow old was the deep-throated laugh. That was when a woman would pretend to be so amused by the words coming out of a man's mouth that she'd toss her hair or roll back her head to display the length of her neck. Paige had that one down.

Sometimes she wondered at what point she had sacrificed her female dignity to gain a lead. At the end of the day, if a little flirting brought them closer to the unsub and brought an end to the madness, it was well worth it.

She delegated the crime tip line to Zachery and excused herself from his view. Jack said to be careful and that none of the local law enforcement could be trusted.

He would have waited on the federal CSIs if he weren't in such a hurry to get the swabs of the trough done. He said that couldn't wait until morning, so here she was "babysitting" a house full of men, including Zachery, two CSIs, and Deputy White, who had returned. She'd focus on the weakest.

Deputy White was drinking his coffee as if it was the only thing keeping him vertical. He pulled it down and let out an enormous yawn.

He caught her watching him. "Long week."

"Yeah it is, and it's just starting." She smiled politely, but this man wasn't her target. He would have been oblivious to any of her attempts to tease out information, but she had to try. "Did you know Earl very well?"

"Nah. Well, a bit. I mean he grew up in the county. He was around. I was around." He took another draw on the coffee, the suction from his mouth made a slurping noise when he pulled back.

"So you didn't really get to know him?"

"Nope." As he spoke the single word, he exhaled a stream of coffee-polluted breath in her direction.

"Well, that's too bad. I've heard he was a great guy." She twisted the words from the CSIs that *Earl would never do this.*

"Like I said. Couldn't tell ya."

"His buddies are going to miss him."

"Bet they will."

"What are their names again? My memory's not the best

sometimes," she lied.

The deputy didn't even give her a sideways glance. It told Paige he was putting in the time. Any experienced law enforcement officer would realize the vital importance of a good memory.

"The older one's Kevin, and the blondie is Charlie."

"Thanks." Paige smiled and excused herself. She headed down to the laundry room where *the blondie* was. Even though she had a reliable memory, most times the CSIs blended together and remained nameless, but this one, her target, she would approach as if interested in him. "Charlie."

The young investigator who was probably a few years younger than Brandon was hunched behind the dryer taking photographs of the find. He spoke with his back to her. "Yeah."

She might have to work a little bit for this one, but she had confidence in her abilities. "Do you have a sec?"

He looked over his shoulder at her. "Guess so." He stood up, bracing hands on his thighs as he rose.

"You were really close to Earl."

"Yeah, I was." His eyes went from her to the pictures of the cut marks on the victim. "I still can't believe he did this. It's like a nightmare."

Paige tilted her head to the right. "I can imagine." She added a slight pout to her lips. "What was he like?"

Charlie's eyes held hers. They hardened and misted over. "Not like this." He pointed to the pictures. "He was a quiet person, kept to himself."

"He didn't have a lot of friends?"

"Not really, but he was a good guy."

His statement made them both go silent for a few seconds. The horror of the photographs, the fact Royster shot at Jack and Brandon and held a gun on Zachery shattered any preconceived notion that Royster was a good man.

Charlie snapped the latex gloves off and ran both hands down his face. "I see it in your eyes. I understand how you can't believe that."

"Had he been different lately?"

"You mean besides how he became obsessed with his brother's disappearance years ago?"

"Yeah." She had to play this close. She couldn't disclose they suspected another unsub. "How did he respond to the find two days ago?"

Charlie went quiet, and Paige feared she'd lost him.

"What did he tell you, Charlie?" Paige put out a hand to the CSI's shoulder. He didn't recoil from her touch, unlike Brandon, who always stepped back to avoid contact.

Charlie's head dropped forward. Paige gave him a few seconds. When he lifted his head, tears were pooled in his eyes. "He wasn't right. I just assumed it was the crime scene. It was pretty intense for around here."

"It would be intense for pretty much anywhere." She pressed her lips, careful to turn them only a quarter upward to reveal the hint of a smile. It was to provide support yet not detract from the severity of the conversation.

"We went out last night, and he really wasn't himself. He went on about the next couple days and that they'd be interesting."

"Interesting?" Paige pulled her arm back.

"That's what I said. Oh God—" Both hands went to his face again.

"What is it?"

The hands peeled from his face. "He said he was curious about how fast the FBI worked. I didn't think anything of it at the time." Charlie's gaze dropped to the floor before matching with Paige's eyes. "The rumor upstairs is Earl sent a picture of that new agent to Bingham. Was that part of his game?"

"Where did you hear—" Paige waved a hand, realizing she knew the answer to the question she was going to ask. They had filled in the sheriff and deputy on the picture. It probably spilled over to the CSI. "We might never know

for sure, but it appears Agent Fisher was the next target."
Seconds passed. "You still don't believe all this," Paige said
the words seasoned with sympathy as she opened a hand and
gestured around the room. The CSI's eyes fell. It was time to
open this man up. "You said you were close with Earl. Would
you consider yourself his best friend?" She smiled at him.

"Yes, ma'am."

"Oh, please don't call me ma'am, it makes me feel old." She
let out a small laugh, a teaser.

"It's a sign of respect. You can't be much older than me
anyhow." He returned the smile.

She had him. "Some days I feel a lot older, lately, at least
forty."

"Forty? No way. Wouldn't believe it."

He didn't need to know she was that age exactly. She let
out a deep-throated laugh and rolled her head back and to
the side. She executed the move flawlessly.

"Hey, you want to go out sometime?"

Maybe she had executed the move too faultlessly. Her
smile faded. "The big guy wouldn't like it."

"Your boss?"

Paige nodded. At least another twenty seconds of silence
passed, the tangible kind shared amongst strangers, with
each person wondering what the other was thinking. Paige
broke the silence. "Did Royster have a girlfriend?"

Charlie blurted out a laugh. It stifled when he noticed that
her face was expressionless. "You did see him?" She nodded.
"He wasn't exactly the hottest guy in the county."

"Not bad." She was being generous. In all honesty, when
she saw Royster for the first time, she didn't take a second
glance—and it wasn't just the number of CSIs she was used
to running into. He didn't have anything that stood out and
made him memorable.

"Seriously?" Charlie laughed. "You'd be the first hot—"
He cleared his throat. Paige smiled. "Anyway, country
women have great stamina, as I'm sure you do, but Earl's

allergies weren't exactly a magnet for them. Not that it really mattered, Earl preferred men."

All Paige wanted to do was run upstairs to Zachery and call Jack. This was the fine jewel of information they needed. Statistically, team killers were a pairing of two or more men. "Was he with anyone recently?"

"Oh, please don't spread the word too much. Others on the team didn't know. It's still a religious community around here, closed to new worldly ways."

"I understand."

"He's had a thing with someone for years. They even talked about getting married, but that's illegal here in Kentucky."

"They could have left and got married in a state that supported it."

"No way. Earl's heart was in Kentucky, nowhere else."

"What is the name of the person Earl was involved with?"

Charlie seemed hesitant to answer, and it reaffirmed why they couldn't trust anyone around here. Potentially, anyone could have been the person wearing the other boot in the picture. Paige put her hand on his shoulder again. "He'll need to know what happened and why. Let us explain it to him."

Seconds later, Charlie answered, "Quinton Davis."

"A black man?"

"An American."

"Of course, I didn't mean anything by that."

"I know you didn't." Charlie let out a deep breath. "Guess that comes from years of defending the guy."

"You said others didn't know."

"I said the other guys on the team didn't know. You really think in a small town like this you can keep rumors from spreading?"

I PULLED OUT THE LAPTOP again and scanned the history of Bingham's followers.

"You're back on that Twitter thing again."

"Yep."

"Hmm."

"Why do you do that?" The question slipped out. I wished I could reverse time like in my novels.

"What?"

"Hmm. You say that a lot."

"Hmm."

I detected the hint of a smile. He activated the hands-free signaling the end of another conversation. When Nadia answered, he said, "Where are you with the followers?"

"Have you noticed the time? Nope, probably not. Little Nadia here is putting in OT to get this done."

The clock on the dash read ten.

"You started on this yesterday." Although the smile wasn't visible, it was audible in Jack's voice. For an instant, I was jealous of their relationship. At least, he called her by name.

"Like I've said before, we're not on TV here. In real life, things take a little longer."

Jack glanced at me. "She likes to pass the blame, too."

I knew he referred to my comment earlier about not being familiar with testing DNA years later and how I had come back with the academy not having taught me everything.

"I'm almost through them all, and nothing useful jumps out so far. Most of the followers are not even from places the Redeemer lived." Papers were shuffled in the background; there was clicking of keys on her keyboard. "But you have a new follower, Brandon."

Jack pulled down the street toward Royster's house.

I had gone to the Redeemer's page, but he hadn't posted anything since yesterday. I never made it to my own page. "Let me guess, Bingham is now one of them?"

"You'd be correct. Be careful out there."

"The kid's gonna be fine."

"You don't know that—with all due respect."

"He's with me—" The phone system notified us of another incoming call. "Gotta go. Call if you get anything else."

"Of cour—"

"Talk to me."

The caller ID read Paige Dawson.

"We have a lead."

Nineteen

Jack cranked the SUV into a U-turn, and we were headed back to the country roads. All it took was the relaying of Paige's findings, and we were after a man named Quinton Davis of Sycamore Street.

Paige said they were fine and still waiting on the CSIs to process everything. Deputy White had headed out to get them food and coffee. They were doing better than we were, and they were definitely doing better than I was. It was time to put my training to use.

Paige said that we couldn't have someone from the county provide death notification, not even the sheriff. Despite the fact that the community was tightly connected, they seemed to have missed that Earl Royster was a homosexual— apparently down here that was a big deal—and because I had missed out on notifying Nancy Windermere about her daughter, Jack figured it was my turn this time.

Quinton Davis could have played linebacker with his thick torso and weight of at least two sixty to three hundred pounds. He studied us after we announced ourselves as FBI.

"We're here about Earl Royster."

Arms crossed, uncrossed, and then he slipped his hands into the pockets of his shorts. "Why come here?"

I answered honestly, "We know you were romantically involved."

Quinton looked down the street before stepping back and allowing us into his house. "Come this way." He directed us to the living room and a burnt orange sofa.

Quinton took a seat across from us in a reclining chair that dated to earlier than the sofa. "What's Earl up to now?" He smiled. His teeth were tainted yellow against his dark skin. My guess was due to age and lack of hygiene, not a nicotine addiction as the place didn't smell of cigarettes.

I swallowed deeply. The plan was to simply notify him of his boyfriend's death, gauge his reaction, and check out his residence—what we could see of it anyway—and get out. We were to keep a low profile to not scare him away if he was the unsub we were still looking for.

"It's not good, is it?" The man leaned forward, rubbed his hands on his thighs. He knew what was coming. His earlier reaction had been a mask to hide it.

"I'm afraid not."

Jack watched me, and I knew what he was trying to communicate, *Get to the point.*

"Earl Royster was shot late this afternoon."

"Oh—" A hand covered his mouth. It dropped as quickly as it made contact, leaving his gaping mouth exposed. His eyes searched for details.

"We went there to question him—"

"You shot him?" His bottom lip quaked, tears pooled in his eyes.

"No, I—"

"You did." Quinton's eyes darted to Jack.

I came to his defense. "Earl held a gun on a federal agent."

"No, no, I don't believe it." He shook his head.

"Has he been strange lately?"

Quinton's eyes hardened. "You should go."

I looked at Jack who, instead of moving to leave, settled into the couch.

"We just need to understand why he would do something like that."

"Why? So you can make yourself feel better?" Quinton rose to his feet and came toward Jack. "You took him away from me."

I stood between them. Jack didn't move. I put a flat hand out toward Quinton, hoping he would stop there. He didn't until pressure was applied. My hand flattened and pressed into the meat of his chest. He kept going until my wrist bent back. His frame towered over me, dwarfing my six foot two by easily another three inches. "I'm going to have to ask you to step back."

"This is my house."

The message contained in his eyes was one of conflict. He was a large man, but I pounced on the weakness evidenced beneath the surface. "You are also suspected of involvement with what Earl was, so I suggest you back off."

"What do you mean?"

I wanted to look back at Jack. We had discussed this on the ride over—what to disclose, what to withhold, but, as was normally the case when it came to communicating with Jack, there were holes in the conclusions. Heck, there were even voids in the middle of the context. "Sit down back over there, and we'll talk."

Quinton held eye contact for a few more seconds before complying.

I flexed my wrist in relief when he retreated. Now that the pressure on it was gone, the joint ached from having been held back. I dropped onto the orange sofa.

"What do you think he did?" Quinton dropped a hand on the arm of the chair.

"This is still part of an open investigation—"

"Don't feed me that bullshit. I won't eat it." Quinton didn't get up, but moved to the edge of the chair. It groaned under his weight.

"He fired on us—" I gestured between Jack and me "—when we showed up to talk to him. Once the situation calmed down, he pulled a gun on another agent."

"You said you got the situation calmed down? That *situation* was my husband."

"Husband?"

"The great state of Kentucky might not allow it, but we were where it mattered." He balled up a hand, thumped it over his heart.

"You obviously knew him better than anyone." I glanced at Jack, asking in silence where I should go from here.

Jack said, "Evidence in our investigation thus far convicts Earl Royster as a murderer. He—"

"No way." Quinton got up from his chair. "I can't believe that. Don't you talk to me after you killed him!" A thick finger wagged at Jack.

I readied to come to his defense again if need be—although, based on what Jack had done back at the house to the CSIs, Quinton should be more afraid of him.

Surprisingly, Quinton just left the room. Jack and I shared a look which ended with him exhaling a deep breath and shrugging a shoulder. I didn't miss the message in his eyes, *Study the house, Kid*. Even his pet names for me were coming through in telepathy now. I might need therapy when this was over.

The living room was outdated, yet decorated modestly. There was an oak mantle over the fireplace. A mirror hung over it, and flowers in a vase showcased in front of it, no framed photographs anywhere. *Had Royster been this man's entire life?*

An abstract painting with slashes of bright colors hung crooked on a wall beside a bookshelf. It pointed out the obvious missing element to most living rooms. There was no TV. My attention went back to the bookshelf which was filled to overflowing with books of different thicknesses and sizes. The ones that couldn't fit in vertically with their spine displaying were layered horizontally on top.

I walked over to the shelf. If Quinton returned, I would tell him I loved books and was curious what ones he had. My eyes worked as fast as they could, taking in the titles, the colors, the images. I spoke quietly to Jack, "No Bible and no book on the coinherence symbol."

When I turned to look at him, I noticed the front window coverings. The drapes were a jacquard pattern, and the only reason I knew that was because my wife insisted on buying similar curtains. She went on about how classy the pattern was and kept repeating its name as if she were an educated interior designer. It was probably the only one she could name.

Quinton came back into the room with an Ale-8-One in his hand. It was already half gone. He stopped beside me.

I forced a smile. "You love to read."

"Yep." He dropped into the sofa chair.

I headed back to the couch. "Lovely curtains."

"Drapes. Thank you." Quinton swigged some of his soda.

"Why did you leave the room?" I asked him.

Quinton held up the soda bottle, cocked it at an angle, and put it back to his lips.

"I think there's more to it. Did Earl ever hurt you?"

He held the bottle to his lips and cradled it there as if he considered taking another sip.

"He can't hurt you now. He's gone."

Quinton put the bottle down on an end table. The room was quiet enough to hear our breathing.

I was afraid to break the silence for fear Quinton would withdraw for good, but I also feared not prying into what he had to say. "What is it?" I leaned forward, my elbows coming to rest on my knees. I clasped my hands.

He took a deep, jagged inhale and stood up. He moved slowly, yet methodically, and lifted the T-shirt he wore. My stomach heaved at what he revealed.

Quinton kept pulling up his shirt. As he looked down at his torso, I glanced at Jack. The incisions weren't as deep as the ones on the victims, and the lengths were shorter, but they were laid out in the same pattern—the method of counting to five with lines. Quinton had eight lines—one set of five and three running vertically a few inches to the right.

Most of them were scarred over. One was more recent.

"He said that it would liven things up." Quinton dropped his shirt. His eyes read of pain and shame.

"How long had he been doing this?"

"Years now—five, six?"

"And that one?" I pointed to the fresh wound.

"Last night when he came home."

"Why did you put up with this?" I mentally compared the stature of Earl to Quinton. Quinton could have easily overpowered him.

"Where else was I s'posed to go? I loved him. He did love me."

"He had a strange way of showing it," Jack intervened. The abruptness of his tone combined with the words spoken caused both Quinton and me to look at him. "I'm not saying anything you don't know. You don't abuse the ones you love."

"I disagree. Those are the ones that get the most abuse," Quinton said.

Interesting debate, and currently I sided with Quinton.

"Let me guess, he apologized afterward." Jack's tone was still dry, he patted his shirt pocket.

Quinton's eyes went to Jack's pocket, and then flitted to Jack's eyes. He must have noticed the bulge of the cigarette pack. The message in his eyes was *No smokin' in here.* Quinton didn't comment on that audibly but what he did say was horrifying. "He would cut me with a knife from the kitchen drawer. As he did, he'd complain about it being too dull, not being the right kind." Quinton dropped into the chair again. "Afterward, when I had stopped screaming, I would cry from the residual pain. Earl'd look me in the eye, touch the back of his hand to my forehead, caress it, and say, 'Shh, baby, don't cry.'"

Twenty

The forensic investigation vehicles were no longer in front of Royster's house. Deputy White's cruiser was parked on the road, and Sheriff Harris was standing in front of the chain link fence talking to Paige. Her hands were dug into her pockets, her arms fully extended. She rocked so slightly, one might not even notice, heel-toe, toe-heel. She did that when she was tired and ready to move on. She paused mid-tilt when we pulled up.

Jack walked between Harris and Paige and headed to the house. "We've got to talk."

"Excuse me," Paige said to Harris, putting a hand to his elbow.

I glanced over at him, and in the casting from the streetlights, the man appeared to have aged over the last five hours.

Paige must have noticed my assessment. She leaned into me. "He had a hard time at the Windermeres'. Sally was their only child. Nancy couldn't have kids after her."

"Hmm." The noise came from me, and I wished I had swallowed it.

Paige held an arm out in front of my chest and stopped walking.

"What?" I turned to face her. Maybe if I played it dumb, like I hadn't realized it, she would move on.

She was smiling. "You're starting to sound like him now."

I let out a breath I hadn't realized I was holding. "Please, don't say that."

"It's bound to happen. You spend that much time around someone."

"Stop there." I was smiling now.

"Well." She held the door open for me.

I put an arm over her and got the door. "Ladies first."

"Thanks." She ducked to fit under my arm and watched me as she passed through.

I smelled her perfume, sweet and lightly floral. I remembered our nights together—and her laugh, not the fake one she put on to be flirtatious or seductive, but her sincere laughter that came out when she was vulnerable. "No problem."

I turned back and looked at Harris. The toe of his shoe stubbed at the pavement, and his head faced downward watching it. I couldn't help but think that if a seasoned man like the sheriff found notifications hard, would it ever get easier?

My mind went to Quinton's face, how it had fallen as his eyes had filled with tears of denial. In that moment, I had taken everything away from him.

"You coming, Kid?"

I watched Harris for one more second before closing the front door. "I'm here."

The rest of the team was gathered in the dining room. Deputy White came out of a side hallway, the rush of water from a toilet filtered in the background. He tipped his hat to us. "I'll be outside. Give you folks some privacy."

Zachery spoke when the front door latched shut. "I contacted the supervisor in charge over at the crime tip line. They pulled their records and searched for anything that matched Royster's voice using the tip about the cows as the sample reel."

"Surprised they have that technology," Jack said.

"The center was donated to the county by a rich man. Nothing but the best, they say. Anyway, just got the call a few minutes ago, and nothing came back."

Jack turned to Paige. "Any further progress on the computer files?"

"I've made copies of the files to forward to Nadia to see if there are any more encrypted files."

"She's got a lot on her plate. Slingshot, maybe you can study them, too?"

"Sure." I dragged out the word a little too long. Jack noticed.

"You can or you can't?"

Normally a field job was just that—away from computers. It felt like a demotion. I turned to Jack. "Can."

"All right then."

"I'll make another copy," Paige said.

"Anything else you have to tell me?"

Paige and Zachery shared a look, shook their heads.

"All right then. We saw Quinton Davis. His background file seemed to match up with the man himself. He lives under the radar, keeps to himself, reads a lot. Really wouldn't peg him as Royster's killing partner."

"It's quite common for couples to kill together. Typically, when you're talking romantic involvement as well, the couple consists of one man, one woman, but the dynamics are based on one dominant, one submissive," Zachery said.

"Obviously, the male being submissive." Paige arched her brows to accompany her sarcasm.

"Yeah, that's it." A small smile showed on Zachery's lips.

I cut the joviality short. "We believe that Quinton was the submissive one in their romantic relationship, making Royster the dominant."

"That right there tells us the unsub we're looking for isn't Quinton," Zachery filled in the obvious. "We already know Royster had a submissive personality when it came to his involvement with Bingham."

"Very good." Jack's sardonic statement was accompanied by an upward turn of his mouth for only an instant. "Because we know all of this started with Royster's need for answers, he became vulnerable, a follower. That means whoever was with him during the torture and murder was stronger than he was."

"But that's not all," I started. "Royster abused Quinton."

"Abused him. How?" Paige asked.

"Cut him, just like the victims." My statement sank in the air as if it were a tangible element susceptible to gravity.

"Quinton was his practice?"

I held out my phone to show them the picture Quinton had allowed us to take of his torso.

"Oh my God." Paige's eyes dragged from the small image to align with my eyes.

"And if you think that's bad, wait until you hear what Royster would say afterwards." I waited until they were all watching me. "'Shh, baby, don't cry.'"

"Creepy." Paige shivered.

"Yeah, and he'd say it while caressing Quinton's forehead with the back of his hand."

"Royster was one sick shit." The statement came from Zachery.

"Seems that way. Do you think maybe we're looking at this the wrong way—" My cell rang, and Jack looked at it. Even he recognized the ringtone as belonging to Debbie. I hit ignore. "We assume that Royster was the weaker of the two followers, but what if the other person was weaker?"

"No." The single word came from Jack.

"No?" Sometimes I wondered if he chose to disagree with me simply for being able to do so.

"No. Royster was the follower to whoever else was in that picture." Jack took out a cigarette and lit up. A puff of white smoke accompanied his next words. "Quinton said Royster complained about the knife not being the right one."

"That shows Royster was trying to imitate what he saw," Zachery finished Jack's thought.

Jack nodded as he took another drag.

Somehow watching him do this made everything fill in for me. "We know Royster had a submissive personality; therefore, we know the other person in that picture wasn't put in place by him. He was recruited directly by Bingham. With Bingham in prison, this follower took over in every way, including leading Royster."

"Quite likely. The man was relatively weak."

"He kept his relationship with Quinton secret for years." For some reason, I came to Royster's defense.

"Weakness. He shouldn't have been ashamed of what they had."

"It was weak for him to hold back because he didn't want unnecessary public backlash including the potential loss of his job?"

"You think he'd be fired over what he had goin' on with that man?" The sheriff came into the dining room.

All of us turned to him. I asked the obvious. "You knew about it?"

"Course I did. Most of us did. Small place, or haven't y'all picked up on that yet? The only ones who thought it was a secret were Earl and Quinton."

"And nobody cared?"

"Nobody but Earl's brother."

"Robert knew about it."

"Listen, if you're gonna parrot everything I say, it'll be a long night."

I noticed Zachery's smile at my expense.

"What did Rob think of his brother being homosexual?" Paige asked.

The sheriff put one hand on his holster, the other to his hip. "He didn't like it. Said it was wrong. Said the Bible said it was wrong."

Maybe that's why Royster had been easily manipulated by Bingham. Bingham was an advocate of scripture, a preacher of confess, repent, and be forgiven. If that man accepted him for who he was, who was his brother to condemn him?

That could have turned his mission of finding justice for his brother to one relating with Bingham's mission, but we still didn't know for certain Robert was a victim of Bingham, and if he was what the motive would have been for killing him. "How did Earl handle that?"

"Robert was still his brother. That's why he took it so hard when he went missing."

Silence passed, except for the sound of a ticking clock that made its way from the direction of the kitchen.

"Well, people, time to go." Jack sucked on the cigarette and headed to the front door. The pile of ash built up on the end no doubt proving as a motivator to get outside.

"Night, Sheriff," Paige said.

"Oh, I doubt that. We'll be watching the place, making sure there are no looters." He pointed at the broken front window. "In the morning, we'll get it boarded up."

THE RIDE BACK TO THE hotel seemed never-ending for only being about a twenty-minute drive from Royster's, but my head pounded. I blamed it on the stench of secondhand smoke that had saturated my clothes and no doubt seeped into my flesh. I could barely wait for a hot shower to wash it away.

Zachery had called shotgun like a child, yet he was the genius, leaving me in the backseat with Paige. At least relief from the smell of cigarette came in subtle waves of her perfume.

Zachery dropped his head back on the headrest. "We're definitely looking for someone close to Bingham, someone loyal."

Maybe if I focused on the case, the headache would subside. "He doesn't have any living relatives. He never had children, so it's safe to rule out those."

"The farmers he worked for valued him, said he was hardworking, but I don't think it went beyond that," Paige offered.

"He attended the Lakeview Community Church but wasn't a member. No one's mentioned him being close to anyone else we haven't already spoken to." My phone rang. It was Debbie again. I glanced at the clock on the front dash. Just after eleven. As far as I was concerned this was my time. I answered.

"I've been trying to reach you."

"I know."

"You've been ignoring my calls."

I shifted my position to face the door. I held my cell in my left hand and sheltered my face hoping it would dilute my voice. "I'm working." I heard Paige say something about visiting more members of the church.

"All day and night?"

"It's part of the job."

"It's late. You're still working?"

"I've got to go."

"Brandon."

"Yes."

"Take care out there."

I hung up without saying another word to her, and the awkwardness of doing so transferred to Paige who paused in the middle of speaking.

"You were talking about visiting more members of the church to see if anyone else was close with Bingham," I prompted her to continue.

"Yes." She studied my eyes, and somehow managed to penetrate them in the glow of the dashboard lights that filtered to the back seat. "Maybe some of them would know more about who he was close to if he mentioned anyone specifically."

"Good idea." Jack pulled into the parking lot of Betty's Place for Paige and Zachery to pick up their SUV.

Somehow, it took until now for me to realize my other reason for a headache—lack of food. Just seeing the lights off in the restaurant made my stomach growl.

"You and Zachery visit those on the congregation list tomorrow. Slingshot and I will pay our new friend another visit."

Paige and Zachery got out of the vehicle, and I couldn't help but think, *Why do I always have to talk with Bingham?*

ALL I HAD WANTED TO do was peel myself out of my clothes and take a hot shower, but the lights of the hotel lobby summoned me in the search for a vending machine.

The night clerk sat behind the front counter, feet up on the desk, watching *Criminal Minds*. He didn't look much older than twenty. The door chimed notifying him he had a customer; he nodded absent-mindedly.

"Just looking for something to eat."

"Over there." He pointed to a vending machine.

I studied my options which weren't plentiful: a few types of chocolate bars, small bags of peanuts, and packages of microwave popcorn, which had me wondering how that would sell seeing as the rooms didn't have microwaves. Along with that was a couple varieties of chips—plain and nacho. Any other time, if I wasn't so hungry, I'd take a pass on all of it. I reached into my pocket for some change, selected the peanuts and a Snickers bar.

"You're one of the FBI Agents, ain't ya?"

"Yes, I am."

"I have mail for one of ya." The guy walked to the counter. "Brandon Fisher."

"That's me."

He extended a card-sized envelope, the same as the one sent to Bingham at the prison—the envelope that had contained my picture. I put the food on the counter and turned the envelope over. No return address. I looked at the front. No postmark. "Someone dropped this off?"

The guy shrugged, glanced back at his program.

"Do you know when?"

He shook his head.

"Do you have cameras in here?"

He gestured behind me toward a large one mounted in the corner of the room.

"I'll need to see the footage."

"You'll have to speak to the manager in the morning."

"Right now. Call them. Wake them up. Now."

The guy held up both hands in surrender. "K."

His statement returned my eyes to the envelope. Even though I held it and its contents were unknown, I knew whatever was inside wasn't going to be good. *Call it a hunch.* "Call them. Now."

He picked up the phone, pecked the buttons with his bony fingers. "He's not going to be—" He stopped talking to me and spoke into the phone. "It's Kyle…"

I heard him speaking, but his words blurred. Everything from the last three days merged. Eleven rooms, ten bodies, one empty grave. Confess your sins and be forgiven. Don't, and be punished. The Redeemer was a new follower on Twitter, but he had reached out from cyberspace and become my stalker in the real world.

I worked a thumb under the seal of the envelope and tore open its length.

The hotel employee hung up. "He said it doesn't work."

"Great! Just great!" I grabbed the peanuts and bar from the counter, walked a few steps and spun around. "Who was working today?"

"Ellen, I think."

"When's her next shift?"

"She'll be in at six."

He spoke to my back and the chimes of the door. My heart beat rapidly. I stopped in front of the lobby, tucked the food under one arm and slipped the contents out of the envelope. Two pictures. When I realized of what, the food fell to the concrete.

LIKE KINDERGARTEN CHILDREN, they were to be all tucked

in and accounted for by eight. Lights went out at eleven. Bingham despised life behind bars. He lay on the top bunk, but he didn't sleep.

His cellmate snored beneath him loud and deep enough to send vibrations through the metal frame. The inconsistent rhythm jackhammered into Bingham's head, interrupting his thoughts at the peak of enlightenment.

Three years in this hellhole to date, two with this hog beneath him. Every night, it was the same noise. The man seemed to fall asleep at the directing snap of fingers.

Bingham had never been that obedient. He didn't see the merit in following the leading of another man. After all, who were they to guide him when they were imperfect sinners without recompense?

He had found a way to repentance through reconciling for others' sins. His cellmate let out another loud snore. The man should fear sucking in his entire face with the depth of his inhalations.

Bingham took his arms out from under the scratchy, wool blanket that covered him.

He lifted his arms, intertwined his fingers, and cracked all his knuckles at once. As each of them shifted into tighter alignment, he thought of those he had saved and those who were loyal to him despite adversity. He smiled.

I RAN THROUGH THE HOTEL parking lot—and, as if I were in a nightmare, the more I willed my legs to move, the heavier they became. I reached Jack's door and slammed the side of a balled fist repeatedly against it.

I heard him swear, but I didn't think I woke him up. As I continued to knock, more voices came from inside, and I assumed he was watching TV. He opened the door three-quarters of the way. No glow came from the TV.

He stepped around the door wearing a white T-shirt and gray boxers. He held his Glock 22 ready to fire if he didn't like his late-night visitor. "What the hell are you doing at my door?" The gun didn't move.

I extended the photos along with the envelope. "This was dropped off today."

He looked from my eyes to what I held out to him and lowered his gun.

"This is a picture of my house back in Woodbridge, and that—" I rearranged the photos to place the other one on top "—is my wife. I tried calling her, but she's not answering." I brushed past him into the room. "I need to get back there now."

"Did they see who dropped this off?" Jack took the photos, held them at an angle, and looked at me. Something in his eyes told me he didn't really want me in his room, and if it had been anything but the current circumstance I'd be out on my rump.

"The security camera's a dud. The lady who was on shift starts at six." I couldn't obtain a satisfying breath. All I could think about was Debbie being kidnaped, tortured, and murdered. I thought of the circular graves, the empty one, the void begging for the unsub to fill it. I knew it was nonsense as there was no way they would ever gain access to Bingham's property, but I also realized it could be repeated elsewhere. After all, we knew files were being sent to us regarding similar murders in Sarasota.

Jack dropped onto the end of the mattress. I noticed then how the sheets were unkempt, pulled back, and bunched up at the end of the bed. I remembered the voices I had heard earlier. The TV wasn't on. Maybe he'd shut it off before answering the door. I didn't know why, maybe it was the jittery way Jack was acting, the more accommodating manner, but I believed someone else was in this room—but it wasn't any of my business. I pulled out my phone and dialed home again. The hollow rings droned in my brain. I might never speak to her again. All I imagined was her captured and begging for life.

"Kid, we'll head out first thing in the morning—"

"In the morning? She could be dead by then."

"We'll call the Prince William County PD, have them drive by the house, and check things out. We have to keep a level head."

Prince William County PD covered Woodbridge.

"Easy for you to say."

"Yeah, I'm the boss. It's my job. Besides, running into Woodbridge, all hotheaded on a mission isn't going to accomplish anything. You should know that."

"You're talking about how I came at the CSIs?"

Jack shrugged his shoulders. I realized another thing about Jack Harper; he never let anything go. He held onto it, good or bad, and used it as a grading chart against all future actions, like my earlier mention of the academy and how it hadn't taught me an aspect about DNA, and suddenly I was a finger-pointer of blame.

"I'm going."

"Okay, how do you know this isn't another game, huh? Maybe Royster dropped this off before or after the photo to the prison. Besides the man's dead."

My jaw tightened, and a hand went over the gun I still carried in my holster. "We don't know he dropped those off, and you're telling me Royster flew to Woodbridge, snapped the photos, and came back here, all for a joke. Maybe the other unsub who we haven't caught yet did this. Maybe he has Deb."

Jack leaned across the bed to the nightstand and opened the drawer. He pulled out his phone, a pack of cigarettes, and a lighter. "Listen, Kid, how do you know she didn't take off to a girlfriend's, go visit her mother?" He straightened back to a seated position, flipped open the cigarette pack, and lit one up. The rooms were non-smoking, not that anything seemed to matter to the man except for his nicotine addiction. "Isn't that possible?"

I gave the question a few seconds' consideration. "Still, her phone? Shouldn't she at least be answering that?"

"It's late. She probably turned it off."

"Then it would ring straight to voice mail. It doesn't." I paced the room. As I headed toward the bathroom door, Jack sprung from the bed and redirected me.

"Call her mother, call her best lady friends, and I'm sure you'll find her."

"And if I don't? They'll all be panicked for no reason. Until I know for sure—"

Jack put a hand on my shoulder and removed it almost as fast as it had made contact. "We'll find her." He pressed some keys on his phone. "We've all been on the go since early. It wouldn't be safe to be on the roads, and that's not even mentioning the pain of arranging the flight back to Washington from Louisville."

Woodbridge, Virginia was about thirty minutes outside of Washington.

"You're being careless."

Jack hung up the phone and glared at me. "When you've seen all I have, then we can talk. I know when to react, I know when to get wound up, but I also know how to control it." He jabbed the phone toward me. "That's the part you have to learn. Look at the evidence. We have pictures of your house and wife. Could Royster have gotten these offline like he did your Twitter pic?"

I pulled the photos from the bed where he had left them. I studied the photograph of my house, trying to be objective. I convinced myself to breathe in deep, allowing myself to believe Jack's other scenarios. Debbie was over at her mother's or at a friend's. Wherever she was, she was safe.

My eyes went to the garden bed at the front of the house. It was just as I remembered before leaving, but the hanging flower basket on the veranda, I didn't remember that. The porch stairs were missing paint. A week, maybe two weeks ago the way time moves, Debbie and I had applied a fresh coat. We had a couple beers afterward and ordered in pizza while watching mindless television programs.

I looked back to the basket. I remembered it now. It had dried out from the sun, and Debbie had thrown it out. I had razzed her about her inability to keep plants alive. She had blamed Mother Nature.

"This photo is at least two to three weeks old."

"Okay, then. What does that tell you?"

"I don't know. What do you want me to say?"

"Think clearly. The photo of you was pulled from the internet. The whole point was to play with you—"

"Was it?"

"Oh Lord, here we go." Jack looked heavenward which I found hypocritical for a nonreligious person.

I took a few steps but circled back to where I had started. "What if Royster mailed the photo to the prison as a confession of his sins? He knew that we'd be watching Bingham, and he knew if we didn't find out about the picture sent there, we'd find these ones."

"You just said a minute ago that we don't even know if it was Royster who dropped these ones off." Jack pointed to the photos in my hand.

"No, now I'd put money on it. Paige said the other CSI, Charlie, commented on how Royster said he was curious about how fast the FBI work. Royster said he didn't mean for anyone to get hurt. I believe he was willing to die for what he had done."

"It doesn't explain why he shot at us."

"He missed us with every single bullet. Like you said, if he wanted to hit us, he would have."

"Okay, let's say you're right—"

"I am right."

Jack's eyes shifted, moving over me, but he didn't say anything.

"So now I have to figure out why these photos. Why did Royster drop these off?"

"Same thing, Kid, if you're right. If we failed to track him by the photo dropped off at the prison, this would ensure we'd come after him."

"So he wanted to get caught. Suicide by cop." Jack shrugged. "A man is dead."

"A man who took part in the brutal murder of at least one person."

Our eyes deadlocked, and reality latched on. "Jack, even if Royster dropped off the photos, it doesn't explain why I can't reach Deb."

"Take a close look at the pictures." Jack gestured toward them, calm and composed.

He was right. I couldn't help Debbie by being hysterical. "Well, the picture of my house is an older one." I thought of the internet. "I got it. He took the photo of my house from Google Earth. That would explain why it's not a current photo. They only update every so often."

"And the picture of your wife?" Jack walked past me to the door and flicked his cigarette onto the pavement outside.

The photo was a bust only. Debbie wore a collared white shirt. Her smile wasn't sincere but likely in response to the photographer's prompt.

"He got this off the internet somewhere too. Just a sec, I'll be right back." I hurried to my room where the laptop was on my bed.

When I came back out into the relative darkness of the lot, I noticed a figure slip out of Jack's room. Based on the size of the frame, it was Paige.

Jealousy ignited the blood in my veins, but I reined in my focus.

Jack's hotel door was still open. I let myself in, put the laptop on the long dresser with the twenty-inch tube TV, and logged on. "Debbie works for a law firm. She's a clerk there, but I remember her saying something about how they were taking staff photos." I went to their website and pulled up the employee page. I pointed a finger at the screen. "Yep, that's where the son of a bitch got it." I let out a deep breath and, as I did, my eyes scanned to the bathroom door. It was no longer closed. My heart cinched. Paige was sleeping with Jack.

"There you go. The pictures were taken from the internet and not in person." Jack pulled out his cell phone, dialed a number, and held it to an ear.

I knew he was right. The words and the conclusion were logical. Yet, without hearing Debbie's voice, it still left way for doubt. "I just wish I could reach her." I pulled out my cell again.

"Everything will be fine."

"Didn't think you believed in making promises."

"I don't believe in—" Jack held up a finger and spoke into his cell. "Chief Fayette…Yes, I know you'd rather I call you by…Yes, Bob."

Jack bantered with the man for a while. It must have been the chief's direct line. Maybe they were golfing buddies, not that I saw Jack having enough patience to be successful at the sport.

I listened closely as the tone of the call changed. Jack expressed his concern over an agent's wife being in danger. They spoke for a few minutes about family and something about *we'll have to do that again* before Jack tossed his cell on the dresser near the laptop.

"She's a pretty woman." Jack bobbed his head toward the screen.

"I think so." I wasn't about to get into an in-depth conversation about it. It was bad enough the man was sleeping with my former lover. "You and the chief are close."

Jack stepped toward me. "It's late, let's get some sleep. A couple cruisers are going to your house to check things out."

"And—"

"Once they do, they'll call you," Jack answered my question hearing only one word. He closed the lid of the laptop and handed it to me. "Night."

Twenty-One

As I peeled out of the cigarette-saturated clothing, it made me wish the damage being done to my lungs from the secondhand smoke could be removed as easily.

I left the phone on the bathroom counter and set the ring volume to outdoor. I had tried Debbie several more times before giving up on reaching her. Although pain still registered in my chest, Jack's calmness had a way of dousing my concern with logic. Royster was dead, and we didn't have proof he and the other unsub were in communication.

I ran the shower almost hot enough to scald. A thousand sharp needles pricked my skin, but as I got used to the temperature it somehow transformed into a warm hug. I stayed in there until the water ran cool.

Pulling back the shower curtain, I looked at myself in the mirror and instinctively put both hands on my abs. I had kept myself in good athletic shape between the gym and my love for boxing. If I wasn't at work or home, I was normally doing some form of exercise.

The assessment turned to thoughts of Paige sleeping with Jack. I found myself making the comparison. He was older while I was younger. He was in good shape for his age. I was in terrific shape, *and younger*. A smirk tugged the corner of my mouth.

I pulled a towel from the bar and swept it around my torso. Why I was comparing us, rating us as Paige's lovers

when my wife was possibly missing, went beyond my logic.
I loved my wife. Paige was part of my past—and, seemingly,
part of Jack's present.

THREE QUARTERS OF AN HOUR had gone by and the phone still
hadn't rung. I kept trying Debbie from the hotel line to keep
my cell line free, still no answer. I gave more thought to
Jack's suggestions of her going to her mother's or a friend's.

Debbie worked to avoid her mother. She felt like a
disappointment to her because she hadn't given her a
grandchild, but it hadn't been for a lack of trying. We got
pregnant once. We celebrated. When Debbie lost the baby,
we grieved. The doctors said Debbie had fetal-blocking
antibodies which meant her body's immune system viewed
the baby as a threat.

We tried a few more times, but Debbie had never been the
same, and in the last few months she hadn't even mentioned
children. It wasn't even something we talked about anymore.
I sometimes wondered if she knew how I really felt about
them. It's not that I didn't like children, but I didn't believe
that alone was enough reason to bring them into the world.

I wedged a pillow in the small of my back and leaned
against the headboard. I put the laptop on my legs and turned
on the television at a low volume—more for company than
entertainment. There was no way I'd fall asleep until I heard
something from the Prince William County PD. Thinking
of them made me think of Jack and his direct access to the
chief.

Jack didn't have to ask for his call to be directed. Jack
had the chief's home number. When I mentioned them
being close, he clammed up as per his usual reaction to a
conversation he didn't initiate.

I brought up the internet. It was good for more than
pictures. I typed in *Robert Fayette Prince William County
PD Chief of Police.* As the results came up, I found one of
particular interest.

Fayette had served time in the United States Army Special Forces from the eighties to early nineties. Jack had served until ninety with his last post in Panama in eighty-nine. It was possible they had both served in the same unit.

I went back to the search results and picked another link. It sent me to a personal blog belonging to Stephanie Tavers and showed a picture of Fayette with his arms wrapped, one around a woman and one around a boy who was tall as Fayette. A little girl sat in front of them, legs folded and showcasing a toothless smile. The photo was at least twenty years old comparing it to the way the chief looked now.

I read the caption beneath it: *My dad is someone special. I'm sure every little girl believes that about their father, but with mine, that conviction grew within me as I aged. We're thankful he returned to us.*

I scrolled down the page and found a photo of a much younger Jack standing beside the chief. Both were in uniform.

The caption read: *My father's hero.*

I had heard the vibration on the nightstand before I heard the ringtone. I answered before the first ring finished. "Hello."

"Special Agent Brandon Fisher? This is Officer Spalding of Prince William County PD."

"My wife, is she—"

"No one is home, but there's no sign of forced entry or a struggle. We peeked into some of the windows that were open."

"Curtains were open?" That was unlike Debbie. She normally loved to let the sunlight stream in during the day but hated the thought of parading in front of passersby at night.

"The ones in the bedroom and the front living area."

"But everything looked fine?"

"Yes. As I said, no sign of a struggle. Maybe she just went to a friend's for the night. We have a watch out for her car and will let you know if anything comes of it."

I let out a jagged exhale.

"I'm not sure what else we can do at this point. As I said—"

"I know. No evidence of a struggle. Keep me updated."

"Of cour—"

I hung up before he could finish and dialed Debbie's cell again which repeatedly rang. This time it switched over to voice mail. Hearing her voice merely as a recording made my stomach tighten. My heart sank. I didn't want to imagine her in the hands of a killer, being cut and tortured because of me. Bingham said I was the sinner, the one deserving punishment, what had Debbie done? Why were they targeting her? Was it just to get to me?

I sprang from the bed, ready to tell Jack I'd be taking one SUV and driving back to Louisville. As my feet hit the carpet, I knew the notion wasn't founded on logic but driven by emotion. Where would I go once I got there? If I made independent arrangements with a commercial airline to fly home from there, I could forget about my career with the FBI. Really, what did I expect to find that the PD hadn't? I dropped back on the edge of the bed, ran a hand through my hair, and stared at the carpet as if the pattern would provide the answers.

Some people say that we can feel when something's wrong with those we love, like an instinct that guides us as a barometer and somehow can connect souls. Even though my emotions were haywire, raw from worry, somewhere inside I felt she was safe—but what if I were wrong, what if we weren't as connected as I thought?

I thought back to our last conversation, her wanting me to come home and my short and pointed response. I hadn't even said *I love you* in response to hers. Maybe she was mad at me and trying to prove a point by not taking my calls. She had been known to do that before. For some reason, she used the silent treatment as a means of discipline, feeling it was capable of realigning the relationship. I didn't see it the same way. I knew that stereotypically men were supposed to suppress their feelings and not be willing to share them even when prodded, but I wasn't that type of man. It wasn't that I wished to discuss how I felt about things at regular intervals, but communication was a basic necessity for a functioning relationship, and to assume otherwise was deceiving oneself.

Maybe that was why it had been easier to fall into Paige's arms while at the academy. At least I had molded that plausible excuse into a justifiable one. Thinking about Paige made me wonder about her current relationship with Jack. I found it strange how jealous I was over them being together, no matter what the depth of their arrangement. Knowing Paige, I figured it was more of an arrangement than a deep, meaningful coupling. Paige wasn't the settling type of woman. She loved her freedom and independence even when it came to her lovers. She had always provided me space and had respected that I had obligations that didn't involve her.

I closed the lid of the laptop and put it on the dresser. I left it plugged into the wall to charge and turned out the light. I had to trust that Debbie was going to be okay.

The pictures from Royster's computer would have to wait. I flicked the TV off and settled into bed.

Twenty-Two

The alarm went off at five. The last time I had looked it had been four as I had spent most of the night tossing and watching the clock, worried about Debbie. I checked my phone by the bed, almost expecting to see a missed call or notification of a message. It was unlikely that it would have rung without me hearing it, but I needed visual confirmation.

I dialed home, and there was still no answer. I repeated with her cell phone and received voice mail there as well.

Where the hell is she?

It's said that we are more in tune with our true feelings when we first wake up. Something that you didn't think affected you can have you stirring with pain in your chest. This morning, I had that ache. It squeezed my chest, limiting the depth of my breaths, but I had to focus and be logical. I wouldn't make a good FBI Special Agent if I flitted around on a whim and followed where my gut and heart drove me. Emotions lead to carelessness, and carelessness to error.

I waited it out until six, then I headed to the front lobby. None of the team was even up yet, including Jack, which I found ironic given his speech yesterday about tardiness.

A woman about my age held a phone to her ear, "Tell Kate to get out of the bathroom…Nick!" The woman rolled her eyes. "You do it. Your sister can't hog it all day…Figure it out." Her eyes met mine. "I have to go. Mom has work to do." She set the receiver down. "Can I help you?"

"Are you Ellen?"

"Yes?" she answered it with the arched brow of a question. Her hair was cut to the level of her jaw and blonde, although dark roots disclosed it wasn't her natural color.

"I'm Special Agent Brandon Fisher."

Her eyes said, *Well, good for you.*

"You were given an envelope for me yesterday."

"I remember." She looked past me to the front door, causing me to turn around. Paige, Zachery, and Jack walked in.

Paige didn't make eye contact, and Zachery put a hand on my shoulder as the two of them went past headed to the vending machine. Jack stopped beside me.

I gestured toward Jack. "This is Supervisory Special Agent Jack Harper."

Another silent response that I took as, *Okay, what do I really care?*

"What did the person look like who dropped it off?"

Her lips pressed downward. "Just an average guy, nothing too noteworthy about him."

I brought up a photo of Earl Royster on my phone and turned it toward her. "Was this him?"

Ellen reached for the phone and accidently brushed my hand. She pulled back. "That's Earl."

"So you know him?"

"Yeah, I just said his name." She passed a glance to Jack.

"Why didn't you say that to start with instead of describing him as an average guy?"

"Well, he is." Her arms crossed. "And how would I know you'd even know who the heck Earl was? Is he in trouble?"

I ignored her inquiry. "Did he say anything when he dropped this off?"

"Why are you so interested in him?"

"Did he say anything?"

"Just to give the envelope to you. He went over to the vending machine, bought a bag of Doritos." She shifted her weight as if bored by the conversation.

"You remember the Doritos?"

"Yeah, I've always liked Earl. He liked," she rolled her hand but didn't say what she was thinking.

"You knew about his sexual preference?"

"Everybody did. He's the only one that thought it was a secret. We even know about Quinton. They've been lovers for years. I always thought maybe I could turn him around, ya know?"

I didn't want the conversation to become about Ellen and her attraction to Earl. "Was there anything different about him when he dropped this off?"

"He was muttering a lot. Earl's always been a mumbler, but yesterday I couldn't make out more than the odd word."

"What word?"

Ellen thought for a few seconds. "None of it really made any sense to me. Something about 'didn't mean to hurt anybody' and 'don't cry.'"

I slapped my palm on the counter, walked to the front door, and took out my cell.

Ellen asked, "Is he all right?"

"He'll be fine." Jack stepped beside me. "We'll head back to Louisville after breakfast, drop off the SUV, and fly home."

If that was supposed to be a comfort, it wasn't. Hours had already gone by in silence. Debbie could have been hurt by now, maybe already murdered if the unsub changed his MO. I pressed the cell tighter to my ear, listened to the constant ringing, and looked out to the road as I spoke to Jack, "Surprised you just didn't tell that woman that her dreams of turning Earl straight were over."

I TRIED TO REACH DEBBIE several more times both on her cell and at home.

If she wasn't captured by the unsub, where the hell was she?

Coffee steamed from the mug in front of me, but it didn't

hold much appeal. I had one sip and it gnawed on my stomach as if it were acid.

Paige hugged her mug and watched me. When I looked at her, she adjusted the direction of her gaze. Jack must have filled Zachery and her in on the situation.

If I put more thought into it than required, maybe Paige felt guilty about her night with Jack because she knew I had found out about them. I also wondered if there was more to it. She had broken her own rule and fallen in love with me. If I didn't have Debbie there, I might have become a victim of the relationship as well, but Paige didn't have someone else to go home to. She was a beautiful woman and could easily have her choice of men, but she was deep and complicated. Some men had an issue with that.

"Now, the kid and I are going to head back to Louisville and take a flight back to Quantico. I expect the files from Sarasota should be arriving there today, too," Jack said.

It seemed more was necessary than for my wife to be unreachable to justify a return flight home.

"I want you two to visit the members of the church again, this time asking about Royster. Was he close to anyone there or spend an unusual amount of time with anyone besides the Redeemer."

"Yes, we can do that." Zachery stabbed his fork into a slice of bacon and slid his knife through, cutting off about the length of an inch which he then put into his mouth.

I found the formal nature of the mannerism odd for a guy like him. He struck me as the type who would pick up the slice and stuff the entire thing in there. "What if everything we think we know about the unsub is wrong?"

"We've been doing this a long time, Pending." Another cut-off piece of bacon went into his mouth.

"And those cases all turned out as originally expected?"

Mouth full, he bobbed his head to the side like a rag doll.

"Exactly. What if Bingham captured his victims, tortures them for a number of days, say eleven, but his followers don't?"

"We found the book on the coinherence symbol at Royster's and the pictures of Sally Windermere's eleven cuts. I'd say torture and the number eleven plays a factor even for the followers," Paige said.

"We know Royster was heavily influenced by Bingham," I began. "We also believe that he was the submissive when it comes to this other unsub."

"Okay." Her eyes looked at me now as if to say, *Where are you going with all this?*

"Maybe the unsub we're looking for wasn't as influenced by Bingham as we think. Maybe they were more independent? They didn't remove the intestines."

"Until we know—"

I cut off Zachery, "But why not factor this in? Maybe it's not a straight line." I gestured a straight line with a flattened hand on the vertical. "It could be wavy." I swayed my hand.

"And you're factoring your reasoning on what, Kid?"

I turned to Jack. "Thinking outside of the box."

"Hmm."

I let out a deep breath. "We're trained to think like the killer, get inside his head, figure the why and who, but if we're going to find the who we have to know the why."

"Circles again, Brandon." Paige's voice was soft, but she didn't offer eye contact.

I knew the words coming out were not necessarily coherent but were more like audible brainstorming. "Listen, I'm just thinking out loud."

"You're going through a lot right now."

I glared at Paige. "Don't patronize me."

About a solid thirty seconds passed with none of us saying anything. I released the napkin I had bunched up in my hand out of frustration. "I'm ready to go."

Surprisingly, Jack rose and followed me.

WE LOADED OUR LUGGAGE INTO the SUV. My entire bag

reeked of cigarette smoke. The smell had set up permanent residence in my sinuses.

Jack slid behind the wheel, pulled out a cigarette, and lit up. "All that stuff you were saying back there—"

"Just forget it."

"We need to keep an open mind. Investigations often do change directions."

I turned to face him. "You're saying that I'm right?"

"I'm saying you could be."

All I could think about was getting to Debbie. I needed to hold her and know she was all right. The clock on the dash read eight thirty and having left at about seven thirty, we'd be in Louisville by about nine thirty if everything went according to plan. Hopefully on a flight by ten thirty and home by one.

I opened the laptop, logged onto Twitter and went to the private message section. I wished for some sort of message from him, something to taunt me or to let me know if Debbie was safe. I was disappointed.

"It's a good sign if there's nothing there, Kid."

For some reason, I didn't think it was. My gut, the one that had told me everything was okay, now told me something was seriously wrong. I clicked on the Redeemer's profile page to see the recent tweets made by him, and there was nothing new since the one from Tuesday.

My cell chimed. I answered as I shut the laptop. "Hello."

"Think that was your message alert." Jack siphoned a strand of smoke out the window to the passing road.

My mind blanked for a second. He was right. I was just eager to hear Debbie's voice. I pulled the phone down and looked at the message.

"What is it?"

I read the words in silence; my throat was stitched shut with dryness.

"Kid?"

Bile rose in my throat. Seconds passed. "'The sins of the

family fall upon generation after generation.'" My breath grew shallow. "He's going to hurt Deb."

Jack flicked his cigarette out the window, turned on the lights, and floored the accelerator.

My heart beat so hard, I could barely hear anything. Adrenaline and anger blurred my vision of the road ahead of me and the vehicles around us. All I could think was, if he hurt her, I would never forgive myself. She would have been targeted because of me, because of my sins.

We had to figure out how Bingham was communicating to the outside world, and it had to be more than solely through Twitter.

"What number did the text come from?"

I looked over at Jack, delaying, afraid of what I might see on the phone. A few seconds later, I looked. "It came from Debbie's phone." I was going to be sick. "How the hell? He's got to have. Oh, shit!" My sentences only came out in fractured syllables.

Jack depressed the hands-free. "Nadia, I need you to triangulate which towers an incoming text came in on."

"Course."

I gave her my cell number, the time of the text, the sender. A few seconds passed. "Your wife?"

"Where are we looking?" Jack pressed her.

"Just a sec." More keys were tapped, clicking through the speakers of the car almost like a subdued machine gun. "Here. Oh."

"Nadia speak to us."

"Your wife's phone, is it a BlackBerry?"

"Yeah, it is. Why?"

"I show two users for her SIM card."

"The text, Nadia. Where did it come from?" Jack tapped his pocket but didn't take out the cigarette pack.

"Two users?" I turned to catch Jack's profile. "How is that possible?"

Nadia answered, "It's called cell phreaking."

"English."

"Phreaking? It combines the words phone and freak together. Basically, computer hacking, but when it comes to phones." She tapped more keys as she spoke. "As technology has advanced, most telephone networks are computerized. For example, people can buy spare SIM cards and duplicate them. There are also scanners which allow phreaks to simply brush by a person, and obtain all their information—their SIM info, their banking access, everything. Identities can be stolen."

"The unsub came near my wife." I couldn't breathe.

Nadia remained silent for a few seconds. "It's possible."

"Shit!" I looked at the sign. We were still at least twenty minutes out from Louisville. "He has her. I know it. We waited, and now she's probably dead."

"Remember the MO," Jack said.

"Brandon, before you panic, it's possible that the unsub is extremely technologically gifted," Nadia offered.

Before I panic? "What do you mean?"

"Well," she paused. "I could duplicate a SIM card if I knew the person's basic information, their full name, address, phone number—and I could do it online."

"So the unsub didn't need to be near my wife?"

"Not necessarily, but if that's the case, we're dealing with a very intelligent unsub."

"The text? Where did it come from?"

"Woodbridge."

"He has her." My pulse rushed while my breathing slowed. "Can you tell the exact location?"

"Unfortunately, that's the best I can narrow it—"

"Wait a minute," Jack said. "Nadia, let's say the unsub copied the SIM information from online, would this person also be capable of making it appear the text routed from anywhere they wanted to?"

"Not sure about anywhere, but they could duplicate the original SIM's location."

"Thanks, N."

"Cour—"

Jack hung up on Nadia and turned to me. "We've got to keep calm. We don't—"

"Keep calm? That seems to be your slogan. Keep calm. If it was your wife, how calm would you be?"

"You know I'm not married."

"Fuck, Jack—"

"Watch the language."

"Sometimes, I feel like your child. Don't do this, don't do that. Don't take this call, take this one. It's a joke. I mean, if it weren't for you, at least I would have taken the time to talk to Deb when she called last. I would have asked about her day, listened when she told me—and, fuck, Jack, I would have told her I loved her before hanging up."

Twenty-Three

The front drapes were pulled back as the officer had said. I studied the porch, the potted ferns to the side of the front door. Nothing stood out as unusual. Both looked to be in need of water, but that was normal for Debbie to leave her plants begging for a drink. She said God would take care of the outdoor ones, but when they died, it was still his fault. What she didn't realize was that sometimes even God appreciates a little help.

I looked inside the front window. Everything seemed mostly the same as when I had left three days ago. Debbie's magazines were displayed on the square glass coffee table, and the television remote sat on top of them. Debbie had watched TV at some point since I had left.

A car door slammed behind me. I jumped and pivoted.

"Sorry, Agent, I never meant to scare you." An officer, whom I guessed to be in his mid-forties, came around from the driver's side of a cruiser. His hair was crop-cut which told me he was trying to hold onto his youth.

Another officer, who came from the passenger's side, stood beside him. He was younger than the driver by at least twenty years and likely a rookie.

"It's Officer Spalding." The older officer splayed a hand over his chest. "I believe we spoke on the phone last night, and this is Officer Hamilton."

"Special Agent Brandon Fisher."

Jack came around from the side of my house.

"And that is Supervisory Special Agent Jack Harper."

"Ooh, supervisory special agent. We need to get ourselves some fancier titles." Spalding glanced to the younger officer before speaking to me, "Have you been able to reach your wife yet?"

I shook my head and looked back at the house. Somehow even though external evidence didn't make it appear that strangers had violated my home, it felt as if they had.

"It's hard to control a woman sometimes. They get a mind of their own and off they go."

I came down the few stairs of the deck to within a foot of Spalding. I would have pressed my nose against his if it weren't for Jack's extended arm. "You have no idea what we're dealing with here. You take a quick look around. No sign of this, no sign of that, and assume what you want. You have no idea."

Spalding's eyes went to Jack as if seeking some sort of explanation for my attitude.

"Let's get inside," Jack said. He applied muscle behind his arm and gestured me back toward the house.

"Just so ya know, we drove by a few times to see if the missus had come back." Officer Spalding was speaking to my back. "Maybe she was too comfortable in her boyfriend's bed to venture home."

My fist balled, and I turned around ready to match it with his jaw, but Jack had aligned himself in front of the officer. "It's time for you boys to go."

Spalding looked around Jack. "You wonder why we guys don't like you feds? You think you're all that, but you're no better than we are."

"Nobody said we were. Go." Jack seconded his directive with an extended arm and a pointed finger to the cruiser.

"Fine, we'll leave." Spalding and his partner reached their doors at about the same time. "But we're not coming back."

The cruiser's engine rumbled as Spalding gunned the accelerator.

"Guess we have some enemies on the PD now," I said the words although I didn't really care about the consequence.

Jack waved a hand. "What do we need them for anyway?" A smile cracked his lips.

Inside the house, the air was cool from the air conditioner yet stale, no smells of food or perfume. It was almost as if she hadn't been here for the last few days.

"Is your house always this neat?" Jack wiped his shoes on the carpet at the front door.

"It's all Deb." I wanted to smile as I praised her, but bile churned in my stomach.

The answering machine was flashing notification of a few messages. I figured some would be the click of my hanging up with at least two of them being me begging for her to answer. I pressed the play button. Four of the messages were from me, and one was from Debbie's mother. "Guess that rules out Deb being there." I looked at the missed calls; all were identified numbers.

"See anything unusual, Kid?"

I shook my head as I put the phone down.

I kept moving through the house, methodically working through every room. Upstairs, I went to our bedroom. Clothes were strewn on the floor, some clean, others worn and dropped where they had come off. The bed was unmade, and the comforter dangled precariously over the edge of the mattress. There was a definite contrast to the rest of the house and our room, but that was normal.

Nothing in the room indicated that Deb had been taken. I turned back to the hallway, went downstairs, and made my way to the kitchen. Jack followed.

In the kitchen, a few clean dishes sat in the drip tray. The rest of the counters and stovetop were empty.

"This isn't making any sense."

"What?"

"Well, let's adhere to your slogan, 'Stay calm.' Let's assume he doesn't have her."

"Okay."

"The unsub seeks control and power. They like to have the upper hand. How would they know I wouldn't be able to reach her unless they had at least been here?"

"Maybe it's a series of bizarre coincidences."

I shook my head. "I don't believe that. How would he know I wouldn't be able to reach her?"

"He routed any calls you made to her cell phone to his copy of the SIM card and then didn't answer."

I bobbed my head. "Okay, possible, but what about her not being at home? And don't say coincidence."

"He was here. You like that answer better?" Jack pulled out his cigarettes.

"Don't smoke in here."

I expected him to go out the back door and light up outside. Instead, he pushed the pack back into his pocket. "What would get her to leave?"

"No stranger, I can tell you that. I mean, I think about ruses the unsub could have used. Maybe coming to the door telling her the house was infested by something dangerous to her health, but she's not gullible."

"What about a friend having problems or a family member that might need—"

The lock on the front door turned. Jack and I pulled our guns, flattened against the walls, and readied to fire if need be. Light footsteps tapped on the hardwood. They stopped in the living room, and the radio turned on. Alan Jackson sang the chorus of "Pop a Top."

The footsteps resumed, and they were coming toward us, the steps now landing on the ceramic tile of the hallway to the kitchen.

Jack held an index finger to his lips. He gestured with the other hand for me to wind around to the dining room side.

"Stop there!" Jack's voice sounded like a roar as it bounced off the plastered walls.

Glass shattered on the ceramic. "Who—"

I knew the voice. "Deb?" I lowered my gun.

"Brandon?" Fear registered in her voice.

"Deb." I came around the corner to find Jack holding his gun on her. I put a hand on his wrist for him to lower the weapon. Pasta sauce oozed out of a grocery bag on the floor like a blood pool.

"What are you…who is he?"

"You're okay." I hurried to reach her without caring where I stepped. I needed to hold her. As I pulled her tight, I kissed her lips then her forehead. I put a hand behind her head coaxing her to rest it on my shoulder. It only stayed there briefly.

"What's going on?" Deb pulled back, arms crossed. She looked to Jack, to the gun that was now secured in his holster, to the mess on the floor. "You're cleaning that up."

"No problem." I couldn't pull my eyes from her. She was okay. She was fine. "I love you."

"What are you doing here?"

"Where were you last night?"

"Last night or for the last couple? You don't listen to me when I talk, do you? Of course, you're too busy with this new job of yours." She passed a condemning glance to Jack.

"Hon, this is Supervisory Special Agent Jack Harper."

Jack extended a hand for her to shake. She tightened her crossed arms. "You still haven't answered my question about what you're doing here."

"This is my home."

"I'm not stupid, Brandon. I know something else is going on here. Why the guns?" She glared at Jack. "He was ready to shoot me."

"You didn't answer your calls."

"Did you call my cell? I had it with me." She twisted her purse around to the front of her, reached in, and pulled it out. She rocked it right to left. "No missed calls. Thought you just didn't care. Too busy."

"You're okay?"

"Don't I look it? Why are you acting strange?" Her arms loosened, and she bent over to pick up the spilled contents of the bag.

I put a hand on her elbow and directed her to regain full height. "The case I'm working on—"

"You think I'm in danger." Debbie laughed. "It's like in the movies."

"This is serious, Deb." The stark soberness of my expression killed any amusement that had graced hers. "I'm going to ask you again, and I need you to answer. Where have you been?"

"Chantilly at Karen's. I told you that two nights ago when you called me."

How did I forget that conversation? For a second, I berated myself for not listening to her when she had told me that. I excused it based on what I had witnessed with this case. "Your sister's laid up."

"Right. The doctor told her she needs to stay off her feet for the rest of her pregnancy. Ken's working night shifts and can't be there to help out with the kids."

Her sister Karen living nearby was part of the reason Deb agreed to move from Florida.

"I need you to do me a favor." I rubbed my hands on her forearms and peered into her eyes. "I need you to promise me that you will."

"What?"

"I want you to go back. Stay with her until I'm finished this case."

"What is it?"

"I can't answer that. I just need to know you're safe."

"I'm not running from my home because some psycho is fixated on you. I'm not afraid."

"If you knew what he was capable of you would be."

"You're trying to scare me?"

I recalled how I explained to Jack that my wife wouldn't

leave the house for anything less than a good reason. Even faced with a murderous psychopath she was prepared to stay and fight.

"We're getting you a new cell phone."

"This one works fine."

"Trust me. Please, just a little."

"Fine."

"And please go back and stay with Karen."

She let out a sigh. "If it means that much to you."

"It does."

DEBBIE TOLD US SHE'D LEAVE with one condition. She didn't want cops posted outside the house while she packed and didn't want them following her. I had given her a tight hug and a kiss on the forehead before we left. I knew I had a job to do, but all I wanted was to make love to her and hold her close.

Jack didn't say anything until we arrived at Quantico, and he pulled into the parking lot. "Be happy we should have other things to do here, Slingshot."

"It's not like we knew she was okay."

"If you listened when she spoke you would have known where she was."

"If you weren't always rushing our conversations—"

Jack slammed a flattened hand onto the steering wheel. He didn't say a word. We both just sat there looking at the other cars until my phone rang. I answered.

"I hear Chantilly is a lovely place."

It wasn't Debbie. It was someone using a voice modifier.

"You son of a bitch! I'll kill you when I find you!"

A laugh from the caller sent chills down my spine. "First, you must find me."

"You stay away from her!"

"Are you going to stop me?"

The line went dead.

"Fuckin' shit!" I gripped my phone hard and faced Jack.

"He knows where Deb's sister lives. He's been close."

We both jumped out of the SUV and went straight to Nadia's office. She was wading through screens of codes.

"The triangulation for the call just made to his cell. Now," Jack barked.

Nadia jumped, and a stress ball fell to the floor. She spun around in her chair. An HB pencil sat clenched in her teeth. She took it out of her mouth as she nodded hello.

This was the second time I had seen her. The first had been during a quick orientation of the base office and personnel. Her dark hair swept just past shoulder length and held the shine of expensive hair products. The rusty-orange frames of her glasses would have been popular back in the seventies; nevertheless, they suited her.

"You said a call just now?" she asked the question as she bent over to pick up the stress ball.

"Yes." The word came from Jack's lips like the hiss of a snake.

"All right then."

Any other time I would have found amusement in the contrast between Jack's attitude and Nadia's relaxed nature. I thought it ironic as Jack always told me to calm down.

Nadia turned back to face the screen. She typed on the keyboard, and within seconds the triangulation filled in on the screen. Her finger traced the perimeter. "It's coming from within here."

"That's a five-mile radius around my home—"

My cell chimed notification of a new text message.

Twenty-Four

Paige loaded into the SUV beside Zachery. She let him drive because he preferred to, and she couldn't care less whether she drove or rode shotgun.

They were leaving the Smith home after speaking to the wife Ann. They belonged to the same church where Royster had been a member and which Bingham had attended. As with the other four families, they had visited they didn't have anything to offer. Paige suspected the unsub wasn't a local. She brought the concept up to Zachery. "It's like Bingham and this unsub didn't even exist around here—and since everyone knows everyone and everything about everyone…"

"Do you think they came to Salt Lick to kill?"

"I'm leaning that way." She glanced at Zachery's profile as he drove. "If that's the case, there's another connection to Bingham. What are we missing?"

"Not sure yet, but it would have to be someone tight with Bingham and comfortable with the area."

"It could be a former resident or a non-church member, maybe a visitor from Florida." Zachery looked at her. "If the cases are connected, the unsub could have helped with the murders in Florida and followed Bingham out here."

The onboard phone rang, and the caller ID came up *Harper*. Paige depressed the hands-free button. "Hel—"

"I need you two to get over to the prison, pronto."

"Boss?"

What Jack told them next ignited a fire in the base of

Paige's gut.

PAIGE AND ZACHERY INQUIRED AT the visitor's desk and were directed by a uniformed officer to the prison warden. The officer had a thick torso and expansive hips which stretched the fabric of her pants to full capacity. She gestured for them to stay back a few feet as she rapped her dark knuckles on the doorframe.

A man's voice called out from the inside. "Ye-eah."

"FBI here to see ya. They says it urgent."

"Let 'em in, Dorthea."

Paige entered the room and could tell by the way the warden took a second glance he expected Jack and Brandon. "I'm Special Agent Dawson." She extended a hand across the desk. The man stood to reach it. He pressed down on his shirt, and she noticed how unusually tall and slender he was. She gestured to Zachery, "And this is Special Agent Miles."

"Clarence Moore." His handshake, firm and brief, contained both confidence and power. "Pleased, I'm sure." The warden shook Zachery's hand and sat down behind his desk again. He laced his long fingers together. "What can I do for ya?"

"We need to see Lance Bingham."

"I 'ssume you're working with that other man and the young kid."

Paige kept a smile from developing. She knew how much Brandon hated being referred to as kid. "That's right."

"Bingham's out in the yard right now. Recess as we term it 'round here." He smiled. When no one said anything for a few seconds, he picked up a phone and directed a person by the name of Tom to retrieve Bingham. Moore hung up the receiver with his attention on Paige. "Let me warn ya, he might be in lock-up for assaulting a neighbor, suspected of these other horrid crimes—" a hand waved across his desk "—and he might appear to be near ninety, but the man ain't dead. If you know what I'm talking about."

"I'll be fine." She spoke the truth. When it came to the dark side of humanity, she had seen a lot. A man who killed his entire family because he couldn't afford them due to a layoff, a serial who stalked maids from work-wanted ads, a serial who took tongues as trophies. Yes, Lance Bingham of Salt Lick may hold a sick record—countless mutilated and disemboweled bodies—but he would be no different than the rest of them. He'd have an agenda, and if she could tap into that, even give him the impression she understood, she'd have a way in.

THE DOOR OPENED WITH A buzzing noise as the man who would have been his victim's last horror was escorted into the room. With a guard on each arm, they guided him to the table and secured him to the restraints there. The amped up security made her wonder if the warden was spreading the reason for the FBI's interest in Bingham.

Paige told Zachery she had this under control and even asked that he not be in the room. She knew he watched through the window in the door and sensed his concern through the pane of glass.

Bingham had an unassuming physical appearance and thin lips, an underlying smile tattooed on them. The glint in his eyes told Paige she was looking at a different creature from the ones she had met before.

"What do you know about this?" She produced the two photos that were dropped off at the hotel, the one of Brandon's house and the one of his wife. She held a third picture in her hands. This was what prompted the call from Jack and the directive to speak with Bingham. As she flung the picture of the scantily dressed woman, she felt an involuntary catch in her throat. *She's Brandon's wife.*

"I 'pologize for my appearance. They took my razor." He rubbed at the growth on his face.

She wouldn't become distracted from her goal. She leaned in her chair and flung an arm over the back of it. "Earl

Royster." She studied his reaction. Nothing. "You two were close."

"If you know everything, why do you need me?"

"See, that's the thing, we don't." Paige smiled at Bingham, attempting to use her female charm to lure him into speaking. "We don't know what he ever saw in you. You're easily what twenty, thirty years older than he was. Surely, he'd have more intelligent friends, and more engaging conversationalists to be around because, from what I see, you rarely speak."

Bingham's eyes narrowed.

"I mean he had lots of buddies, but losing his brother, he had a hard time with that. Is that why he turned to you?"

Bingham's eyes snapped to hers and dropped to her mouth just as quickly. She knew he watched her lips as she spoke and she put effort into manipulating them to her advantage—a small pout here, the hint of a smile there.

"He looked to you for comfort, didn't he? He saw you as a caring individual who had his back. He knew you from church and saw that you were a hard worker with the farmers in the area."

A small twitch in his cheek revealed she was chipping away at his pride. He didn't want to be thought of as weak, empathic, and caring, least of all a simple farmhand.

"And you gave him friendship and supp—"

Bingham smiled. "Ain't none of this true."

"No? Well, then you'll have to educate me because from what I see it is."

He looked down at the photos. "It was supposed to be a joke."

"What was, Lance? Can I call you Lance?" She pulled out his first name and added an element of huskiness to her voice.

"The pictures." Bingham's expression went serious, and any sort of control she had gained evaporated with a figurative hiss to steam. "None of you can prove I did anything wrong."

"We know about the other murders in Sarasota Florida."

She paused. He didn't blink. "We know about some of your victims right here in Salt Lick. Earl's brother was one of them." She stretched the truth.

He tapped an index finger on the table.

"Why go after Special Agent Fisher?"

"Special Agent la di la. Nothing special that I see there, but you do." He leaned in, closing the distance between them. "You do, don't you?" His mouth rapidly transformed into a wild smile.

"Why his wife?"

The smile disappeared. Bingham's gaze lingered in her eyes making her uncomfortable, but she refused to break the eye contact. To do so would demonstrate weakness and give Bingham the upper hand. She needed to maintain control. "Who is this person? Who is your follower?"

"You told me already that Earl must have been."

Paige smirked. He bit. "How many did he help you with?"

Bingham guided her eyes to the table and the photograph of Brandon's wife. "She's beautiful." Seconds of delay followed those two words. "That must bother you."

JACK BRAKED HARD ENOUGH THAT the nose of the SUV dove. He put it into park, and I jumped out and headed up the porch steps. Police cruisers were already at the house, including the two officers we had met earlier.

"I didn't think you big shots needed us," Spalding said as he pulled up on his pants and adjusted his holster.

"We need you to block the street. No one in. No one out." I heard Jack's firm words. "Now."

"Yes, boss." Spalding's words were followed by a chuckle, but he complied with Jack's directions.

"The only way he could have got that picture is from inside the house." I turned the handle and turned to Jack. "It's unlocked." Deb's car was in the driveway, but if she was there, wouldn't she be outside wondering what was going on with the police cruisers? And why wasn't she answering her phone?

I cracked open the door, gun readied as was Jack's. I heard more sirens from the local PD coming closer.

"Take it slow," Jack cautioned.

"Deb." I called into the house and looked through to the kitchen as I wound along the wall, vigilant in case the unsub was here. "We shouldn't have left her alone," I spoke in a whisper. "I can't believe the unsub knows about Deb's sister." Not only was I worried about Deb's safety but also for her sister and her family's. I continued down the hallway, placing foot over foot, back to the wall, gun ready.

"One thing at a time."

"Deb," I called out more loudly than the first time.

I heard banging upstairs. I pointed upward. "There. Did you hear that? Deb?" More shuffling of feet, and a slam of a dresser drawer.

"You go first. I'll stay behind and watch your back."

Adrenaline forced my steps forward, suppressing my fear beneath layers of bravado. I approached the base of the stairs cautiously, straining to hear anything. Nothing but silence seeped over the upper landing like a thickly laid fog. I faced upward and raised my gun to match. There was no one there, no shadows casting against the exterior wall of the staircase.

I took each stair slowly, careful not to agitate the old wood of the home, but it didn't matter. Even the lightest placed step caused the treads to groan. I turned around to Jack, who directed me to face forward with a tightened jaw and a scowl.

Keep alert, keep vigilant, take in your surroundings, and keep your eyes ahead.

I recited what I had been taught, hoping the words would drown my guilt over pulling Debbie into this. If anything happened to her, there wouldn't be a purpose in living.

I focused on the upstairs landing. A shadow darkened the doorway of our bedroom, casting its length into the stairwell. I picked up speed. Jack closed the distance between us.

In the hallway, my heart sped up causing my breath to deepen, threatening to expose my position.

Jack motioned that he would be going to the right of the doorway, and I was to take the left. He sprang in front of the opening. His eyes said it all, someone was in there.

I nodded to Jack and took the lead inside the room. My gun readied, I would have no hesitation to take the shot. "Put your hands up! Now!"

The yell that pierced my ears would likely cause them to ring for hours.

"What the—" Debbie's one hand went to her chest while the other ripped out the earbuds. "You scared the shit out of me." She glared at both of us before settling her eyes on my weapon. "You're holding a gun on me."

It wasn't until her words made it through that I realized it was still pointed at her. "What are you doing here?"

"What am I—" Her face scrunched up, and she let out a snuff of air from her nose. "I'm getting ready to go."

"You need to come with me. Now." I put my gun back in its holster.

"Brandon, you're acting strange."

"I just need you to trust me."

"I am trying to. You told me to go back to Karen's. That's what I'm trying to do here."

I noticed the opened suitcase on the bed. Some clothes were already inside. I didn't look forward to what I had to say next. "You can't go to your sister's now."

"Brandon." Two hands went to her hips.

"Come with me." I put an arm around her and guided her out of the room.

She spun around, pointed at Jack, and asked me, "What's he doing?"

He was standing on our bed, his hands gloved, poking around the light fixture on the ceiling.

"We'll talk outside."

"Brandon."

I leaned in and whispered in her ear, "Just trust me."

"Fine."

I moved her out to the backyard and for a moment took in the cloudless sky, the chirping birds, the whirring of lawnmowers. Another beautiful Virginia morning, and yet here we were dealing with an unsub bent on destroying all that was truly beautiful and distorting it to a twisted view of righteousness.

We stood on the back deck facing each other. Debbie's arms were crossed. "You better tell me what's going on."

"The case we're working on—"

Her head cocked to the side, and I could read the reflection in her eyes, *You put us in danger*.

"It's complicated."

"Say it, Brandon. I'm in danger?" The arms tightened. One long strand of brown hair fell from the clip that held the rest. I reached out for it, peered into her eyes, and nodded.

"I can't believe this. It's a job, Brandon." She shifted to the right, moving just out of reach.

"It's not just a job."

"What else is it?"

The direct question rendered me silent for a few seconds.

"Like I thought. For a job, you put our lives in danger. Great. Just great!"

Every time she said the word *job*, it came out with such disdain that it angered a portion of my soul. "The FBI swear to protect—"

"Save the brochure for new recruits." She said the words, but after she did her eyes snapped to mine. "I didn't mean it like that."

"No, I think you did, but I get it. You weren't really into this career choice from the start."

"It's not that. It's just, it's dangerous."

"Damn right, it's dangerous!" I averted my eyes from her.

"Brandon."

I watched a squirrel run across the yard and up one of the

giant oaks.

"Brandon."

"What?"

She placed a hand on my arm. "Where do you need me to go?"

PAIGE'S EYES WERE FASTENED TO the photo of Brandon's wife. Bingham was right. The woman was beautiful, and it would be a lie to say it didn't bother her on some level, but she was jealous of the woman for more than her looks. She got to spend her life with Brandon. "Why would it bother me?"

"You love him."

"Special Agent Fisher is a colleague of mine, a member of the—"

"Then you love him." Bingham's lips curled upward. The smile chilled Paige.

"Who is helping you on the outside?"

"Round and round you go." He emitted a small laugh.

"Earl Royster is dead." She dropped the fact, callously with unwavering eye contact.

Bingham tapped a finger on the table. Paige counted— eleven total. A smirk still on his lips, he said, "I suppose that creates a problem for you."

I TOOK THE SUV AND left Jack at the house searching for cameras and audio recorders. Nadia volunteered her place, and it was deemed a safe house for the time being. We picked up her key on the way.

She lived in a condo building in Logan Circle. When she told me the address, it had me wondering how much money she had. Logan Circle was a historic district in D.C., and condos there would have ranged up from half a million.

"It's only going to be temporary until we find the guy." I parked the car, and Deb looked through the window at the building.

"How does she afford this place?"

"Good question."

"I'm sure I'll be fine here—for a little while." She straightened and undid her seat belt.

"I wouldn't ask you to do this unless it was for your safety."

"I know."

She got out, and I followed her to the back of the SUV. She opened the back door and went to haul out the suitcase and the one bulging overnight bag. I came in between and took them from her.

"I want you to stay in contact. I call, you answer."

Her hands went to her hips. "If the same applies to you. How do I know this psycho won't come after you? You've got their attention obviously."

"You let me worry about me okay?" I walked toward the building. She didn't need to read my face, or she'd witness the truth. As much as I wanted to think positively, uncertainty hindered the vision.

Her sandals flapped as she walked along the sidewalk behind me. "Not fair."

"Don't start, Deb. It's for a few days until we catch this guy."

"How do you know you will?"

"That's what we do. We catch the bad guys."

A hand reached out to my shoulder, causing me to turn to face her. "And what's your track record?"

I hated it when she did this. She had a way of tapping into my perfectionist nature. She knew I was technical and critical. "It's about to have an arrest on it."

"Uh-huh." She brushed ahead of me and flung open the front door. "And how am I supposed to explain this to my work?" She held the door, her eyes fixed on mine.

We had discussed how imperative it was for her to stay away from anywhere or anyone familiar. She wasn't to leave Nadia's condo, and that included going to her job. Even to me, those restrictions equated capture.

"I'm going to go nuts inside four walls for days."

"You could be in a place with six."

Her expression went sour. She got my implication—a coffin. "You think they'd kill—"

Her words died on her lips as we stepped into the lobby.

"She lives in a hotel."

High ceilings held recessed lighting that cast almost an enchanting glow over the area. A few seating areas were laid out, and minimalistic artwork hung on the walls. The combined textures of the wood flooring and color of the walls welcomed one with the warmth of a sun-kissed beach.

"May I help you?" A concierge called out from behind the front desk. His eyes said, *And who are you?*

"I believe Nadia Webber called ahead."

"Oh yes, most certainly. Mister Bond, is it?" His eyes passed judgment and skepticism the same way mine had when Nadia had told me the cover name she'd assigned. She'd said it would be fun.

"Yes, it is."

He kept watching me but didn't say anything. I could only imagine what was going through his mind.

"The elevators?"

"Right there, Mister Bond." He passed a glance to Deb. "Enjoy your stay."

I put an arm through Deb's. "Let's go."

She leaned into me and whispered, "Mister Bond?"

"Long story."

"Uh-huh."

As we waited for the elevator, Deb swayed forward and bumped the purse she held dangling in front of her against her knees.

"You have to take this seriously, and, yes, they could kill you." I picked up where her last sentence had left off. I didn't want to underestimate the potential threat.

Her eyes locked with mine, and she stopped swaying the purse. "All right, then. Guess I'm jail-bound."

"Don't say it like that—" Her soft laugh stopped my words

there.

She smiled. "Not really much of a prison here." She glanced around. "I kind of wanted some time off work anyhow. More time to write."

"Brat." Debbie had worked on one book over the last three years.

"What, now you're jealous?"

"Maybe. A little." I wrapped an arm around her and pulled her close to me. As her head bent to rest on my shoulder, I brushed her hair back and kissed her forehead.

The motion transported me back to Quinton and the words Royster would say after cutting him, *Shh, baby, don't cry.*

The other unsub was still out there.

Twenty-Five

I hated leaving Deb in the condo alone, even though she'd be safe there. The unsub didn't know anything about Nadia's existence, and if they had attempted to follow us, I had made more than the necessary turns to weed out any suspicious vehicles.

Back at the house, Jack and a few CSIs were combing the ceilings, through pieces of furniture, and the bookshelves. We had a collection of Agatha Christie books on the one, and I hurried over to the guy. "Please be careful."

He looked at me as if to say, *It's not my first day on the job.* The man was old enough to be my father.

"Where's Special Agent Harper?"

A rubber-gloved finger pointed to the ceiling.

I bounded up the staircase two steps at a time. Jack was in the bedroom, a haze of smoke around him. I waved a hand in front of my face. "Put that thing out."

He went over to one of the windows, lifted the old pane and flicked the butt outside. "You should really put in a screen."

"What did you find?" I asked pointing to a small device that was on the quilt.

"That is a camera."

I picked up the bag and examined the contents. It was small enough to fit on the flat part of my thumb. "This is a camera?"

"That."

"What about audio?" The unsub needed to have some sort of ears on the place to know about Deb's sister Karen. I ran a hand along the base of my neck and paused to rub it for a few seconds. "We need to get someone watching my sister-in-law's place, too."

"Already handled. Called in Chantilly PD."

"So, obviously, this creep was in my home, in my bedroom, defiled Deb's privacy."

"Obviously."

"You're going to be like that now. At a time like this?"

"You really need to harness your emotions, Kid, or they're going to kill ya."

"When? How?" My thoughts were on the unsub.

"Questions that need answers."

"Okay, one thing at a time." I drew a deep breath and looked at the bagged evidence in my hand. The unsub had held this and had put it in place. "When would he have come here? How could he have known?"

"*Obviously*," Jack mocked my use of the word. "Bingham is still in contact with him. We know it's not Twitter. By the way, Nadia called and she's almost finished getting the backgrounds on all the Twitter followers. She also has the evidence files from Sarasota."

I nodded. My mind dwelled more on the home invasion than the cold cases. "The unsub must have a means of affording transportation."

"And their communication is current. It was only three days ago that we found the bodies." Jack patted his shirt pocket for another cigarette.

"Don't even think about it. As it is, Deb's gonna kill me when she gets home." I waved a hand in front of my nose. "We'll need to get that smell out."

He smiled and pulled his hand back. "If your windows had screens we could leave them open."

Jack's phone rang, saving him from my two hands that wanted to encase his throat. At least I had only imagined it and hadn't acted on the growing compulsion to do just that. *See, Jack, I have control.*

"Harper here…I'm putting you on speaker." He pushed a button on his cell to increase the volume. "It's just me and the kid."

"Hey, Brandon."

"Paige?"

Jack looked at me. "I believe you two know each other."

Another opportunity to display self-control when I wanted to say, *I believe you know each other, too.*

"There's no way we're getting anything from the guy. He…" Paige paused, letting out a groan. "He talks in circles, and he doesn't just answer questions with questions, he's even better than that. He's not going to tell us how he communicates with the unsub."

"Can't say it surprises me," Jack said.

There were a few seconds of silence in which I was certain Paige wondered why he had sent her to speak with Bingham if that were the case.

"The other church members didn't have anything for us. What do you want us to do now?"

"Drive back to Louisville tonight and get back here for first thing in the morning. Nadia's got a bunch of evidence for us to work through. We'll need all the help we can get."

"Sure thing."

Jack ended the call, and a CSI yelled up the stairs. "We found it."

I was the first to hit the staircase.

The CSI held it up in gloved hands. "Found it sitting on the stones for that candle over there, pretty much right in front of us this whole time."

The CSI pointed to the dining room table where Deb had a curved dish showcasing three pillar candles on a bed of rubbed stones. She had said they added a decorative touch.

"Any latent prints?"

The CSI smiled. "A partial."

"What about the range of this thing?"

The smile faded. "I'm not a tech, but some of these things can have a huge range."

"We're talking a mile, a few?"

"A few. I think I've even heard tell of some of them being enabled with Wi-Fi."

"Meaning connected over the internet?"

"Yeah." He gave me a look that communicated, *Did you just fall onto the planet?*

I was starting to believe the advances in technology hurt us more than they helped. "Great."

Jack pulled out a cigarette, stuck it in his lips but didn't light it. "Think of it this way. The unsub likely planted these devices in the last twenty-four hours. Your wife went to her sister's yesterday morning. I'd assume he came in after she left."

"So he could still be around the world. Really, what's to say our unsub isn't rich?"

"We know Bingham doesn't have money. There's nothing in his accounts, and he lost his house."

"After his sister died." I spread a hand over the gun in my holster. "Before that his sister paid the property taxes. What if Bingham left all his money to her?" I shook my head. "And if he did give everything to his sister, where did it go when she died? We know it didn't return to Bingham, and she didn't have any children—"

"Hmm."

I took that as Jack being impressed.

"How do we know this person isn't some recluse from Salt Lick that no one knows about?" All of the possibilities were causing a stress headache to set in. "But then I guess we'd have them by now because they would have been watching the crime scene. Something would have tipped us off to them."

"Would you have suspected Royster's involvement?"

He had me there.

"I'll have Nadia run a background on Bingham's sister's financials and see if we can find out where the money went."

"And one more thing, why would Bingham leave all his money to his sister? The man was only going away max of five years. Did he figure he'd be found out?"

Jack pulled his cigarette from his mouth and latched his eyes onto mine.

Twenty-Six

The next morning, Jack and I were at our head office wading through forty boxes on the eleven Sarasota murders. They accounted for suspect interviews, character references, issued warrants, and recorded notifications that were made to next of kin for those who were identified.

The murders were pegged between the years seventy-one and eighty-four. The bodies were found in eighty-six. Five of them remained unidentified. The average cooling off period between kills was estimated at one to two years.

I had asked Jack why the FBI wouldn't have been called in on the case back then. He couldn't provide me with a satisfactory answer, and with all leads exhausted, the case had gone cold.

We had the boxes carted to an empty office which had appeared large enough before they were piled inside. Now there was barely standing room around a conference table the size of my dining table that seated six adults comfortably. Some boxes didn't even make it inside the room but sat outside the doorway. The box belonging to the first victim was on the table.

As Jack had said, *Always start at the beginning*. He had also added that if we could establish a connection, a trigger, an emotional connection between Bingham and the first victim, then we'd have something to move on.

He held up a mug full of sludge, at least that's how he

termed the coffee from the break room, to his lips when Paige and Zachery walked in. "You made it." He spoke with the mug against his lips, took a sip, and set it down on the table. "You should have brought us something to eat." Jack dropped into a conference chair. He finally succumbed to his exhaustion. I had given up on standing over an hour ago.

The clock read just after ten in the morning, and we had been working since five.

Zachery's eyes went over the room, taking in all the boxes. "It looks like it."

"That's what happens when you have eleven murders, lots of paperwork," Jack said and passed me a glance. "Yeah, get your writing hand ready, Kid. Ours is going to look similar—"

"It's already starting to, but the only difference is we're going to catch the bad guy." Zachery smiled.

"Cocky and confident as always." Jack returned the smile.

Paige and I weren't really part of the conversation between the other two. She watched me with that fawn-like quality to her eyes again—soft, wanting, knowing, and vulnerable. When she looked at me like that, did she have any idea how it affected me? Today, though, all I could think was: *Do you look at Jack the same way?*

"Glad your wife was okay." She smiled at me, the awkward, slightly forced kind that had me questioning the truthfulness of her words.

"Thanks." I held a file in my hands and put my attention back on it. "The first victim's name was Anna Knowles. Her picture wasn't one recovered from Bingham's cell."

"Maybe Bingham had a special connection with her, or the murder wasn't intended," Zachery said.

"Possible. Anyway, she was a mother and left behind two children, one boy and one girl, and a husband. Detectives interviewed the man at length. There were at least a few boxes dedicated to him from what I could tell. He claimed his wife dropped the daughter off at a babysitter's and never returned."

"Sounds like you've got this under control." Paige smiled again.

"Yeah we pretty much have the case solved." I glanced up from the file and smiled at her.

"You can be such a smart-ass sometimes."

"And I don't even have to work at it."

"Why doesn't that surprise me?" She took a folder out of the box and took a seat at the table. Zachery followed her lead.

"So what else do we know?" Zachery tapped his palms on the table.

"The husband was suspected of his wife's disappearance back in seventy-one, but friends and family confirmed they were a loving couple. When her body was found in eighty-six, the husband was cleared based on lack of evidence. There was no way to prove his involvement. A Detective Jenkins was the lead on the case. He'd visit Knowles once every year until his early retirement back in—" I lifted up his background that we had pulled "—back in 2001."

"How were the bodies found?" Paige leaned across the table, her elbows bent, and she cupped her chin in her hand.

"They were digging up the property for a new land development. At first, they thought maybe it was an old graveyard, but the land didn't have a record of that, and when they realized they were all killed the same way, they knew it wasn't a mistake in paperwork misplacement," Jack said.

"Did Bingham own the property? Why not just trace the bodies back to him?"

"There was no connection to Bingham whatsoever." I put the file I had in my hands back on the table. "Basically, it was in an industrial area. The building had been used as a feed mill and abandoned long ago. The city owned it for years but never did anything with it. It just sort of sat there."

"Making it an ideal location."

"Pretty much, yeah."

"How did they die?"

"Just like with our case, the last victim was preserved by the burial. They had the coinherence symbol cut into their torso. It's believed they all suffered the same way." I tossed a photo toward Paige and looked at Zachery. "Guess you were right."

"I can be sometimes, Pending." He smirked.

"Were they disemboweled?" Paige studied the photo.

Jack answered, "Asphyxiation. Speculation is a plastic bag because there was no trace left behind."

"It would be consistent with Bingham's personality of wanting power and control. Still, why would he change his MO? Why start tearing out intestines and grinding them up for pigs?" For a woman, nothing seemed to faze Paige.

"And the eleven murders there started with a woman. In Salt Lick, it was a man. He just continued his pattern," I said.

"Hmm."

I glanced at Jack briefly, unsure how to translate that grunt.

"I guess we have to figure out why the change in murder method, also, why he chose the people he did."

"He said to you," Jack directed his words to me, "did he not? 'Confess your sins and be forgiven, don't and be punished'?"

I nodded. My eyes traveled to Paige who refused to make eye contact.

Zachery moved forward on his chair. "We know Bingham's got some sort of God complex. Basically, he believes he's righteous for killing these people. No doubt his follower would as well. Bingham would have instilled this."

"We need to figure out the first murder and work forward. Honestly, I have a feeling that's where we'll find our answers," Paige said.

Again, I nodded.

"But why would they have targeted you—and your wife?"

"My wife? To get to me, toy with me. Royster had mentioned no one was supposed to get hurt."

"But people did get hurt," Paige interjected.

"When Royster had said no one was supposed to get hurt, what was he referring to?" Zachery asked.

I let out a rush of air. "Good question. Maybe just the victims he took part in killing?"

"Well, that would be the last one in Salt Lick, Sally Windermere," Paige said, "but maybe there's more? I mean his brother went missing back in 2005."

"What about the time lapse between the Sarasota killings? Do the files comment on that, Pending?"

I eyed all the boxes before settling my gaze on Zachery. "From what we see, one to two years."

Zachery reached for a file. "Guess it's time for me to get reading."

"The rest of us can pretty much leave now. Zach will be done in twenty minutes." Jack rose from his chair.

"With the file in his hand?" I asked.

"No, all forty boxes."

I watched Jack, unsure if he was being blatantly sarcastic or serious. In the time I studied Jack's face, Zachery had closed the first file folder and was reaching for another.

Paige stood up but didn't back away from the table. "The one thing bothering me is: Did they look to the city and government officials? Someone had to be responsible for watching the building."

"Where were you to question the fifty squatters, plus the city board?"

The voice came from the doorway where an older man in his late sixties stood wearing a visitor's badge clipped onto his shirt pocket. Deep lines were carved in his face. His gray mustache was filled in more than the top of his head where hair formed a trace outline around his skull.

I looked between him and Elise, who was one of the administrative clerks entrusted to accompany him back here.

Jack asked the question, "And who are you?"

"Marty Jenkins." The man walked into the room as if it was his office and we were invading his privacy. He latched his hands in front, making no motion of a handshake.

Jack addressed Elise, "Who is he?"

"Do you talk about most people as if they're not there when they're standing right in front of you?"

Elise's eyes enlarged, and she backed away with a shoulder shrug and opened palms.

Jack addressed the man who already had his hands in a file box. "I have to ask that you get your hands off there, Martin Jenkins. This is part of an open investigation."

"Like I said, it's Marty, my given name by my mother. She didn't believe much in calling people something others would distort by abbreviating."

I had noticed Paige smirk before she raised a hand to conceal it.

Jenkins sunk a hand inside the box and pulled out a file. "Anna Knowles. Nice lady. At least that's how her friends and family saw her."

"You're the detective from the Sarasota murders." Jack came up beside the man.

Zachery glanced up between flipping pages.

"Now I know how you got to where you are." Jenkins's attention went to Zachery and the flipping sheets of paper. "What's he doing?"

"And yet you made detective." Jack glared at Jenkins, who smirked in response.

"Lead detective for the Sarasota murders actually. Eleven vics, five with no identities."

"We read that in the file."

"The papers were calling him the Symbolic killer. They always have to have a name." Jenkins glanced at Paige and me. "It makes our jobs easier to label them."

"I take it this has been your life's work." Jack's hand

skimmed over his shirt pocket, went down the side of his torso, and came to rest on his hip.

"Retired already, Agent. Although I'm sure you pulled my background. You know being a retired cop isn't all about golf memberships and yacht clubs. I'm just happy to have the mortgage paid off."

"So what—"

"Am I doing here?"

Jack didn't say anything.

"My little girl went missing back in the early eighties. She was never found. I hoped that one of the vics would be her."

"Wish they would have been," Paige said, her words containing disgust.

"Closure, that's all. Do you know what it's like to go to sleep at night wondering where the hell your daughter is?" He let out a breath. "If not, then you can't understand."

"I understand you want closure, but why—"

"Like that? Because I'm not naive enough to believe the world is a good place—"

"Special Agent Paige Dawson." She crossed her arms. "I take it your daughter wasn't one of the bodies found."

"Not that we've been able to prove."

"What about MtDNA? It was discovered back in sixty-one. Samples would have been taken from the remains." Zachery put the file down on the table. "Its full name is mitochondrial DNA, and it has proven to be a great aid in solving old cases where the remains are skeletal. This DNA can be pulled from hair, bones, and teeth unlike nuclear DNA." He glanced at me. "That's the common DNA you normally hear about. Anyway, MtDNA can be used to match an individual with a family. It only takes on the characteristics from the maternal side. It's fascinating really." He paused as if assessing to see if his words were sinking in. "It remains unchanged for thousands of years, only undergoing a significant mutation after sixty-five hundred years. Some believe our ancestry traces back to an African woman from two hundred thousand years ago."

Jack raised a hand to Zachery as if to say, *Enough of the forensic lesson.*

Zachery continued. "The technology's available to us. Why haven't you gotten the unidentified female corpses tested to see if one was your daughter?"

"Her mother died years ago, and I wasn't really a part of their life—not that I wanted it that way—but we were kids when she got pregnant. I was eighteen, her sixteen. I proposed. She wisely said no. Anyway, life went on. My daughter's mother has a sister, Tammy Sherman, but she can't stand the sight of me." Jenkins took out his wallet and extended a photo to Jack. "Her name was Donna. She was just nineteen when she went missing."

Jack looked at the photo, and then handed it to Paige and directed her to pass it along. "Did you file a missing persons?"

"What was the point? I know those types of things get lost in the system."

Zachery handed me the photo. As my eyes settled on it, I recognized the face immediately. My head snapped up to face Zachery, who shook his head.

Jack took the file that Jenkins had put on the table and put it back in the evidence box. "We'll let you know if we can identify her."

"Oh no, you're not pushing me out of this investigation."

"There's no way—"

"One officer of the law to another."

"Retired," Jack corrected him.

"Isn't there one case that means so much to you that you lose sleep over it? Have you seen the bags under my eyes? I'm not here for a pity party, but I'm not leaving."

"We can have you escorted."

"You could, but I see in your eyes you won't."

Jack didn't say anything for twenty-five seconds. I listened to the clock in the room tick off each one. "You help familiarize us with the files, the suspects, and the investigation, but the minute—" Jack pointed a finger at Jenkins "—you are more in the way, out you go. Understood?"

Jenkins saluted Jack, soliciting another hidden smirk from Paige.

"But first if I could consult with my team."

"Is there something you're not telling me? You found her, didn't you? You recognize her?"

"I just need a few minutes with my team," Jack directed Jenkins. The man complied and left the room. Jack closed the door behind him.

"My god, Jack, his daughter was one of the photos found in Bingham's cell," Paige said.

"We have to tell him," I urged.

Jack turned to me. "Absolutely not. At this point, all we have is a photo. The rest has to be proven." His eyes scanned all of us. "Are we clear on that?"

We all nodded.

## Twenty-Seven

We spent the next few hours going over the case as Jenkins recalled it. Zachery had read the entire contents of the record boxes and could relate to most of what Jenkins said, but what Jenkins did offer was a live recounting, not something simply documented and left for interpretation.

"So why didn't you refer the case to the FBI?" Paige asked the question of Jenkins.

We were all seated around the table in the cramped office. An evidence file box had been pushed to the middle of the table to allow room for an extra-large pizza box. The pizza brought in for a late lunch had disappeared in a record time of ten minutes.

"And what, let you have the glory?" Jenkins smiled at Paige, and she returned it. "There wasn't any immediate danger. No evidence the killer would strike again."

"There were eleven bodies in shallow graves."

"Yes, but no evidence to indicate there would be more victims. The last victim was pegged at two years before the find."

"But that was the estimated time between kills. Some were two years apart, some one. The one year, two people were killed. You couldn't have based it on that." Jack had a tight grip on his pop can. "You made a risky decision." The implication wasn't missed by Jenkins.

"It's my fault more people have died?"

"It could have been prevented."

Paige intervened, "How did you find out about our case? I mean it's great you're here to help, but—"

I picked up on the not-so-subtle glare Jack projected toward Paige.

Jenkins snapped open a can of pop and pulled off the tab. "Gets caught in the 'stache." He took a swig.

"But how did you find out? The open case we're investigating hasn't been reported in the papers."

"Your open case I know nothing about, but I still have friends in the department. They know the stake I have in the Symbolic killer case."

I glanced over at Jack. Maybe it was time we let the retired detective in on our case. After all, he had too much to lose by exposing the case to the public. "We call him the Redeemer."

Jenkins's eyes squinted, pinching the skin around his eyes and showcasing more wrinkles inflicted from the passing of time and a hard life. "It has a sort of ring to it. I take it with your case he also carved the symbol into the vic's torso?"

"Not exactly."

Jack rose from the table. His focus honed in on me. "We don't share details of an open case with a civilian."

"Agent—"

"Supervisory Special Agent Harper. It's not up for discussion or debate. You are here to help us, not get in the way. Those were the ground rules to not kicking you out the door on your ass."

Jenkins rose to match Jack. Both men were the same height, making for even eye contact. "You need my help."

"That has yet to be seen." Jack pulled out a cigarette, perched it in his lips, and went to leave the room when his cell rang. He answered, "Harper."

"What not Supervisory Special Agent Harper? Guess he cuts down when he answers a phone to save time," Jenkins said this to the rest of us as he dropped back into his chair.

I caught Paige smirking again. This time she didn't bother

to hide it.

Seconds later, Jack spun around to face us. "We have the same rough timeline as did the detective here, just every one to two years."

Jenkins's face scrunched up, almost as if he didn't appreciate being identified by a title and not a name. *Maybe he should get to used it*, I thought.

"So what happens every one to two years that sets this guy off?" Paige asked.

"Like I said, rough timeline. The ninth victim came seven years after the eighth and Sally came three years after that."

The room fell silent as we contemplated some justifiable reasoning.

"Maybe he didn't bury his victims right away?" I suggested, piercing the silence. "Or he kept them somewhere else?"

"No, that doesn't make sense." Zachery was quick to dismiss my idea. "And there's no evidence to indicate the burial chamber was a secondary grave."

Jenkins's eyes widened at the mention of a burial chamber, but a glare from Jack kept him silent.

"He took pause to work on the tunnel system and layout."

"This guy had an elaborate thing going?" Jenkins's brows pressed.

"That would explain one to two, maybe even a three-year gap, but what kept him occupied for seven?" Paige got involved.

"What if," Zachery started, stopped, started, "what if Bingham—"

"You have a name." Jenkins's head snapped to face Zachery.

I saw the words in Zachery's eyes like a flashing reader board, *Oh shit*.

"I meant to say the killer."

"The killer's name is Bingham? You know where he is? Let's go pick him up." Jenkins leaned forward.

"First of all, you're not going anywhere." Jack flicked his lighter, no doubt dreaming of lighting the cigarette in his lips. "And second of all, yes, we know who the killer is. We have to prove it thanks to the whole innocent-until-proven-guilty mandate."

"Then let's prove it. Let me help you." Jenkins's newfound eagerness was extinguished by the rest of us going silent. "There's more to it. You don't think he worked alone."

None of us responded.

"Yes, that's it. Well, damn." Jenkins looked around at the boxes. "It would make sense that the killer—Bingham you said?—wouldn't have acted alone. How else would he subdue the victim?"

"I'm going to ask you to leave now." Jack stepped toward Jenkins.

"I can't leave now. Besides, you just said, I'm not going anywhere."

"Why don't we just tell him, Jack?" Paige made the appeal in a soft tone that I was familiar with it but shouldn't have been. It took me back to the times she talked me back into bed when I should have been home with Deb. "He could be of help."

Jack looked around at all of us, his gaze settling on me. "What do you think, Kid?"

"Honestly?"

"Amuse me." If he didn't get a nicotine fix in the next couple of minutes, we might have a massacre take place in this room.

I glanced at Paige and Zachery trying to draw the courage to speak my opinion. Jenkins didn't look impressed that he was being discussed as if he were not there. I faced Jack. "We should." I wanted to wince after the words came out, just the facial expression on Jack, the way his jaw tightened and his eyes hardened over.

Nadia spun around the doorframe and nearly bumped straight into Jack. "I found something." She handed him a piece of paper. "That's a list of the followers who stood out to me from the Redeemer's Twitter account, but that's not why I'm here. I found Kurt McCartney's wife. She changed her name from Martha McCartney to Denise Hogan—and here's an interesting tidbit. She's currently living in Sarasota, Florida."

Jack pointed at me and Paige. "You two, get ready to go."

Paige's brows pinched downward in confusion. "You're his—"

"I know what I am, but for this trip, you'll be the mentoring agent. Go, you have a plane to catch."

"What about Deb?" I asked.

"She's safe, and Zach and I have it under control."

I didn't understand why he was sending me on a plane with Paige. Why not send her and Zachery or come with me himself? But with the glazed-over look in his eyes, I knew there would be no arguing with him. His decision was final.

Twenty-Eight

The flight to Sarasota was just under three hours. I hated planes—particularly the lift-off and the landing. If only there were some way to just be in flight without the necessary bumpy navigation required on both ends of it.

Paige had passed me a few glances as we took off. She must have noticed the grip I had on the arms of the chair, but she never made a comment. In fact, she hadn't said much since we'd left the office.

"Do you know why us?"

Her head was pressed against the headrest as she turned to face me. "Punishment for something," she said seriously, but a small smirk at the tail end of her statement disclosed they weren't intended to be taken as such.

"Jack doesn't like planes?"

Paige laughed. "Jack's not afraid of anything, Brandon. I think the man could have a rocket launcher aimed at his face from five feet away and still think he'd walk."

"I asked him, but he didn't really give me a straight answer."

"He thinks we'll make a good team." Her eyes scanned my face, paused on my lips for seconds, and rose back to my eyes.

"Why?"

She faced forward. "He said you come from Florida, and I'm a woman."

"I've noticed." I had hoped the statement would garner a smile from her, even a slight upward curve—nothing. "What does your being a woman—"

"Everything. Denise Hogan might be more open to talk to me."

"We don't think we're looking for a female unsub, but we're approaching her like she's our only link."

"She is in a way. We've spoken with the family of the other suspected victims. We've exhausted those areas. This woman is the only one we haven't—and doesn't it make you wonder why she'd change her name and move all the way to Florida?"

"Sarasota, no less."

"That's right. A little close to home for you."

I studied Paige's profile. She was tired. Even her curls had lost their regular bounce. The time was just after eleven, and the plane would touch down by midnight.

"When I asked Jack why us, he didn't offer much. Just that if I liked being an agent I'd be getting on the plane."

"He's testing you."

"Excuse me."

"He wants to know if you can handle it. He wants you right in the middle of the investigation so that he knows if you're right for the team."

"A trap?"

Paige laughed and turned to face me again. Exhaustion had etched into her expression and it faded quickly. Her eyes were slightly bloodshot. "Like I said, a test. Despite what you think he doesn't want you to fail. He just thinks you will." She said the last sentence at a lower volume, but I still heard her.

"Well, that's just great."

"Don't take it personally."

"How else am I supposed to take it?"

"Jack knows people, Brandon. He knows whether a person is a fit for the team within a short time. With you, I don't think he's sure."

"I'm eluding him."

She smiled. "Guess so."

"You seem to know him pretty well." The words came out, and her smile disappeared.

"None of your business."

"I didn't mean anything by—"

"Of course, you did, but what I do is my business, understood?"

She held eye contact until I nodded. Her association with Jack was rubbing off on her. The way she added *understood* was something Jack would say to make a point.

"I mean who are you to judge—" She shook her head and stopped talking.

We spent the rest of the flight in silence.

Twenty-Nine

P art of me expected to wake up to a ringing phone, the other to a knock on the door. Neither happened. Surprisingly, I woke up on my own in a hotel room where sunlight filtered in around the drapes. The alarm on the side table read nine thirty.

I missed Deb with an ache in my chest. I wondered how she was making out at Nadia's and worried about her safety. I thought of calling last night, but by the time we got in, it was too late.

I picked up the cell to make the call, but it rang on the way to my ear. ID showed that it was Jack. I took a deep breath and sat up on the bed. I stretched my neck left to right and softly slapped my face to wake up. "Special Agent Fish—"

"Where are you?" Jack's voice carried more aggravation than had been there before we'd left yesterday. He seemed to be a man who needed sleep, and this case had us going on the minimum human requirement.

"At the—"

"Don't tell me you're still in bed."

I sprung from the bed as if he could see me and drew back the drapes. The bright sun blinded me, and my eyes instinctively shut for seconds until they adjusted. When they opened, I looked around the room. "I'm not."

"Hmm."

I knew what that one was for. He didn't believe me. "What is it, Jack?"

"Don't change the subject, Kid. I'm the one who asks the questions. Where's Paige?"

I hesitated to answer because I didn't know.

"Is she in the room with you?"

"Jack?"

"I know about the two of you."

I dropped into a sofa chair by the window and watched vehicles whizz by on the street below. Everyone in a hurry with a place they needed to be, even on a Saturday.

"Kid?"

"It's not like that."

"Hmm."

"It was a long time ago." Why did I feel like I owed him an explanation?

"Is that the sin the Redeemer wanted you to confess?"

"Let me guess, it's only because of pillow talk that you know about my affair with Paige." The words charged out infused with a fuel of their own.

"You know about us." There wasn't any shame in his voice, neither any regret.

"I do."

"Well, then."

"Surprised you sent me away with her. Late nights, far away from home," I said with my eyes on the bed. I had thrown back the sheets and comforter in my haste to get up. I pictured Paige lying there and played this like a poker game. "She's here now if you want to talk to her."

"Sure."

He was calm, non-judgmental. He had called my bluff. *Now what?* "She's still sleep—"

There was a knock on the door followed by my name being called out.

"Let her in. I have news for both of you."

Jack must have heard the knocking. I detected amusement in his voice. He won this round. I unlatched the chain, unlocked the deadbolt, and opened the door. Paige stood in the hallway holding a tray with two extra-large coffees and a paper bag clenched in her hand. She looked at my boxer shorts and smiled. She passed me the tray, and I balanced it with one hand as I held the cell to my ear with the other.

"It's Jack."

She nodded and placed the bag on the dresser before taking the tray from me. "Good morning, Jack."

"Put me on speaker now," Jack directed.

I depressed a button and held it out for Paige to hear him.

"We've been here most of the night, but we're getting somewhere. The results also came back from the pig trough. There were traces of human DNA."

My stomach tossed. Paige's face scrunched up, but her apparent disgust was thinly layered as she reached for a coffee, took the lid off, blew on it, and then took a sip.

"You're going to shut them down." I remembered the petite woman whose pig farm had been in her husband's family for generations.

"Don't have much choice but to report it to the FDA. Human meat was consumed by their animals which people then ingested."

Paige paused, resting her lips on the edge of the cup. "That takes your appetite away." She looked at the paper bag she had brought with her.

"Yeah," I echoed her sentiment.

"You guys heading out to see Denise Hogan now?"

"Some of us, or should I say one of us, needs to get dressed first." Paige's eyes went back to my boxer shorts.

She wore navy dress slacks that fit her snuggly and rested on her hips. She had tucked her white shirt into them which only further accentuated her fit figure. The holster and her gun wound around her waist as a bulky piece that didn't seem to belong and appeared to weigh her down.

"Keep me posted. We're taking a break for a couple of hours to get some sleep, but if something comes up, I want a call immediately."

"Of course," Paige reassured.

"By the way, how are things going with Detective Jenkins?" I asked.

"Anything comes up, call." Jack avoided my question and disconnected.

Paige and I were smiling. "He really doesn't like the guy, does he?" I commented.

"Can't say I blame him."

"Really? You had me fooled. You seemed to be captured by his cop stories."

She shrugged a shoulder. "Guess I can be a good actress."

THE ADDRESS PROVIDED FOR DENISE HOGAN was a modest apartment building of five stories. Paige and I had eaten the blueberry scones she had picked up for us on the way over. It took time for the image of people consuming human intestines in their morning sausage to fade away for our appetites to resurface. When we left the hotel, we took a taxi to a car rental where we picked up a four-door sedan that rocked as if we drove on waves, not a paved road.

I spoke with a mouthful, "Think she'll even be home?"

"It's Saturday morning. There's a good chance."

"I still find it strange that she wouldn't have reported her husband missing."

"Sounds like someone who has something to hide, and the name change and relocation go right along with that. It's a good thing I'm here."

"You expect us to get that out of her?"

"Not we, me." Paige smiled. "Woman to woman."

"Just for that you think she's going to open up to you?"

"Guess we'll see."

"WONDER IF THE BUZZER'S EVEN WORKING." Paige dialed the intercom again for Denise Hogan's apartment.

The main entrance was a cramped space not much larger than an average-sized cubicle in a high-rise office building.

Our elbows touched when she dropped her arm back down. Paige moved quickly to pull her arm in.

A woman opened the door and stepped into the lobby. She was wearing cut-off jean shorts and a sleeveless tee. Her hair was in a tight ponytail. Her bangs were trimmed square across her brow boxing her face. She shimmied between us to reach the door to the streets. Her face was familiar. Paige picked up on it at the same time I did. We both went to go out the door at the same time. The woman had already put at least a dozen paces between us.

Paige yelled, "Denise Hogan!"

The woman slowed down, glanced over her shoulder and started into a run.

"I hate it when they run." Paige made the complaint then fired off ahead of me.

The sidewalk was relatively barren. Only a stub of a man walking a pug headed toward us. Moving past him I noticed the resemblance between the man and his pet. It wasn't a compliment to the man, and I nearly tripped over the dog.

"Hey, watch it," the man called out to me.

I kept running and passed Paige. About a foot away from our target, I called out to her, "Miss Hogan."

"Go away!" Her arms flailed as if they would somehow keep us back the wilder they moved.

"We need to speak—" I reached out for her shoulder.

"Get your hand off me." Denise Hogan stopped and jerked her shoulder to free my grip. The way she stood there with her hands on her hips, I knew she wasn't going anywhere. Deb was the same way. Placement of hands on hips grounded her. I pulled my arm back.

"What do you want?" Her breathing was calm despite the mini cardio workout.

Paige came up beside us and ran a hand from her forehead back through her hair. "We're federal agents, Miss Hogan. We need to talk to you about your husband—"

"I'm not—" Denise stalled, her gaze passing between

Paige and me as if she were trying to read our eyes. After ten seconds of silent penetration, her hands came off her hips. She lunged away from us.

"Oh no, you don't!" Paige fired off after her and caught Denise by the back of her shirt. I jogged the few paces to the two women.

"You are going to talk to us—"

"You can't make me do anything. I have rights." The hands never went to the hips. Her arms crossed, a running shoe tapped the sidewalk. The foot stopped when Paige tightened her grip on Denise and moved closer.

"We can talk out here on the streets or someplace private."

Denise let out a rush of air as her eyes ignited with anger and blended with hopelessness. "Private."

"Works for us."

THE TEAKETTLE WHISTLE COULD EASILY be heard at the other end of the apartment. I couldn't think about drinking hot liquid when the temperature was eighty-seven in the shade and the humidity level was headed for an all-time record high.

Denise had led us back to her apartment where she asked if we wanted anything. She kept busy in the kitchen which was open to the living area where Paige sat on the sofa and I on a reclining leather chair.

Paige began, "So your husband Kurt McCartney—"

Denise dropped a box of tea bags to the kitchen floor. "What about him?" She disappeared behind the counter as she bent to pick up the box.

"He went missing and was never found."

"That was a long time ago." Her hands appeared unsteady as she dangled a tea bag by its string in a mug.

Denise took a seat on the couch with Paige, folding her legs beneath her and holding the cup as if it were her savior. Based on posture one might conclude she was relaxed, calm, and open to conversation, but her energy said otherwise.

She placed the mug on the side table, and her right hand picked at the cording on the arm of the sofa.

"You were only twenty-three at the time."

She reached for the mug and blew on the tea. She held it to her lips but must have reconsidered taking a sip as steam wisped in front of her face. She pulled it down.

"It must have been scary not knowing where he went."

Denise turned to face Paige. "If you think you're going to analyze me, read me, and get into my head, you are mistaken. Kurt and I were a long time ago. Twenty years ago, in fact. I've moved—"

"We found him."

My eyes snapped to Paige. Her words were a lie as that hadn't been confirmed yet.

Denise remained perfectly still. Even her facial expression went unchanged.

"You're not surprised."

She shook her head and crossed her arms. Her hands rubbed her arms as if fending off a chill, which in here wasn't physically possible.

"What do you know that you're not telling us?" I asked the question, and both women looked at me. Paige's eyes said, *Back off*. With Denise's, I wasn't sure.

Paige reached out and touched a hand to Denise's shoulder. The woman jumped at the contact. "It must have been really hard. You weren't married long."

Seconds passed in silence. "Long enough to know marriage doesn't mean happily ever after."

Paige and I looked at each other as Denise reached for the tea and managed a small sip.

"You weren't happy."

"We were okay." She drew out the last word almost to the length of two. "You know what I'm talking about." She pulled her legs out from under her, crossed them toward the window away from us. She compressed her thin frame tightly against the arm of the sofa. "Love, marriage, babies, they can be overrated. We had good times but mostly bad," she paused and faced us. "I had nothing to do with his disappearance."

"We never said you did."

With the way Paige handled Denise, I knew why Jack had put her on a plane. She had a way of touching people that weren't even open to it.

"He was found in a grave back in Salt Lick," Paige said, continuing to build on her earlier lie.

Denise sucked in her bottom lip, and her left hand rubbed her right arm faster than before until a wild spark lit in her eyes. "You think I did it!" Her arms flailed wide as she got up from the couch. "It's time for you to leave."

"Please, we just have a few questions." Paige didn't move from the couch.

"You think I did it. I wouldn't do it. How could I do it?"

"Please."

Denise sighed and sniffled. She slipped a finger under her nose and consented to Paige's plea. She dropped back onto the sofa. "I couldn't have done it." Denise shivered.

"But you know who—"

"I didn't say that."

"We know you're afraid—"

"You have no idea what you're saying. None."

"We'll protect you."

"Protect me? Where were you to protect Kurt, huh? Guess he can rest in peace now, can't he?"

"The person who did this is behind bars—"

"Both of them?" Denise buried her face in the mug of tea.

"You know there was more than one? Do you know who did this?"

"I know what they sound like. I will never forget what they sounded like." Her eyes squeezed shut, tears seeped from the sides.

"Why change your name?"

"Same reason I got the hell outta Salt Lick. So they couldn't find me again."

"*Again*?" I leaned forward.

"I didn't mean to say again."

"I think you did."

Paige's eyes lectured me for taking over her interview. "They had you, but you escaped?"

Denise let out a snorted laugh. "You don't escape from them."

"They let you go?" Paige asked.

"It should have been me that died not Kurt." Denise stood and lifted her shirt. Three vertical scars on her torso served as a permanent reminder of her time beneath Bingham's blade.

"Why not report him missing?"

"They told me if I ever reported it they'd come back after me and finish the job."

"Do you know why they stopped?"

"Not really. They kept saying she's the wrong one, she's the wrong one—over and over again."

"Can you describe the people who did this to you?"

A headshake. "They must have drugged me somehow. Everything was blurry images. I sensed more than I saw. It was like beams of light and energy moving over me and around the room." She shivered and hugged herself. Her eyes closed. "The room was damp. I remembered being cool yet sweating. And the smell—" she inhaled deeply "—musty—no earthy." Her eyes opened. Tears fell down her cheeks. She let them fall. "One was smaller than the other. I still remember what the one would say to me." She bit down on her bottom lip hard. "They would touch me."

"You mean cut you?"

"No, I meant touch me." Denise blinked hard, more tears squeezed out and fell. "Not like sexually." She inhaled deeply. "The smaller one, they caressed the palm of their hand on my forehead and swept my hair back. They leaned into my ear and whispered, 'Shh, don't cry.'"

Thirty

Paige and I hit the sidewalk not long after Denise's recounting of the torture. Every time the unsub sliced her, he or she would whisper the words, *Shh, don't cry*. The statement sent shivers through me, and I wasn't the one who had lived through the ordeal. I was amazed that she wasn't more affected by that day. "I'm not really sure how much creepier you can get. Can't believe she doesn't remember everything."

"She remembers plenty, but her mind's shut off portions she can't deal with."

We asked Denise if she would be able to identify the voice if we played it for her. She had let out a wail and asked us to leave. Paige stepped in to console her and appealed to the good side of human nature—that of wanting to find justice for others. If her dead husband wasn't enough motivation after all these years possibly knowing someone else could be next would be.

"And I wonder if it's Bingham that's saying 'Shh, don't cry' Royster's lover commented that he said the same thing. Is it something that Bingham passed onto his followers or just something our unsub does?"

"Well, we know Royster wouldn't have been with Bingham back in ninety-one, or at least the evidence doesn't lead us there. People only said they got close after Royster's brother disappeared back in 2005, so the other person we're looking for may have learned the trait from Bingham. In turn, they taught it to Royster."

My phone rang, and it was Nadia from the Quantico office. "Your wife wants to talk to you."

"Sure, put her on." I found it strange that Debbie hadn't called me directly.

"Brandon?"

"What are you doing out of the condo? Is everything all right?" I held a hand over my other ear as some teenager ran down the sidewalk yelling for someone's attention. "I'm having a hard time hearing you. Speak up."

"I can't do this, Brandon."

"Can't do what? You have to stay put until the case is over."

"I can't be a prisoner every time you have a case. It's not fair to me."

"We'll talk when I get home."

"Please, Brandon, don't make this any harder."

Why was she using my name so much? "I'm just in the middle of—"

"I'm leaving, Brandon."

My arm dropped. My breath stalled. I knew Paige stood in front of me, but my focus wasn't on anything in particular. There was something in Deb's voice, in the way she kept repeating my name. I chose to play to ignorant. "You can't go back to the house. Where is Nadia? Put her back on."

"You're not listening to me. Again." The last word hurled through the airwaves as a punch to the gut.

"Why?" The single word contained all of the heartache that seized control of my thoughts.

"We just want different things. You know it. You can't keep pretending forever. We married young—"

"We were in love."

"Were, Brandon, or still are?"

What does she want from me?

"We'll talk when I get back," I said.

"I won't be—"

I took a deep breath. This happened to other people, not

us. "You're—" I wanted to say *ending our marriage over the phone*, but I knew Paige was listening to the conversation.

"You can reach me on my new cell," Deb interrupted. "You have the number?"

"Of course, I—"

"Be careful, Brandon. Come home safe." She hung up leaving me with more questions than answers. My world had been devastated by an earthquake, the very foundations cracked and crumbling.

Come home *safe? Where exactly was that now?*

"Brandon, are you okay?"

Paige's question broke through. I held the phone to my ear as if Deb remained on the other end.

"Are you okay?" She put a hand on my shoulder.

I dropped my arm and clipped the cell in its holder. "I...I'll be fine."

"Brandon?"

I looked in her eyes. "We have a case to solve."

We held eye connect for a few seconds before she removed her hand.

I respected that she cared enough not to pry and allowed me distance to deal with this *thing* that happened to other people. I needed to focus first on the case, second on my marriage. Once I got back, the unsub up on charges, then I would talk with her, and she'd see the stupidity in splitting up. I would prove to her that I still loved her.

"I don't think—" I jacked a thumb to the apartment building behind us "—she's in any trouble."

"No imminent threat that we have reason to suspect anyway. Ninety-one was twenty years ago now. She'd be dead if they wanted her to be."

"She said her husband was a drunk and a cheat." I looked away from Paige when I said the last word. Had I ruined my marriage by sleeping with Paige? Had Deb known all this time?

"And we know the first victim in Salt Lick, Bingham's

brother-in-law, beat on his sister."

"He's definitely exacting punishment on those who are sinners."

"And he seems to be picking his victims from church congregations. Denise said they went to the Lakeview Community Church a few times."

"People who should know better than to sin." The words slipped from my lips, and the revelation hit. "There's a year or so between kills. It's not about availability. It's about gaining the victim's trust."

"But Denise Hogan couldn't ID Bingham."

"Couldn't or wouldn't? But we can't make her talk."

Paige shrugged.

"Bingham didn't get close to his victims so he could manipulate them into his home. He got close to them to know their sins—"

"And exact punishment?"

"Exactly."

"THAT WOULD BE A UNIQUE profile for a serial killer," Zachery said. "Most aren't familiar with their victims. It's statistically stranger-on-stranger murders."

"That's the norm out of a textbook, but statistics are always proven wrong." Paige smiled at me.

I was still numb from Deb's words, *I'm leaving, Brandon.*

Paige and I were back in my room at the hotel on a conference call with Jack and Zachery. The retired detective Jenkins was there as well. My attention kept drifting to the mini bar. I knew alcohol wasn't the answer, but it sure helped at times. I needed to get home, talk to Deb. I would make this all better if I could. With Denise Hogan's statements, there wasn't a need for us to be in Sarasota any longer.

"We do know that Bingham is a definite narcissist," Zachery said. "Narcissists are pros at getting close to people for their advantage. Normally, they would want their victims to know who was killing them. It gives them power, elevates them."

"If he did pull all his victims from church members, they would make perfect targets. They're taught to believe the best about people," I added.

"Are you saying those who go to church are gullible?" I recognized the voice as belonging to the detective.

I didn't answer. I wasn't in the mood to debate religion. No one said anything for ten seconds.

"So your conclusion is that Bingham became friends with those he killed," Jack summarized, "and that he did so with the purpose of finding out their sins to punish them."

"Yeah, or maybe it just happened. As he got close, he noticed their weaknesses and snapped? Maybe he has some sort of bad experience with religion, a controlling parent or something."

"That would coincide with the statistics of a narcissist. There're certain factors from childhood that can contribute, such as a strict upbringing," Zachery said.

"We need to look more into Bingham's background and find out who he was in Sarasota."

In response to Jack's words, Paige gave me lopsided smile as if to say, *Guess we won't be going home quite yet.*

"Keith Knowles, Anna's husband, found God after her death. It was his reason for defending the fact he would never hurt her. Maybe he made the change because he sought forgiveness." Jenkins offered this.

"We've spent hours going over the case, and you're just telling us this now?" Jack's voice held anger.

"I didn't realize it factored into this."

"There's a good reason you're retired."

"Hey."

The following thirty seconds of silence had Paige and me looking at each other expectantly and latching eyes wondering if we should break it. Jenkins did.

"Knowles became a priest actually."

"Which church?"

Jenkins named the church. "And I believe it's still around."

"And Knowles? He still around?"

"Don't know."

"Yet you suspected him of killing your daughter?"

"I haven't for years."

"Why, because he found God?"

I imagined them in locked eye contact. One older man against the other, both stubborn, both refusing to back down.

"There wasn't any evidence."

"That doesn't stop a good detective."

"Jenkins could be on to something with this," Zachery said.

Jack groaned. "I'll have Nadia locate Keith Knowles and get a congregation list together from the seventies. Maybe Bingham will be on it, or, at the very least, maybe someone is still alive who knew Bingham."

"Because he was born here?" I asked. It seemed like a fishing expedition without adequate tools, basically a string tied onto a stick to catch a shark.

"Is there something else you'd like to do?"

"I just thought we were finished and would be headed back."

"I'll have Nadia send the list. Get back to me on what you find—"

"Jack." I pictured his finger poised over the disconnect call button.

"Yes."

"Did anything come back on the surveillance devices? The fingerprint on the audio recorder?" I asked, desperate.

"I'll let you know once we do." He terminated the call.

The space between Paige and I fell silent.

"Brandon?" Paige pierced the quiet.

I could feel her gaze on me, but I couldn't look at her.

"You sure you're okay?"

I inhaled a deep, jagged breath. "I just thought we'd be

headed home."

"This shouldn't be too bad."

"We're sitting around waiting on a list of people."

"Sometimes the job involves waiting."

"I'd just rather—"

My cell rang, and I answered without checking the identity of the caller. "Hello." There was nothing but dead air. "If this is you, you son of a bitch—"

"Whoa, I see you're still a fiery redhead."

It took me a moment to place the voice. I answered anticipating it being Debbie wanting to retract her earlier decision. Then with the silence I had assumed it was the unsub, but it was neither. "Randy?"

Randy Whalin and I were best buddies before the move to Virginia. He had never settled down and teased me about the decision to marry young whenever he had the opportunity.

"How goes it as a special agent for the FBI?" He put on an uppity voice and laughed.

He made me smile despite my mind being a tangled mess between work and personal. "On a huge case, actually."

"Oh, your first time out? You've had your cherry popped." Randy thought of himself as a player, and I had to admit the guy did all right. "When are you coming home? The bars aren't the same without you. I need my fall guy."

"Aw, touching, man, but I'm working."

We used to frequent a bar called Sassy's on Main. I always made Randy look good by acting like a sleaze. Randy would jump in and save them from the drunk, grabby guy.

"That sucks."

"Yeah." My eyes scanned the hotel room. We were sitting around waiting on a list. "Maybe we could meet up for drinks." I glanced at Paige, who cocked her head to the side.

"I thought you were—"

"Forget what I said. I'm actually in the city."

"Really?"

"I'll explain later. Sassy's for eight?"

"Date." Randy laughed. "I really need to get laid."

I was smiling when I hung up.

"Sassy's?" Paige's fawn eyes watched me. She wasn't going to like this.

"It's a bar."

"We're working."

"Do we not get any time off the clock?"

"Not much and not during an investigation on the scale of this one. It's not a nine-to-five job."

"I'm familiar with the FBI website Paige, but it's an old buddy of mine. It would mean a lot right now."

"I don't know."

"You might even like him."

Her eyes hardened over. "I'm in a relationship."

"You're sleeping with someone. There's a difference."

"What are you saying, Brandon?" Paige stood there, her expression full of anger and pain.

"I didn't mean—"

"Yes, you did."

"Just a few drinks before bed."

She didn't say anything, and a text came through on her phone. She checked it out and didn't say anything.

"I take it that's not the member list."

"Good work, Sherlock." She left the room, slamming the door behind her.

I was feeling too sorry for myself to go after her. I turned instead toward the mini bar.

LANCE BINGHAM SMILED. Those feds thought they were so intelligent by screening his mail, but they didn't know he had the perfect system worked out. They likely never would figure it out, and that was why he was really the one in charge of the investigation. They only found what he left for them.

He hadn't always been a country hillbilly who fed hungry hogs. He'd been places, been educated, not that it was from any school nor did he have a diploma to frame and hang.

Life taught him more than any textbook ever could.

He knew the feds would have connected the bodies from Florida already, but he had been younger and, dare he admit to himself, more careless back then. He hadn't had as much restraint. The method of killing had been different, but he still had fond memories of the self-control he had demonstrated in wielding the knife in a rough circular motion, but all the willpower climaxed when he had placed the plastic bag over their heads and suffocated them. They had thrashed but to no avail.

Bingham's smile widened.

Their fighting for their life and losing the battle had brought elation to him. The steps to get to that point drained him of control. The kill was the release. It was up to him whether they would live or die.

The guard led him out to the courtyard.

He squinted as the contrast between the darkness of the prison and the light of day proved blinding for a few seconds. It made him think of the Bible story where God blinded the man on the road striking him in punishment for his sin.

The smile on Bingham's face sobered. He was sent to do serious work. He didn't kill simply for pleasure. He killed to cleanse the Earth, and it wasn't like he set out knowing this was his mission in life. As with higher callings, it struck him as an epiphany one day. He had deeply cared for his first kill, loved her even. At least what he knew of love, but it didn't mean anything at this point. She had betrayed everyone.

Bingham sat on the top of a picnic table in the prison yard and rested his feet on the bench portion. The warden walked by, looking condescendingly on him and the other inmates, a thing which Bingham found hypocritical as the warden wasn't a religious man. He was in no position to judge the people here. Yet it wasn't Bingham's place to teach the warden either. People who weren't drawn to God didn't know any better and couldn't be held accountable for their sins.

Those who knew and yet sinned committed the greatest sin.

With the warden's back now to him and knowing he wouldn't circle back around, Bingham pulled the envelope from the waist of his pants. This was his favorite time of day. Just knowing that someone else carried on the good work until he reclaimed his freedom would get him through his sentence.

He carefully handled the envelope, tearing it along the seam. He pulled the paper from its sleeve and smelled it. For an instant, he felt transported to the last kill when there had been three, a triad of power, before acting on an impulse that had landed him in prison.

Bingham looked over the yard at the imbeciles with whom he shared the correction facility. They dribbled a basketball and collected in clusters. Another guard came along and broke them up. They were worthy of confinement. They acted on their own agendas. He had acted on the highest authority.

Bingham smiled as he unfolded the letter. The words caused the smile to fade and become replaced with consuming anger.

"WE'VE BEEN OVER THESE FILES at least fifteen times now."

Jack smiled at Zachery. "I'll trust your count to be accurate."

Between the records and trying to access the memories of the retired detective, they hoped to derive some relevant information to get them closer to the unsub.

Jenkins appeared more ready for sleep than to be of any assistance. He dragged a hand down his face and gently slapped himself before dropping his hand to his lap where he clasped it with the other one.

Nadia walked into the room. "Boss, I have something. It just came over now. I swear to you."

Jack looked at the file she held in her hands. It was labeled

SURVEILLANCE EQUIPMENT—THE REDEEMER CASE NO. R238923. "They were to call me with the findings."

"Like I said, they just showed up."

"Hmm."

Nadia held up her hands in surrender and stepped back toward the doorway.

"How's the congregation list coming?"

She took another few steps backward. "Almost there. I've contacted the church administrator. It should be—"

"The minute it gets here."

"Yes, boss." She cleared the doorway.

Jack could handle another cigarette right now. Something in his gut told him they were narrowing in on the unsub. He patted his pocket as if for some reason to delay the opening of the folder and the forensic findings. He knew Zachery and the old man watched with impatient eyes. Jack opened the folder and read what was inside. "Get that kid on the phone now!"

Thirty-One

The ringing phone cut through the minute trace of happiness that had come from the few small bottles of whiskey I drank back-to-back from the mini-bar. I sat slumped forward, watching out the window over the street. People all had somewhere to be, people waiting on them. I had no one now. I tore off the lid of a fourth bottle and swung it back before I answered.

"Special Agent Fisher."

"Kid, we got a hit on the fingerprint from the recording device."

I sat back, the fresh swig of whiskey soothing me. Even the sound of Jack's voice didn't have the ability to jar me sober. "Who?"

"The guy's name is Peter Robinson. He's on file for assaulting his wife a couple years back, Apparently, he held a knife on her—but, Brandon, he's in Sarasota. He owns a pawnshop on the corner of Clark and South Lockwood Ridge Road."

"We'll go now." I stood, holding the cell between my ear and shoulder, and hoisted up the holster around my waist. The combination of rising quickly and the whiskey had me lightheaded.

"Round up local PD. Go in hot, but just remember that he could be the unsub we've been looking for."

Go in hot. I always thought that was something they said in the movies.

"I'm texting the information to your cell, and, Kid?"

"Yeah."

"Don't mess this up."

"You can count on—" The line went dead.

If Jack knew I was drinking on the job, I wouldn't have to worry about my career factoring into my marriage.

"ARE YOU GOING TO APOLOGIZE?"

"I don't believe I did anything."

"You basically called me a slut."

"I'm not in the mood right now."

Paige leaned in toward my mouth and sniffed. "You've been drinking."

We headed down the elevator to the lobby. Local PD had been called in.

"If Jack finds out—"

"Is he going to?"

Paige's jaw tightened, and she turned to face the elevator doors. "No."

SOMETHING MUST BE SAID FOR flying through a city at the speed of seventy miles per hour with cruisers trailing behind, sirens wailing, and their lights reflecting off the glass buildings like a kaleidoscope.

Paige drove while I rode shotgun because, as she said, I wasn't in any shape to drive. The rental sedan rocked as if on stormy seas. Any more whiskey, and it would be revisiting.

"Let me take the lead with Robinson," Paige said.

I didn't say anything, and she glanced over. She swerved through traffic like a ribbon weaving through a basket. How she managed with only half her attention on the road, the rest devoted to me, I didn't know.

"Why were you drinking anyway?"

"Call it lunch."

She scrunched up her face. "What—"

"We've been putting in overtime. The way I see it, lunch is

my time. On my time—"

"It's after four in the afternoon, and you drink yourself shit-faced?"

"I'm not—"

"Just don't let it happen again—and don't fuck this up."

"Does this mean we're good?"

"Not even close." The car jolted forward as she pressed on the accelerator.

I couldn't wait for the ride to be over.

THE PAWNSHOP, that was its actual name, was located on the corner of Clark and South Lockwood Ridge Road, as Jack had said. The windows were plastered with posters announcing cash advances, discount electronics, and *We Buy Gold* advertisements.

Paige parked the car near a fire hydrant. She had that look—brow furrowed, eyes narrowed—that said she wasn't one to be messed with.

"You follow behind, watch my six."

"Not a problem."

"Don't even try to be funny at a time like this. We know what this guy is capable of."

"I got it."

"All right then." She directed a few police officers around the back of the building to secure the perimeter.

I held the door for Paige.

A teenager wearing earbuds rifled through an assortment of classic rock CDs. Her head bobbed up and down like one of those bobbleheads people put in their car's rear windows.

Paige put a hand on her shoulder. The girl jumped.

"You need to leave." I grabbed her elbow and guided her to the door where I passed her off to a police officer. With the girl secured outside, Paige and I readied our guns and approached the counter.

A black man moved behind a display rack of watches that towered on the counter. All we could see was the top of his head and his arms.

"Peter Robinson, FBI."

He stepped to the side of the display. His eyes went to our guns. "What the—"

"We need your hands in the air now!"

He complied with Paige's direction, his attention steadied on our drawn weapons.

"You're coming with us."

"I don't think so." His one arm went under the counter.

"Lift your arms in the air!"

"You can't make me." His arm extended under the counter.

"Last warning. Hands in the air!"

"I can't go to—"

Paige had a shot off before I completely assessed the situation.

"Fuckin' son of a bitch!" Robinson staggered back a few steps. Blood spurted from his shoulder. He put a hand to it.

"Next time you won't be so lucky." Paige moved in closer to him, her gun readied to fire another round. "Let me see both your hands."

Peter Robinson raised his good arm in the air. "I can't go to jail."

Sergeant Haynes of Sarasota PD came in the front door and spoke into a phone. "We need a bus on Clark just east of South Lockwood Ridge Road for a GSW."

"Stay back from the counter. Keep your arm in the air. Face the door." I headed toward the counter, taking my steps slowly. "You mess up in any way my partner will shoot to kill."

Peter Robinson's eyes begged for mercy.

Shoot to kill. I had been trained for this if the situation deemed it necessary. I swallowed back on the smell of whiskey that came up from my lungs and made eye contact with the suspect.

Paige stepped behind the counter. "Hands behind your back now."

He complied. "I didn't do it."

"Do what, Mr. Robinson?"

"Whatever you think I did."

Paige snapped the cuffs on, wrenching his wounded shoulder back. Peter Robinson let out a wail.

"Is this 'cause I'm black?"

"Yeah, that's it. The whole world's out to get you." Paige tugged on his arms. "Let's go."

The wails of the ambulance siren were approaching.

"This is where I would normally say you take the car and I'll go with Robinson, but—"

I read her eyes, *You shouldn't even be here.* "I'm fine."

"Where the hell do you think I'm goin', lady? You shot me."

Paige ignored the man and spoke to me, "You sure?"

"I'm fine," I repeated my words.

She studied my eyes as if by staring into them she'd have an answer on whether or not to believe me.

The wails of the sirens muted as they arrived on scene. The paramedics got out of the bus almost as if they simply pulled to a stop and tucked and rolled.

One headed straight to Robinson but glared at Paige. "You cuffed him."

"Damn straight I did."

"You shot him then cuffed him?" He examined Robinson's shoulder while talking to Paige.

"Nothing slips past you."

"I'm going to need you to uncuff him."

"If you knew what he's done you wouldn't—"

"So much for the innocent until proven guilty BS, I guess. I always figured it was a line of crock."

"You're talking to a federal agent."

"And you're talking to a paramedic, and this isn't my first time out. The man has rights."

I noticed the small twitch in Paige's cheek. She broke eye contact with the man and undid the cuffs. "He's not leaving my sight."

The other paramedic came to them pushing a stretcher with a medical bag on it. As they worked on Robinson, Paige's eyes didn't leave the man.

"IT WAS JUST A LITTLE BULLET." Paige paced while I leaned against the wall.

We were at Sarasota Memorial Hospital waiting on Robinson to come out of surgery. Paige insisted that we stay right outside the operating room just in case he made a run for it. I tried to convince her he wasn't going anywhere.

I had followed behind her in the rental sedan while she rode in the ambulance. We met up here at least an hour ago, and she hadn't stopped talking about Robinson or the paramedic who thought he was "the ruler of the world"— her words.

"We should probably call in and let them know how we made out," I proposed.

"And what? Tell Jack I shot the guy?"

"He'd probably be proud of you." I smiled at her, and she returned it.

"Yeah, he probably would be." She laughed and ran a hand through her hair. "God, it's been a long week."

"Why we deserve some down time."

"I thought you had some of that today already."

For some reason her saying that brought everything to the surfaced again. The ache inflicted from Deb's words had never left, but at this moment they weighed me down further.

Paige shook her head, and her eyes softened. "I didn't mean anything by—"

"I know. I was stupid. First case, and I—"

"Agents."

Both of us turned to face a decorated officer. He was probably about the same age as Paige, in his early forties.

"I'm Brennan, Chief of Police." He rested a hand on his right hip, but a finger rose and pointed toward Paige. "I believe we talked on the phone."

"We did. Thank you for cooperating with a federal investigation."

"You might not be thanking me in a bit. Is it true you shot the suspect?"

"In self-defense. It was a non-fatal wound."

"We never recovered any weapons at The Pawnshop. I fail to see how Mr. Robinson could have posed a threat."

"He was told to leave his arms in the air, several times. He failed to obey that direct order—"

"So you feel that gave you the right to shoot a Sarasota resident?" The chief glanced at me.

I came to Paige's defense. "He didn't comply. He gave her no choice. Statistically, most pawnshop owners are armed for protection—"

"Do FBI agents run around shooting people based on statistics these days? You must believe that all black kids are in gangs, all serial killers are white and in their thirties."

Paige glared at me as if to say, *Stop trying to help me.* She addressed the police chief. "I appreciate this is your city but, this case—"

"Let me guess, top secret. Something above my pay grade."

Paige's phone rang, and mine chimed to announce a new text message.

"I have to take this." Paige answered her phone.

The chief studied me from my shoes to the top of my head and ended with eye contact. "Don't get me wrong, I respect the FBI, but you come to town, don't even notify us you're working on an investigation, and then call us in to back you up. It hardly seems fair—"

"I was just about to call you…" Paige turned her back on us and spoke into the phone.

"We notified local authorities at the point necessary."

Seconds passed. Brennan spoke. "You feds have everything worked out. Politics—never did like them much."

I wanted to say, and yet you're the police chief.

"It got a little out of control...Yes, he's in surgery...He'll be fine. It's just a little shoulder wound."

"On an unarmed man," Brennan spoke up no doubt hoping the caller would hear him.

"Yeah...That's the police chief...What can I say? I'm good at making friends...We'll keep you updated." Paige shut her phone and spun around, a finger was aimed straight at Brennan's nose. "Don't you ever talk when I'm on the phone again." She held the eye contact for about thirty seconds before pointing the finger at me. "You stay here. I'm going for a coffee."

"Sure."

"You want one?"

"Sounds good."

She drew her pointed finger from me to the chief. "Don't say a word to him."

The sound of her shoes on the hospital floors was rushed and angry. Her arms swung more than normal with her stride, and her hips swayed like a pendulum.

"She's a firecracker," he observed.

"You have no idea."

"What are you here for anyway?" He jerked a thumb toward the operating room. "What do you think he did?"

"We can't say."

"Yet you want our cooperation." He slipped his hands into his pockets.

"We have the man now."

"And you're sure of this?"

The man's prints were lifted from the audio device. At the very least, coincidental evidence pointed to this man being the Redeemer's follower, but none of this could be shared with Brennan.

"Huh, no answer. You just remember you might need us again."

"And if we do we'll notify you immed—"

"Agent, don't make promises you're not authorized to

make. You smell of a newbie." He inhaled deeply as if he were a hound picking up on a scent. "Otherwise, I can't see you letting her lead you around by the balls."

"She's—"

"Don't deny it son. She's the senior while you're the junior."

"The title's Special Agent actually."

"Aren't you missing the pending part?"

"Well, if you have something else to do we have this covered."

"Do they let you drink while on duty as an FBI agent?"

My eyes darted to his. "Excuse me."

Brennan smiled. "Good day, Special Agent."

Thirty-Two

The operating room doors swung open, and Doctor Hopkins, who performed Robinson's surgery, came out.

Paige pushed herself from the wall.

"Mr. Robinson is going to be just fine," Hopkins answered before Paige verbalized the question.

Paige didn't respond with a smile or project any sense of relief. "When can we speak with him?"

"He's in recovery right now. It will take a few hours for the anesthesia to wear off. Even then, things will be a little hazy for him."

I looked at my watch. Five fifteen.

"Thank you, doctor," Paige said.

"Uh-huh." He backed into the operating room.

"This is just great," Paige huffed, crossed her arms, and stood there tapping her foot. "What are we supposed to do? Just wait around for hours? What about the church members? Do you have the list yet? You got a text hours ago when I was talking with Jack."

With the excitement from then until now I hadn't checked the message. It had begun as procrastination in fear it would be Debbie with more bad news although I wasn't sure how much worse it could get.

"You still haven't checked it?"

I pulled out my phone and opened it. One unread message. I noticed the sender and clipped the phone back in its holder.

"You still haven't read it."

"It doesn't matter."

"It's her, isn't it?" Paige's face softened.

"Her?" I turned my back on Paige and walked down the hallway.

"Your wife." Paige followed behind.

I stopped walking and faced her. "Robinson will be fine here. We can call in the local LEOs to watch over him." Also known as law enforcement officers.

"After we made such good friends with the chief of police?" Her lips cracked in a sarcastic smile. "Nice subject switch by the way."

"I don't want to talk about my life right now. How about we just go have a couple of drinks with Randy, come back in the morning. Robinson's head will be fresh then."

"I don't know."

"Paige, I'm going. I'd like you to come, too. There's nothing we can do here tonight. You heard the doctor. Even in a few hours, Robinson's head will be hazy. Maybe if you hadn't shot him…" I was smiling, but Paige didn't notice until her arm extended to strike me.

"You think you're funny."

"I know I am."

"Huh." She put an arm on my shoulder, patted it. "Let's go then, but we're coming back first thing."

I held up a hand as if swearing an oath.

"All right, I'll let them know when we'll be back."

My cell vibrated with another text message. I made myself look at it. "It's Nadia. She said the list is taking a little longer to get her hands on. She's having a hard time reaching the church administrator."

Paige smiled and looped an arm in mine. "Guess we do have the night off. You're sure he's not going anywhere?"

"Where's he gonna go? You cuffed him to the stretcher."

DEB'S TEXT MESSAGE FROM EARLIER in the day, the one I wished had been the congregation list, went through my mind: I've been thinking about this for a long time, Brandon. I don't want you to feel responsible for my decision.

Paige must have sensed the text was bothering me on the way to Sassy's, not that she had any idea what it said, but she kept trying to make small talk.

"So this bar? You and—"

"Randy."

"You used to go there a lot?"

I smiled. This diversion tactic helped somewhat. "Every Friday night for wings and pitchers of beer."

"Pitchers? Why should I be surprised?"

Paige and I had gone back to the hotel from the hospital and changed into more casual apparel. Both of us wore blue jeans. I wore mine with a white shirt, and Paige paired her jeans, which clung to her figure flawlessly, with a black sleeveless collared shirt.

"So besides wings and beer, what does this place offer?" I noticed Paige's attention go to the clock on the dash. "You said eight, right?"

"Yeah, we'll be a little late."

"Hope he understands."

I laughed. "Randy's probably further off from making it there than we are."

"Tell me about this guy." Paige rubbed her hands on her thighs.

The motion made me jealous of her hands. "He's a guy's guy. He likes to think of himself as a player, so you might want to be careful."

"I can handle my own."

"I know you can."

Her smile faded. "Do you think Robinson did it?"

"He has a background, and his fingerprint was on the audio equipment."

"I'm just not sure he's intelligent enough."

"Why 'cause he's black?" I laughed, just teasing her. I knew she wasn't prejudiced in any manner, nor was I.

She cocked her head to the side and slapped my arm. "It's just all we really have at this point is a print."

"So you shot an innocent man."

She let out a rush of air. "Maybe I did. Guess we'll have a better idea when we get to talk to him."

"If you didn't shoot him we might be now—"

"Brandon, one more word and—"

I twisted an imaginary lock over my lips.

SASSY'S HADN'T CHANGED SINCE THE last time I'd been here. Gold letters contrasted against the red painted brick. The wrought iron fence outlined the patio where about ten tables lined the front. The patio butted up against the sidewalk and lent itself to foot traffic. To get an outside table, especially on a night like this one, would be nearly impossible. Music droned through exterior speakers, and inside it filled the place with a cacophony of noise as it mingled with the raised voices of its patrons, but people didn't come to Sassy's to talk. They came to have a few drinks, watch a game, and kick back.

"Nice place." Paige smiled as she pressed into my side. "A little loud."

"Yeah, it's perfect."

She bumped an elbow into my ribs. I instinctively wanted to wrap an arm around her, but somehow, I found the willpower not to.

A table of college students roared, making Paige jump. She laughed. "Oh, I need a drink."

"Your wish is my com—"

"Buddy." I heard the word and felt the jab to my lower back.

"Randy."

We reached our arms around each other and patted each

other's backs. When he noticed Paige standing there, Randy backed out of the hug.

"That was just a bro hug."

"Uh-huh." She smiled at him. The way she looked at him stung me with jealousy.

Randy swung an arm back and hit me in the abdomen. "You going to introduce me?" he asked with his gaze going to Paige.

"Randy, this is Special Agent Paige Dawson. She's on my team with the BAU."

"Would you listen to him talking all proper?" Randy extended a hand to Paige and introduced himself. "He probably told you all about me. Don't believe anything he said unless it's good."

"He didn't say a lot about you."

"Oh, that hurts, man." Randy laughed. "And here I have nothing but great things to say about you." Randy patted my shoulder before tucking his hand into a jean pocket. "How are you doing? How's Debbie? You're looking well."

Hearing her name hammered in the reality that my wife no longer loved me.

This happened to other people—not me!

"Why don't we get that drink?" Paige redirected, and Randy looked at her then at me before letting the matter go.

"I'm always ready for one."

"Don't I know it," I said.

"Don't listen to him. He already had a wee nip this afternoon."

"On the job?"

"That's what I said." Paige laughed.

I watched the two of them walk up to the bar ahead of me. They would make a good couple. Both of them loved their freedom but craved human connection. It made me miss Deb even more.

FOR THE NEXT FEW HOURS, we drowned our logical thinking

in the amber liquid of frivolity. We moved to a table on the patio about ten, and none of us seemed in a hurry to leave. The light from the moon and the manmade lights of the patio cast a sort of spell.

We talked about Randy's work as a graphic designer and how his bosses seemed to think they owned him like a piece of property. They would interrupt him when he was designing and treat him as if he wasn't doing anything.

"They're just making really stupid decisions." Randy gulped some beer. "Why pull me off a job that's going to make the company money to redesign the company van? Stupid."

"We all have bosses who don't get it," I said. Paige glanced at me. "At least your bosses call you by name."

Randy tightened his grip on the beer mug, lifted it to his mouth. "You don't have a name?"

"Guess I haven't earned one yet."

Randy scrunched up his face. "Okay." His single word carried the invitation, *Please, elaborate.*

"I'm referred to only by nicknames."

"So he likes you then."

"I'm not a pet."

That comment made Randy and Paige laugh.

"To him, I'm Kid or Slingshot."

"Oh, I like Slingshot." Randy took another swig.

"You wouldn't if you were me."

"This guy takes himself too seriously sometimes, doesn't he?" Randy jabbed his beer mug toward Paige, who lifted a shoulder.

"And he's always going around saying 'hmm.' What the heck is that supposed to mean anyway? Speak like a human being."

"Brandon, I think that's enough," Paige said.

"What? I'm just telling the truth."

"Jack is a great man."

"You're only saying that because you sleep with him." The

words came out, and her cheeks flushed red as if she were slapped. "I'm sorry."

Paige leaned back into her chair and crossed her arms.

"Don't mind him. He can be a donkey sometimes," Randy said.

"You're telling me?" She wouldn't look at me. Instead, her focus was on another table where a group of four held mugs of beer up in a cheer.

"He's probably just jealous." Randy looked over at me with a smile.

I wasn't smiling. Randy didn't know about the past affair with Paige, but his assessment was right.

"We should get back," Paige moved forward.

I settled into my chair, cradled the mug of beer, and took a slow, deliberate sip. "He doesn't get people. Jack is the most unfeeling person I know."

"You don't even know him."

"Explain him to me then, would you? He doesn't believe in hope—"

"False hope."

"He misleads people. That woman is going to lose the pig farm that's been in her family for generations."

"There was," Paige stopped talking, cognizant of Randy taking every word in.

"He made her believe everything would be fine when he knew the truth was going to be the opposite."

"He's been through a lot in life. It hasn't been easy—"

"We all have shit to shovel. No excuse."

A waitress came to the table. "Can I get you guys anything else?"

"Cup of coffee for me," Paige said.

Nothing was worse than being stranded somewhere without the ability to leave, but since both of us had kept drinking we were in no position to drive.

"Anyone else?" the waitress asked. Both Randy and I declined. "All right, then, I'll be right back."

"And he smokes all the time. I'll probably have lung cancer when I get older."

"If you hate it so much, leave the team. No one's making you stay." Paige excused herself to Randy and took off down the sidewalk.

Randy looked to me. "You're just going to let her go?"

I sunk my lips onto the rim of my beer glass. "She can handle herself."

"Wow, I don't know what being an FBI agent is doing to you, but you're a different guy." Randy got up and left me there.

I DRANK PAIGE'S COFFEE AND ordered a refill. The crowd at Sassy's was starting to dwindle. No doubt most had left in search of a hot night club.

"Can I get you anything else?" The waitress had long since cleared the table of the beer pitcher and glasses. Our plates and the platter of the appetizers we ordered had long been taken away.

"Just the bill."

She smiled at me and nodded.

She was a polite waitress, but her interest in her customers never went beyond her job. She never gave me the look most women did, the inquisitive kind that pried into your mind and tried to solve your problems. It may have been what I needed anyway—a stranger who would simply let me brood over my feelings. My wife no longer wanted to be married, but I would make it right. I would make Deb see that we could work things out.

I heard Paige's laugh before I saw her. When she and Randy came into view, she slapped his arm. Her head arched back, exposing the length of her neck.

"Oh, he's still here." Randy came to the table. "We were hoping you would have covered the bill by now. We can go for another walk." He smiled at Paige who returned it.

"I was considering making a run for it." I smiled, too,

although I had to force it and its appearance didn't showcase for long. "So how was it?" I asked the question of Paige. "I hope he treated you right."

Paige remained standing. "Fine. We should really get going. I'm okay to drive."

I got up and extended a hand to Randy, who pulled me into a hug. He felt the need to explain the affection again. "Bro hug."

"Well, that's how you guys started the night so it seems fitting you would end it the same way." She extended a hand to Randy. "Nice getting to know you."

When they shook hands, their connection lingered. Their focus was on each other.

"Early morning." I pulled out forty bucks to go toward the bill and set it on the table.

"Yeah, we better go." Paige didn't even glance at me. She slipped her hand out of Randy's and backed away.

"Good luck with the case you're working on."

"Thanks."

Our backs already to him, I waved a hand over my head.

BY THE TIME WE REACHED the hotel, it was just after midnight. I was tired and ready to crawl into bed, but what I wanted even more was to feel needed. Paige talked about Randy most of the drive, how he was a real decent guy, maybe just a little confused about his direction in life, but otherwise "stellar." Although I loved the guy like a brother, jealousy interfered with my vision.

On the drive to the hotel, I had leaned back on the headrest and inhaled Paige's perfume. It hadn't changed since we had slept together. Nostalgia transported me to the past, to the afternoons we'd slip away to a hotel room where we'd make love and afterward fall asleep in each other's arms. I remembered waking to her perfume and the smell of her. I remembered the showers we took together and how the soapsuds lathered on her skin.

"It was fun tonight," she said, as we both stood in the hotel hallway. Both of our rooms were on the tenth floor next to each other's.

"Yeah."

"Why do you say it like that?"

As she was in front of me, I realized again how small she was in comparison to me. I recalled how when we had hugged her head dropped at the height of my collarbone. "Like what?"

"Like you don't mean it."

"No, it was good to see him."

"He is a great guy." Paige smiled.

"He's all right."

"He's all right? I thought you guys were best friends?" Her eyes peered into mine.

"Anyway, I'm tired."

"Don't change the subject again." Anger flashed in her eyes.

"I'm not trying to. I'm tired. I'm calling it a night."

"What aren't you saying, Brandon? Why don't you get it out?"

"Night, Paige."

Her hand came out and pulled on my forearm. "Don't leave like this."

"Like what?"

"You're that stubborn?"

"I'm not sure what you're talking—"

"You're jealous."

I did my best to conjure a sarcastic laugh. "Of what?"

Seconds passed. Her eyes locked on mine. "You can be such an ass."

"You can be such a b—"

"Don't even say it, Brandon. You don't have the right to say who I like, who I see, who I sleep with. You understand that? Because if you don't, you better start." She walked to her room, slid her passkey through the lock, and cracked the door open. She turned to me before slipping inside. "You have no right." She slammed the door behind her.

I didn't realize what I was doing until it was too late. My fist rose and knocked on her door. She cracked it open enough so that I had access to enter her room. I put my hands on her neck, tilted it back, and kissed her. I became intoxicated by her taste, her smell. She let me maneuver her as if she were moldable clay, as if she had waited for this moment.

"Brandon," my name was carried in a hushed whisper, a partial moan.

I took her mouth with the hunger of a man who hadn't eaten for days. I made love to her tongue, to her lips, to her neck. I wanted her, but as I kept indulging in the forbidden, Deb's face haunted my thoughts. I pulled back, jagged breaths escaping. I swallowed deeply, bit on my lip, trying to sedate the insatiable hunger that couldn't be satisfied. I ran my hands down her arms and held her hands. Her eyes were misted with tears and narrowed with a sexual craving. They weren't the eyes of a stranger but the eyes of a known lover.

"I'm sorry, but—"

"I—" She swallowed deeply, her breath uneven. "I understand."

I took her mouth again before pulling back.

"I love you, Brandon."

I swept a hand through her hair. "I know you do." I couldn't allow myself to speak the words in return even if I thought I felt the same way. "I'll see you in the morning?"

She nodded and closed the door slowly behind me, leaving me alone in the hallway.

Thirty-Three

The banging on the door pulled me from a dream where Deb was crying and telling me she took back everything she had said. Deb lifted her shirt and there were slice marks in her torso. My breathing was rushed from the dream-transformed-nightmare.

The knocking on the door repeated. "Open up."

I got up from the bed and nearly tripped and fell on the hotel carpet when my foot got wrapped up in the comforter that lay on the floor. I undid the chain and opened the door.

"What took you so long? We have to go." It was Paige, and she was already dressed.

I turned around to look at the clock on the nightstand. In my fuzzy state, I seemed to have forgotten it was not visible from the door. "What time is it?"

"Six. Get dressed." She glanced down at my boxer shorts and smiled. "Do you own a six-pack of the plaid ones?"

Instinct wanted me to reply, *You can find out if you want*, but the reality was until I knew for certain Deb was gone, I was a married man. "I'll be out in five." I inched the door closed with Paige being pushed backward into the hallway.

I only had time to turn around, and Paige banged on the door again. I didn't open the door but yelled out to her, "Five minutes."

I was impressed that I had adhered to the time limit I gave myself. Five minutes later, I opened the door dressed, armed, and ready to go. Paige wasn't as impressed. She was leaning against the far side of the hall. She pushed off with a foot when I came out.

"I need to tell you something, I should have told you yesterday."

"Sounds like a confession."

She waved a hand. Her cheeks flushed a light hue. "It has nothing to do with last night. All the same, I'd like to forget any of that happened."

The flash that fired through her eyes disclosed her pain. She didn't forget, nor did she want to. "Sure."

"I should have told you yesterday," she paused. "Jack's here."

"What—"

"Kid, you're up. Good thing we've got work to do."

My head snapped to face down the hall. Jack and Zachery were walking toward us.

Was this still part of my sleeping cycle? Was I having a continuing nightmare?

Paige leaned into me and whispered, "I should have told you yesterday."

"You knew?"

She nodded, and her eyes pleaded for forgiveness. "He told me when I took the call at the hospital."

"You knew," I repeated.

"You were going through something bad yesterday. You needed time to wind down."

We held eye contact until the other two reached us.

"Paige, good morning," Jack said.

"Morning." She dragged her eyes from mine to look at Jack.

"Pending." That seemed to suffice for Zachery's greeting.

"Why do you look like a deer in headlights, Kid? I'm sure Paige told you we'd be coming."

"Yeah, of course." The latter two words took a while to form. *She did tell me but only after I knew.*

"We're going to put this animal behind bars where he

belongs. I understand local PD is guarding him." Jack patted his shirt pocket for his beloved pack of cigarettes.

My throat was dry of moisture.

"You all right, Pending? You look a little peaked."

"Yeah, I'm fine."

Zachery laughed. "You don't do mornings very well."

"I'm fine."

"Well, all right then. Let's go," Jack said as he led the way down the hall, Zachery beside him, Paige and I trailing behind. "You two haven't forgotten how to hustle, I hope."

"No, boss, we're coming." Paige hit me in the forearm and we quickened our pace.

My brain didn't want to wake up. "You don't think it would be too much to get a cup of coffee to go?"

"In the car," Jack replied.

"You rented another—"

"We might be the government, Kid, but we still have a budget. I got a set of extra keys for the rental sedan."

"When did you get in? How?"

"Save the questions for Robinson, Slingshot."

SARASOTA'S FINEST WAS POSTED OUTSIDE Peter Robinson's room. The officer's head leaned forward, his triple chin resting on his chest. Jack slapped his arm.

The officer let out a few snorts and jolted awake. "I'm watching him."

"Looks like you're doing a great job."

The officer smiled at Jack, stood, and extended a hand. "I'm Officer Benson."

"You've been here all night?"

"Uh-huh." The head nodded rapidly, the extra weight the man carried jiggling with the movement.

"By yourself?"

The smile faded. He finally seemed to pick up on Jack's sarcasm. "Yes."

"No one else—" Jack glanced up and down the hospital

corridor both ways "—to sit with you?"

"No."

"You better hope he's in there." Jack left the officer standing there, gasping for a full breath.

Zachery, Paige, and I followed behind Jack. Peter Robinson was asleep with his mouth open. Feathered snores reverberated in his throat.

Officer Benson stood in the doorway.

"Good news for you because not only do you get to keep your job, you won't have to go to prison."

Benson put a hand to his chest and nodded.

Jack smacked his hands together, and Robinson woke with an outburst. "What the—" His words died as he looked at all of us.

Jack held up his creds. "Supervisory Special Agent Jack Harper."

Robinson appeared dazed, his eyes jumping to each of us.

Jack motioned for Zachery to dismiss Benson into the hallway.

The door clicked shut, and Robinson struggled to sit up. "I didn't do anything."

"You didn't help kill twenty-one people?"

Robinson's eyes watered, and he swallowed forcibly, causing his Adam's apple to heave. "Kill? Twenty-one?"

Jack fanned a bunch of the crime scene photos on the bed including one of Anna Knowles, the first victim in Sarasota.

"Brilliant, actually." Jack paced around the end of the bed and came up on the man's left side. "You have a masterful mind."

"I—" A hand flattened over his mouth. Seconds passed. "I couldn't kill nobody."

"You beat your wife."

"Now, that damned bitch she deserved—" His words stopped there.

"Did they deserve it, too?"

"You're twistin' my words outta order."

"Where were you earlier this week?"

"Whatcha mean? I was at my shop where I always am. Who's lookin' after it now?" Robinson appealed to me. I must have struck him as the weakest of everyone.

"You don't worry about your shop," Jack said.

"Don't worry 'bout my shop? That there's my livelihood. It helps me eat, have clothes." The accusation of multiple murders seemed to have snapped him from his sleep-induced haze. He collected the pictures together with his one free hand. The other remained cuffed to the bed. "Get those away from me. I've never liked dead bodies."

"But if they deserved it." Jack paced a few steps back to the end of the bed. "Can anyone prove you were at your shop four days ago?"

"The cash register can. I had sales."

"Anyone could have rung them through." Jack pulled a cigarette from the sleeve of the pack.

"You can't—"

Jack perched it in his lips unlit.

Robinson let out a sigh. "I work by myself."

"That's not what your tax returns claim."

His dark eyes flitted around the room, not fixing on anything or anyone.

"You falsified your returns. That's a federal crime. You can go to prison, be levied with huge fines."

He scratched at his right ear and adjusted his position on the bed. "It wasn't supposed to mean anything."

Those words reminded me of Royster's when we had showed up at his home. He had said, *No one was supposed to get hurt.*

"What you mean is you never intended to get caught."

"No, no, that's not—"

"That's exactly the truth, Mr. Robinson, but we're not interested in your evading the tax laws." Jack pulled the cigarette out of his mouth and held it between the middle and index finger of his right hand. "We're interested in why you did this." He pointed the cigarette in the direction of the photos. Robinson picked one up. "You're proud of those, aren't you? They deserved it after all."

"I—" Robinson studied the one in his hand and glanced at the others that were on the bed. "They have the coinherence symbol carved in them." He talked with his eyes back on the photo.

"You know what that is."

Robinson looked up at Jack. "It doesn't mean I put it there."

Jack dragged the visitor's chair from the corner of the room, positioned it beside Robinson's bed, and dropped into it. "What fascinates you about the symbol?"

"No, I ain't never said I was fascinated." Robinson shook his head.

Jack leaned back, crossed his leg, and let his left ankle rest on his right knee. "I know very little about it. It's religious?"

It was interesting observing Jack and how he handled Robinson. When I expected him to attack, he retreated. At this point, when I assumed he would lunge into matters, he remained quiet. His eyes never left the suspect.

This was an intimidation tactic taught to us. It was supposed to put the suspect at unease. The unrelenting eye contact was to make it harder for them to gauge the interrogator's thoughts. The intensity of being watched with such scrutiny made the human mind question itself. An innocent party could project guilt, manifesting itself in several ways such as fidgeting, or facial or body language. It was up to us to discern the motivator—fear or guilt.

"Maybe I know a little about it. I'm not ignorant."

Jack remained silent.

"It can represent many things from religious to philosophical to ideological teachings."

"It's fascinating how basic shapes and linear strokes can be the subject of such debate and intrigue over the centuries." Zachery stepped forward. Robinson's eyes went to him. "The interpretation of the symbol can virtually be endless, but the one thing always agreed upon is its simplicity and divinity of the number one. It's purity."

"Eleven inner points were consciously chosen in its design. Eleven represents perfection. The attributes of purity doubled in strength," Robinson added.

"It's time for you to answer that question, Mr. Robinson, why did you kill those people?" Jack resumed control over the interrogation.

"She shot me!" A pointed finger shot in Paige's direction. "An unarmed black man."

"The man suspected of being a serial killer." Jack drew Robinson's attention back to him.

"I told you. I couldn't kill anyone, deserving or not."

"But you like to decide."

"Do you not make decisions in life? Judge or condemn others for theirs? Then you and I are no different."

I noted the change in Jack's eyes. He picked up on what I saw. There was defensiveness that resided in Peter Robinson. Along with it came pride. The fact he knew so much about the coinherence symbol indicated intelligence. All of those factors corresponded with the characteristic traits Bingham demonstrated and that his follower would need, too.

"Life should be order. Instead, chaos is what rules," Robinson continued. "You have technology invented to simplify, yet we are busier than ever. Movements to save the environment that end up destroying it further."

"You believe you have ideas that would benefit everyone?"

"I know I do."

"Like what?"

"Oh no, I'm not sayin' and someone else be taking the credit."

"I'm going to ask you again." Jack uncrossed his leg and leaned forward. "Where were you four days ago?"

"Wednesday? I told you. I'm always in my shop. I can prove it. My cameras actually work." He looked at Paige.

"And it'll have you on camera shooting me. That should come in handy."

Paige lifted a shoulder.

"We're not here to talk about the shooting. We're going to need that video footage, and our experts will verify that the date stamp hasn't been tampered with."

"I can assure you it hasn't."

Jack rose from the chair, leaving it where he had dragged it. He scooped the photos from the bed.

"You're letting me go?" He looked at his cuffed hand. "Undo me."

"You will be in here for a couple days. We will have police officers posted at your door. You get free, try to leave, and they'll shoot the other shoulder."

"And I'll be getting' myself a lawyer." Robinson called out from behind us.

In the hall, Jack said, "Paige and Zach, you get to The Pawnshop and get that video footage. The kid and I will stay here until you get back."

"Do you think Robinson did this?" Paige asked.

"Too early to tell, but he knows about the coinherence symbol and has the right attitude."

"And he didn't seem really affected by the pictures," I added.

"Good point, Pending. The average person would be sick or stare in shock. Robinson did none of those things."

I would have smiled at Zachery for the compliment but didn't want to give him the impression his opinion meant anything.

"The way I see it, this doesn't count into his hours of holding time. These are bonus hours," Jack said.

Zachery smiled at him. "That's why you're the boss."

"Don't start kissing ass now, Zach. I don't much like a man's lips there."

"And you would know the feeling?" Zachery was laughing.

A smile smeared over Jack's lips. "Don't get smart."

"Yes, boss."

"We need to find a way to link Robinson with the murder victims. Get into his life."

"And find his motive. What would prove as a stressor to him?" Paige asked.

"Let's get started then. It's already nine in the morning, and we have a long day ahead of us."

Thirty-Four

I f efforts equated results, Nadia would have the congregation list by this point. She knew they were pursuing a lead, but until it was proven Robinson was the unsub, she was to continue as directed, but if she didn't get some cooperation from the church administration, Jack would be banging on the church doors himself. They would be doing themselves a favor to respond to her messages.

She'd rather be at home under the sheets, but she knew Jack's patience had a low threshold. Even trying to convince herself that she was in on a Sunday as a favor to him didn't work. She wanted to get this guy. Anyone who was still free to roam the streets after killing those people wasn't suited for life.

Nadia flicked fingers across keys and moved the mouse rapidly around the screen. She would do what she could to narrow this down for them if it took all of her time to do so.

For some reason, the thought of Deborah Fisher's face when she had handed the phone back after calling Brandon resurfaced in Nadia's mind and tugged on her emotions. The man responsible for these murders, the one free to do so again, had been the final stressor in their marriage. In a way, Nadia felt responsible for having provided the phone for her to call Brandon, and when Deborah had hung up and said her goodbyes, it had given Nadia a nauseous twist in her stomach. The unsub they were looking for was intelligent and mobile. He had found Deborah once to target Brandon's emotions, and he could do so again.

Nadia typed faster. Images and data filled the screen. She'd have to think creatively and get the congregation list another way.

Zachery tracked the cord from the video camera to where it went through a hole cut out in the drywall.

Paige kept her eyes on the place where she had fired her weapon; a hand instinctively went to her replacement firearm.

"The recording device is in here." Zachery tapped the doorframe and glanced at Paige.

She looked up at him.

He took a few steps to her. "You all right?"

"Yeah, I'm fine."

He moved backward as if he expected her to follow. When she didn't, he pulled in closer to her. "You had no choice."

"I warned him to put his arms up. I did so more than once."

"You followed procedure. He could have had a gun behind the counter."

"But he didn't." Paige's eyes went to the counter. Her mind kept replaying the moment she pulled the trigger.

"This isn't your first time, Paige. You filled out some paperwork—"

"I assure you more than *some*. Some is when you unclasp the clip over your gun. Some is even when you draw your weapon. Some doesn't apply when it's discharged." She didn't look at him as she walked behind the counter.

"Robinson's going to be fine."

She noticed the impatient tone growing in her team member's tone of voice. "You're right." She nodded and took a deep breath, hoping it would rid her of the negative thoughts, but anyone she had shot before had been armed.

Shooting an unarmed man, did that make her as bad as the killers she hunted?

"The door locked?" She went up behind Zachery, brushed him out of the way, and twisted the door handle. "Yep."

"Did you want to shoot it out?"

Paige cocked her head to the side. "You think you're funny."

He smiled and scanned the store for something that would work. "Ah, here we go."

"A wrench set?"

Zachery opened the case which must have held fifty different sizes. What he came out with wasn't a wrench.

"An Allen key." Paige smiled. She understood now. "Smart."

"Don't tell anyone, but I'm not half bad at home repairs. With the job, I just rarely have time for them."

Paige went to the counter where she remembered seeing a pile of paperclips and came back with one for Zachery.

He nodded a thank you and got to work. The lock was of standard interior security and the door was opened within fifteen seconds.

Inside was an old wooden desk with mismatched file trays overflowing with paper. A computer monitor, dating back about a decade, took up most of the desk space, and the CPU tower hummed from the floor.

The trail of black electrical cords from the hole in the wall led to a videotape recorder.

"Tape? Who actually uses that anymore?"

"He did mention his concern over the environment. Maybe this is one of his creative ways," Paige offered.

Zachery traced his fingers over the machine and looked in the clear plastic door where the video cassette was. "It's not rollin'. He must have run out of tape."

Paige scanned the shelves that were bracketed to the wall. Video tapes were stacked on each other, labeled one through three. "Number four must be the one in the machine from yesterday. That would explain why it ran out of tape. It looks like he has one for every four days and then reuses them?"

"If that's the case then Wednesday would be tape number one."

"Just let me know when it's ready." Paige left the room with her eyes on the counter. She replayed the image in her mind of the bullet impacting Robinson's shoulder, how it had jerked him slightly backward, and how the blood had projected from it.

She had shot an unarmed man.

She turned around. Zachery wasn't watching her but was paying attention to the video machine. She stepped behind the counter and walked down to where Robinson had been standing. She picked up on the metallic scent of blood. It had dried a darkened red, almost black, on the floor and behind where some had splattered on the wall.

The back of the counter was open-faced with a shelf for storage. A thick layer of dust covered every surface. It was littered with more trinkets from another age. Walkmans in their original packaging were lined up and organized based on color. Paige picked one up. She remembered how excited she had been when her father had bought one for her. She had felt like an adult being able to put on the headset and tune out everything except for the sound of REO Speedwagon and Bryan Adams.

She put it down, her fingers leaving prints in the dust on the packaging. She kept moving along until she reached exactly where she shot Robinson.

"Paige."

Zachery's call pulled her from her thoughts. "What?"

"We're ready to go here."

"Just a sec."

Zachery stood in the doorway between the office and the storefront. She knew he watched her, but she didn't care. She had to see for herself that there was no weapon behind here. She bent down and there were stacks of CDs, most of them dance mixes from the late eighties and early nineties and cassette tapes of artists she had never heard of, still wrapped in cellophane.

"Paige?"

"I said, just a sec."

She heard Zachery's footsteps approach the counter. He looked at her from the customer side. "What do you expect to find down there?"

She ignored him, and her eyes kept scanning.

"The local PD—"

She glared up at him. "I know what they said, but come around here and look for yourself."

"We don't like to fire our weapon Paige, but sometimes it's the job." Zachery walked around.

She lowered closer to the floor to see the underside of the counter. There was evidence of strapping that could have held a gun. "The chief despises FBI. His people might, too."

"You're saying either he or his people removed the evidence?"

"It sounds ludicrous out loud."

"Kind of, actually. Why would—"

"Maybe someone couldn't make agent and wanted to cast a bad light on the FBI's competence with me in the sightline."

JACK AND I SPLIT OUR time between passing glances at each other and trying to coerce Robinson into talking. We'd go into the room, push for several minutes, and when Robinson sealed up, we'd leave the room. Sometimes we left the room when Robinson was in the middle of a rant. Jack said it would have tortured the man as a narcissist not having all his words heard, and he was right. Although Robinson had mentioned a lawyer, he never demanded one.

"Ready for another round, Kid?"

"Of course."

"You recognize these?" Jack held up a small video recorder and the audio piece in evidence bags. I knew they were duplicates of the real thing. Robinson would view them as official evidence.

"You must think I'm an idiot." Robinson's dark skin pinched around his eyes as they narrowed on Jack. "Course I do." He dropped his head back on the pillow.

"I thought you were going to deny that."

Robinson's head lifted. "And why would I do that?"

"We found these in an agent's home. We lifted your finger—"

Robinson looked at me. "It was you? You're the agent?"

A twitch swelled my cheek.

"I didn't kill nobody."

"So you admit to placing these in the agent's home?"

Robinson spoke with his eyes on me. "I don't even know who you are."

Jack walked to the bags of clear liquid, likely morphine; they dripped through plastic tubes and fed into Robinson's hand. Robinson watched him nervously, his eyes shifting from Jack's face to his hands back to his face.

"Answer the question directly. Did you plant these in the agent's home?" Jack's hand reached out to the plastic tube. "All it takes is one small bubble of air."

THE CHIMES ON THE FRONT door of the pawnshop sounded. Paige and Zachery rose to full height.

"Are you agents all right?" It was a Sarasota police officer, and he had let himself go around the middle. His hairline had receded, and the hair he did have was parted perfectly centered. He stood there poised with both hands on his hips.

"We're doing fine in here," Paige answered.

"I just didn't see either of you or hear anything."

"We're fine."

He waved a hand at him and he left.

Paige snapped her head to face Zachery. "What was with that?"

"I believe that was a cop trying to either cover for himself or someone higher up."

"Did you notice how he said agents?"

"It's almost like he sees us as elevated in status and doesn't respect the fact."

"We have to find out what's going on here. I'm not going to face investigation or have a mark on my record because some eager ass-kisser wants to smear the bureau's name."

ROBINSON'S BODY SHOOK. "Please don't. I told you. I didn't do it."

Jack held the plastic tube in his fingers. "Didn't do what?"

"Any of the things you're accusing me of. I didn't kill those people. I didn't go into the agent's house." He turned to me. "Please believe me. Make him stop."

Jack released the tube. "See all you have to do is cooperate. Now tell me where you were back in seventy-one."

"Seventy-one?" Robinson's breath was choppy. "You're the FBI. How can you not know?"

"Answer the question."

The record on Robinson didn't show much more than the charges brought against him for beating his wife. The records showed that he had lived in Sarasota all his life and that he had a means of travel. He owned a Toyota Prius, and his financials showed a substantial rate of return.

"Here."

"Does the name Anna Knowles mean anything to you?"

Robinson blinked slowly. He opened his eyes to Jack. "The name does sound familiar." His eyes widened. "How could I be so stupid?" The question came out as a monologue. "Those murders discovered a while back now." He looked to Jack. "That's what you think I did?"

"She was murdered in seventy-one. Her body and ten others were found in eighty-six."

A hand waved back and forth. "Nope. I didn't do it."

"You keep saying that but haven't convinced me of it."

"Isn't your job to prove I did it?"

Jack took a seat back in the chair that was still near the bed. He leaned in toward Robinson. "I will."

"Just because there's strapping there doesn't mean a gun was." Zachery looked at Paige.

"Robinson was reaching under the counter when I told him to stop. There was a gun there, and he planned on pulling it on us. You can't convince me otherwise."

"Don't you think we have enough on our hands with this case? Let's just do the job we came here to do—"

"I need to know."

"I'm not sure what you'd expect to find. You suspect a cop removed it."

"Please, just one quick look around."

"Quick. Then we have to watch that video and make sure Robinson was here the time of the break-in."

"Deal." Paige let her eyes wander, starting up close and then taking in more of the store.

Zachery stepped from behind the counter and Paige followed him. They moved methodically. Paige's phone rang, and she answered, "Special Agent Dawson…Yeah…We've got it. We're about to watch it. We're on it…Oh, Jack…I need you to ask Robinson something." She stepped into the office, out of Zachery's hearing range, and told him about the strapping under the counter. She didn't elaborate on her suspicions, but Jack would have pieced it together.

She hung up and called for Zachery to join her in the room. "Let's watch the video."

"You asked Jack to talk to Robinson about what was behind the counter, didn't you?"

Paige focused on the video player. She didn't even want to consider the shot not being a good one.

"You do realize if he had a gun there, he's not going to admit it."

"Just hit play."

Zachery hit the button and the screen filled with the counter of The Pawnshop with Robinson as the lead actor.

"With such archaic machinery, how do we know the date

and time stamp are even accurate?"

Zachery tapped the current readout which was correct and smiled.

Paige returned his smile and took a deep breath.

They continued to watch Robinson manage the counter. He took a five-minute siesta in the afternoon. They forwarded through the video.

"Not too busy here, is it?"

"From what we've actually watched, maybe five customers so far."

They kept watching, forwarding periodically, and Robinson was where he said he was the entire day.

"There was no way he could have been in Woodbridge planting surveillance equipment in Brandon's house," Paige said.

"We're going to have to let Jack know the guy didn't do it."

"You volunteer to tell him? He's not going to be happy about this one. He came all the way down here certain we had the unsub."

"There's still more to prove, and we're where everything started. Either way, it's advantageous being here. Besides, you and Pending wouldn't want to be alone when it comes to the church congregation list."

"If Nadia ever gets it put together."

"I know she never normally takes this long, but remember it's not current church records either."

"And she does have a lot of evidence to sort through and analyze. She has the photos we recovered from Royster's computer still, for one." Paige looked around the office, then back to Zachery. "Why do you always call Brandon Pending? He hates it."

Zachery smiled. "Maybe that's why."

Paige rolled her eyes and dialed Nadia. "I know you're swamped, but I need you to do something for me."

ROBINSON WATCHED AS JACK SLIPPED his phone into a pants

pocket. Jack opened his mouth to say something when his phone rang again. Jack answered and I observed Jack's facial expressions, how they ranged a full spectrum of emotion from surprise to disappointment to anger. This was where the range ended. He closed the cell, held it in his hand, and looked at me. If I was reading his eyes correctly, Robinson wasn't our unsub. Jack's next words confirmed it. "Your alibi for four days ago stands."

Robinson smiled. "See? I told you."

"We need to know who you sold these to." Jack held out the bags containing the surveillance equipment.

"I don't keep names."

"We need to know when."

"Five days ago. Yes, that's it."

Jack looked at me. "So Tuesday. Do you remember who you sold them to?"

"Why would I—"

Jack rose and moved to the morphine drip.

"Stop." Robinson's chest heaved. "I don't remember. Truthfully I don't."

"We need to see the video feed from that day."

Robinson's face tightened in a wince. "I don't have it."

"Hmm."

"It's to save the environment. Every four days I record over the previous four days."

"So today's tape would have had Tuesday on it?"

Robinson gave it some thought. "Yeah, that would be right seeing as I wasn't there to change the tape out last night."

"We'll be taking it."

"Sure, whatever you need to do. I didn't kill those people."

"We'll have it analyzed by specialists. If there are ghosted images for them to recover, they will. You better hope you're on there selling these surveillance pieces." Jack dragged the chair back to the corner from which he had originally taken it. The legs scraped the vinyl flooring, causing a high-pitched squeal. "Do you own a .38 Special?"

Robinson didn't say anything.

"Answer the question." Jack patted his shirt pocket and pulled out the package of cigarettes.

"It's licensed."

"Where is it?" Jack's phone calls obviously tipped him off to more than one thing.

Robinson's eyes darted to the end of the bed, to his feet.

"We're not leaving until—"

"Behind the counter. I wasn't going to shoot them." He glanced at me, back to Jack. "I was just going to scare them. I swear."

"You let an agent feel guilty over shooting an unarmed man." Jack headed for the door.

"That's not a crime," Robinson called out behind us.

In the hallway, Jack suspended a cigarette from his lips for a brief instant before pulling it out. "Robinson has the revolver registered in his name. Paige had Nadia pull the registry when they found strapping under the counter. Robinson just said the gun was behind the counter, but local PD said there wasn't one."

"Someone on the police force took it? But why?"

"Questions that need answers, Kid. We'll start by talking with the chief of police."

Thirty-Five

The Sarasota police station was a modern building of architectural wonder. Its many windows allowed sunlight to stream in creating a bright, uplifting interior. The periwinkle blue used as an accent on the exterior took up a solid presence in the lobby where the front face and wall of the reception area were painted the same color.

The female officer sitting behind the window watched the four of us approach. She offered a sincere smile. "Can I help you?"

Jack held up his creds. "We need to speak with the police chief."

"Brennan's not in today."

"We need to reach him."

She took a business card from a plastic display that was kept on her side of the glass and extended it to Jack. "It has his cell listed there."

Jack took it but never looked at the card. "What about Sergeant Haynes?"

Sergeant Haynes was the superior in charge of the officers who had come to The Pawnshop. He was the one Paige was put in touch with to arrange for the backup.

"He's here." She dragged out her words in such a way as to turn them into a question. She picked up her phone and dialed an extension. "You have someone here to see you... Okay." She hung up. "He'll be right down."

Minutes later, a far door opened, and he stepped out. "Agents."

I remembered him clearly from yesterday. He had walked through the door to The Pawnshop after the shot was fired. Sergeant Haynes was a man of average height and of common features, except for a distinguishing mole on his chin.

"We need to speak with you—in private."

The sergeant's eyes skipped over all of us, settled back on Jack. "This way."

He led us through the building to a conference room where he took a seat at the end of the table and gestured for us to sit around it. "So you have your unsub?"

"We have evidence that someone at The Pawnshop tampered with evidence."

"You come in here and accuse the Sarasota PD of a cover-up?"

"That's exactly what we're doing. We know Robinson had an S&W .38 revolver registered to him."

"There's no record of it being found at the shop."

"You want to try again?"

Haynes remained silent.

"Robinson said it should have been there."

"I...I don't know what to say. I know nothing about it."

"Is this because you don't like us in your city, and you actually want to pin something on the FBI?"

"That's not true." His eyes went to the empty water pitcher in the middle of the table.

"Your chief made it clear to my agents—" Jack nodded toward Paige and then to me "—he was offended by the fact we never notified him of our presence here."

Haynes clasped his hands on the table. "It is common courtesy to—"

"Is this the excuse for removing evidence?"

"Of course not."

"We ran quick backgrounds on the officers who were

at the scene yesterday, and Officer Bryant applied to the academy."

"You think he took the evidence to make it appear as if your agent shot an unarmed man? Why?"

Jack's eyes narrowed.

"No. There's no way one of mine would—"

"Robinson said he had the gun behind the counter," Paige reiterated.

"He must have forgotten he moved it and misplaced it somewhere."

"What we're thinking is that Officer Bryant was more unhappy about the feds being here than the chief, and he wanted to drag our reputation down—namely mine."

"He's a good cop. Sometimes a little hot under the collar, but a good guy, nonetheless."

"Consider this little meeting a professional courtesy. Bryant has interfered with a federal investigation," Jack said.

"I'll call him in."

"You do that."

Nothing was moving fast enough for Nadia's preference. Normally, information was only a few clicks of a mouse and pecks on the keyboard away. The older detective roamed the hallways, pensive and agitated. He had been redirected into Nadia's space several times now.

"If we catch you wandering again, Mr. Jenkins, we will ask that you leave." The security agent led him in again and dropped him off with Nadia. "Keep an eye on him."

"What, am I a child?" Jenkins's gruffness manifested into a verbal pout.

The security agent left with enlarged eyes at Nadia that said, *He's your problem now.*

"You work twenty-four hours a day?" Jenkins walked around Nadia's space, touching her in-tray, her stapler, and adjusting her phone so it sat perpendicular to the edge of the desk.

Nadia reached out and put the phone back at its original angle. "Please just sit over there."

"Police work used to involve a lot more fieldwork than it does these days. All the forensics and computers weigh down the investigations." He dropped in the designated chair.

"All the science has made it possible to convict criminals that may have otherwise gone free."

"You're defensive about your work."

"Of course, I am." Nadia turned back to face her monitor. She almost had a completed list of congregation members. She still hadn't heard back from the church administrator but had gone about things her own way—donation tax receipts. The process took longer, but she expected Jack would be calling soon for an update. She had rehearsed her defense for not having the answers yet.

A name came up on the computer screen, and her hands stopped moving. She verbalized her thinking process. "Bingham and Knowles."

The chair Jenkins sat on groaned when he shifted his weight. "You're working on the church membership list, right? Knowles shouldn't come as a surprise. That's why you're looking at that church in the first place."

Nadia ignored the man's words. She couldn't believe she didn't connect the two until now. "I know that name from somewhere else, too." She turned around and tapped on the keys, the screen flashing and filling in with information. "Oh my god." She kept her fingers moving over the keys. More windows opened on her screen. "It's been here this entire time." Nadia picked up the phone to call Jack.

With the receiver to her ear, an e-mail notification flashed up in the bottom right hand of the computer screen. She went over to the program and opened the e-mail. Jack had asked her to locate Keith Knowles, and this file held her answer. As the report filled the screen, Nadia's jaw gaped open.

WITH THE FOUR OF US crammed into the rental sedan, it weighed down the car enough to make it less of a rocky ride. We were headed to the Catholic church where Knowles had served as a priest, hoping they'd be more cooperative if we showed up in person. Nadia still hadn't come through with the list, and Jack wasn't impressed by the delay.

"I miss the SUV," Zachery said from the front passenger seat.

For a man of over six foot myself, I related to the statement, but my mind wasn't on discomfort. It was on Debbie. I missed her, and kissing Paige last night, wanting her the way I had, had been wrong.

Jack's cell rang. He didn't hesitate to pull it to his ear and answer while driving. He spoke for a few seconds and hung up. He swerved the car around a slowing moving truck and picked up speed.

"Jack?" Paige placed a hand on his headrest.

"That was Nadia. Keith Knowles is a follower of the Redeemer's on Twitter—"

"Keith Knowles had a connection to the first victim—"

"And he had a connection with Bingham. Apparently, Bingham donated money to the same church Knowles became a priest at. The good news is Knowles is still in Sarasota."

THE ADDRESS FOR KEITH KNOWLES brought us in front of a modest brick bungalow at the east end of town. All four of us got out of the car.

Jack banged on the oak door. "FBI."

Zachery stood beside Jack; Paige and I hung back.

The evening air had turned humid with the threat of impending rain. The sounds of the neighborhood—voices, laughter, screaming children, and lawnmowers—carried, empowering it with a sort of life force.

Jack's fist rose again and lowered when the door opened.

The smell of roast beef, onions, and baking potatoes filtered out. My stomach churned instinctively.

"Keith Knowles?"

"Yes?" The man responded with a heightened tail on the end of his single word. He looked past Jack to the rest of us and adjusted his glasses. "Who are you?"

Jack announced himself and gestured to the rest of us as being a team from the BAU of the FBI.

"Why do you want to talk to me?"

"We're here about your wife. We'd like to step inside."

"She is dead."

"Yes, we know."

Knowles hesitated, but he ended up consenting with a nod and another adjustment of his glasses. He stepped inside his house and held the door open for us.

One observation I made of Jack was the man never asked for anything, he presented everything as a directive.

"Come sit in here." Knowles directed us to the living area, and then excused himself. "I just need to turn the oven off. You have me right at dinner hour."

Family portraits hung on the wall, and a large wooden cross was centered between them.

Knowles returned a few minutes later. "You're here about Anna?" He played out the sign of the cross on his chest and took a seat.

"Where were you five days ago?"

"Tuesday?" The older man adjusted his glasses again. "I don't understand."

"Just answer the question."

"I was with a church group for children."

"What time?"

"From eight until five. It was a Bible camp day."

"I assume you have people who can verify this."

Knowles ran a hand over the top of his head. "At least twenty. Why are you asking me these questions? I thought you were here about the man who killed Anna." Pain saturated his tone of voice.

"We are." Jack leaned back into the sofa pillows.

"You think?" Knowles placed a hand on his chest. "There is no way I would have done that to my wife. No way. Detectives came, and they took my statements, my alibis. I endured days of interrogation. I spent nights behind bars while Anna's killer had freedom." Knowles balled a fist and punched it into his thigh.

"You went on to become a Catholic priest."

The fist loosened. "That is right. I sank my life into the Lord to deal with what had happened to Anna, to all those other people. There is so much evil in this world."

"You thought by preaching you could change the world." I caught the cynicism in Jack's tone, and Knowles didn't miss it either.

"The Bible can affect you more than one might realize. It's a hard thing to quantify, but it has only positive effects when put into practice."

"You retired two years ago now."

"Just because I am no longer a priest doesn't mean that I don't live by the Word. I practice peace—"

"Hear confessions."

"But, of course. To be forgiven, one must confess one's sins and repent."

Bingham's words refreshed to the forefront: *Confess your sins, or don't and be punished.*

"And you believe you have the power to forgive sins?"

"As a priest, I served as a mediator between man and the Lord."

I watched Jack's face take on an uncomfortable contortion. "What about Lance Bingham? Does that name sound familiar to you?"

"Of course."

"From Twitter?"

"Twitter. I've heard of it. That's some online social networking thing, right?"

"Right."

"I don't even own a computer."

"We show you as Bingham's follower. Maybe the Redeemer sounds more familiar to you?"

"Follower? I'm not sure what you're talking about. The Redeemer is our Lord and Savior." Knowles clasped his hands on his lap. "But either way you'll find no computer here as it allows a place for the Devil."

"You said you know the name Lance Bingham, is it because he donated money to your church?"

"Lance was a nice guy and a family friend, an active member of the church before Anna. We had been friends before I became a priest, before Anna went missing." He stopped talking for a few seconds, and I heard voices which sounded like they were coming from a television.

"You said a family friend, so you were close?"

"Very close. Every Sunday, he came for dinner. I tried to tell Anna he was a troubled soul, but she wouldn't have any word of it. She said that he just had a hard past and that he needed people who could look past imperfection and love him for who he was."

"Troubled soul and a hard past," I said, stepping into the questioning session. It brought a glare from Jack and a sideways smirk from Zachery.

"He had a horrible temper." Knowles looked at me. "As told by him, anyway. We were never witness to it."

Controlled rage would fit Bingham. We knew Bingham to be an organized killer, one who gave thought to his method of operation, targeting of his victims, the outplaying of their torture and then demise. In his mind, his actions were justifiable, and he felt no remorse over the kill.

"What was his childhood like?" Paige asked.

Knowles turned to her. "His parents weren't very good people, if you ask me."

"You knew them?"

"Only what Lance told us, but he'd seal up and excuse himself a lot of times the subject came up."

"What did he say?"

"His father was a religious man. 'Very zealous,' as Lance put it on numerous occasions. Now Lance never came out and said it, but I think his old man beat the church into him—and maybe it took, too, because Lance was an outstanding example for—"

A man came through the doorway to the living area. His hair was clipped short, and he wore wire-rimmed glasses like his father. "Who are these people?"

"Don't you worry about it."

"They're cops?"

"This is my son, Reggie." Knowles halted eye contact with any of us, and his head bowed forward if only a little. "These are FBI agents investigating the murder of your moth—"

"It's about time!" Reggie adjusted his glasses as his father had earlier. "She's been gone forty years."

"You would have been young at the time," Jack said.

Reggie's eyes snapped to him. "I was a baby."

"It is harder on a small one than you would think," Knowles said.

"I turned out just fine."

Knowles's jaw went askew for a second.

Reggie shoved his hands in his pockets. "Dinner's going to be ready soon, so if you would all leave now."

Knowles stood. "This here is my house, Reggie, and if you want to continue living under my roof, you listen to me."

Jack stood, and the rest of us followed his lead. "We might have more questions moving forward."

"Of course." Knowles was angry, as evidenced in his eyes and the subtle pulse in his cheek. "You know, just because her body was found, I still don't have full closure. Capture the man who did this to her. Please."

IN THE CAR, Jack spoke first. "We need to get a background on that kid."

"You heard him. He would have been a baby at the time of

his mother's murder," Zachery countered.

"Like you mentioned before, what's to say Bingham had a partner from the beginning? Maybe this kid found Bingham and, like Royster, fell prey to his manipulation tactics. He could have filled his head with talk about his mother."

Zachery played out the thought, "And he started killing other people?"

"He had a rough start in life. His mother was murdered, his father was so grieved he turned to the church and made that his family."

"Did you notice when Reggie said he turned out all right he didn't accredit his father for that, and in turn his father didn't back up Reggie's self-assessment," Paige added.

"Oh, I noticed, and it seemed like he didn't even want his son in our presence," I said.

"Hey, good point, Brandon. He did seem embarrassed by him. I noticed that as well."

"So the question is why." Jack make a call on his phone. "Nadia you're on speaker. I need you to pull a background on a Reggie Knowles, likely Reginald."

"Of course—and about the list—"

"You're finished it?"

"No, I'm not having any luck getting a hold of the church administration. I'm going about it the long way. That's how I knew about Bingham donating—"

"Keep us updated. And Nadia?"

"Yeah."

"You have a videotape coming to you for early morning delivery. I need you to rush review of the footage—"

"No problem."

"It's been recorded over."

There was a pause on Nadia's end, then she said, "I'll do what I can."

"I trust you will. Call right back with Reggie's background info." Jack ended the call and spoke to us. "Knowles said that Bingham had a strict upbringing."

"Perfect environment to create a narcissist. They feel they need to be perfect, and when they inevitably fall short, they feel the need for punishment. This results in an obsessive-compulsive disorder where they feel they always have something to prove and need to excel against their contemporaries. That's based on statistics anyway," Zachery said.

"We also need to think outside the regular parameters with this case because Bingham targets those he gets close to, contrary to statistics on serial killers. He has such control that he's able to take time with his victims. He has mastered the art of manipulation, so that he can even turn an enemy into an ally—thinking of Royster." Jack's cell interrupted him. He answered. "You're on speaker."

"I have the background," Nadia paused there.

"And?"

"It doesn't look good, boss. There's no present address on file for him. His last known was jail back in ninety-three when he was twenty-two. He had been serving time for drug possession and B&E with a weapon. He landed a homeowner in the hospital with a broken arm and rib, but that's not all." Nadia took a deep breath. "There was a psychological assessment attached to the file. He expressed a desire to hurt living things. You know those cards that are held up and the doctor says, tell us what you see—"

"Nadia, point."

"He always pictured a wounded animal, a bird without wings, dogs without legs, mice without tails. You get it. We have to get this guy, boss, but I've done a quick trace in the system, and nothing's coming up. Like I said no current address, no credit cards, and no phone numbers are registered to him."

"It's all right. We know where he is."

"You know—"

Jack executed the perfect U-turn and we were on the way back to the house.

Thirty-Six

Lance Bingham prided himself on two things—self-control and intelligence. Of course, he realized the two inevitably relied on the other. Without intelligence dictating the result of action, restraint would be impossible.

He sat at the cafeteria table with men wedged so tightly on either side, it made it hard to lift a fork to his mouth. Brushing his arms against theirs made him want to tear their limbs off. He imagined them lying on the floor bleeding out.

The images of blood brought a sense of accomplishment. He had taken control over the lives of numerous souls, more than law enforcement would ever discover. They would define him a serial killer. He might have a mission and purpose in life, but he'd wear the label with pride. His smile widened before he killed it by stuffing a forkful of mush into his mouth.

Anna—Anna had been special. She had barely screamed when he'd cut her. He had pride in the self-control that he had exhibited. Normally, their cries were what steadied him. He took pleasure in death, but the execution was equally as, if not more, important.

The discovery in eighty-six had been responsible for his move to Salt Lick. He remembered the face of Detective Martin Jenkins as clearly as if he were standing in front of him today.

Another smile formed and was destroyed by another mouthful of food.

The memory brought with it an inner satisfaction. The detective had no idea he had been talking to the killer.

Bingham stabbed his fork into his plate, and the fat guy to his right made the mistake of looking at him. Bingham felt rage flutter through his veins, an uncontrollable pulsation. His hands shook. He thought of it. He imagined it. He had to harness control of it. Slowly, the shaking calmed and then stopped.

He wouldn't ruin everything over this piece of shit. He was too good for that. He killed with purpose, not simply for pleasure, and he had taught his followers this, but they had disappointed him. They had made a mistake. They had led the investigation to them simply because they could not operate as he had—with control and intelligence. They felt they could get close to the feds without being touched. They felt they could invade the young agent's home—*special* agent's—he corrected sarcastically in his thoughts. What an arrogant young man he was, but, still, they could never know exactly how Anna had started everything.

JACK DIRECTED PAIGE AND ZACHERY to the rear of the house, and the images of Royster's residence flashed through my mind. We were approaching this the same way. I imagined bullets hailing through the front window. Instead, the front door swung open. Reggie Knowles stepped onto the concrete steps. "What are you—"

"Going somewhere? It's dinner hour."

"I don't need to explain myself to you." Reggie went to move by us.

"Turn around. Hands behind your back."

"Why?"

"Now!"

"Okay, okay."

Jack snapped on the cuffs and said, "You should remember how this feels."

Reggie projected a wad of spit toward Jack's face which

barely missed and landed in the grass.

"And you just assaulted a federal agent."

"This is bullshit!"

Jack yanked back on his arms, turning Reggie around to face the road. He pushed him forward. Reggie planted his feet.

"Dad!"

Paige and Zachery came back around to the front of the house. The door opened again, and Keith Knowles stepped outside. He seemed to have aged since we left the house less than ten minutes ago.

"Dad, tell them I'm innocent. Tell them!"

All of us watched as Keith Knowles retreated into the house and closed the door.

"Dad!" Reggie's legs buckled, but Jack hoisted him up.

"He can't save you from where you're going."

Reggie hurled a wad of spit again, and this time it hit Jack's left cheek.

"You are so going to be wishing you didn't do that," Zachery said.

Jack said nothing.

"AGENTS, HOW NICE TO SEE YOU AGAIN." Sergeant Haynes came down to the interrogation observation room.

Other officers had led us in and directed us here for the process to begin. Jack was in the room with Reggie Knowles.

Haynes stood beside me and stuffed his hands in his pockets, something I surmised he was good at by this point. An observer who no longer got his hands dirty but allowed his subordinates to stain theirs with lies.

"You still aren't going to tell us what's going on here."

"We will when it's necessary," Paige answered, "and it's not yet necessary."

"You're the one who shot that unarmed man at his pawnshop."

"He was only unarmed *after* your officers removed

evidence."

The sergeant rocked on his feet. "That investigation is in process."

"Well, then I suggest until you finalize it, you keep your mouth shut about it."

I smirked, impressed by Paige's ability to stand up for herself.

The rocking stopped, and the sergeant's hands dug deeper into his pockets. His eyes focused through the glass.

"Your record speaks for you." Jack paced the room, holding a beige file folder that contained a printed copy of Reggie's background.

"That was who I used to be."

"A leopard never changes his spots. Isn't that how the saying goes?"

"Maybe one an old person knows."

"Seems to me you're not a kid yourself. You turned forty last month."

Silence.

"You feel like a kid?" I knew Jack's tactic was to play to Reggie's pride, test the waters.

"I'm not a kid." He drew out every word.

"You like to hurt things."

Reggie didn't say anything.

"But, I mean, if they deserve it—"

"Then they deserve it."

"Fair enough." Jack took a few steps around the table. "How did losing your mother affect you?"

"I was a baby."

"But you grew up without her."

"Dad had other women, at least until he really found God."

"You say that mockingly."

"He may have appeared righteous, but the man isn't all that pure."

Jack sat across from Reggie. "Why do you say that?"

I knew Jack was working to get close to Reggie, to open him up so that he would expose himself. Once Jack felt he had established a connection, he would turn on Reggie and this would serve to ignite him and hopefully result in a confession.

"He's not unlike anyone else at church. I don't even know how he was approved to be a priest."

"What do you mean, 'not unlike anyone else at the church'?"

"No one is all good." Reggie rubbed a flattened hand on his throat.

"Your father did things."

"Everyone sins. Ask God." Reggie laughed. "But as long as you confess and repent, you shall be forgiven."

"You don't believe that?"

"Not at all."

"You have a record."

"I'm true to who I am. I don't hide behind some self-professed righteousness."

"Where were you five days ago?"

Reggie didn't even take the time to think about it. "Scoring coke on the corner of MLK and—"

"You do realize you're telling a federal agent this."

"You need to prove it."

"You just gave me your confession."

"Then I shall be forgiven." Reggie took a bow from the chest up across the table.

In the observation room, Sergeant Haynes said, "The guy's not so bright. Isn't drug possession part of what landed him in jail before?"

"He knows we still have to find him in possession," Paige said before glancing at Zachery and me.

Inside the room, Jack didn't say anything for nearly a minute.

Reggie adjusted his seated position.

Jack opened the file on the table. "You were sent to juvie

in eighty-four. You were thirteen, and then you spent some time in jail for drug possession and armed B&E. You assaulted the homeowner. We want to know what you've been up to since you got out in ninety-three."

We knew the first murder in Salt Lick dated back about twenty-five years ago, at which time Reggie Knowles would have been behind bars.

"You're the fed. You tell me."

Jack looked to the mirrorpane and ran a finger across his neck.

"We need to ask you to leave, Sergeant," Zachery requested.

"Leave? This is my police station."

"This is a highly sensitive case."

Haynes looked among the three of us, and when he realized we weren't going to back down, he left the room.

Jack confronted Reggie with the truth. "You have anger in your soul."

"How would you presume—" Reggie's words stopped there.

"You have pride in who you are."

"Like I said, I'm true to who I am."

"Most people with your record would have kept it going, but you haven't seen behind bars since ninety-three. Maybe it's just because you haven't gotten caught."

"Caught? For what?"

Jack spread out photographs found in Bingham's cell on the table and added one of Anna Knowles. It was included to elicit an emotional reaction from Reggie, and it seemed to work. "Do you know Lance Bingham?"

Reggie's eyes moistened as he picked up the photograph of his mother. "I never even got to know her. I only saw pictures and heard stories."

"Lance Bingham?"

Reggie didn't answer Jack but spewed words of no consequence. "I was with my father a lot at this Bible camp for kids. It's one of the rules for living under his roof. How pathetic am I? I'm forty and living with Dad."

"Bingham?"

"I've never had a religious bone in me. I don't understand what Dad gets from it. I guess that's why we're all made differently."

"Answer my question about Bingham."

Reggie's eyes finally rose from the picture of his mother. "I don't know who that is."

"Not even from Twitter? Maybe the name the Redeemer sticks with you more?"

"The Redeemer? And Twitter? You have to own a computer."

"Or at least have access to one."

"I don't know who that is."

"See, I think you do."

After a few hours of interrogation, Jack took the photo of Anna Knowles from Reggie's hand.

"No, please."

Jack stuffed it into a folder with the rest of the pictures and left the room. The door slammed hard behind him. "It's not our guy." Jack patted his shirt pocket.

"How do you know for sure?"

"He doesn't know Bingham."

"Because he said so." The words left my lips, and I felt like an idiot for allowing them to be birthed.

"We have to prove he does, and we can't. He was a baby when his mom died, a delinquent kid afterward. Why would he pay attention to some friend of his father? We'll verify his alibi for Tuesday and pull up all the information we can get on him. We don't even have enough for a warrant to search the residence for a computer—and until we can connect him to Bingham and Salt Lick," Jack paused. This was the first time I noticed the case having any sort of real impact on Jack. "We'll hold him overnight. Maybe he'll have more to say by morning. Let's call it a night." Jack pulled out a cigarette from the package.

Thirty-Seven

We had dinner in the hotel restaurant, and when most groupings would be eating dessert and coffee, we were sipping on drinks and talking about what we were going to do after, but hours later, we still hadn't gone anywhere.

"You going to have another?" Paige asked me with a glass of merlot to her lips.

"I'm fine." Everything from this case weighed on my mind along with my marital problems and the active attraction to Paige. I never should have kissed her last night, and I had no right to feel jealous when another man showed interest in her.

"The kid probably has a bedtime to adhere to." Jack laughed and took a draw on his vodka martini.

Zachery laughed. "What is it, ten thirty?"

"Try closer to midnight." I endured a few more minutes before excusing myself and heading back to my room. I needed to be alone.

I dropped on the bed with my arms crossed under my head and stared at the ceiling. I needed to call Deb. I dialed the new cell number. It rang once before an automated voice said, "The number you are trying to reach is no longer in service."

Are you fucking kidding me?

My first reaction was anger, but it gave way to heartache and worry. I dialed the number again and met the same result. Maybe I had recorded the number incorrectly. I scrolled through the calls to my phone until I came to the one she'd made yesterday, and I dropped my hand. She had called me from head office.

It hurt to breathe as if my heart were full of metal shards that pierced my lungs with each inhale and exhale.

I had to convince myself she was safe. I just hated what the flipside to that meant—she had disconnected her phone.

I took a deep breath, the exhale working its way out slowly, painfully. *Deb was all right. I wasn't.*

I undressed and pulled my MP3 player from my luggage bag and popped in the earbuds. Nothing like a workout would cure this. I needed the volume loud and the physical intensity draining. I started with jumping jacks as nothing got the heart beating faster. After a minute of these, I moved onto jabs, upper cuts, and then side and roundhouse kicks.

As I was nearing the end of the workout, I heard a pounding on the door even over Nickelback's "Burn it to the Ground." I pulled one bud from an ear. My breathing was still labored when I opened the door. "Paige?"

She stepped into the room and put a hand on my chest. She didn't seem to care I was soaking wet. "I need you to listen to me." She looked down at my boxing shorts. "Why are you always in your underwear?"

I went to move to the bathroom for a towel. She grabbed my arm. "I didn't come here to talk."

"You just said you needed me to lis—"

Her lips pressed against mine, and as her mouth opened and mine reciprocated, I knew I didn't possess the strength to back away this time. Deb's face went through my thoughts but dissipated as fog does once the sun breaks through the clouds. I pulled Paige to me and cupped her breast in my hand. She moaned under my touch, and I under hers. I led her to my bed and made love to her. My thoughts weren't on Deb, on my failed marriage, or on Jack and how he might feel. They were simply in the moment, living and breathing

Paige. It had been too long.

AFTERWARD WE HELD EACH OTHER and spoke of everything except promises and expectations. I told her about Deb, and she ran a hand down my chest and listened. We finally fell asleep. When my eyes opened, a couple of hours had gone by. The alarm clock read two forty-five. I nudged her. She groaned.

I rose from the bed, put on a pair of jeans and a T-shirt.

"Where are you going?" Her voice was groggy, yet laden with more sexual appetite.

"Don't worry about me."

"Of course, I worry about—" Her last word faded from exhaustion, and she sat up. "It's late."

"We fell asleep."

"Where are you going?"

For some reason when I looked at her now, I saw her differently. I cared about her, dare even say loved her, but she was involved with my boss. Now that we could possibly be together, life still kept us apart. I realized the irony of it and appreciated life a little less.

"You should get back to your room. Jack—"

She lifted the sheets to cover herself. "Jack?"

"We can't have him finding out about—" I rolled my hand "—this."

"*This*?" Spoken as if she was offended.

I was saying everything wrong. "I mean—"

"You think I'm sleeping with him?" Paige's mouth tilted upward to a smile. She shook her head, amused at something. "I kind of led you to believe that."

I dropped on the end of the bed. "You mean you're not."

"Heavens, no."

"You were in his hotel room back in Salt Lick."

"You knew?"

"Why were you there?"

She pulled her legs in and tucked her head to her knees.

"Fine, you don't want to tell me."

"I was just talking to him."

"Just talking?" Anger raised the hair on the back of my neck.

"Yes, just talking."

"Why haven't you denied my accusations? Why make me believe—"

"I guess I just wanted to make you—"

"Jealous?"

She pressed her lips and nodded.

I got off the bed. She followed.

"Brandon?" Her hand touched my arm. I turned and looked at her. I pulled her to me and caressed her forehead. I kissed her there, and then her lips. She tried to pull me back to bed, but my mind was interfering.

"I'm sorry."

"You're sorry? Sorry for what?" She sounded slighted and got up and gathered her clothes.

"I just have to think."

"Now you have to think?" She stopped outside the bathroom door.

"Please don't take this personally."

"How can I not take this personally?" She slammed the bathroom door behind her.

THE LOUNGE OF THE HOTEL was like many others with dim lighting and candlelit tables. Bottles of alcohol were showcased on glass shelves behind the bar and bathed in seductive illumination, making what should be enjoyed in moderation a call to those desperate at heart. Right now, I was one of them.

I sat at the bar and ordered a double Manhattan. Less than a minute later, the bartender sat the drink in front of me. The glass looked like crystal, yet I suspected it to be a cheap knockoff—something pretending to be one thing when it was something else altogether. Just like how before Salt

Lick, I thought Deb and I were okay. Now I realized I had deceived myself.

I took a sip of my cocktail, enjoying the potent flavor of the whiskey as it filled my mouth. I listened to the music of a piano, assuming it was simply a recording until I spotted a man playing, tucked around the corner. I hadn't even noticed at first how big the lounge was. I got up, taking my glass with me. I heard the breaking of billiard balls before I saw the tables.

A few black oak pool tables lined with red felt were there. A stained-glass light fixture consisting of three pyramid-shaped shades hung from a black iron bracket and illuminated the tables.

The man on the piano played "The Way You Look Tonight."

Playing pool at the one table was a familiar face. As I walked toward Jack, I extended a hand.

He looked at my hand as if it were a foreign concept to shake hands as a greeting. He rubbed a piece of chalk on the end of a pool cue. "You play, Kid?"

I retracted my hand. "I have a couple of times."

"Twenty a game too steep for ya?"

I shook my head. "I should be able to handle it."

"You wouldn't make a good poker player. You some sort of pool savant?" Jack set up the rack.

I had been made. The truth was I had spent most of my teenage years at a billiard hall not far from here. I smiled at him, but it faded when I noticed the martini on the side table.

Had he been drinking since we'd left the restaurant hours ago?

"Your break," he said.

"All right then." I drank some more Manhattan before setting it on the table beside Jack's martini. "I'm not taking it easy on you just 'cause you're the boss either."

"I wouldn't expect you to."

I pulled a pool cue off the rack, and as I chalked the end, all the conflict from the last week, from the last several months, paraded through my mind. I blamed the reflective nature of my thoughts on the alcohol and the soft background music.

I bent over and lined up the shot. Three balls went into pockets, two stripes and one solid.

"Pretty impressive, Kid."

It took three shots for me to miss and for it to become Jack's turn. He lined up and took a few shots in a row himself. When he missed, he straightened out and headed for his martini. He drank until there wasn't much left in the glass.

"It's been kind of a rough week."

Jack wasn't facing me when I said this. The glass he had sat down, he lifted again. When the glass went back to the table, it was empty save the olives. "If it's too much for you, you can leave anytime."

"No, that's not what I meant."

Jack turned to face me. He held his pool cue in his left hand. The concentration in his eyes and his pursed lips told me he only needed one reason to send me home.

I gulped some Manhattan as if it would provide some courage to speak up to him. "I was just commenting."

"I'm not your buddy, Kid. I'm the team leader."

"I just thought—" I gestured toward the drinks and the billiard table.

"You thought wrong."

We stood there by the table, me sipping the Manhattan and Jack eating the olives from his martini.

Jack broke the silence with, "Your turn again."

I didn't move. "Is there something I've done wrong? Something you don't approve of? I'd like you to be straight enough to tell it to my face."

Jack watched me, and even though I had asked part of me feared hearing something about my job performance. I couldn't handle being told I was a failure at the one thing I had wanted to do with my life, the thing that had cost my marriage.

"You have one great weakness."

I prepared myself to hear about how I had a temper and needed to learn self-control. I expected to hear how I tended to overreact. I put my glass to my lips.

"You're too positive."

I took a small sip.

He went on. "You think we catch all the bad guys, that we can stop the evil in the world."

I slowly lowered the glass. "If you don't think that way, why bother—"

"You believe in hope even when there is none."

With Jack's last words, I sensed the sadness which emanated from both his eyes and body energy. I realized that despite the tough exterior, he cared more than he calculated worth the risk.

I drained the rest of my drink, took my shot, and rid the surface of a few more striped balls.

Jack took his turn and cleared the table of the solids with the exception of the black ball. "Right corner pocket." He lined up the shot and drew the cue stick back.

Smack! Thunk.

"Looks like you won." I fished out my wallet; not even a buck was in there. "I'll have to get it for you."

"You make a bet and don't have the money to pay up?"

"Figured I would have won against an old guy like you." The words came out, and I wished I could have swallowed them, but I noticed the hint of a smile on Jack's lips. "I'll have it for you in the morning."

"Not a problem, Kid."

"I'm going to call it a night. I'm sure we have a lot ahead of us." I turned to leave.

"Hmm."

I stopped walking. "What does 'Hmm' mean, anyway? It's not even a word."

Jack's eyes met mine. "It can mean a lot of things."

"Like what? What does it mean now?"

"It means you hear something you don't like and you clam up. You're like a kid."

"And that drives me nuts, too. I'm twenty-nine. I'm not a child. I'm not in need of another father."

"Never said you were."

"You act like it sometimes. Don't take this call, don't take that one." Jack scowled, and I think I might have gone too far, but I was tired and feeling relaxed from the booze. "And I have a name," I added.

The corners of his mouth tweaked upward, even though a full smile never formed.

"You call Paige and Zachery by their names. You call Nadia, Nadia. Me, I'm either Kid or Slingshot—which I resent, by the way, because I scored well over the acceptable percentage on the gun range."

"I've told you before, a name is earned."

"We're not some Indian tribe. We're individuals doing a job. It's a career, nothing more."

"Hmm."

I raised my hands in the air. "Night."

"Kid."

I groaned and turned around. "What?"

"This isn't like TV." He chalked the end of his pool cue as if he were completely unaware that I was questioning everything in life.

I had a woman in my room who loved me, yet I wasn't exactly sure how I felt about her. I had a wife I loved, but she had called to end our marriage and disconnected her phone—and to top off the metaphorical sundae, I had a boss who viewed me as too positive and inexperienced to deserve a name. I could punch something. "Not like TV?"

"We're not best friends just because we're on the same team. First and foremost, this is a job. I need to know I can trust the people on my team."

"And you don't trust me?"

"I'm not saying that, Kid, but we mind each other's personal space and respect it. Do you have a problem with that?"

I said nothing.

"Good. Then, I'll see you in the morning. You better have my twenty."

"Not like TV," I mumbled Jack's words as I entered the hotel room.

"Brandon?" Paige's voice called out from the darkness.

I flipped the light on.

"Oh, thanks for blinding me!"

"What are you—"

"Don't ask me what I'm still doing here." She shimmied to a seated position on the bed. "I'll help save you from yourself. I'm not quite sure why."

I didn't say anything. I tossed the contents of my pockets on the dresser.

"Where were you?"

"Just downstairs." I took off my shirt and sat on the edge of the bed beside her.

She moved behind me, scooping her arms around me. Her fingers weaved through my chest hair. She sniffed the air. "You smell like whiskey."

"There's a good reason for that."

"What did I hear you say when you walked in? You mumbled something."

"It doesn't matter."

Her hands stopped moving. "If I asked, it does."

"I ran into Jack down there. We played a game of pool. What is that man's problem anyway?"

"We've been through this. He's seen a lot—"

"And it gives him an excuse to make everyone around him miserable."

"Jack cares too much about other people. That's his problem." Paige pulled back her arms and slid back until she rested against the wall.

"Cares too much?" I laughed.

Paige never smiled. "His mother is in her eighties, boarded up in some nursing home. She's losing her mind to Alzheimer's. He spends as much time with her as he can which, as you can see with this job, isn't much."

"I didn't know that."

"Maybe if you actually talked to the guy."

"I try to, but he either seals up or grunts. He kind of reminds me of that sow at the pig farm."

Paige smiled. "He's not that bad."

"You're not with us when we try communicating."

"He's just not trusting with new people."

"I wish he'd get over it."

"And he saw a lot of horrible things during his time with the Special Forces."

"You know what he just said to me?"

Paige studied my lips when I spoke.

"It's not like on TV."

She let out a small laugh. "Not like on TV?"

"Yeah, as in we're not all best friends, connected by the job, and I mean as if he had to say the job isn't like on TV. The horror we've seen in the last week speaks for itself." Her smile was contagious. I leaned into her and kissed her lips. Afterward I pulled back. "Do you think I'm too positive?"

Paige attempted to cover an outburst of laughter with a hand.

"It's not funny."

"No, you being too positive, that is funny." Our eyes locked, and her expression turned serious. I found mine responding in the same manner. Her eyes went to my lips, then mine to hers. I kissed her again. We made love, and at some point afterward, Paige fell asleep. I didn't think I would.

Thirty-Eight

Morning came too soon, and it felt like I had just fallen asleep when the alarm sounded at seven. I swept a hand across the side of the bed Paige had been on to find it empty. I strained to see if light came from the crack beneath the bathroom door. It was dark, and I didn't hear anything. She must have slipped out and gone back to her own room.

I got up, showered, and met everyone at Jack's room where he had ordered in room service for breakfast. He figured with the privacy of the room it would be a good place to discuss where we were with the case.

"We've tried going about this the traditional way," he said, pausing to put a forkful of scrambled eggs in his mouth. After swallowing, he continued. "Bingham is an organized killer, and we expect no less from his followers."

Zachery sat on the arm of the sofa, balancing a plate on his lap. Paige sipped a cup of coffee.

I said, "Bingham's followers seem to desire involvement in the investigation. Look at Royster. He dropped off the pictures of me to the prison and the hotel. He knew it was going to come back to him. Heck, he was armed and ready for us."

Paige lowered her coffee cup. "He even said to his CSI buddies that he wanted to know how fast the FBI worked."

"And he wasn't afraid of getting caught. He felt he deserved to die for the murder, or murders, he had been involved in, and then the unsub we're looking for was blatant enough to go into your home, Pending."

I stood up from where I was on the sofa. "I agree and wonder if they're acting on their own or from direction somehow."

"One thing's for certain, our unsub loves the cat-and-mouse game. They have narcissistic qualities like Bingham and believe they're untouchable." Jack placed his plate on the nightstand beside the bed where he was sitting.

"They won't be remorseful either," Paige said. "We also need to figure out how Bingham communicates with them. The prison warden hasn't contacted us, so no new mail. It has to be another way."

"Twitter hasn't been active since his message from Wednesday, that's five days ago now."

"We've got to be overlooking how they communicate, or maybe the unsub is acting on their own now." Jack looked at Paige. "We need a background check pulled on all the prison guards."

"I'll get right on it." She got up from where she sat at the table and pulled out her phone. "Nadia…"

Jack turned to me and Zachery, leaving Paige to her conversation. "We know a stressor for Bingham sprang from his childhood. He saw others who didn't live up to Daddy's standards and felt inclined to punish them as his father had punished him. We need to figure out what motivates our unsub."

Paige hung up the cell and sat back on the chair folding her legs beneath her. "She'll have the backgrounds for us as soon as possible."

Jack nodded. "We know there was something special about Anna Knowles. She started the entire cycle. What was it about her?"

Jack's question sat in the air as if it was rhetorical, and at this point it might as well have been because none of us had the answer. Jack continued. "We've visited the family of the victims—"

"There is one person we haven't spoken to," I said.

Everyone looked at me, and for a moment I wondered if I should have kept quiet. Maybe what I had to say wasn't relevant.

"Speak, Pending."

"Well, we spoke to the A.W.O.L. wife of McCartney, Anna's husband, and interrogated the son, but didn't they also have a daughter? Maybe she remembers something about her mother or Bingham? She's older than Reggie."

"She was only a year when her mother was murdered," Zachery said.

"Yeah, but it sounded to me like Bingham was a family friend long after. Keith Knowles didn't express anything like Bingham had disappeared. Besides, to do so would attract attention. We also know there were more victims in Sarasota after Anna, and he didn't move to Salt Lick until eighty-six."

"Oh my God, Brandon. The guy tortured and murdered his friend's wife and hung around for Sunday mass and family dinner." Paige's face paled.

"Yeah." The room held a tangible silence for a few seconds. "And he must have come across innocent because the police never questioned him at length. It tells me he kept a low profile and didn't stand out."

"The perfect malignant narcissist," Zachery said. He got up and put his plate on the table.

Paige straightened her legs out from beneath her and made another phone call. "Nadia…Yes, I know you're working on it. I have something I need right now. I'll hold on the line." She glanced around the room at us as if to say, *You'll see.* She turned to face out the window and spoke lower. Minutes later, she hung up. "Amanda Knowles is the daughter's name. Her background check comes up spotless, and she lives right here in Sarasota. She's a teacher at a local theological school."

Jack looked to Paige and me. "I want you two to go and see what she remembers about Bingham. Maybe he slipped up with her and mentioned something he shouldn't have, like another name or at least something we could go on." Jack pulled a pack of cigarettes off the nightstand and lit up.

"Isn't it a non-smoking ro—"

His glare silenced me.

"I ALWAYS GET THE JOB when a woman's involved. It's almost like Jack admits males and females don't communicate properly."

"I think it's just Jack who doesn't communicate properly with either sex."

"Leave it to you to say that."

We had dropped Jack and Zachery off at the car rental for another set of wheels. With us headed in different directions, it was needed. They were going to the police station to ask more questions of Reggie Knowles. Paige and I were en route to the Bible College where Amanda Knowles worked as a theological scholar. According to the file, she had never married, wasn't living with anyone, and rented a bungalow in the east end which wasn't far from her father's house.

I looked over at Paige from the passenger seat. "I still question whether this is a good use of our time. It just seems there's something else we could be focused on right now."

"Hey, this was your idea. Besides, we're still waiting on the church list from Nadia. It should be coming through soon, hopefully. At least I hope so, or Jack's going to do a backflip." Paige glanced from the road to me. "But we'll have you back to him before you know it. Don't worry."

I smiled and faced out the window.

"So I guess we're not even going to talk about last night."

I turned back to her. "What about it?" Her eyes narrowed but opened fully when I smiled at her. "It was great."

Paige returned the smile. "It was."

"Then what else is there to talk about?"

She bobbed her head from side to side. I watched as her expression changed from one of light-heartedness to a serious nature. "Maybe talking about where we go from here wouldn't be a bad idea." Her arm rested on the window ledge, and she put a hand to her forehead. She pulled into the driveway of the college at a fast speed, causing the rental sedan to heave over the one-inch curb.

I didn't say anything because there wasn't anything to say. We had a case that deserved our focus. I had a marriage that had crumbled, but I still held out a faint hope of reconciling. When Paige had shown up in my room last night, she had known the risks and that there would be no promises.

"This is a non-denominational bible college. Our purpose here is to unite people of all ages, ethnicities, and backgrounds to Jesus Christ and to produce Spirit-filled disciples." The woman behind the front counter spoke as if rhyming off the contents of an information brochure. Her nametag said Maureen, and she couldn't have been older than twenty-five. Her dark hair flowed in wild curls over her shoulders.

I glanced at the brochure that I had pulled from a plastic display holder.

"You will find all of this in there." She pointed at the pamphlet. Her smile showcased teeth. "What can I help you with today?"

It only took a five-minute greeting and brief orientation to come back around to why we were there.

Paige held up her creds. "We need to speak with Amanda Knowles. We understand that she's—"

"Yes." Maureen smiled. I wondered if the expression ever changed. She probably scowled when she went home. At the very least her smiling muscles would be sore. "She's teaching her class right now, but—" she looked at the computer monitor on her desk "—another thirty minutes, and she'll be available. Would you like to wait?"

Paige nodded.

"You can take a seat over there, and I will let her know."

Paige and I walked to a bank of about ten chairs. "She

didn't even blink when you showed her your creds."

"Weird, wasn't it? I'm used to some sort of reaction."

"I think the lady just smiles to get through her day. Can you imagine manning that front desk?"

We both looked back at Maureen who sat there watching us. She smiled and gave us a little wave.

"I'd shoot myself."

THE LADY WHO WALKED TOWARD us was lean and tall. She wore a black business suit with a red blouse. Her hair sprang like flames from her head in a wild frizz, as if she had washed and blow-dried without any aid of hair products. Her green eyes were deep and hard to read. "I'm Amanda Knowles, and you are?"

We both held up our creds.

"The FBI?" Amanda glanced back to Maureen from the front counter who smiled at her. "What could the FBI want with me?"

"We just have a few questions about a family friend. Lance Bingham."

Her arms went like they were going to cross, but instead she slipped both hands into her jacket pockets. The pockets were only deep enough to cover her fingers, her thumbs latched over the fabric. "Why would you think I'd have anything to say about him?"

"We understand he was a good friend—"

"Of my father's. They were of the same age, both involved with the church." Defensiveness sparked in her eyes.

"We're not implying anything improper here," I said.

"I would certainly hope not. Bingham was a good man."

"Was or is?" Paige interjected.

"These days, I wouldn't have a clue, but he was a good friend years ago."

There was an awkward undercurrent to this conversation. Amanda knew something she preferred to keep a secret. At first Bingham was her father's friend, and now she referred to him as a good friend as if implying he was one of hers. I also noticed how when the mention of an improper implication came up, it was Bingham she defended.

"Is there somewhere we can talk privately?"

"I don't see why—"

"We're looking into the murder of your mother as well as the other ten bodies found in eighty-six." Paige fed her the relevant information and avoided disclosing the finding in Salt Lick.

Amanda's eyes fixed on mine. Seconds later, she spoke, "We can go to the conference room in the library."

She led us down some hallways and slid a security card through a reader to gain access to the library.

"Good day, Miss Knowles." A young girl, with her hair tied back into a French braid, smiled at Amanda.

"Good day, Monica. How are your studies coming along? I'm not taking it easy on you just because you're my best student." Amanda winked at the girl but kept walking.

Inside the conference room, Amanda sat at the end of the table. Paige and I sat across from each other.

Amanda tapped the table with her index finger. "What is it you want to know about Mr. Bingham?"

I counted as she tapped her finger. *One, two, three...*

"We want to know what kind of a person he was."

"Why are you looking at him? He had nothing to do with any of this. Police never even considered him a suspect at the time. He is a decent man."

Four, five, six...

"You still keep in contact with him?"

Seven, eight...

"I never said that. I just assume he is because he was."

"You teach theology here?" Paige changed the direction of the conversation. "What is that exactly?"

"It educates minds to open up and explore the world around them, to assign meaning to the greater being of the universe. Really all of us do this in our ways, Agents. You find your work to be the Lord's—"

Paige shifted in her chair.

"This makes you uncomfortable?"

"I just don't consider it the Lord's work."

"Au contraire. You bring the wicked to justice." Amanda looked at me. "You are learning the way."

This woman had almost an uncanny sense of perception. With her eyes on me, my skin tingled. I tried to discount it as paranoia.

Nine, ten...

"Let me show you two something."

Eleven...

She tapped the table one last time before getting up. "It's a little drive from here, though. Is that all right?"

Amanda looked at me when she asked the question, and despite instinct telling me to say no, this woman knew something.

Thirty-Nine

We followed behind Amanda's Kia for about thirty minutes. She led us north outside of the city to the east and pulled into the parking lot of a country church. Boards were on the windows, and a padlock secured an outside basement door.

I turned to Paige. "We should have called in and let Jack and Zach know where—"

Amanda rapped her knuckles on the driver side window. Paige put her window down a sliver.

"Don't worry, it's a friend's building. I know it doesn't look like much, but Bingham brought me here all the time as a little girl. It used to be glorious at one time." When Paige and I didn't move, Amanda said, "It will only take a minute. Call it in, if you like. I watch them cop shows."

Paige reached over and put a hand on my forearm. I knew Amanda had noticed the action. I wondered if Amanda had picked up on the underlying connection between us.

"All right, we have a few minutes," I said.

We got out of the car and followed Amanda to the basement door. She pulled a key out of her jacket and slipped it into the padlock.

"You said a friend's place. Is it Bingham's?" Paige asked the question, even though we knew Bingham didn't show any properties registered in his name except the one in Salt Lick, Kentucky. Paige glanced at me as if to say, *We should have called in.*

We should have, but we had been wrapped up in a heated conversation about what last night meant and where it would go from here. For a good portion of the drive, we weren't even speaking to each other.

Amanda smiled at us. "Not sure what that matters." She pulled the lock off and swung the door open. "If you want to, follow behind me." She phrased it more as a directive than an invitation.

I wasn't looking forward to descending into the basement of an abandoned church. With this case, the two married together too well—the isolated burials and the religious connotation.

"You said Bingham brought you here when you were young?" Paige took the stairs slowly with well-placed hands on the walls for balance.

A few steps down, my heart rate increased and my breathing became labored. The smell of dirt transported me straight to the burial chambers in Salt Lick.

Amanda opened another door at the base of the stairs and flicked on a light. "Lance also had a fond place in his heart for this place. He said this is where he really learned about God and became enlightened."

I pulled my cell from its holder and brought up the messaging screen. Jack and Zachery needed to be notified of where we were. We were careless and stupid for not calling it in.

"Enlightened?" Paige pulled from Amanda's statement.

"Yes. It's when you know what God has planned for you. You realize where you fit in and what differences you can make in this world. In a sense, you were enlightened when you chose to become FBI, as I mentioned a bit at the college."

I had only a few more steps to text the words I needed to before it would have Amanda's attention. I pushed a few keys, but my large thumb impeded my progress.

"What about you?" Amanda looked around Paige to me.

I quickly tucked the phone behind my back. "About me?"

"Why did you become an agent?"

"To make a difference."

"You could do that being a police officer, a teacher, or many other things. That answer is very vague." Amanda kept walking into the basement but faced us.

All I needed was a few seconds of her attention on Paige to finish the message and send it. "My father served his country."

Paige glanced over a shoulder, her eyes saying, *I didn't know that.*

"He was FBI?" Amanda asked.

"Navy."

"Impressive. He knew that in order to bring peace, people must sometimes fight."

"I guess so."

"Still doesn't answer about you."

The conversation held the veneer of new friends getting to know each other. Yet the situation was much different, and any interest was expressed to extract and manipulate.

With each step deeper into the cellar, the intensity in Amanda's eyes deepened, and she watched our every move.

I would have to play along. "I like to travel. Speaking of which, have you ever been to Kentucky?"

Paige turned to face me, and the impact was so quick, I never saw Amanda lift the gun. Paige crumpled to the dirt floor of the basement.

My training kicked in. I went to draw my gun, but my cell was in my right hand. I hit what felt like the send button.

My God, I hoped it was the send button.

"Don't even think about it." Amanda glared at me from the other side of a gun I had no doubt was loaded. Her green eyes were clouded with rage.

I looked down at Paige, seeking evidence of breathing. A raise of her shoulder brought hope.

"Don't worry about her. She'll wake up. It was only the butt end of the gun. You'd only have to worry if I had used the other end."

"What are you—"

"Hand me your phone and gun—now!"

I assessed my surroundings and my options. The basement was unfinished. Its walls were brick blocks, and the floor was flattened dirt. On the wall to the right was a marker board with scribbling on it, none of which I could decipher. Beside it was a large golden cross and a poster of the coinherence symbol. There was an inset in the wall that I assumed led to another room. To the left of the space we were in, there was a coffin. My breathing froze for a few seconds.

Why was there a coffin here?

I tried to rationalize that it was an old church, and maybe it had been left behind.

I looked down at Paige and back up at Amanda. I knew what my next step would be. I tossed the phone.

With her attention on it flying toward her, she didn't catch me drawing my gun. Amanda caught the phone and connected eyes with me. She raised her weapon and aimed it at Paige. "You put your gun down now or she dies. You have eleven seconds!"

Eleven.

My chest compressed. The height of the ceiling only hovered above my head a few inches. I didn't want to become her eleventh victim, and I didn't want Paige to either. I lifted my hands in surrender, realizing that if there ever was a time to turn to God, now would be it. I watched Amanda as I bent down and laid the Glock on the dirt floor.

"Now step back ten feet." Amanda waved her gun.

As I stepped back, I assessed her weight at approximately one hundred and ten pounds to one hundred and twenty-five, shy of my weight by at least sixty pounds. If only she wasn't armed, I could easily overpower her.

"Why are you doing this?"

"Doing what?" Amanda smiled.

The facial expression reminded me of Bingham in prison,

and how he'd smiled when there was no reason to, how he held my gaze and tried to read my thoughts. His words slammed to the forefront, *Repent and be forgiven, or don't and be punished.* "Are you here to exact punishment on me?"

Amanda laughed loudly.

I watched as she picked up my gun, tucked it into the waist of her pants, and closed the distance between us. I studied the grip she had on her gun. She held it tight enough her knuckles were white.

"On Paige?"

Amanda kept moving toward me.

"Why did you break into my house?"

As she came closer, my breathing tightened. If we were both unarmed, the odds would be in my favor, but, armed, Amanda had the upper hand. My mind replayed the crime scene in Salt Lick. The bodies and how they were mutilated, how they were tortured for days before having the final incision be the one that claimed their life.

"Only those who ask the right questions get them answered."

"You're a smart woman."

"Flattery only works on the vain and simpleminded. I am neither."

"You killed people."

"Only those who deserved it."

That was a confession, yet it made me sick to realize one normally confessed when they felt they would get away with it. "You're going to kill me."

"You are arrogant and cocky. You are proud. Scripture says pride comes before a crash. That too is a punishable sin, but there are greater sins, namely hypocrisy."

I wouldn't die without a fight. I studied her movements, but her eyes followed mine.

She stopped walking a few feet from me. Her eyes faltered from mine for only a fraction of a second. I moved forward and grabbed the barrel of her gun. She struggled to gain control of it, pulling back and to the side.

"Let go—"

A bullet whizzed by my head. It bit the upper tip of my ear. Adrenaline infused my bloodstream. My strength grew. I would kill her if that's what it took. She fought back with the power of a man. She punched me in the left eye, and I hit her in the abdomen.

She wailed.

I thought I broke a rib with the blow, but it didn't stop her fighting power. Instead, the pain seemed to have empowered her.

I tried to pull the gun from her grasp, but I had to be careful that a stray bullet didn't get fired again and somehow wind up striking Paige.

Amanda gripped the gun tighter than before. I punched her in the face. She faltered backward. I mustered the strength and roundhouse-kicked her to the chest. The gun flew a few feet across the floor. She lost balance; her legs came out from under her.

I came at her as a predator to take its prey, but a kick to the solar plexus was substantive enough to propel me backward. I came at her again, my focus on reaching the gun, on winning this struggle.

I saw her hand reach into a pocket and come out, but it was too late to avert the result. Electric juice from a TASER shot into my chest.

My body slumped to the ground, my arms and legs paralyzed. My eyelids fell closed.

"I never meant for this to happen." Amanda struggled to her feet. I heard her movements. She went to where the gun had come to rest and picked it up.

I fought to open my eyes. The basement was a blurry haze.

I feared for my life and for Paige's. I didn't want to wake up to being tortured and disemboweled. Our deaths would result from our negligence in failing to notify Jack and Zachery of our whereabouts, but hadn't all the evidence so far pointed to a male unsub? Jack's words came in waves of conscious thought, *We need to think outside of the regular parameters with this case.*

I felt Amanda loop her arms under my shoulders and hoist me on an angle. She dragged me across the floor, but I couldn't move. I couldn't fight against her. I couldn't scream. She dragged me in bursts of strength, alternated with moments of catching her breath.

I willed my body to fight. No strength came.

"You will be fine." Her words were calm.

My eyes willed to close, but I focused on keeping them open. She dragged me past Paige. It was too hard to focus. My thoughts were whirling and were not rational.

Amanda kept pulling on me, until she stopped. "You will rest peacefully in here and be out of the way."

My eyes flashed open, enlarged, and a surge of pain attacked my forehead.

The coffin! No!

I screamed loud enough the world should have heard it, but it only ricocheted inside my head.

She yanked on me, hoisting me slowly and methodically until I was inside. I blinked tears. My fear being realized, and yet I was powerless to fight against it.

"You must sleep." I barely felt the brush of her hand on my arm, even though I saw the hazy silhouette of her reaching toward me. "When this has passed, you will be resurrected."

I lost the fight, and my eyes shut. I felt the faint caress of a hand across my forehead and heard the words, "Shh, don't cry."

Forty

Jack flicked the cigarette butt out the opened driver window. He and Zachery had rented a Hummer H3, the only vehicle left in the lot. Accounting would be on them about it when they got back. People had the illusion the government's budget was extensive, but it had limits like everyone's and sometimes even more so. A requisition form was nearly required for pens.

The Knowles kid had checked out and they were headed over to the Catholic church. Jack's cell chimed with notification of a new text message. As he pulled it out to check the message, it rang. Caller identity announced it as Nadia. He pushed the button to answer. "You're on speaker."

"I have something you're going to want to hear. I have all the backgrounds on the guards from Kentucky Correctional. None of them stood out except for this one: The guy is a nephew to Keith Knowles. It's his sister's kid—and that's not all. The guard's name is Sean Atwood, and he's normally posted to Bingham's wing of the prison."

"Hmm."

"Boss?"

"Gotta make a call." Jack hung up and dialed.

"Clarence Moore here." The prison warden answered on the third ring.

"Special Agent Jack Harper—"

"There still hasn't been any mail for—"

"Is Sean Atwood working today?"

"Yes?" There was a question contained in the single word. He was curious why they cared. "He works regular day shifts Monday through Friday, and every other Saturday."

"I need you to pull him, detain him. I'll call Sheriff Harris and take care of the rest."

"Agent?"

"This isn't an option."

"Okay, but what am I supposed to tell him?"

"Make something up. Bring him to your office. Make him think he's done something great to deserve praise. Don't make him feel threatened or like he's done something wrong. Understand that?"

"Yeah." Moore remained quiet for a few seconds. "Is he dangerous?"

"Just do as I've asked."

"Okay," he drew out the word.

Jack hung up the call and lit another cigarette. "We're thousands of miles away while our unsub could be back where we started."

BINGHAM LAY ON THE MATTRESS, staring at the ceiling. There wasn't much else to do in prison except for track time in your mind as you waited for release, but time wasn't what went through his thoughts. He relived his kills, every one of them. He remembered the way they smelled, how they presented themselves righteous to the world yet sinned in their souls.

Everything had been perfect until now. Anger tainted the recollections.

His follower had been stupid, leading the FBI right to their doorway. They had always been too elevated in mind to think they were vulnerable. For a quality that was potentially great, it could be a weakness to exploit. He feared this would be theirs, but what he cared about more was that if they went down, so could he.

The truth wouldn't continue. People would sin without

consequence.

Bingham heard the voices in the hallway and recognized the man speaking as the prison warden himself. They were a few cells down. Bingham listened carefully.

"You're doing a great job here. I need to speak with you about it. Jamie's going to take the post for a bit."

"Okay."

The man agreeing to leave was Sean. Bingham balled his hands into fists.

JACK PULLED THE HUMMER OVER to the curb and dialed the sheriff. He explained the importance of bringing in backup to go after Atwood. As the profile indicated, he would be extremely intelligent and dominant-natured. When he hung up, he checked the text message that came in. "Did that kid fall and hit his head?" He held the phone out for Zachery to read.

"*We're with Amanda at*...what does that even say? *XJUCRJ.*"

"Your guess is good as mine, but you're the genius. I need you to figure it out."

Zachery kept looking at the text. "He added 'at'...but at what? The next word is just gobbledygook."

"Love it when you talk technical."

"So they left the college with Amanda, but why the change to garble?" Zachery depressed the speed dial for Brandon's phone. It rang through to voice mail. "There's no answer."

"Try again."

Ten more rings. No answer.

"Try Paige's."

"It went straight to voice mail."

"Shit! What the hell is going on?"

"I'll try Brandon's again." A one-second pause. "It's straight to voice mail now. Someone has shut it off."

Both men spoke at the same time. "Amanda."

Jack continued. "Our evidence lends itself to a male

unsub."

"You were the one who mentioned just this morning this case was outside the norm. Look at Bingham's killings. For a serial killer, he gets close to his victims first."

"Shit!" Jack pounded the wheel. "Atwood isn't our unsub. He's Bingham's connection to Amanda."

"Oh no." Zachery maneuvered his body in the seat to face Jack.

"Share it now."

"When Paige and I visited the family of the girl, Sally Windermere, her fiancé's parents remembered her coming to the house a few times with a new friend. Sally had said it was a girl she'd met at church, but the parents never remembered her from there. They couldn't remember the girl's name, but said they thought it started with the letter A."

Jack dialed Nadia. "The unsub has now been identified as Amanda Knowles. Paige and the kid are with her. We have a text from the kid's phone, and I need you to triangulate and find out where the text message was sent from."

"Just a sec." Nadia clicked some keys. "I'm not showing it on."

"The message just came in."

"I'm not sure what to say, but the phone's not on."

"Both Brandon's and Paige's did ring straight to voice mail," Zachery said.

"What about the kid's personal phone? Track that."

"On it." Seconds later. "It's not on."

Zachery gave Jack the look that said, *Since you don't allow personal calls, that would make sense.* Jack wasn't being pulled into the guilt trip. "What about Amanda Knowles? Does she have a cell registered to her?"

"One second." Nadia dragged out the word *second.* "Yes, she does and…it's not on either."

"Shit! So you're telling me there's nothing you can do, and that our two agents are out there on their own? Is that what you're telling me?"

Nadia said quietly, "I'm sorry, boss."

"Don't be sorry. Find them."

NADIA HELD THE PHONE TO her ear for a bit after Jack hung up. What was she supposed to do?

Nadia, think.

Then it struck her. The photographs she had from Royster's home computer. She hadn't had much time to go through them. Maybe they would lend a clue as to another location. Maybe something would stand out among them.

She studied the screen and the picture of the two work boots that were side-by-side. She enlarged it. There was a logo embossed on the side of the beige rubber. She brought up the website for the company to get the ratio of the logo on the full boot and returned to the photo. She made the calculations and she had the proof. The foot on the left was a size eleven, the same as Earl Royster, but the foot on the right was significantly smaller. She dialed Jack.

"You know where they are?"

"I can tell you that the unsub we're looking for is definitely female. The picture of the work boots, the one on the right is a size nine, so unless the man had unusually small feet, this is a common size for a woman."

"Shit!"

"Boss?"

"I let them walk right in there."

Zachery said, "They didn't have to go along with her."

"Go along with her?" Nadia asked.

"They were going to just ask her a few questions about Bingham, what she thought of him, whatever, it doesn't matter now. They went somewhere with her. We don't know where, and now we can't reach them. I don't believe in coincidences," Jack said.

"What alerted you in the first place?"

"The text message, but it's jumbled up."

"Send it to me. I'll see what I can—" Nadia's screen flashed up with a new e-mail. It was marked urgent, confidential, and highly sensitive. The subject was: *Sally Windermere, victim number ten, forensic evidence.*

"Nadia."

"I'm here. Just a sec…" She opened the e-mail, and as she read the finding, her stomach flopped. "You're not going to believe this, boss. Give me a sec, and I'll call you back."

"Nad—"

This time she hung up on him.

PAIGE OPENED HER EYES. The room was dimly lit. She strained to hear anyone or anything.

Where was Brandon?

She was on her side, her neck cocked at an unhealthy angle toward the ground. Her head pounded, and her neck ached. She went to rub it and found her arms constrained. She stretched out and realized her feet were tied together with rope. She pulled in her legs, tucking them as far to her chest as she could and rocked herself to a seated position and looked around the room.

The lights were off, and the only illumination came through two windows at the other end of the room. When she noticed the poster on the wall of the coinherence symbol and a large cross, fear labored her breath.

She saw a coffin in the corner with a silver lock securing it shut and moved toward it, inching her way there like a worm, knees to chest, pull, knees to chest, pull.

"Brandon?"

She felt he was close, yet far away. She feared he was dead inside there. They had upset Amanda's killing method by getting too close. She could break from the norm and kill without holding and torturing. She would still have a male for her eleventh victim.

Paige called out louder. "Brandon?"

Silence.

She rested her forehead on the cool wood of the coffin

and cried.

"DID I MISS ANYTHING WHILE I was gone?" Amanda walked into the college foyer, passed a smile to the receptionist. She was a simple woman, easily manipulated.

"No, I don't think so." She smiled back, pleasantly. "How's your aunt?"

"She's still having a rough go of things, but we're hopeful." Amanda slid a hand along the counter. "Have a great afternoon if I don't see you again."

"You too, Miss Knowles."

Amanda opened the door to face her one o'clock class. She smiled at her students—bright, intelligent minds who were interested in exploring the greater power of the universe. In this room, she had the ability to influence them and to make a difference.

"I WANT ALL OFFICERS OUT looking for her Kia. If she so much as goes on the highway, we'll know about it." Jack barked the order to Chief Brennan.

"And now you want our help?"

"It's not a request."

"You're pulling out the 'feds trump local,' are you?"

"Whatever it takes." Jack lit up a cigarette and sought the nicotine high that never lasted anymore.

"Then I don't have much choice." Brennan disconnected the call.

Jack hung up and merged back into traffic. "Cocky bastard."

They were stuck in a stream of cars. There was barely any forward movement.

Zachery hung up from his call. "I just got off from the car rental. They don't have tracking systems in their cars."

"Son of a bitch."

"We'll find them. I know it. We've faced worse."

Jack looked over at Zachery. "I don't believe in hope."

"Maybe it's time to start?"

Jack's cell rang, and he answered, "You're on speaker."

"It's Nadia. I just received an e-mail from forensics. Doctor Jones in Salt Lick pulled a hair off the tenth victim, whom we have already identified as Sally Windermere. The MtDNA is a match to Anna Knowles."

"The killer is related to Knowles." Zachery elaborated, "The MtDNA profile from Knowles would have been on file to help identify the remains back in eighty-six."

"And there's more: The DNA has been confirmed as belonging to a female, but it has markers similar to that of Bingham's."

"Bingham didn't have any children," Jack said.

"At least not according to any legal record."

"And we're certain it ties back to Anna Knowles as well?"

"Yes, sir."

"So Lance Bingham and Anna Knowles had an affair, she got pregnant with Amanda, and Lance found out about it."

Zachery drew out the rest of the scenario. "This must have been his initial stressor. He grew up with the need to be perfect in the faith. When she got pregnant as the result of adultery, he saw his reflection in Anna, yet held her responsible for the trespass."

"So then the question is: How did Amanda find out who her father really was, and can we prove Bingham knew about her being his daughter?"

"We need a conference video call set up to connect us with Kentucky correctional and Sean Atwood immediately. Route it through the Sarasota PD. We're headed there now."

"Right on it."

The call ended.

"For some reason, traffic's not even moving." They might have moved three feet since the start of the phone call.

"It might be better to leave the car and run there," Zachery suggested.

Jack hesitated but took the keys from the ignition and got

out. "Smoking hasn't killed me yet, running shouldn't."

"Hey, asshole, back in your car!"

Horns honked, and people were swearing. Not that they could see it, but Jack was smiling.

Forty-One

My skin was drenched with sweat, and my heart palpitated wildly. My eyes opened to darkness. My breathing was labored as I reached my hands out to feel the size of the space in which I was enclosed. As they touched the sides, I remembered I was inside of the coffin.

I pushed on the lid. It didn't move. I paused, attempting to get a solid breath and to get my heartrate under control. Nothing I thought of was successful.

"Help!" I didn't want to die in here. I banged on the lid.

"Brandon?"

I heard Paige's voice, but it was shallow as if in the far distance.

"Are you okay? Brandon?"

"Get me out of here!" I could barely breathe. The confined space was suffocating, constricting my chest as a boa constrictor would. I tried to shift my position, but there wasn't adequate room to move much.

"There's a lock." I sensed hopelessness in her voice. "My hands are tied up behind me, and I can't get you out."

I banged both hands on the lid of the coffin as if sheer determination and will to escape would break the lock and lift the lid. My efforts were pointless. I stopped moving and again tried to focus on breathing.

This wasn't personal. The killer wasn't after Paige or me. We had interrupted her plans.

I focused on my breathing. *Inhale. Exhale.*

I said, "I think I know who her eleventh target is."

JACK AND ZACHERY FLASHED THEIR creds to the officer at the front desk. She was the regular one they had come to know over the last couple of days as Rita. She released the lock on the secured doors for them to enter.

"I'll call ahead of you," she yelled out to them.

They rode the elevator to the floor where Chief of Police Brennan and Sergeant Haynes were pacing outside of a conference room.

"It's all set up." Chief Brennan held out a hand to gesture them into the room.

Both local law enforcement officers followed behind Jack and Zachery. Inside the room, there was a table that would seat eight comfortably and a television on a mobile cart at the end of it. The screen showed a man sitting inside a private prison visiting room. A plastic coffee cup sat in front of him, but he kept running a hand through his hair.

"That's your Sean Atwood," Sergeant Haynes said. "Apparently, he hasn't said too much to the sheriff down there. Where is Salt Lick anyhow?"

Jack ignored his question. "Have we heard back from the cars sent to the college?"

"They're still about ten minutes out." Haynes pulled on the collar of his shirt.

Brennan sat back in his chair. "I believe it's time you gentlemen tell us what's going on here. We've been very cooperative. I've authorized the use of our city's resources to assist you with whatever you need. In return—"

"You've only done what you must and won't be charged with obstructing justice and standing in the way of a federal investigation."

"I understand you have two agents out there." Brennan clasped his hands on the table in front of him. "It's all about time, time we don't have."

Jack held eye contact with Brennan.

"We are fully prepared to back you, but if we knew what was going on we'd have a better chance of—"

Jack thought of the pack of cigarettes in his left shirt pocket, but he wouldn't be able to satisfy that calling, at least not right now. He studied the chief's face, and then directed his words to Sergeant Haynes. "A week ago, ten bodies were discovered in Salt Lick, Kentucky. That's a little blip on a country road in the middle of nowhere. The property owner is in prison, but on charges unrelated to murder. His name is Lance Bingham." Jack watched the two men, but the name had no impact based on their facial reactions and body language. "The victims were held for about eleven days and tortured daily before being killed. They were sliced and disemboweled alive."

Haynes's pasty skin paled another shade.

"But there was reason to believe the job wasn't finished. There was another burial site—"

"For an eleventh victim," Chief Brennan piped in.

"That's correct."

"How did you end up here?"

"The find in eighty-six."

"Find? Ah, yes." Brennan's eyes lit with the recollection. "I remember that. Eleven victims. You believe they're connected."

Jack bobbed his head. "Along with other things, Bingham's history traces back to Sarasota. We don't believe it to be a coincidence."

"You said the man's in prison already?"

"Lance Bingham is. His follower isn't."

"His follower?"

"Bingham didn't work alone. Evidence indicates he may have started off that way, but it didn't stay like that."

"Shit." The word escaped from the sergeant's lips.

"Our investigation had led us back here, to the beginning, and now we believe our unsub is Amanda Knowles."

The room remained silent for at least thirty seconds before the volume on the television was turned up and communication was confirmed online with Kentucky Correctional.

Sheriff Harris paced behind Atwood.

Jack did the questioning. "Do you communicate with your cousin, Amanda Knowles?"

Atwood looked around the room. The sheriff pointed at the camera.

Atwood stared in the lens. "She is my cousin."

"Did you bring unauthorized mail to Lance Bingham, an inmate in your wing?"

Atwood reached for his cup but didn't lift it.

"Answer the question."

"Yes." He looked to a corner off camera. "Please don't fire me. I need this job."

A wrist brushed in the way of the lens and clearly belonged to a black person. Also based on Atwood's words it must have been the prison warden.

Jack reclaimed the interrogation. "This mail, was it passed between Lance Bingham and your cousin Amanda Knowles?"

Atwood moved the cup around on the table.

"Answer the question."

"Yes."

"When was the last time something was passed between them?"

"Saturday."

"What was it?"

"I don't know."

Jack punched a fist into the conference table. Although Atwood couldn't see him, only hear him, the bang caused the man to jump. "You don't know what you gave him?"

"Amanda just told me to pass it along."

"It? What was it?"

"An e-mail."

"What did it say?"

"I…I don't know—"

"Not acceptable."

Atwood ran a hand down his face. "She sends them sometimes to me, for Bingham."

"Keep going."

"I'm not to read them. She…she puts his name in the subject. I'm just to print and deliver."

"So you have no idea what the one from Saturday said?"

Atwood shook his head. "No, I respect their privacy. What is this about anyway?"

"You are an accessory to murder."

"Whoa, wait a…" Atwood straightened. "I didn't do anything. Bingham killed some cows and assaulted a neighbor, that's it. He's not a bad man. What's going on here? Accessory to murder?" His voice cracked at the highest pitch of his question.

"You helped a serial killer communicate with his partner."

"He killed cows. His partner? Amanda?"

"Bingham's killed a total of twenty people that we know of. We suspect Amanda has killed at least one and helped in others."

"No. Not possible. Nope."

"Keep him locked up, Sheriff. Absolutely no contact with the outside world. We don't need him alerting his cousin that we're coming after her."

"I didn't do anything. Mandy, she would never—" Atwood lowered his head.

Another phone rang in the conference room. The sergeant silenced the connection to the prison and answered the incoming line. "This is Sergeant Haynes. You're on speaker with Chief of Police Brennan, FBI Agents Harper and Miles."

"It's Officer Millbrooke. Amanda Knowles isn't at the college. They said we just missed her."

"Son of a bitch!" Jack slammed the side of a fist into the table.

"But there's more. They said that she has a sick family member right now and she's been missing classes lately."

Zachery turned to Jack. "It could account for her being in Woodbridge at Brandon's house."

"Did they say what family member?" Jack asked and turned to Zachery. "Possibly the next target?"

"No, they didn't remember."

Jack directed Sergeant Haynes, "Turn the audio back on." Haynes hit the button for the feed to Kentucky Correctional.

"I need you to think about this real hard."

Atwood's head lifted.

"If your cousin isn't at the college, where would she go?"

"I don't know. Home maybe."

"Where else?" Jack raised his voice. They had already sent uniforms there.

"I don't know. I don't know her that well."

Jack turned to Zachery, and in a lower voice mocked Atwood's earlier words, "Yet she would never kill a person." Back to Atwood, he demanded, "When did she and Bingham start communicating?"

"Um, back about six years ago. They met when she came up for a family visit."

"And you never questioned why your cousin wanted to talk to Bingham?"

"I didn't think it mattered—"

"No, you just didn't think."

IT WAS A BEAUTIFUL DAY. The sun was shining. There wasn't a cloud in the sky. Amanda smiled at herself in the rearview mirror and reapplied lipstick. The feds were not a match for her intelligence and planning.

She had no doubt they would be looking for her car at this point. She saw the message that left the agent's phone and had considered sending a follow-up one but thought better of it. All they really knew was that they were with her—somewhere.

The less communication, the lower the risk of leading them to her—and it was hard to factor in the ripples caused by change. Everything had a timetable and had to go according to plan. As it was, the schedule had been accelerated.

She had exchanged her Kia for a co-worker's Ford Taurus Wagon. The woman was dedicated to the outworking of good, so she didn't think anything of it when Amanda told her that she had car trouble and needed to reach her sick aunt. She had used that excuse to get some time off work last week, and people had poured in the sympathy speeches. People were so easily manipulated.

Amanda reached into her bag on the passenger seat and pulled out the nine-millimeter. She would do what needed doing.

MY BREATHING SLOWLY CAME UNDER control, but periodic heart palpitations kept reminding me of the need to get out of the space as soon as possible.

"Brandon?" Paige hit the top of the casket, I assumed with her head because she was bound. "Brandon?"

"I'm here." Another heart flutter. My eyes were heavy. "I keep going in and out."

"You said you know who her target is."

"Yes." My eyes shut, and I struggled to keep consciousness.

"Brandon?"

"Do you—"

"Brandon?"

"Phone?"

"No, and my gun is gone."

"We need to call Jack." Somewhere in the back of mind I knew I had the solution, the way to communicate to the outside world, but my thoughts were unfocused and scattered. My clothes were drenched with sweat.

"Brandon?"

My eyes shut again. My throat was dry. I couldn't speak.

ELEVEN 343
. . .

The phone on the conference table rang again. The officer who called said, "We found her car in the college parking lot."

"Yet you're certain she's not there?" Chief Brennan asked the question.

"She definitely signed out. The receptionist even confirmed she left about thirty minutes ago."

"She switched out her car with someone else's," Zachery said.

"Interview everyone at the college and find out if anyone lent their car to her."

"There's over two hundred faculty members."

"We don't want to hear excuses, officer. Do the job as assigned," Chief Brennan said.

"Yes, boss."

Paige moved, trying to struggle herself free of the constraints. Her shoulders ached along with her neck and back. Brandon hadn't responded to her calls for him. She had to find some way to get him out of there. First, she needed to free herself of the ropes. They bit into her wrists. She inches across the floor toward the alcove on the other side of the room hoping to find something there to cut the ropes.

The distance across was at least ten to fifteen feet, possibly as much as twenty, but if she remained focused, she had no doubt she'd reach the room.

"Brandon?" She called out to him one more time, careful not to speak too loudly. She didn't know where the woman had gone, but faintly remembered hearing a car engine and feeling its vibrations through the ground.

No sound came from the coffin. She moved faster toward the alcove, but once she cleared the doorway, she wished she had stayed where she was. Her heart beat fast from just the action to get here. Now her heart sped up for another reason.

Paige's eyes fixed on the empty circular burial site.

Amanda would be back and victim number eleven would be put to rest there. Brandon didn't think it was them. Paige wasn't willing to bet on anything right now.

There was a doorway on the side of the room. It had a keyhole. Paige moved toward it. If they weren't Amanda's intended victims, was number eleven behind the door?

Her head turned to the left. She heard it first, then felt the vibration. A car pulled in near the church. She had to get back to where she had woken up.

She inch-wormed across the dirt floor, making faster progress back than she had on the way there. The car's engine was cut.

She sucked back on the pain that shot through her back and neck. She paused as she heard the key go into the padlock on the exterior basement door. She had seconds. She wasn't going to make it.

She estimated the length of space to go—about five feet. There was no way she would make it by inching forward. She pulled her legs into her hips and fought to find the balance and strength it would require.

Footsteps were on the stairs.

The options were do this or die. Paige coached herself, and she found the strength to hoist upward to her feet. She hopped along the dirt floor closing the distance to where she had been when Amanda had left.

The handle turned on the door.

Paige dropped and rolled to her side where she had rested before. She heard the door open and shut.

JACK STOOD FROM THE CONFERENCE table. "We can't just sit here waiting on all of this to play out."

"What do you want us to do?" Sergeant Haynes asked.

"Get us a car. We're going out to the college. Send another car to Amanda's house in case she does return, and we'll go pick up the Knowles kid again, Reggie. Maybe he knows more than he told us."

"Certainly."

Jack's cell rang, and he answered to Nadia.

"Two things. One quick update: some fingerprints lifted from the photo mailed to the prison came back to Royster, so no real surprise there, but the other news is huge. The video from The Pawnshop has been analyzed, and it's still not perfect, but it's definitely Amanda Knowles who bought the surveillance equipment."

MY EYES FLICKERED OPEN. My breathing was weak, and my pulse faint, but, for some reason, my thinking seemed clearer. The air inside of the casket was stifling, and I'd quickly be running out of oxygen. I must have been in here at least an hour, maybe over that. All I knew was the oxygen was depleting, and I didn't have much time left. With that thought, my heart palpitated. I had to coax it back into an equal rhythm. I was about to call out for Paige when I heard her scream. My instant reaction was to sit up, and I bumped my head on the coffin.

Amanda barked out to Paige, "To your feet!"

"Please don't! Let go! I'm a federal agent!"

"You're in my territory now."

Paige yelled out, "There's another burial site ready—"

I heard the slap and felt the vibration. Someone had dropped to the floor. As I shifted, I felt the bulge in my back pocket.

"Get up!" Amanda yelled at Paige.

"She has a gun!"

I knew Paige yelled these things for me.

"You get around. You didn't think I'd see your marks on the dirt floor?" A brief pause. "It seems you even visited your friend in the coffin."

Amanda reveled in the psychological mind games with her victims. Just as Bingham had, she kept them alive, tortured them, and taunted them with the possibility of hope, and when the spark extinguished, took their lives. Her waiting to kill us would be her demise because the longer she kept me alive, the less chance she had of walking out of here.

I shimmied in the tight space, careful to move slowly and not cause the wood of the coffin to creak. Sweat dripped down my face, my breathing labored as my heart continued to palpitate.

Focus.

I maneuvered a hand beneath me and reached into my back pocket.

My personal phone, the one Jack would have preferred I left at home. I kept my hands still and listened.

Their voices were low. They were moving away.

I pulled out the phone and shimmied to the side to free enough space to bring it up to me. I bent at the elbows, slid it open, and turned it on. My eyes watered at the brightness of the screen, but as my vision came into focus, the news was good and bad. There was reception down here, but the battery was almost dead.

Shit!

I might not have enough to make a call, but I needed to try. I pushed a button and it beeped. My heart sped up as I worried Amanda would hear it and stop the call from being made, but I heard another door open. It was distant, and I assumed it had come off the alcove.

I pushed the numbers for Jack's phone and cringed as every digit beeped.

JACK DROVE IN A POLICE cruiser with the lights on. Zachery sat beside him.

"We're going to find them, Jack."

"We don't have a choice." He had lost too many men in his life and had seen too much bloodshed. If he could at all prevent it, he would. The cell rang, and Jack looked at the caller ID. "It's the kid's name, must be his personal number."

Zachery pulled out his phone and got on the line with Nadia. "We need you to triangulate a call. Live now to Jack's cell."

"Where are you?" Jack asked.

"I know who the eleventh target is…"

"Kid—" The connection hissed with static.

"Target number eleven is—"

"Where are you?"

"She has us at—"

Jack tossed his cell in the console. "We were cut off."

"Nadia, do you have it?" Zachery asked.

"Yeah, yeah, just give me a second." Seconds passed. "It bounced off towers northeast of Sarasota. There's a lot of empty land and farmers' fields out there."

"What the hell are they doing out there? See if there are any abandoned buildings, churches. Try churches first," Jack directed.

Zachery hung up the phone and looked at Jack. "We will find them. Everything will be okay."

"Stop saying that." Jack pulled out his cigarette pack and lit one. After inhaling deeply, he said, "Amanda Knowles found out Keith wasn't her real father—"

He pressed harder on the gas.

GOD, HOW I HOPED NADIA had tracked the call and that, at a minimum, I had saved a man's life.

I heard voices from outside the coffin but only caught mumbled words.

I needed out. The haziness had somewhat cleared, and it was easier to assess my options. I thought of punching through the lid of the coffin but realized the unlikelihood of that. The space was too tight to muster a punch or a kick that would contain enough strength. On top of which, wood coffins were built to withstand six feet of dirt and not cave in. Unfortunately, my only way out was if someone let me out.

If I yelled and screamed, it would take what little bit of oxygen I had left. I would risk killing myself. If I stayed quiet, Amanda may leave me in here to die.

I had to think of how she operated. She had learned from Bingham. She would be organized, but Paige and I had thrown her plans into confusion, causing her to deviate from her predetermined course and improvise. She had crossed over from being in control of her emotions to an illogical and disorganized state of mind. At this point, she would prove her point and that might mean killing us.

Paige had yelled out there was another burial site and that Amanda had a gun. If Amanda had lost all control, she would have just shot Paige.

The vibrations of footsteps were headed toward me. The lock on the casket struck the wood. As the lid opened, my eyes squinted from the brightness.

Amanda held a gun on me. "Get out now—and do as I say."

"Where's Paige?"

"She's sleeping."

"Did you kill her?" Rage raised the hairs on my neck.

"Get out and do as I say." Her fiery red hair sprang as wild flames around her face.

I held up both arms and got out of the coffin.

"In there." Amanda cocked her head toward the corner alcove, but her eyes and the gun remained fixed on me.

I walked to the corner and looked at the circular grave. Images flashed through my mind of the sites from Salt Lick and the bodies of the victims.

"In that door."

Inside, Paige sat on the floor, her legs bound and her arms behind her back. Her eyes were covered. There was a gurney, and I recognized the man on it. There were two vertical slashes in his torso already.

"Daddy, we have two friends who will be joining us." Amanda graced his forehead with the touch of her fingers.

JACK POUNDED ON THE DOOR to Keith Knowles's house. "FBI!

Answer the door!"

Both he and Zachery held their guns ready to fire.

"We're going in." Jack stepped back and looked to Zachery who charged at the door. It opened, and Zachery had to catch his balance from the momentum.

"Where's your father?" Jack asked the question as he entered the house with Zachery behind him.

"You can't just come in—"

"Where is your father?" Jack repeated the question, his nose gracing the end of Reggie Knowles's.

"He's not home."

"Do you have any idea where he'd be?"

Reggie shook his head.

"Listen, Kid, we need you to keep calm. We have reason to believe your sister has him."

"Has him?"

"Do you have any idea where she would take him?"

"Take him?"

Jack pushed Reggie into a hallway wall. With one hand splayed on Reggie's chest and the other wielding the gun, he said, "Anywhere special to her?"

"I can't think of any—"

Jack's cell rang. He kept the eye contact with Reggie as he backed up and answered. "Agent Harper." He balanced the phone between his ear and shoulder and clipped his gun back in the holster.

"I found a church on Utopia Road up around where the signal triangulated. It's been abandoned for five years now. Its name used to be the Redeemer Church of Christ."

"Send the directions to my phone."

There was no response.

"Nadia?"

"I just got the financials back on Lori Carter, Bingham's sister. You're not going to believe this, but in her will she left a few hundred thousand to Amanda Knowles. Hang on a second. There was a stipulation: She was to buy the church on Utopia Road."

"That's where we'll find them."

Jack went back inside. "Reggie, you're coming with us."

"What? Why? What did I do?"

"We need to keep an eye on you."

Zachery took Reggie's arm and guided him to the squad car.

Behind the wheel, Jack asked Reggie, "Does your father have a cell phone?"

"Yeah."

"We'll need that number."

He rattled it off and Zachery dialed.

I GOT DOWN ON THE floor beside Paige and brushed a hand on her arm, doing so carefully so as not to alert Amanda.

Keith Knowles lay with his eyes closed; his chest rose and fell evenly. He was either asleep or sedated. Beside the cot, a table held a scalpel, a bottle of rubbing alcohol, a jar of cotton swabs, and a towel stained with blood.

"What are you looking at?" Amanda waved the gun at me. "You try to understand, and you will fail. You could never understand why I do this."

The fire in her eyes advised my instinct that it was best to remain silent.

She kept the gun on Paige and me as she brushed the back of her free hand along her father's hairline. "He deserves to die, to gain repentance, to be forgiven."

"You do God's work."

She turned to face me. She studied my face, the contortion of my mouth, my eyes. "That's right."

"All the people you killed deserved to die."

Amanda smiled. "Yes, that is right." Another brush of her hand caressed her father's head.

I had to try to appeal to her intelligence, make her feel unique, elevate her. "Help me to understand."

The smile disappeared. The hand came off her father's

head.

"Did he make you feel less than perfect?"

Amanda's facial expression hardened, and then fell. "Keep quiet!"

I held out my hands. "Please let her go. It will show a sign of good faith to let her go."

"No!"

"They will be here soon."

"You told them where I am? You have sinned!" Spittle flew from her mouth.

"It's the FBI. They have ways of finding people." I used the term *they* in an effort to separate Paige and me and to make us more relatable to Amanda.

"They won't find us here." She picked up the scalpel from the table, wielding it in the hand that had moments ago caressed her father's brow. "You don't seem to understand that I'm in control here, not you, not the FBI." She moved closer to her father. "You made me do this to him." She slid the knife into his torso, holding the skin taut with the side of the other hand that held the gun. The man let out a moan that turned into a wail. "See what you made me do."

Her attention was more on her father than on us. She laid the gun at an angle across the man's torso, and although her hand was close to it, she wasn't in control of the weapon. This was my opening except I knew the moment I'd move she'd turn on me with both the gun and the knife. There wasn't much time to think about it. I had to act.

Amanda moved closer to her father. She looked down at him affectionately, yet there was something more in her eyes. She was losing control, quickly. If I didn't move now, the man would die.

I brushed a hand on Paige's thigh trying to communicate through touch and energy that I was making a move.

"Shh, don't cry, Daddy." Amanda caressed his forehead.

The man's moans were low as if he'd been sedated and the drug kept him groggy and not fully aware of the level of pain his body was experiencing.

Amanda watched over him, hovering there as a loved one tends to a sick relative in a hospital. I moved toward her slowly, still uncertain how I was going to gain the control in the room.

"THE PHONE CONTINUALLY RINGS STRAIGHT to voice mail." Zachery referred to Keith Knowles's cell.

"She's got him." Jack pushed the gas on the patrol car harder. They had called in backup, and their sirens wailed through the city streets and out to the country roads. They served as a reminder that law enforcement couldn't stop all evil from happening, but they could hopefully hold the guilty accountable and prevent some of it.

"How did your sister know that Keith isn't her father?" Jack glanced in the rearview mirror to their captive passenger.

"What do you mean not her father?" Reggie curled his lips backward and up toward his nose.

"You didn't know," Zachery said, shifting in his seat and looking through the bars separating the front from the back.

"No, but she was always different from the rest of us. I just thought she was the black sheep. They say every family has one."

"She never said anything to you about finding herself or who she was." Zachery did his best to lead the man along.

"Mandy always talked about that sort of crap. How can you find yourself? Are you lost? Anyway, a while back, she got on it more, started withdrawing from us."

Zachery turned back around to face the road.

Jack glanced over at him. "She did find out the man she thought was her father wasn't."

Reggie's voice came from the back. "She got in arguments with Dad more. I don't know what about, but they'd yell for hours until one of them would storm out of the house. Normally, it was Mandy. She has a temper, especially when she doesn't get her way or people can't relate to her viewpoint."

Jack looked back in the rearview to the caravan following behind them—five more squad cars and two ambulances. He was ready to take this woman down, save a man's life, and get his team back alive.

MY HEARTBEAT SOUNDED IN MY ears, dulling my sense of hearing, yet awakening my perception in other areas. Amanda's movements seemed to slow down. I broke down her passes in segments. Her attention was solidified on her father. It was almost as if Paige and I no longer existed.

"You could have told me. I would have forgiven you." Her words came out in a whisper.

She moved the knife over his torso again. She was preparing to lower the blade, the time to act was now. I rose to my feet quickly and executed a roundhouse kick to the small of her back. She let out a roaring scream and crumpled to the ground. Her gun fell just out of reach. The blade remained in her hand.

"You must pay!" She slinked across the floor toward me, the bloody knife jabbing at the air, hungry to strike more flesh.

I closed the distance between us, careful not to get slashed by the swaying blade. The gun was near Paige's feet, four feet away. Amanda must have noticed my calculating as she made a move toward it. I lunged across the floor at her and attempted to pin her to the ground. The blade flew wildly, swiping the air with deadly force. She squirmed and moved beneath me, trying to get control, trying to strike me. I lost my grip on her. The blade swiped past my head. She kneed me in the groin. The pain took my clear vision but reinforced my desire to survive.

"You can't stop God's work." Amanda made a move for the gun, and I roped my hands around her ankles.

Her legs kicked in an attempt to free herself and buy the other required few inches to reach the gun. I pulled back on her, but she extended and reached the gun. The blade dropped to the ground. The gun pointed at me.

"Get off me or I will shoot her!" Amanda glanced at Paige, but for too brief a time for me to make any movement toward her. If I did, I'd have a bullet between the eyes.

"I will do what I came here to do." Amanda scooped the knife from the ground and rose to full height. Her attention was on me, the gun aimed at my forehead. "Try something like that again, and they'll be collecting your brain matter from the floor."

I sat there, filtering dirt through my fingers, feeling powerless, but as Amanda brushed the skirt of the cot, I noticed a black mass under the bed. Amanda moved more to the right, and the light in the room revealed its identity. This would be how we'd get out of here alive.

JACK AND ZACHERY NOTICED THE rundown church from a distance.

He turned on the radio to address the other cars. "Sirens off, now!"

"Copy." The officer from the other cars came back, even though it wasn't necessary as everything went to silence.

Jack looked to Zachery. "We don't need to scare Amanda into doing something. Her mind works differently. If she feels threatened, she won't back off; she'll go at it stronger which means no one will walk out—"

"You think she's going to kill Dad," Reggie interrupted.

A SMIRK LIFTED THE CORNER of my mouth as I viewed the find as a buoy among stormy seas.

Amanda's attention had become fixed on her father again.

I moved across the floor slowly, inching my way toward the underside of the bed. My fingers grazed the grip of the gun. If I could get just a little closer—

A foot kicked me in the abdomen. I curled like a poked caterpillar, both of my hands cradling my gut.

"You must want to die." She aimed the gun at me; a flicker in her eyes darkened them. She sat the gun on her father's torso and came at me with the scalpel. "You want to feel their pain before you go? Be cleansed of your sins?" She came down toward me, the knife gripped tightly in her hands.

"Were they all sinners?" I had to buy time for the knot to untie from my core.

"Yes, I told you."

"Even Sally Windermere?"

"She was a fornicator." Amanda came down on top of me and straddled my torso.

"And she alone was guilty? Why not her fiancé, too?"

Amanda smiled. "It was a lady's turn to pay for sins. Now it is a man's, but plans can be modified. You, her—" she bobbed her head backward to gesture at Paige "—and then him. The man who called himself Father."

The man who called himself Father? My suspicions had been completely accurate, but I tested them further. "Why him?"

"He committed the greatest sin: hypocrisy. He pretended to be my father when he wasn't. Lance is."

Hearing the verbal confirmation sent images and audio through my mind as a slideshow. Reggie had said Keith may have appeared righteous, but added the man wasn't that pure, and the way Amanda came to Bingham's defense at the college, terming him a good friend. What had cemented my assumption was her smirk and how it held a familiarity that had first transported me to Bingham. Something in her eyes brought a sense of déjà vu. "I see the resemblance." I extended my arms to reach a gun. My fingertips fell shy of contact.

"You're being snide."

"I'm being truthful. You're intelligent like he is."

"Again, flattery only works on the weak-minded." She leaned down further over me. "Are you ready to die?"

The blade lowered. I reached for the gun. The weight

didn't feel right. I pulled the trigger, heard the click. Amanda laughed. "You didn't think I'd be stupid enough to leave it loaded, did you?"

I gripped on the wrist of her hand that held the knife.

"You can't stop me!"

I squeezed it tighter. Amanda screamed. Her hand released the knife. She came at my throat with both hands. I held her back with one arm and tossed the knife toward the corner where Paige sat.

"To your left," I called out.

"No!" Amanda rose from me and charged toward Paige. I took the gun from her father's torso, aimed directly at her brain stem, and pulled the trigger.

Amanda's body flew forward.

"Brandon!"

I hurried over and pulled the dead woman off Paige. I lifted Paige's blindfold. "The nightmare's over."

Paige took a deep breath.

I traced a finger down her nose and went to kiss her lips.

"Great job, Kid."

I turned around to see Jack, Zachery, and a few uniforms standing behind them.

"I catch the serial killer and I'm still Kid?"

Paige smiled at me as I undid the ropes on her.

"You have to earn a name, Kid."

Paramedics came in the room and tended to Knowles. I pulled up from my haunches, helped Paige up, and went over to Jack. "He's not her real father."

Jack's smile slanted higher to the right, his eyes pinched. He put a hand on my shoulder. "Yeah, we know, Kid. Lance Bingham is. Turns out Anna Knowles had an affair on her husband. When she wouldn't leave him to be with Bingham, he snapped and saw it as his job to punish her."

"Anna was Bingham's stressor."

"And when Amanda found out about the lie, she sought out her real father. Obviously, she found someone she could relate to."

"Obviously," I said.

All of us glanced over at the paramedics working on Keith Knowles.

"Of course, somehow you pieced this all together." Jack's eyes held the question, *How*.

"Well, I had a bit of time to think. If Amanda was Bingham's daughter, it would create a strong enough bond to make her capable of such horrible things. She would follow in his footsteps to feel like she belonged. With her mother dead and uncertain who her real father was, she'd feel like she'd lived her life with strangers. She was the perfect find for Bingham."

"Hmm."

A paramedic said to us, "Looks like he's going to be all right. His blood pressure is a little low, but we'll get him get a trauma line set up and that should improve things. A few days' rest and some stitches, and he'll be fine."

I couldn't help but think, as they loaded the man on a stretcher, how he might be fine physically down the road, but psychologically, he'd have a long road ahead of him. I knew I would.

Epilogue

onths later, we had moved through several cases, most involving another killer after revenge or seeking justice for some cause, but my first case with the Behavioral Analysis Unit would never leave me. The case of the ten bodies buried in a small rural town of Salt Lick, Kentucky, of a man and daughter who felt imperfect measured against godly standards, and who felt it their divine right to execute punishment on those who fell short.

I sat at my desk in Quantico finishing up paperwork from a recent case, but my mind was still on the victims who were murdered in Salt Lick and Sarasota.

The Sarasota PD had concluded their investigation into the shooting of Robinson, and Paige's shot was ruled a good one. Officer Bryant was found guilty of tampering with evidence, was suspended, and would be serving time.

Amanda's body was being buried in the lot behind the church, and Keith Knowles made his stand clear with the words, *Man doesn't have the right to judge, nor truly forgive.*

Even coming from a former priest, who heard and forgave parishioners confessions, he was right. We are all people, basically alike, fragile and strong, and despite these attributes coming in different forms, shapes, and sizes, they are nonetheless what make us unique. Who are any of us to point the finger at another man?

As for Bingham, he faced lethal injection. With connections tying him to twenty murders, there was no way for him to talk himself out of this. Although I supposed, for a man like Bingham, he probably continued to scheme escape despite the odds against him.

Sean Atwood, who had served as the communicator between Amanda and Bingham, was charged with conspiracy to commit a crime. It was still being debated in the courts, though, because it was hard to prove that he knew the contents of the letters.

As for the victims in Sarasota, we were able to obtain identities for three out of the five who had previously remained nameless. We requested DNA from Tammy Sherman, the aunt to Jenkins's daughter, and were able to give the man closure. He said he would finally have some peace in his life.

In Salt Lick, eight out of ten victims were identified, including Robert Royster, Earl's brother, and Kurt McCartney.

I closed the file folder and noticed Jack walking toward me with a cigarette perched in his mouth.

"Special Agent Fisher, are you finished with your report yet?"

I smiled. I had earned a name. It only took nearly being killed and a few more cases, but it had never felt so great to have a name. "Almost there."

"All right, Brandon, but they're serving wings and martinis tonight down at the pool hall." He took the cigarette out for a second and smiled.

"I'll catch up. Just give me a minute."

As Jack walked away, I realized I was satisfied with my choices in life. As for the one thing that didn't belong in any FBI report, Deb had moved out by the time I had returned from Sarasota. She hadn't called, but I had received a letter from a lawyer with divorce papers. Even though life presented tougher situations than any job could, I had come through a stronger person.

"You coming or what?"

I turned to see Paige. She smiled at me, her eyes happy and soft, vulnerable yet courageous.

"It's going to be time to call it a night before we get there."

"Let's go." I closed the file and got up.

Paige had become so much more to me than a team member. She had become my best friend. She had seen me both at my worst and my best and loved me in each scenario. I knew it hurt her deeply that I couldn't commit to a relationship right now, but I also made it clear no one can know the future.

I wrapped an arm around her, and we headed for some cheap wings and beer. Maybe Jack would even give me another chance to earn my twenty back.

Catch the next book in the Brandon Fisher FBI series!

Sign up at the weblink listed below
to be notified when new Brandon Fisher titles are available
for pre-order:

CarolynArnold.net/BFupdates

By joining this newsletter, you will also receive exclusive
first looks at the following:

Updates pertaining to upcoming releases in the series, such
as cover reveals, book descriptions, and firm release dates

Sneak peeks of teasers and special content

Behind-the-Tape™ insights that give you an inside look at
Carolyn's research and creative process

There is no getting around it: reviews are important and so is word of mouth.

With all the books on the market today, readers need to know what's worth their time and what's not. This is where you come into play.

If you enjoyed *Eleven*, please help others find it by posting a brief, honest review on the retailer site where you purchased this book and recommend it to family and friends.

Also, Carolyn loves to hear from her readers, and you can reach her at Carolyn@CarolynArnold.net.

Upon receipt of your e-mail, you will be added to her newsletter mailing unless you express your desire otherwise.

Keep on reading for a sample of *Silent Graves*, book 2 in the Brandon Fisher FBI series.

Prologue

"THE GRAVES LAY SILENT. The graves lay untouched. The graves lay silent. The graves lay untouched."

He tapped his hand against his thigh as he repeated the chant. He had done everything right. He had made sure not to leave anything behind and had chosen only those who deserved to suffer and die.

The way they'd tilt their heads back in laughter, flaunting what wasn't theirs to own, draining their cocktails as if there was no tomorrow. No risk. Nothing to lose.

Chapter 1

Prince William County, Virginia
September

He had promised her a time she'd never forget. It was why she sacrificed comfort and drove in her stuffy BMW into the countryside. The weather had such nerve to reach record heat waves in September. It scorched as if it were the middle of summer.

She glimpsed in the rearview mirror, angling it to better see her reflection.

"A woman has been reported missing…"

Those few words from the radio made it through to her ears. That was top news? Surely, there was a murder, or a stock market drop to report.

"…it's suspected that she may be the victim of foul play. Police are urging women of the Washington, DC area to be careful."

She laughed. Be careful.

A song came on, one she didn't care for, and she commanded the radio off.

She had never been where he had directed her to go, but she was excited to see this Wooded Retreat. Usually, they'd meet up at her house or the Marriott, but he had wanted today to be special—personal.

She had long given up on feeling guilty about her marriage. Her husband was too busy with his prestigious law firm in central Washington. Really, it was his work that killed their marriage—his love for revenue his priority.

Her focus returned to the road and where she was headed. She wasn't used to the country with all its color. She was accustomed to the shades of gray that were intrinsic to life in the city. Maybe there was something to be said for the simple things. She lowered the window and breathed deeply, ready to give the rustic experience a chance.

The air was fresh, despite the humidity, carrying with it the smell of greenery—but there was something else. She inhaled deeper, coughed, and raised the window back up. Damn blasted cows that polluted nature with their stench.

Why would he think she'd be in the mood once she got there?

The thought barely formed, and she had the answer. He was a fabulous lover. Thinking of his hands caressing her skin sent shivers through her and made her lower abdomen quiver.

She turned left when she noticed the rundown diner he had mentioned to her.

The gravel crunched beneath her tires as she went from the highway's asphalt to an unpaved surface. The strip was narrow, barely wide enough to accommodate two cars if one came in the opposite direction. She studied the edge, anticipating the need to do just that. The soft shoulder appeared unforgiving as if it would suck in her car given a chance.

Fifteen miles.

She found it hard to believe this stretch would continue that long. Her eyes went to the woods, being cautious, watching for any deer or other animal that may decide to become a hood ornament. She checked her side mirror. All the dust being kicked up would wreak havoc on the wax job.

So much for showing up looking perfect.

She glanced in the mirror again and touched her fingertips to her forehead. She couldn't let him see her like this.

Driving with one hand, she reached into her designer handbag on the passenger seat and pulled out her compact. She lifted the loaded brush and the air conditioning vent cascaded powder through the air. She blew to keep it from landing on her cream-colored pantsuit and began application. The scent of the powder made her sneeze.

As she reached for control of the wheel, the case dumped on the floor, going straight through her legs, barely missing her pants.

She slammed on the brakes. The mailbox he had told her to watch for, once a bright red, had worn from time. She almost missed the turn.

She couldn't see the house from the road, but her heart beat rapidly now, anticipating what awaited her.

She fished into her bag again, this time for her gloss. She smeared some on with a finger, smacked her lips, looked in the mirror, and declared herself perfect. She was ready to go to bed with her lover.

Chapter 2

WOODBRIDGE, VIRGINIA
SEPTEMBER, TUESDAY MORNING

A COUPLE MONTHS HAD PASSED, but I was still getting used to sleeping alone. Most mornings I would roll on my left side, open my eyes, and expect Deb to be lying there. Every time I did this, it met with the same result. I was alone.

The mornings were hard to take. At night, my mind was usually preoccupied with the day's events, a current case, or the complicated relationship that existed between Paige and me. We had just closed a case a few days ago, and it was easier to let go of that than the continuing innuendos that remained, as fissures, beneath the surface of our relationship. I loved her, in a way, but not on the level she required. She acted as if everything was fine, but I knew—I sensed—it wasn't.

I rolled over and faced the clock. Five a.m.

I returned to my back and stared at the ceiling. It was hard adapting to the early mornings, but these days I usually beat the alarm. Even on days off, my body would wake me.

AC/DC's "Thunderstruck" came on, and, at the same time, my cell vibrated on the nightstand. I rolled over again and sat up. It wasn't like I would be getting more sleep anyhow.

"Rise and shine, Kid."

I rubbed a hand across my brow. Even though I had earned being called by name from Supervisory Special Agent Jack

Harper, periodically old habits would resurface and, with it, the nicknames. "What's up?"

"What's up? Am I some friend now? I'm your boss."

"I'll save professional for office hours," I said the sardonic statement with a grin I'm sure he didn't miss. In this career, there was no such thing as set hours.

"Come in straight to the meeting room today. We've got a new case."

"Sure."

"What's that noise in the background? Have you been partying all night?"

I hit the button and turned it off. "It's AC/DC, classic rock."

"Well, it's not music. Music is—"

"I know—The Rat Pack, Natalie Cole, Michael Bublé."

"Don't knock it, Kid, and there's nothing wrong with Michael."

Yeah, I suppose if you're good with the crooner music in the first place.

"See you soon," I said.

"Don't be late."

I rolled my eyes, wishing the expression weren't lost on the walls of my bedroom, yet thankful he couldn't witness it, or I might be searching for a new job.

I rose from the bed and flicked on the stereo, turning up Nickelback's "Burn It To The Ground" until the glass in this old house rattled. I loved this song, and loud was the way I preferred it.

I had an hour to make it to the office. I wrapped my hands and wrists with tape, and then started beating on the heavy bag I had installed in the bedroom. Deb never would have let it happen, but I didn't have her to worry about anymore.

With each impact, I let it go—the stress, the anger, the frustration, the lack of control. The physical movement drained the negative and infused me with the positive.

Adrenaline pumped through me, and I embraced it, as I

roundhouse kicked the bag. It swung on its chains. I reset the bag and had at it again.

The song changed to the next on the playlist—Poison's "Nothin' But a Good Time".

Damn. Now this was music.

I uppercut and jabbed at the bag mercilessly, going at it as if sucking its life force.

Thirty minutes later, sweating profusely, I headed for the shower. There was no better way to start the day. In a matter of minutes, I'd be facing the next monster to cross paths with the FBI.

I SMILED AS I ENTERED the meeting room just on time. How could one get any more punctual than that?

"You're late, Fisher." Jack was sitting at the table with the rest of the team.

"It's Pending, boss. He probably forgot to set the alarm." Zachery lifted a steaming take-out cup to his mouth, cutting his smirk short. Whenever he could poke at my probationary period with the nickname, he would.

"He even got a wake-up call," Jack mumbled.

"Brandon," Paige said. Her red hair hung in loose curls, serving as a soft frame for her face, but her eyes were cool.

I took all of them in, not sure how they did it. They were there, not just on time, but early. They were all alert, despite the caffeine they clung to as if their lives depended on it.

"Sit. We don't have all day." Jack patted his shirt pocket where he kept his cigarettes. He had probably already smoked a few since waking up.

"Hey." Nadia came up behind me and tapped me on the back as she walked by.

"Hey." I took a seat.

The screen was filled with faces of various women. On the left side, was their smiling before photos. On the right, was the aftermath—their remains, part flesh, part bones.

Nadia clicked the remote she held, and the screen filled

with a picture of one woman. She was beautiful, with long dark hair and brown eyes. Nothing, in particular, stood out about her.

"Her name is Amy Rogers. Her husband is Kirk Rogers."

"Hmm."

I knew what Jack was thinking—money bought results. We were in the Behavioral Analysis Unit to stop serial crime, not for a single abduction. Why weren't the police handling this case?

"He owns the communications company Trinity," I said.

Nadia acknowledged me with a bob of her head. "That would be correct Brandon, but the man has lawyers, and he paid people to do some snooping around. They found out that a bunch of women have gone missing in the area over the past decade. He also has a tight friendship with the chief of police down in Washington. He had him call us in."

"So, we're looking for Amy Rogers? No real concern for the other missing women?" I knew I was being cynical, but the power of a buck, the control and sway it held, sickened me at the best of times.

"We're investigating this case because this is the one we've been assigned." Jack intensified the reprimand with a hardened facial expression.

"I'm not saying anything contrary to that. It's just—"

"I know what you're saying, Brandon. We have a chance to find Amy Rogers before it is too late. To accomplish that, a good place to start is investigating the older cases," Paige said.

I let what she said go. I didn't need another parental surrogate on the team. I already had a father figure in Jack. I addressed Nadia. "Who were these women you had on the screen when I came in?"

"Their naked bodies were found in ditches along I-95 between Lorton and a little west of Dumfries."

"No jewelry or anything?" Zachery asked.

"No."

"I-95 is a major highway, but it's not a huge stretch. What—twenty minutes," Paige offered. "It's likely someone from the area."

"How many women and how long ago do these bodies date back to?" Zachery asked Nadia.

"The oldest dates back to nineteen seventy. Her name was Melanie Chase. She was discovered along I-95 near Woodbridge by the Levine family who was on a road trip. The youngest, age three, had to go to the washroom. There were no rest stops for a distance so the father pulled over for the kid to go, and they got more than a number one."

Woodbridge? That is where I live. "How was she killed?"

"The ME ruled the cause of death as being pulmonary edema."

"Fluid in the lungs." Everyone gave me the once-over as if to say, yes, that would be pulmonary edema. "What about the other victims?"

"Another died of a severe stroke while yet another of a brain hemorrhage. These three old cases, the thirty missing women from Prince William County—"

"Thirty?"

Nadia nodded. "Yeah, that has our interest too, and that's thirty missing women in the last six years. Seems Amy Rogers wasn't the only target."

Zachery quickly compiled the math. "On average, that's one woman every two months."

"Holy crap." The words left my lips without thought, and everyone's attention was on me again. "What more do we know?"

"These three women were married, as is Amy Rogers. None of these women had children either. All were reported by their husbands. All of them were taken from Washington or PW County. It's too coincidental to ignore."

"I agree," Paige said.

Nadia turned to the screen, magnifying on their wrists and ankles. "The three women that were found all had these same markings. It appears the killer had bound them all with linked chain."

"I see there are different nationalities among the victimology." Zachery bobbed his head toward the screen.

"Yes, the only similarities are what I mentioned—married, no kids. Among the law enforcement community, by the time the third victim was found, he had earned the moniker The Silent Killer."

"And here, I thought that was cancer," I said implicating Jack's smokes.

Nadia continued as if I hadn't said anything. "Based on forensic evidence, these women were aware they were going to die but couldn't do anything about it." Nadia's face paled and she swallowed heavily.

"Ketamine?" Zachery lifted his cup but didn't press it to his lips.

"Actually, there wasn't any trace of that in their systems."

"Possibly something herbal then that would inhibit their ability to move and then leave the system quickly."

"If they figured one person was responsible for the death of these three women, why not call in the FBI?" I asked.

"They did, but the case was never taken on. The killer went silent, no pun intended, and there didn't seem to be any threat."

"We're thinking this guy's back and could have Amy Rogers?"

"That's exactly what we're thinking."

Chapter 3

THE NEWS WAS PUBLIC NOW. Another woman's life summed up in the media—missing. Trent Stenson wished he could discredit it as something menial. He was surprised it was worthy of the news, and the reason was likely because she was the wife of some rich businessman—Kirk Rogers of Trinity Communications—and he was worth millions. According to the newspapers, Rogers even got the FBI involved.

His superiors made Trent feel that his contributions held little value. He had the official training and three years on the job, but he didn't rank and was kept under the label of officer. There wasn't much room for advancement within Dumfries PD, but he could always move up to captain. That was the only downfall about a smaller department. People typically retired before they were replaced. It had him considering a move over to Prince William County PD where they had about six hundred officers to Dumfries eleven. PWPD also got involved with the complex crimes—where he saw himself.

He already had a friend there too. Lenny Hanes, a detective from the Violent Crimes Bureau. They even had beers on occasion. Trent hoped that Hanes would put in a good word and help him transfer and advance, but things hadn't worked out that way yet. For the most part, shit floats to the top. At least, that's how some disgruntled cops saw things.

But none of this stopped Trent from doing the job. In fact, he was determined to excel. He subscribed to the advice "anything worth doing is worth doing well."

Amy Rogers wasn't the only missing wife who graced the missing persons database from the area. There had been many others before her. He suspected more would follow.

He looked beyond the front desk, and out the glass doors to the parking lot. It was a quiet night. The PWPD communications center had dispatched only a couple domestics calls and one drunk and disorderly at a local bar. Officer Becky Tulson had that covered.

Yes, it was the perfect time. Management had left for the evening—it was up for debate who benefited the most from their absence. He loved being left alone to do his digging, and these missing women had his attention.

He logged onto the missing persons database and searched the area for women ages twenty-two to thirty. It didn't seem race mattered so he let that parameter go. He searched Prince William County and surrounding areas as far as Washington on the south side.

Thirty faces came on screen. He searched for new ones. He had the others memorized and categorized in his mind— and in his filing cabinet at home. If his sarge found out about the latter, he could lose his badge, but it was worth the risk if it meant bringing even one woman home.

Most of their faces were familiar to him. He scoured this information every day, sometimes more than once day. It had become not a fascination, but an obsession.

Who would take these women? How did the husbands lose track of their wives?

Not that Trent had any experience being married. He was only twenty-four and preferred to hold onto his single lifestyle as long as he could. He didn't need a woman telling him how to live his life.

He dropped forward and cupped his forehead in the palm of a hand for a few seconds. His bangs brushed the back of his hand. Silly how, at a time like this, he thought of his mother and how she preferred his hair cut above his collar. He let it grow out, only trimming its length periodically. The women he took to bed liked to run their fingers through his hair.

The door opened, and a woman in her late sixties walked in. Her blue eyes stood out in stark contrast to her pale face and gray hair. Tears had dampened her cheeks.

"I should have called it in. I shouldn't have driven all the way here." She shook her head, and tremors ran through her body as if she fought off a chill.

Trent rounded the desk. "Ma'am. Slow down. You're safe now."

The radio crackled to life, and Officer Tulson confirmed she was returning to the station.

"Sorry about the interruption. Ma'am?"

In the time he listened to the transmission, the woman had collapsed to the floor. She sat there with her knees tucked into her chest.

"Ma'am. I'll call you an ambulance. You'll be fine."

She reached for his hand and tugged on it. "There's no time." Her eyes seeped fresh tears. "It's there...I found it. I should have called."

Trent agreed with her assessment that she should have stayed put at home and called it in, but he didn't verbalize this. "It's okay. You said, 'it's there' ma'am? It what?"

She nodded, slowly. Her eyes reached into Trent's. Her body heaved with another bout of crying. Her hand covered her mouth, her eyes pinched shut, and her head burrowed to her knees.

Oh, he thought, please don't be another crazy.

"Ma'am, I can help you, but only if you talk to me. Let me help you off the floor." He held out a hand to her, and she took hold. He helped raise her up, but when she reached about halfway, her legs faltered.

"You have a face like my grandson."

He pulled up on her, attempting to straighten her out—this time assuming most of the responsibility against gravity. He feared that, if he let go, she'd crumple back to the floor.

"I could go home and pretend I never saw a thing. I'll shut my eyes, and the body will be gone."

The body?

Morbid excitement pulsed in his veins.

A homicide case—in his lap? Maybe this was the break he was waiting for?

He reined in his emotions which were balanced quickly by the realization that this body was once a human being, or at least he hoped so, although, even that thought sounded wrong to him. He didn't need a crazy making a fool of him. If he took her seriously and an investigation revealed nothing more than a decomposing cow on a riverbank, or even worse, thin air, he'd never make detective.

He considered the empty station. If anyone came in, no one would be at the front desk. "Excuse me. One minute." He spoke into his radio. "Officer Tulson, what is your ETA?"

"Tulson here. Pulling in now."

"Roger that." He turned back to the woman. "We'll just wait for Officer Tulson and we'll make out a report."

The woman nodded. She understood. Good. She had some wits about her.

He studied her in those few seconds. Her eyes, although moist, were cognitive. There was awareness behind them. Her pupils followed his as he took in her face. They were not dilated or pinpricks. She wasn't on medication.

"Honey, I'm home." Becky walked in the front door, her steps coming to a standstill when she saw the woman.

He went over to Becky.

In the limited space of the station, her sexual pheromones sparked making it impossible for any man in her vicinity to ignore them. She had a uniquely shaped face, and, when paired with her confidence, it made her beautiful.

"I need you to watch the front for a bit."

"Sure."

The way Becky's gaze pierced his eyes, he wondered if she read his thoughts. Then she smiled, but only a partial display. The light in her eyes completed the expression.

Trent led the older woman to a conference room, thankful his sergeant wasn't there to take over. If he got in over his head, though, he had someone he could call—Hanes—but he'd reserve that as a final option. Technically, he should have driven her to PWPD, but why squander this opportunity?

"Would you like some water?" he asked.

She was already seated at the table. "Yes, please."

He poured a glass and sat beside her. "My name is Trent Stenson." He dropped the officer part, not because he lacked pride in his position, but what did it matter in here? If he wanted her to relax and feel like an equal, he needed to level the playing field. "And you are?"

"Audrey Phillips."

Holding a pen in his hand, he fidgeted with the pad in front of him. He would rather listen to her recollection of the situation and then make notes, but he had to follow things by the book if he would ever rank. He wrote her name on the form.

"Now, you said you found a body?"

Her face paled further, eyes blank and distant. She nodded.

"This was a human body, I assume."

Seconds had passed before she answered. "Yes."

This would take a long time if all he received were simple answers, direct, concise, and to the point. "Continue." His pen was poised, eager to spread some ink on the page.

"Most of her…" Shivers jerked her shoulders upward and her head twitched. "Most of her was a skeleton, but her face, her hair, it was there. And she was…gray. Is that normal?"

Excitement laced through his insides. Could this be one of the missing women?

"Where did you find her?"

"Out back. On my property." She gave him the full address and waited while he took down the details. "She was in the field. Just…just lying there." She covered her mouth with a hand, lowering it a second later. "We had flooding, but it's receded now. Do you think she came up in the river?"

It was too early to offer an opinion, and they needed men out on the scene. The longer the body remained exposed to the elements, the more contaminated it would become.

"How old do you think she was?"

She lifted her shoulder and nudged it against an ear. "Thirties. I took this. " She pulled out a plastic sandwich bag and extended it to him. Inside was a gold band.

He wanted to scream, you touched the body, but, instead, countered with, "She was a married woman?"

Audrey nodded.

He took the bag and pinched the ring between his fingers. Saying those words out loud caused images from the missing persons database to play through his mind as if on fast forward.

Could it be her?

He studied the ring and got the burning sensation in his gut, the one that contracted it into an acidic raisin. "Can you excuse me for a minute?"

"Yes, of course." Her brows sagged, and the corner of her mouth twitched as if she were confused by his rush to leave the room.

"I will be back. We need to get some officers over to your place."

His heart beat fast, the pressure in his gut not easing up, instead, intensifying. He pulled out his cell and dialed. "Len…you're at home…this is important. You know all those cases we've been talking about? How I think they're all connected somehow? Well, now we have a body."

Detective Lenny Hanes stood in the doorway of his kitchen. He watched his wife cleaning up the dinner dishes and loading what would fit into the dishwasher. Nicole and Brett, both under eight years of age, had been put to bed not long before. Lenny hoped the ringing phone hadn't wakened them.

"You're sure this is her?" he asked into the receiver.

His wife looked at him and he mouthed the words, it's a case.

"When isn't it?" She closed the dishwasher door and started the cycle, leaving him in the kitchen but kissing his cheek on the way by. "See you in the morning?"

Lenny made a sad face. He held her hand until it filtered out of his, keeping his eye on her until she disappeared up the staircase.

"The ring. It matches, I swear to you." Trent sounded out of breath.

"And she took the ring off the woman's finger?"

"Off Nina's finger? Yes."

"Before you get all caught up on—"

"I swear to you, it is. The engraving on the band matches the one noted in the missing persons database and there's—"

"There's what?"

"Audrey Phillips, who found the body and took the ring, she took some of the flesh with it."

Bile hurled up Lenny's esophagus. He swallowed—roughly. "What is wrong with some people?" His stomach tightened, compressing his dinner into a reduced space.

"Don't know. She seems like a sweet woman, but I don't get it."

"People do strange things when faced with extreme circumstances."

Lenny remembered one case where a woman leaned over her husband's body and open-mouth kissed him. She only admitted that he was dead when he didn't reciprocate. The hole in his head and the blood pool around him wasn't enough. He shook the memory from his mind.

"And you haven't told anyone else about this yet?" A

couple of seconds passed. "Trent? You hear me?"

"Sorry, I was shaking my head." He let out a small laugh. "Guess you couldn't see that."

"No." Lenny sensed a mixture of emotion coming through the line. Trent was excited that his fixation on the missing women hadn't been in vain, but, at the same time, he came across as regretful that his assumptions might be correct.

"We're dealing with a serial killer, Len. It's obvious. Amy Rogers went missing just last week. They called in the FBI for her. They need to know about this."

"We can't rush to conclusions. I'm going to notify the chief to let him know about the find and contact crime scene and the ME. I'm heading out to her place now. Stay with the woman there, keep her calm, and let her know we'll take care of it."

"It?"

"The DB, Trent. The victim. You have to learn to think of them that way. Otherwise the job will eat you up."

"I'm not babysitting this woman. I'm going to the crime scene."

"Oh, no, you're not."

"Len—"

"There isn't room for debate here. You have to stay there. That's your job. This is mine."

"So you keep reminding me. Just remember, I connected everything before the detectives of PWPD even had a clue."

"Now you're resorting to digs? Come on, Trent, you know I've got your back. I always have."

"I still don't see detective on my badge, and, yep, I'm definitely in uniform."

Lenny laughed. "Stop sulking. I'll keep you posted." He hung up the phone, went upstairs, and told his wife there was another case. His hours around home would be hit—and more likely miss—for the next while.

"Just take care of you." She brushed a hand on the side of his face, and he kissed her forehead.

"That's why I love you."

"Love you." Her nose went back into her paperback. She would be carried off into a fictional world before he hit the front door.

Also available from
International Bestselling Author
Carolyn Arnold

SILENT GRAVES

Book 2 in the Brandon Fisher FBI series

We know serial killers exist. We don't want to believe they're in our own backyard.

Rookie FBI Agent Brandon Fisher and his team head to nearby Prince William County, Virginia, when a woman's recent disappearance sheds light on thirty other women who have gone missing in the area over the last six years.

Brandon is determined to find the connection—if any—between the cases and prove himself a good agent. He even has high hopes of bringing some of the women home alive, but his new boss seems to have made it his mission to antagonize him. Brandon's not about to let his temper make him lose the career he's worked so hard for, but will he be able to bite his tongue and get the job done? The pressure only continues to mount when some of the women turn up dead and the investigation takes one dark turn after another.

**Available from popular book retailers or
at CarolynArnold.net**

CAROLYN ARNOLD is an international bestselling and award-winning author, as well as a speaker, teacher, and inspirational mentor. She has four continuing fiction series—Detective Madison Knight, Brandon Fisher FBI, McKinley Mysteries, and Matthew Connor Adventures—and has written nearly thirty books. Her genre diversity offers her readers everything from cozy to hard-boiled mysteries, and thrillers to action adventures.

Both her female detective and FBI profiler series have been praised by those in law enforcement as being accurate and entertaining, leading her to adopt the trademark: POLICE PROCEDURALS RESPECTED BY LAW ENFORCEMENT™.

Carolyn was born in a small town and enjoys spending time outdoors, but she also loves the lights of a big city. Grounded by her roots and lifted by her dreams, her overactive imagination insists that she tell her stories. Her intention is to touch the hearts of millions with her books, to entertain, inspire, and empower.

She currently lives in London, Ontario with her husband and beagle and is a member of Crime Writers of Canada and Sisters in Crime.

CONNECT ONLINE
CarolynArnold.net
Facebook.com/AuthorCarolynArnold
Twitter.com/Carolyn_Arnold

And don't forget to sign up for her newsletter for up-to-date information on release and special offers at CarolynArnold.net/Newsletters.

CPSIA information can be obtained
at www.ICGtesting.com
Printed in the USA
LVHW090319150920
666044LV00001B/337